Waterford Street

Also by Desmond Gallagher

Shooting Suns and Things: transatlantic fliers at Portmarnock

Waterford Street

Desmond Gallagher

Kingford Press
Dublin

For Karena, Adrienne, Lorna, Dermot, and Norman

ISBN 978-0-9511565-2-0

A CIP catalogue record for this book is available from the British Library.

enquiries to: info@kingfordpress.com

Kingford Press
Dublin
www.kingfordpress.com

Acknowledgement

I am grateful to the people who read the drafts, particularly Kay Murphy who made invaluable suggestions. The National Library and the local libraries were always willing to assist my research. I was fortunate to have the opportunity to talk with persons of a past generation about tenement life in Dublin, the Rebellion of 1916, and the Irish Civil War – their personal stories were the inspiration for the novel. My wife Lillian was a constant support during the writing and gave sound advice on the text. I thank them all.

CHAPTER ONE

1912

Monday morning. Lily Clancy looked down on the women outside the pawnshop. They were waiting for it to open. They had come with their bundles, some big, some small, mostly clothes and shoes, wrapped in a sheet or pillowcase – a wardrobe redeemed on Saturday, worn on Sunday, to be hocked again today: money to keep a body and soul together.

Some of the items pawned would never be claimed back; the tickets might as well have been torn up at the outset. A Dublin accent rises from the queue, 'Me fella can't get a start anywhere!' This is how it began for many and from then on things would quickly get out of control. Soon any bit of finery you had was gone, then it was goodbye to the man's suit and your good topcoat, the wedding ring had gone as well, and you were left with only the clothes you stood in. For now, you still clung on to the miserable, north inner-city room, your only shelter, but you were behind in the rent and the huge sum of seven shillings and sixpence was now needed. The rent collector had been dodged, but you knew in your heart that it was only a matter of time before the heavies would charge up the stairs and burst into your room and you would be out on the street, what was left of your meagre possessions exposed for all and sundry to gawk at.

Many a time this happened when the man was out. Later, he would come from the pub, buoyed by porter, but he would sober up at the sight of his stained mattress on the footpath. Even a normally good man could swing a blow at his wife; he had to blame someone. Neighbours would rush to calm him and within minutes he would be pacing up and down the street, looking in frustration at the windows of the tenement room that used to be home.

Lily remembered the morning a woman had collapsed while waiting outside the pawnshop; the commotion outside had brought her to the window. A crowd had gathered round the woman, whose head was on the doorstep of the pawnbroker's, her legs stretching indecently towards the centre of the footpath, until the hem of her well-worn skirt was tugged down by a considerate bystander. She was in a bad way and a passing cart was called upon and she was wheeled away to Jervis Street Hospital. Lily hadn't gone downstairs to see if she could help, even though that day there had been nothing to prevent her. Later, she heard that the woman had died. An unfortunate part of living next door to a pawnshop, you couldn't avoid its drama.

From her third-storey window, she looked past the pawnshop queue and watched her eldest son Stephen take his brother Bernard down Marlborough Street to school. She had told them to hurry, but they were sauntering, as if time didn't matter, and she imagined she heard the schoolyard bell. They'll be late! And how many times have I told them to hold hands? The boys went from view and, without wanting to, she looked down again at the women below. She knew some of them to see, from Mass or from shopping, but wouldn't have spoken with them.

She turned from the window and looked about the room at her furniture. A sideboard, dining table and chairs, all in mahogany, a large mirror with an ornate gilded frame, a carriage clock on the mantelpiece – all comforting items she had inherited from an aunt. The furniture also gave a sense of status and every reason to feel secure but seeing the women outside the pawnshop had made her uneasy, even though she knew her lot in life to be better than theirs. Recently, her husband

James had been promoted in the tram company, rising to be foreman in the fitting shop. The wage was higher, and he no longer worked with his hands; instead, he told her he went about giving instructions.

She heard a sound from beyond the folding doors which led to the bedroom and remembered Peter was still inside, and because he was a crawling nine-month-old, with a habit of trying to scale the side rails of his cot, she rushed to him and lifted him out and placed him on the floor – she'd once been a second too slow and saw him bounce off the floor. He hadn't been hurt, but the near accident had frightened her, and she later tormented herself with the thought of what could have happened. She went into her routine of making the beds. A double, then, a single in the corner, where Stephen and Bernard squeezed together, and the cot – she slept in a room with four males.

When Peter was born, her husband had said: 'If you want a girl, we'll just have to keep trying.'

But she was not having any of that!

The north-inner city was full of women with large families, twenty or more – the more children you had, the better the chance of a good number surviving the illnesses that waited for them. But every delivery took a slice from the mother's health. Also, it often meant a large family crammed into one room and not enough money coming in, maybe even none, sleeping on beds of straw, forever hungry. A Sunday treat would be a boiled sheep's head or fish heads, the cheapest of the cheap. She was sure that most of the women who came to the pawnshop lived that way.

The beds made, she lifted the baby and said, 'Now, Peter – let's get your breakfast into you!' She put him in his highchair and filled his bowl with porridge from a pot kept warm by the fire; he was a tidier eater now and no longer flung his food about the room. Afterwards she produced a bottle, which he snatched from her and sucked hard on the teat – she was glad she was no longer feeding him herself.

When he'd had enough, she caught the bottle in mid-air as it dropped to the floor. 'It's time for our walk, Peter. What do you say?'

He beat the tray of the highchair. The word walk was all it took.

'You don't say much, do you Peter?' She smiled at his antics.

She dressed him and carried him downstairs, past the drawing room where the Cullens lived, him and her. He was an official of some type in the nearby General Post Office; she was a cheery, neat woman who always had time for a word when you bumped into her on the landing. She descended the next flight of stairs to the hall. Mrs. Hanley lived here, in the front parlour. She was old, widowed for perhaps an eternity, and the landlady. Her room was off the hall, and she would open her door at the slightest noise to see what was stirring – this is where Lily stored the pram and Mr. Bradley parked his bicycle. The Bradleys lived in the basement flat, where the kitchen would have been in grander times, when the house had had a merchant owner. Lily sometimes wondered how the Bradleys managed, six of them in a small space and only half of God's daylight reaching down to them through the area. She was an energetic little woman, who must have spent all her time at a mangle, and he was a dark-haired, tanned man who worked in the Zoological Gardens. But once in the hallway he'd made a suggestive remark to Lily and ever since that day she had tried to avoid him, sometimes hanging back at the top of the stairs until he had gone. However, she still had time for his wife, whom she kind of pitied.

Mrs. Hanley's house had a lock on the hall door, not like the tenement houses in the nearby streets, where the women who went to the pawnshop lived. They would have little privacy there. Any tramp off the street could sneak in and sleep in your hall or make a mess in the building's single lavatory in the back yard, that's if they even bothered to go out that far.

With Peter tucked under a blanket, Lily stood at the hall door and called a youth from the other side of the street to help her lift the pram down the steps on to the footpath. It was a bright May morning, with a hint of summer, but you always kept the vest on at this time of year in case it was a false start, otherwise you risked pneumonia, according to the old people.

She pushed the pram as far as Talbot Street where she bought a portion of butter, a fresh batch loaf, two pork chops and a string of sausages, then on her way home she slipped into Findlater, the wine merchants, and came out with a bottle under the rug of the pram. 'Don't you kick that bottle, Peter! That's Mammy's medicine.'

By the time she got back to the house the queue had gone from outside the pawnshop. She looked up and down the street and decided it was too good a day to go upstairs. Once inside, she thought, I'll be up there for the whole day. Peter had fallen asleep in the pram and rather than disturb him she placed it against the railings and sat on the granite steps. She often did this in fine weather, just to pass the morning until he got hungry. You'd never know who'd salute you or even stop for a chat, she thought; however, that morning she didn't know any of the people that passed. She complained to herself: A fine how-do-you-do in your own city!

She saw something unusual outside Ganly's pub on the corner – it was Mrs. Ganly, herself, a woman you seldom saw idle, and she on a chair placed outside on the footpath, shaking the handle of a pram. Whose baby is that? Lily wondered. It's not hers or I'd have heard about it. And she hasn't grandchildren. Perhaps she's just minding for someone?

A coal-cart stopped outside the house and Lily forgot about the mysterious pram. The coalman, everyone called him Kevin, shouted to her, 'What's it to be today, missus?'

'I'll take a bag of coal and give me some of the slack, as well.'

'No sooner said –' He put his back to a bag and with a grunt pulled it to his shoulder and ran up the front steps and Lily jumped up and opened the door before he thundered into it. She heard him clattering up the stairs. He would place it on the landing outside their door, as they had no proper coal storage.

Mrs. Hanley appeared at the door to her room, hair unkempt and face dirty. Lily often wondered what it would be like to get at her with a wet flannel and a bar of Sunlight soap.

'Get me a bag too, Kevin' she said, when the coalman came back down. 'And mind you, no rocks in it!'

'You're a hard woman,' the coalman joked, running out the door. He came back with the bag of slack for Lily and took the stairs with endless energy. When he returned, he stood waiting to be paid.

Reaching into the pram for her purse, she moved the blanket too far and revealed the bottle of wine. She quickly covered it, and then dropped the coins into a coal-ingrained hand.

'That's you done, missus,' he said. 'Now it's the auld battle-axe...' He carried in Mrs. Hanley's coal, then, waited, anxious to be on his way, while she turned her back to him and burrowed into the pocket of her apron to find her purse. Once paid, he'd no further time for talk and grabbed the bridle and walked the horse further on down the street, bellowing 'Co-al! Co-al!'

The landlady had followed him out and she stood at the top of the steps to look up and down the street, but the effort drained her, and she turned to go back in. Just before she crossed the doorway, she paused and said to Lily, 'If you're opening that bottle, be sure to bring me down a sup.'

Lily wanted to tell her to mind her own business but held back. Her morning had now been spoiled, and she asked the first man that came along to help her up the steps with the pram. Peter was sleeping and she left him in the hallway while she ran upstairs with the messages; then, afraid he might waken, she rushed back down, however he only woke when she disturbed him. Upstairs, she fed him from a bowl – she'd never liked breastfeeding and had weaned him early. She heard children on the street below. Stephen and Bernard would soon be in for the lunch. She heard them on the stairs. 'What did I tell you boys about going easy? You sounded like beasts going for the cattle boat!'

'Ah, Ma, we're rushing,' Stephen said. 'We've to be back in the playground for a game before the bell goes.'

She watched them eat. Stephen was now nine, a strong boy who never seemed to tire; Bernard was seven, neither sickly nor healthy looking, and despite spending many hours playing outdoors, either on the footpath in front of the house or in the school playground, he remained pale, as if he had never seen the sun. She worried more over him than the others. When he'd first started mixing with children from the street, she'd fretted at the thought of him picking up tuberculosis or scarlet fever or something else contagious but soon realized there was little she could do except hope for the best and pray.

Bernard said, between slurps of tea: 'Stephen got hit by the teacher.'

'Where?'

'It was nothing, Ma,' he said, glaring across the table at his younger brother.

'Let me see.'

He stretched out a palm and Lily stroked the red welts where the stick had landed.

'What did you do?'

'Nothing, Ma…honest.'

'Let me kiss it better.'

'It's alright, Ma,' he said, pulling his hand free. 'We're off, or we'll be late for the game.'

The boys pecked her on the cheek and then rushed noisily down the stairs. She watched them from the window as they ran back to the schoolyard. It was time for Peter's nap, so she cleaned him and placed him in the cot and sat down with the bottle of wine – there'll be plenty of time for a glass before he wakes up, she told herself. She poured the drink and stretched out her legs. 'That's better', she said, after downing the first swallow.

She wondered if she should take a refill. A bird never flew… What harm will a little drink do? She felt good, she felt comfortable. Her eyes rested on their wedding photograph on the sideboard and she fetched it and returned to her chair. Weren't we the handsome couple? They had posed for it at Jerome Studio – James in the navy-blue wedding suit, wing collar and tie, she in a wine skirt and fine white blouse that had been set off by a gold chain Aunt Hannah had loaned her for the sitting.

Everyone said I was beautiful then, she thought. But it was before the first – James still says it, bless him, but what else would a husband say?

She treated herself to another glassful, then, moved to the mirror, where her reflection smiled back at her. You may as well laugh as cry, she thought, patting beneath her chin. She adjusted her dark brown hair and raised the glass in salute: 'Here's to you, Lily Boylan!' She was using her maiden name, as if Clancy were only a borrowed one.

There was a noise from inside the bedroom and she remembered Peter.

'My little man,' she said, waltzing up to the cot. She took him in her arms and danced him round the bedroom, spilling some wine as she spun.

Peter was smiling, yet, even at that young age, some instinct made him hold on tightly. She snatched a mouthful of wine and said: 'You're Mammy's best dance partner, aren't you, Peter?'

He garbled something and his eyes were full of uncertain excitement.

'Would my little man like a drink?' She held the glass to his mouth. He tried to put his nose into it, but she pulled it away. 'No, you're too young, Peter! This is only for mammies…I'll get you your bottle, instead.'

She refilled her glass again and put a saucepan of milk to heat on the fire: soon he was sucking the bottle dry. 'We get on famously, don't we, Peter?' she said, as if he were able to understand her. 'You've your bottle and I've mine.'

Suddenly there were footsteps coming up the stairs and Bernard came in from school.

'It's not that time already?' she said, clumsily attempting to conceal her drink.

'We got off early, Ma.'

'Where's your brother?'

'He's down in the street.'

She felt a stab of worry. 'Doing what?'

'Nothing', Ma…just playing''

She bent down to lift Peter off the floor but stumbled and couldn't stop herself from falling; however, she still had the presence of mind to spread her arms to stop herself landing on him. He thought it was great fun, another game. 'Boo!' she said to him, then, recovering what grace she could, she stood up grinning. 'Must've been a lightness.'

Bernard ran to his baby brother and raised him on to his feet. He held his hands at arms' length while the child flexed up and down on his toes. 'Look Ma, he's nearly walking!'

'You're a grand boy, Bernard. What would I do without you?' She pressed him against her skirt and, at the same time, reached over to pat Peter's bouncing head. 'Mammy's in a happy mood today.'

'I know, Ma.'

'Huh?'

'You've that funny look…'

'You're a grand one…now…now, I must start getting the dinner on for Da.'

Bernard watched her take potatoes from a sack: she began to wash the clay from them – usually, a task she did quickly, but, today, it seemed as if she didn't know what she was doing. He went to the window and shouted down to Stephen: 'Ma wants you!'

When his brother arrived, he signalled towards his mother with his eyes. Lily had noticed Stephen come in, and said, 'And here's my biggest boy…' He took one look at her, then, found the glass and half-empty bottle and emptied them down the sink.

'What're you doing with my drink?' she asked.

Stephen ignored the question and hid the empty bottle at the back of a press, then, rubbing his hands together, he asked: 'Now Ma, what were you going to do for dinner?'

~~~

James Clancy saluted the conductor and alighted the tram at Sackville Street (being an employee of the Dublin United Tram Company he paid no fare). He turned into Cathedral Street and slipped in the side door of the Pro-Cathedral to say a prayer. Benediction had just begun. The regular congregation was listening to the priest intone in Latin. The women wore shawls; some were street traders. They'd have been out from sunrise, pushing their barrows about the streets, selling fruit, fish, whatever would turn a shilling. The men were mostly like James, coming from work, some being labourers, others were tradesmen still in dungarees, an occasional man in a suit, probably a civil servant working in Dublin Castle, or maybe a counter assistant in Clery's or Arnott's, the big department stores.

James knelt beside a stout, Neo-Grecian pillar and bowed his head, his nostrils filled with incense and his mind flooded with prayers: God, look after Lily, my wife – but You know that, as I'm always asking the same – Stephen, Bernard and Peter, my sons – but You know that too – sorry…keep me in work, for which I thank You; bless the Church, priests, nuns…and bless the dead, Father, Mother, sister Eileen…may perpetual light shine upon them…keep us all safe... '

He left the cathedral by the main door which leads on to Marlborough Street and while descending the steps, he heard someone hail him. Barney Cullen from the room below had been walking past. 'Aren't you the holy one?' he said, a grin on his face. 'Most men go to the pub after work, but you go in to pray for the rest of us.'

'I can go to the pub, too,' James replied, slightly irked that he had to defend himself.

Cullen walked with him. 'Don't take it to heart, James, I'm only slagging.'

'I know you are.'

'You should learn to relax.'

'Get me a job like yours, and I'll be an expert at it.'

'My dear sir, keep that one under your hat…it's one of the perks of the Post Office.'

'It's well for some.' James stepped out to avoid a boy running towards him, who was rattling a stick against the railings.

'Maybe I could get you out for a pint of porter some night?'

'Why not, Barney? Knock up some night and we'll do just that.' James parted with him on his landing and climbed the final flight home.

Stephen took his jacket at the door and pointed to his father's favourite chair. Bernard carried the plateful of food to the table.

'There you are, Da...' the boy said. 'A surprise, eat up!'

'Where's your mother?'

'She's asleep, Da,' Stephen said. 'Don't you like the dinner?'

He swallowed a mouthful and smiled. 'It's good, son...really good.' But he couldn't wait to leave the table and look in the bedroom. She was indeed sleeping, and Peter was also asleep, in the crook of her arm.

Bernard followed him in and tugged his sleeve. 'Da, will you help me with the ecker?'

'Sure, son – but a young fella like you shouldn't be getting hard homework.'

Lily moved in her sleep, and he backed away from the door and returned to the table to finish his meal. Later he heard her get up. She came in, tidying her hair. 'I don't know what happened to me...I meant to lie down for only a few minutes –' She noticed the dirty plates on the table. 'You got your dinner, then?'

'Stephen looked after me'

At that moment his son, feeling he was in his father's good books, said: 'Da, can I go out to play?'

'Stephen, you know I don't like you hanging round the street.'

'Let him go, James,' Lily said. 'At least, for a half-hour.'

'Can I go too?' Bernard asked, his face full of hope.

'What about your homework?'

'Oh! I forgot. When it's finished then?'

'It'll be the bed, then, son.'

Bernard's head bowed, as if his father's decision meant the end of all happiness.

'You're too hard on him,' Lily said, as she cleared off the table.

He was frustrated. 'How can you say that to me? I have to protect him...you know the types that are going around the streets at night.'

'But it's not even dark, yet.'

James went to the window. She's right, he thought, there's still time. His concern was that after dark, the brothels in the nearby streets would be a magnet for all types: sailors, soldiers, discontented married men, frustrated single men, and young men with fantasies but no money. He hated the way the neighbourhood changed when the gas lamps lit the streets: it wasn't his world, and he didn't want his family infected by it. However, that evening, he began to have second thoughts about restricting Bernard's freedom. 'I'll let you go, this time,' he said. 'But I'm going down to watch you from the steps.'

Lily smiled, but turned away as he went past, not wanting him to smell her breath. When they left, she took a brown paper bag of mints from a drawer and fell into an armchair. She asked herself: If not for the boys, what would I have done? The thought sickened her. She bathed Peter and put him down. He wasn't sleepy but was content to talk to himself. She made James's sandwich for taking to work the next day, then moved on to wash socks for the boys. When the light started to fade in the room, she lit the gas mantle and waited for the returning footsteps on the stairs. They all came in together and the boys sat down to do the homework – James helped Bernard, as he had promised earlier, while Stephen seemed to now manage on his own. Lily made cocoa for supper and the boys then went to bed.

Finally, alone with his wife, James watched her as she tended to tasks. She hadn't fooled him. He hated it when she drank, and worried over her, unable to forget the weakness in her family. He had seen it on the very first night he'd gone to her home. They had been walking out for nearly six months, which had meant meeting on the street and wandering about the city holding hands and looking in shop windows. Sometimes, they walked the length of the quays and then left the river and went into the Phoenix Park and that was where they had first kissed. Later, they became daring, wrapping their arms around one another in the doorway of a shop, after its closing hour, just up the road from where she lived.

Lily had asked him to her home, the Boylan's, on Christmas Night, convincing him that they shouldn't be walking the streets while everyone else were gathered indoors. He was nervous knocking on her door, but Lily had been watching at the window and rushed out to bring him in. Her mother had welcomed him, then he'd sat in a corner, listening to the conversation of her relatives, while Lily busied herself going round the room with plates of sandwiches and bottles of stout for the men and sherry for the women, smiling at him when their eyes met. Later, her father came in boasting that he had visited all the pubs that he'd drank in during the year to collect his free Christmas drink. He tried to get the relatives to each perform a party piece, as if it were an annual challenge for him. But James had noticed how the mood in the room was changing: one couple made their excuses and left, and in a short space of time others followed. Soon, it was only immediate family and him; Lily's mother was quietly crying, and her father was glowering at nothing.

The tension eased a piece when there was a knock at the door and Lily ran to answer it. She ushered in a man called Alf, a crony of her father's. By now, Mr. Boylan's eyes were just slits. He stuck a glass of whiskey in the visitor's hand and placed him in the centre of the room. 'Now, here's a man to entertain us!' he said. 'None of these can sing nor nothing,' he added, waving loosely about him.

Alf took a mouthful of whiskey, handed the glass to Lily for safekeeping, and started to tap dance and whistle at the same time. Boylan looked on as if it were the best show in town. Then Alf switched his act and began to sing in a sweet voice. James had only ever seen or heard such talent in a theatre. When the man stopped, there was a moment of awkward silence, then Boylan clapped loudly and said, 'This is a man who can do something!' Then those narrowed eyes fell on James. 'Now, it's your turn, boy – if you're going to be courting my daughter, you'd better have a song in you!'

James ran from the room and Lily followed him.

'He isn't always like that,' she said, 'it's just that it's…well, it's Christmas.'

They left and passed the rest of the time walking the local streets, listening to the joviality coming from other homes. He later came to realize that her father was always like that. Now, James was afraid it was a family weakness. If it were, it had been late coming to Lily; she hadn't tasted drink until a night three years beforehand. A childhood friend of hers had died of consumption and she had gone to the wake. He had asked her not to go: 'You'll catch her sickness.' He had taken a stand on the issue and refused to go with her. She had seen dead people before, but the sight of her friend's corpse had shocked her. Someone put a glass of whiskey in her hand and she'd drunk it. Then there were more glasses, the sense and the smell of death eased; she walked home that night hardly able to feel her feet and keep her direction – a dreamlike state, with no sorrow. James had made excuses for her that night. But now, this was different. He feared the drink was getting a grip on her.

James had gone to the bedroom to prepare for bed. He lay back; one of the boys was snoring; Lily was still tidying in the other room. Later he heard her on the chamber pot, then she climbed in beside him. He turned to kiss her, but she slipped away from him, saying, 'You'll wake the boys.' She's right, he thought. The springs creak something terrible. Stephen might guess what's going on, but Bernard's still an innocent. But what do other couples do? Those who have ten, fifteen, maybe even twenty in a room?

CHAPTER TWO

The doors to Ganly's public house were jammed-open to clear the stale smell from the night before. A barman was washing glasses and the cleaning woman was spreading a fresh layer of sawdust on the floor. Tom Ganly, the proprietor, was outside with the Guinness draymen, watching them unload his barrel delivery. He stroked the mane of Sally the draught horse, magnificent in polished harness – she reminded him of his childhood days on the small farm in County Galway. There, he had been surrounded by green countryside, but there had been too many in the family for the land to keep them all, so he'd taken the train to Dublin to look for his fortune. Over the years, with a combination of hard graft and good luck, he had arrived at where he was now. He had no complaints, but while he stroked Sally's coat, he felt something primitive that pleased him; it separated him from the dour surroundings of the city.

A movement above him caught his eye. His wife Biddy had come to the curtain in the living area above the bar to glance down at him. She must have finished dressing the baby, he thought. She was not their own baby girl, in the true sense, because the infant had been given to them: Biddy hadn't known discomfort or pain, this time.

~~~

Nora Moore was the baby's mother. At the age of sixteen, gripping a reference from the parish priest, she had come to Dublin from a remote part of County Roscommon to work in service with a family in Mount Pleasant. The husband of the house had given her gifts, mostly costume jewellery; no one had ever given her anything like that before. 'A secret between us,' he had said. 'Don't tell the madam or she'll want to take them for herself.' So, Nora kept her presents hidden, only to take them out when they were alone together in the house and, at his instructions, she would parade around her room wearing them. He called it a 'show' and, when it was time for him to go (the madam being due to return), he would kiss her on the mouth and leave. Then one day the wife went off to stay with a cousin in Kildare and the husband ran to Nora as soon as the carriage left for the station. He gave her the run of the house, beseeched her to call him Bill, and by nightfall she was fully intoxicated by the new game. It was then that he got into her bed. She knew how to kiss, but that was all – he showed her how to do the rest.

Bill called her, 'Wife', and swore that he preferred her to the dreary madam. It was easy for her to believe him, and from then on, even after the madam's return, she waited every night for a visit, sometimes it lasted only minutes, other times her 'husband' stayed at least a half-hour.

During the day Nora took orders from the wife – 'clean here', 'scrub there' – but it was easy to be willing when you had a big secret, and once when she scolded her for daydreaming, she bowed her head in silence but grinned when her back was turned. The husband seldom spoke to her when the madam was about, and if he did, he barked at her, but it was an act, and he would later beg forgiveness. 'You know I don't mean it.' Soft words, persuasive strokes of her long dark hair.

When Nora started to put on weight, she thought she had been eating too much. The man never stopped coming to her, saying he loved her new shape. Then one day there was uproar in the drawing room, and she heard her name being repeated, over and over, and her instinct told her she was in trouble.

The madam summoned her and commanded the husband to stay in the room and watch; he had retreated to a corner, like a kicked hound. 'Miss Moore, I have no choice but to sack you,' the woman said.

Nora could hear the grandfather clock ticking in the background. She had an urge to look out the window at the trees in the avenue; anything to distract her numbed mind from what she had just heard. 'But why, madam?' she asked, her voice trembling.

'You know why, you cheap hussy!' the woman spat. 'You're not having a baby under my roof!'

'A baby?'

'Don't you know you're pregnant, girl?'

Nora looked around at the husband of the house, but he'd climbed a ladder on the pretext of searching for a title on the upper shelf of the bookcase. She was confused, didn't really understand. She had been told that babies were born under heads of cabbage. Now, the reality that it had to do with her weight gain began to sink in and a panic grabbed her.

'Where else can I go, madam?' she pleaded.

'It's of no concern of mine, Miss Moore – and I hope to never set eyes on you again.'

Nora climbed the stairs to her room and changed out of the uniform she had been supplied with. She hung it in the wardrobe, then gathered up her few belongings and wrapped some old clothes round the costume jewellery that Bill had given her. The room was given a last look – it had been a palace compared to what she'd ever had in County Roscommon, and now she had lost it.

Downstairs, the wife was stone-faced as she oversaw the eviction. She made sure that there was no contact between the sacked maid and her husband, not even eye contact.

Nora went out the hall door, heard it being slammed after her, and, as she had never had the need to use the tram nor any other Dublin public transport, she started to walk in the general direction of the city centre; she wasn't going to put herself in the way of further embarrassment by looking for directions. She was exhausted by the time she got to the city, and as she was passing the door of a large church, she noticed many people going in. It was a novena, a time when the faithful laid siege to all their favourite saints, hoping that all their intentions would be answered. She found a seat in the back, half-resting, half-praying. She was still there when they came to close the doors that night. Out of the shadows, a priest came up to her and said, 'We're closing, miss.'

She didn't know what to say.

'Have you nowhere to go?' he asked.

'No, father.'

The priest sighed. He had heard the same reply so many times. The homeless, he thought, drift into the house of God and think it's a rescue shelter. But what they needed most was money to pay the rent. He regretted that neither he nor the order had money to hand out and could only give assistance to the needy when they, in turn, had received donations. He knew for a fact that the cupboard was now bare, for even the rich seemed to have decided that they were going through hard times and were keeping their money for their own security. He was guiding her to the main door when he realized she was pregnant.

'My child, where's your husband?'

'I don't have one, father.' She felt the priest study her. She was trembling at the thought of having to go out on the street

'What's your name, child?'

'It's Nora.'

He hurried off and returned some minutes later wearing an overcoat. 'I'm Father Nix and the best thing I can do for you, child, is bring you to the sisters...you'll be cared for there.' She followed him outside into the dark and watched him turn a large key in the door of the church. 'We'll leave God and his holy saints to rest for the night,' he said, smiling at her. 'Now, follow me and let me do all the talking when we get to the sisters.'

The priest knocked, but at first there was no response, the convent remaining in darkness. He persisted with the assuredness of a bailiff, until there came a glimmer of light in the hallway. A voice came from behind the solid door: 'Who is it?'

'Sister, it's Father Nix. I have a good Catholic girl with me who needs your help.'

The nuns took her in, but never let her forget that she was in shame. Washing the corridors of the convent was too good for her, despite her condition. Nora cried herself to sleep every night. She could have left the convent but was too terrified to face the unknown world outside. At least she had food to eat, no matter how bad it was, and shelter from the weather. And, most important of all she felt that the nuns knew more than she did, for she'd no idea of what was to come, of how her baby would be born.

When she went into labour, she was sure that she was going to die. She prayed wildly and loudly. A midwife was called; the woman bossed her, shouted confusing instructions at her; and no one wiped the tears and sweat from her face. She went into a panic when the baby's head stuck out. 'There's a big hole in me!' she screamed.

'You fool, this is how it happens!' the midwife shouted.

Then there was a moment of complete confusion, exertion to the point where she thought she would faint, and then everything went quiet. There was a flurry of activity between her legs, then, she heard a cry and raised herself on her elbows to look. There was nothing to see, except the midwife with bloodied hands. 'You made an awful racket, whoever you are,' the midwife said to her.

Nora paid her no attention. She looked beyond her and saw two nuns washing the baby. She heard one of them say: 'She'll be called after the Blessed Virgin.' Nora's elbows no longer had the power to keep her up and she fell back into a sleep. The nuns whisked the baby away and had her baptised Mary Theresa. But she cried throughout the night, keeping the nuns awake. For peace and quiet, Mary Theresa was returned to Nora, but when she needed to be fed, she was whisked away. A week later, the reverend mother came and told her that the baby would be going to a good Catholic home.

She was confused. As a child, she had been told to respect the nuns, but she didn't want to part with her baby. A scullery maid had overheard that the adopting couple would come the next day. She liked

Nora and, risking her job and the shelter of the convent, she told her what was to happen.

Nora fretted for the rest of the day, afraid to let Mary Theresa out of her sight; she even brought her with her to the toilet, but she had to let her go when she cried to be fed and couldn't calm herself until her return. That night, when all was quiet, she dressed her, putting two yellowing cardigans on her, one over the other, wrapped her in a rug, and prayed to God that she'd be forgiven for stealing it from the sisters. She crept from the room and padded down the statue-lined corridor that formed the spine of the convent. The scullery maid had left a side gate open. She found the kitchen, went outside into the garden, and found the gate.

She ran from the convent, clutching her baby, and only slowed when she felt it was safe. It was cold. She blew on the infant's face, hoping to keep her warm; she did not know the streets she was walking, and was penniless. The night seemed endless. Finally, the dawn came, a streak of yellow on the sky above the rooftops and people began to move about on the streets, the lucky ones who had work to go to, but they passed her as if she didn't exist. She yearned to be back in County Roscommon, where at least someone would bid her time of day, but she couldn't return with a baby, bring shame on the family.

~~~

Biddy Ganly had risen at seven o'clock. She had been out to Mass and on her return had put the kettle on the stove to make tea. She would bring a cup into Tom – a ritual, while he counted the previous day's takings – then, she would settle down with a cup herself before she faced the bar, faced another day, just like the one before. Out of curiosity, she went to the window to see if that young woman with the baby was still on the street – she had noticed her on the way home from the church and wondered about her.

She looked up the street, but there was no sign of her, then, she looked straight down and saw her sitting at the kerbside, directly outside the pub. The woman's back was to her, and the head was bowed forward; Biddy thought she might have been asleep. But it wasn't her business – or so she told herself – and she went back to her cup of tea. Tom came into the room; he hadn't put the razor to his face yet and he'd a hand in his pocket, clearly scratching his private parts. She thought: how many times have I told him about that?

'How were the takings?' she asked, already knowing his answer.

'Pitiful,' he said. 'There's no money left in this town…and, if there is, the Ganlys aren't seeing any of it. And, you mark my words, Biddy, it's going to get worse.'

Biddy went back to the window, expecting the woman and child to have gone. They hadn't moved.

'Tom,' she said, 'come and see this.'

He came to her shoulder and looked down on the street. 'Well?'

'I think there's something up with that girl…it's not natural to be sitting out in the cold like that, and a baby in arms, too.'

'I hope she gets a move on soon,' he said, 'or, she'll be in the path of the delivery.'

Biddy returned to check at the window every few minutes, then, unable to hold back any longer, she went down.

'Are you waiting on someone, luv?' she asked.

Nora couldn't talk; instead, she started to cry.

Biddy knelt beside her and saw the baby's face for the first time – it looked blue and pinched from the cold. She touched Nora's hand, a block of ice. 'Tom! Tom! Come down here, quick.'

She extracted the baby from the girl's grip and handed the bundle to her bewildered husband. 'Run up, man, and put this poor creature close to the fire!' Then, she helped the stranger to her feet and brought her inside.

Nora felt as if she had landed in heaven. Mary Theresa had been bathed in warm water in front of the fire, then, smelling of soap, she was dressed in new clothes, which Mr. Ganly had been sent out to buy. She was crying for food and Biddy presented her back to Nora, but she stared back at her.

'Go on, girl,' she said. 'Feed her…I'll make sure my husband stays out of the way.'

Nora realized what she was asking. 'I've never done it –' She was about to explain that the feeds had been taken care of by the nuns in the convent, then, she remembered that she couldn't reveal that. By now, Mary Theresa was beyond consolation.

'Go on, child,' Biddy urged. 'Put her on before she loses her mind.'

'How?'

Mrs. Ganly had no idea of Nora's lack of knowledge and thought she was having trouble opening her clothes. She leaned over and undid her buttons for her, then drew the top of her dress back, revealing a marble-white shoulder and a veined breast inflated with milk. Nora's instinct was to cover up, but – as she was holding the crying baby – she had no free hand. Next thing she knew Biddy had guided the baby's head: a frantic mouth was searching, the nipple was found, and Nora was startled. She'd seen young calves being suckled on a farm once and realized this must be the same thing.

But Mary Theresa broke loose from the breast and started to cry again.

'She's not getting it, child!' Biddy snapped. 'Keep her calm…stroke her head…it'll come for her.'

Nora guided her daughter's face to the nipple, no longer thinking of her embarrassment, but determined to make the feed. She did as the woman had told her, and soon she knew it was working, as a trickle of her milk escaped from the mouth and ran down the side of Mary Theresa's smooth face.

'That's better,' Biddy sighed, as if she had just pulled a perfect pint in the bar. 'She's a good sucker…when she's full, we'll put her down and then we'll look after you.'

Nora woke in the afternoon on a couch. The fire was stacked high with coal and the kind woman was moving about the room, humming to herself. The man – the woman had called him 'Tom' – came in to have a cup of tea with them. Firstly, he had to inspect Mary Theresa. 'It's a good job we kept the cot,' he said, satisfied that all was well. 'And how is the good mother?' he asked, drawing up a chair.

Nora just smiled at him, as no words could tell how she felt. She looked around the comfortable room, a China cabinet, children's photographs on the walls, a piano tucked away in a corner, and standing in the opposite corner, the cot, and her sleeping baby. She thought of the night before, walking the streets, and for a terrifying moment she realized that her baby could have died from the cold. And, it would have been all her fault, because she had left the convent. Now, Mary Theresa is safe, warm, and comfortable, the way she should always be. She asked herself: Would I be able to give her that? No, was the answer. She had nothing, and nowhere to live.

She looked at the Ganlys. If she were to imagine a mother and father for her baby, they would be like this couple. It was a snap decision. 'Missus, will you look after my baby?'

'Good gracious, child!' Biddy said. 'Do you know what you're saying?'

'I've nothing, missus,' Nora pleaded. 'And you've everything.'

Biddy turned to Tom. He knew he couldn't refuse his wife, not on something so important.

Tom gave Nora two guineas to help her on her way and took her to the railway station. She never wanted to see Dublin again, however, she wept silently in the corner of the carriage as the train moved off.

And that was how the Ganlys came to have a baby in the house.

CHAPTER THREE

B iddy Ganly tucked the blanket round the baby's legs. Mary Theresa should have fresh air, she thought, and, as the day looked like being a dry one, she had pushed the pram out to the footpath. She would watch it through the open door while she washed glasses behind the bar. By now she was getting used to women stopping and looking into the pram. 'She's beautiful, Gawd bless her!' they would shout into the bar. And she would shout back out: 'Isn't she just!'

That morning, Lily was passing by. She stopped to let Peter see the baby.

'Wouldn't you like a sister like her?'

But, instead, his eyes were on an approaching dog. It stopped and cocked a leg against the Ganly's pram. Biddy ran out of the bar, holding a mop, screaming at the top of her voice. The animal looked at her as if she had no right to move it on, then seemed to have second thoughts and padded away. She stood, weapon in hand, watching the dog explore the rest of the street. It was then that she saw Lily watching her.

'The cheek of that!' she said. Lily was someone she knew to see.

Lily smiled and nodded.

'If he shows his face round here again, he'll get it from me!' Biddy had declared war on the dog.

Lily felt a need to explain her proximity to the pram. 'I was showing the baby to Peter. What is her name?'

'Mary Theresa.'

'Isn't she just gorgeous! And her clothes...'

'My husband doesn't skimp on her.'

'Anyone can see that, Mrs. Ganly.'

Later that evening at the dinner table, she mentioned how she and Peter had seen the Ganly baby.

'Ganner is in my class,' Stephen said, 'and he says the baby was left on their doorstep.'

'Mind what you say!' his father said. 'You shouldn't believe everything you hear.'

'But it's true, Da... he told me.'

'That doesn't make it true, son.'

'But, Ganner says his ma was never fat. The baby just –'

'Wash out your mouth, Stephen! I won't have you talking like that!'

'But Da...'

'No "buts" out of you – that's the end of that dirty talk!'

The room went silent, except for the noise of knife and fork, and food been eaten in a mechanical way. He could be right, Lily thought, as she hadn't noticed any show on Biddy Ganly either and she'd only bid her 'Hello' about a month before. If the story is true, then she is indeed a lucky woman. Imagine, a baby landing like that on your doorstep, no carrying, and no labour, that's the way all babies should come.

During the following week, a tenement building collapsed two streets away, its front wall falling outwards. She had heard that a man walking past was killed, also a bedridden woman on the top floor. Others were lucky, and only a few ended up in the Mater Hospital. She thought: who'd want to live in one of those? They say it's past fixing and will have to be torn down.

Many families were split-up as the now homeless tenants squeezed in with relatives, friends, or good neighbours, while they waited to get a room. Also, the rats moved from the rubble of the building, and one got into the cellar of Ganly's pub.

Next day, Lily was going past with Peter, just as a drayman stood on a long tail. He cursed loudly and the rodent scurried up one of the wooden planks used for rolling the barrels into the cellar. Lily saw it dart across the footpath and then climb into Mrs. Ganly's pram. She ran over and picked up the baby. The rat jumped back out and ran through the open doorway of the pub. There was uproar within, then the barman let out a whoop. He had caught the rat with the swing of a hurley stick. Biddy Ganly ran out to check on Mary Theresa.

'She's safe,' Lily said, cuddling the baby.

Biddy muttered, 'Thank you,' but it was plain from the look on her face that she didn't want her touching Mary Theresa. She disappeared inside to check the baby for bites; she wouldn't be happy until the infant was stripped and examined from head to toe. And that poor wretch of a mother, she thought, placed her baby with us for a safe rearing. And this goes and happens!

Lily returned to her own pram and said to Peter: 'Did you see what nearly happened to your little sister?' But he was in a contrary mood and kicked against the floor of the pram. 'Some brother you are! You're only happy when you're being pushed round the streets.'

From that day on, whenever the pram was put outside, Lily would walk past, even if the trip were out of her way. She would steal a look at the baby, and then talk to Peter about her. She began to think of the baby all the time, daydreams of holding and cuddling her. She even thought of becoming pregnant again but shuddered at the idea. There was now an emptiness inside her that drinking didn't help.

Then one morning without thinking about it, she lifted Mary Theresa from her pram and cuddled her. The infant smiled at her. Lily glanced around: the street was empty. She placed her in beside Peter and wheeled the two of them away. Her heart was pounding. She expected someone to shout, 'Stop!' But no one had noticed.

Without direction, she pushed the pram into Sackville Street, passed the entrance to the Gresham Hotel, and moved on down the street towards Nelson Pillar. The capital's main street was full of noise: tram cars slapping along, horses pulling carts which rattled, and a handful of motor cars that puttered and chugged, the drivers muffled up and wearing eye-goggles. A flower seller called to her, 'Flowers, luv?' but she walked past her, as if she didn't exist. She stopped to look in Clery's windows, hoping to see clothes for her new baby, however, all she saw were mannequins displaying finery for the gentry. The clock over the store's entrance chimed; she would have to hurry home to meet the boys coming in for lunch.

Meanwhile, there was uproar at Ganly's. Biddy had discovered the empty pram and sent the barman running to the DMP station at Store Street: the response was immediate, a constable on a bicycle was sent to investigate. As he listened to the hysterical, publican's wife, he asked himself: Who in their right mind would take on the feeding of an extra mouth? Nevertheless, he wrote down all the details with great care, then, after downing the ball of malt that Tom Ganly had stuck into his willing fist, he remounted his bicycle and wobbled off on a search of the nearby streets, just to show that the DMP was doing something. However, his choice of direction was unfortunate, for as he was leaving the street, Lily was entering it at its opposite end. But, if truth were known, it wouldn't have dawned on him to stop and search the pram of a respectably dressed woman going about her daily business.

When Stephen and Bernard tumbled in at lunch hour, they saw the baby and were told that she would be staying with them while her poor unfortunate mother was in hospital. Lily was relieved that the boys accepted her story, their natural curiosity seeming to have left them, temporarily. Soon they were off again, rushing back to the schoolyard. She had fooled them, so far, but she worried over facing her husband, and the questions he would ask.

Mary Theresa started to whimper; it was close to her feeding time. The hole in the teat on Peter's bottle had been widened for his use and the milk kept gurgling in her throat. Lily would send the boys out to buy a new one later. Meanwhile, she only allowed the baby to suck small amounts at a time. This frustrated Mary Theresa, but, in the end, the feeding was successfully finished: it was now cuddling time. She smiled down at the baby and the smile was magically returned, but, at that moment, Peter demanded to be fed and broke the spell.

~~~

Everyone in the school now knew that Ganner's new sister had been 'took', but it never occurred to Stephen and Bernard that she was the one and the same baby they had seen at home. The whole of Marlborough Street and the surrounding area was now talking about the disappearance, or, put more plainly, the kidnapping. Men who had no work and time on their hands became extremely interested in tracking down the baby, for surely the finder would receive free porter for at least a month from the grateful Ganlys.

James hopped off the tram in Sackville Street, gave his customary wave to the driver and, keeping to his routine, went into the Pro-Cathedral to pray, then he ambled towards home, letting the cold air refresh his mind after a difficult day in the tram sheds. There was more activity on the street than normal; he was unaware of the baby snatch.

Lily told him the same story that she had told the boys. 'We're minding her…isn't she adorable?'

He was glad to see her happy.

That night, Peter slept in the big bed between them, while Mary Theresa, being the visitor, was given the privilege of using his cot. James found out the hard way that his youngest son was a kicker. Maybe he'll run out for the Dublin team when he's grown-up! Feeling his sore back in the morning, he crept out early and left for work without wakening anyone.

He was in the fitting shop when he spotted a messenger coming towards him, along the aisle of lathes: it was a summons to Mr. Kershaw's office. Kershaw was the chief engineer and when James arrived, he was looking over drawings spread across a table. 'I'll be right with you, James,' he said, without raising his head. 'Feel free to read the newspaper…I won't be a second.'

'Take your time, Mr. Kershaw.' James picked up the Irish Times and scanned the front page. There was a report that King George V would not be making a return trip to India in the foreseeable future. He had no interest in the diary of royalty, it all seemed so distant to him, and he turned to the inside pages and came across an account of a baby stolen from a pram in Marlborough Street: a baby girl, brown hair, pink dress. He felt his legs go weak. He thought of the infant in his home, and remembered her hair, her dress, but it couldn't be the same child, he convinced himself – that description could fit a thousand baby girls.

Then, why am I feeling like this? Don't I trust Lily and what she's told me? He was annoyed with himself for letting such thoughts enter his head and closed the newspaper.

At that moment, Kershaw looked up. 'Sorry to keep you, James, but I need to go over the overhaul schedule with you.'

'Certainly, Mr. Kershaw.' But as he listened to his boss, he couldn't get rid of a nagging doubt.

~~~

Lily stayed inside that day. She gave Stephen a half-crown and a list of messages to be bought on the way home from school. He put on a sour face, but it brightened when she promised him a penny for himself. He ran out with Bernard, under strict warning not to lose the half-crown. She was now free to prepare Peter and dote on Mary Theresa. Later in the morning when her chores were done, she had more time to hold her, even let her put her mouth to her breast, which she knew would give nothing, and the infant fell asleep that way.

At lunch hour, when she heard the boys pounding up the stairs, she pulled her clothes together and placed the baby back in the cot alongside Peter. Stephen burst into the room and placed the messages on the table, along with the change from the half-crown, and waited for his penny. Bernard stood beside him and shouted: 'I helped!'

'No, you didn't!' Stephen said.

'Yes, I did. I should get money, too.'

'Will you two be quiet,' Lily said, putting her finger to her lips. 'You'll wake her.'

At that stage, Peter was already awake and standing with arms outstretched, one step away from climbing the rails of the cot. She lifted him out, gave Stephen the promised penny, and compromised by dropping a halfpenny into Bernard's palm. 'That's for being such good little men.' While they devoured their lunches, she asked if there were any new happenings at school.

'Ganner's new sister's been taken,' Stephen said. 'They think the gypsies got her.'

'They're looking everywhere,' Bernard added.

'Go on,' she encouraged, hoping for more news. She now felt panicky and imagined the size of the search party; everyone would be the publican's friend. They would be scouring the streets as far away as St. Stephen's Green, every bundle under a shawl would be eyed with suspicion.

She stayed away from the window for the rest of the day. When school was over, she asked Stephen to put on the dinner.

'Ah, Ma, I'm supposed to be in goals for the football!'

'I need your help, son.' She pointed to the baby. 'I have to attend to her and Peter...'

He looked as if someone had cancelled his birthday.

'They'll manage without you, Stephen,' she said. 'At any rate, what did your father tell you about playing football in the street?'

James climbed the stairs, greeted Mrs. Cullen as she was going in her door, and faced the final flight, unable to rid his mind of the newspaper report. He thought of the baby asleep he had left that morning. No, he thought, Lily would never do anything like that. She was holding the baby when he entered the room.

'Look, Daddy is home,' she said.

James managed a smile, trying to appear normal. He went to Peter who was playing with hand-me-down toys, and pot lids, and when he lifted him into the air the boy shrieked with pleasure, his legs flailing like a frog lifted out of a pond. 'And you, Big Fella, what do you think of our visitor?'

'He loves her,' Lily said. 'Don't you, Peter? We all love her.'

James prepared a basin of hot water, stripped to the waist, and washed himself down. Lily put Mary Theresa into the cot, tied Peter into the highchair, and then put the plates out on the table. As she did so, she caught young Stephen's eye and winked at him. It was their secret that he had made the dinner.

That night, Lily was feeling more tired than usual. She had prepared her husband's lunchbox for the following day and set the table for his breakfast. 'Are you going to bed?' she asked.

'I don't think I could sleep,' he said.

'Why? Aren't you tired? I'm exhausted looking after the baby and Peter.'

'You haven't told me whose baby she is.'

'You wouldn't know her...she was in a terrible state and it's the least I could do.'

'What's her name?'

From a few days before, Lily suddenly remembered a woman in the shoe shop placing a deposit on new shoes who hadn't been shy about letting everyone within earshot hear her details. 'May Sheridan, but you —'

'Where's she from?'

'The Diamond,' she said, waving her arm in the general direction of the area called Gloucester Diamond. She was relieved when her answer seemed to satisfy him; she asked him again to go to bed. Later when he lay beside her in the dark, she was surprised when he threw another question at her: 'And, when is this baby going back to...to May Sheridan?'

'The little thing will be with us till her mammy's back on her feet – what else would you have me do?'

~~~

James looked for Seán Brady from the Gloucester Diamond who worked in the company's power station (he wanted to ask him about Lily's friend, May Sheridan).

'Sheridan? Let me think...it doesn't ring a bell – but, yeh know yourself, there's so many in the houses nowadays. It's hard to keep up with the comings and goings.'

She's in hospital,' James said, 'and she recently had a new baby girl.'

'Sorry, can't help yeh, pal,' Brady said, shaking his head.

'May Sheridan,' James repeated. 'I thought you'd have known her.'

Brady looked closely at him. 'This woman owes yeh money, or something?'

'No, it's nothing like that!'

'I'll tell yeh what I'll do, I'll ask the other half...she knows everyone.'

'You're a star,' James said, hoping that Brady wouldn't visit a pub on the way home and forget about it.

That evening when he got home, Peter was clean, happy-looking and sitting in his highchair; Mary Theresa was snoozing in the cot. The rooms had been cleaned, dinner was ready to go on the table and he didn't get a smell of drink from his wife. During the meal, he asked the boys, 'Any more news in the playground of the missing baby?'

'No, Da,' Stephen replied. 'But, Ganner says his ma is in a fit over it.'

'Is that so?'

'He says there's no living in the –'

'Stephen,' Lily interrupted, 'you finish your dinner, son, or it'll get cold.'

'Maybe, we should let the boy talk?' James said.

'We don't want them gossiping about the things that go on behind Ganly's closed door,' she answered. 'It isn't right...'

In conscience, he had to agree. When the dinner was over, he went to the window. 'It's still bright,' he said. 'There's plenty of time to go out for a walk.'

'All of us?'

'No, Lily, just you and me.'

'I couldn't leave the babies.'

'Take them with us.'

'They'd get a chill.'

'Then, the boys will mind them.' He looked towards his sons, but they didn't look interested. 'Well, maybe they won't. Not even for wages.'

'Wages!' Stephen said. 'How much, Da?'

'No, it's a bad idea,' he said. 'It's putting a lot on you...'

Bernard now looked excited. 'We can do it, Da! You and Ma go out for a while.'

'Do you hear that, Lily? They're letting us go out.'

She looked anxiously at the baby in the cot, and to Peter, who was now struggling to get out of the highchair. 'Can we trust –'?

'I can trust them,' he said. 'They'll only get paid when we get back, and everything will have to be as we leave it. Now, put on your coat, woman.'

She had no excuse now and soon was linking him down Sackville Street, watching other people stroll by; a pleasure they used to enjoy before the children came along. One could parade up and down the street and watch the people and the diversion wouldn't cost you a farthing. As they turned for home, the lamplighter had started at the bridge end.

'Did you enjoy that outing?' he said, as they arrived at the steps of the house.

'Yes, I always loved a stroll out.'

'Remind you of the old days?'

'James, you make us sound ancient.'

'You know what I mean. When we were courting.'

'James Clancy, don't tell me you're going all romantic...'

'What's wrong with that?' he said, at the same time opening the hall door. It was dark in the hallway, and he moved her against the wall and looked for her lips. They were slightly open, and he had a shiver of excitement, a sensation he hadn't felt for some time. He pressed against her and she broke for air, releasing a girlish giggle. Suddenly a voice came from the front parlour: 'Who's out there?'

'It's all right, Mrs. Hanley. It's only us,' Lily called back.

There was a long delay, as if the message had to travel a long distance. Then another question: 'What's going on out there?'

James kissed her again, enjoying the sense of mischief. 'Tell her what we're up to,' he whispered. 'I dare you.'

'What's got into you,' she said, pushing him away.

'What's that?' the voice demanded.

'Nothing, Mrs. Hanley, I'm just taking a blanket out of the pram.' She put her hand to her mouth, muffling another giggle.

There was another long silence, then: 'Well, don't make so much noise.'

~~~

The next day Seán Brady came up to James on the shop floor. 'I found your May Sheridan.'

'Oh?' He wasn't sure if he wanted to hear any more.

'As I told yeh, the missus knows everyone.' He gave him directions to the house, to the floor where the flat was. 'But she was thrown by the baby bit...'

James thanked him, but, in a way, he was sorry, for he now had a decision to make – act on the information or ignore it. He thought of little else that day, while he worked, while on his way home in the tram and while he tried to pray in the Pro-Cathedral, however, all the time he clung to the hope that Lily was telling the truth. He sat across from her, ate little dinner, knowing what he had to do. He could have gone straight to the Ganlys, but he'd convinced himself that he still hadn't real cause. And, he thought, why put her in this position without being sure?

Rising from the table, he tried to be casual as he lifted his coat and said, 'I'm going out for a short walk.'

'Wait, James,' she said. 'I'll come too.'

'You don't have to…'

'I want to. The boys will mind the smaller ones, won't you, boys?'

The table had been cleared and they were at their homework. 'Ah, Ma!' Stephen said. 'Not again – I wanted to go out to play.'

'Young man, you know it's too late for that,' she said.

Her husband was already at the door, hoping she would change her mind, but she ran to the bedroom and came out in hat and coat.

'Will we get wages for tonight too?' Stephen asked.

'And me too!' Bernard said.

'We don't want to be giving you bad habits,' she said, 'but do this one thing for us and we'll see about taking you to the Zoo on Sunday.'

The boys smiled.

James was frustrated; he wondered if she somehow had known that he was heading out to find May Sheridan. Outside, he felt her arm slip under his. At the top of the street, without thinking, she turned for Sackville Street as they had done the evening before, but he stopped her and said: 'Let's head this way, instead.'

She looked up the street towards the tenement buildings of Summerhill. 'Why would we want to go that way? There's more to see on Sackville –'

'I know that, but let's go this way… for a change.'

'Some change! You know I like the other way.'

'Just the once,' he coaxed, guiding her towards Summerhill.

Lily hated Summerhill. The way the women sat outside gossiping on the steps all day, their children running through horse dung in their bare feet, the loud and foul talk coming out the doorways of the public houses. She was afraid its smells would turn her stomach and she held her breath for long periods and didn't relax until they passed the Parade and stood on Ballybough Bridge and watched a canal barge pass below. They waved to the boatman, and watched as the vessel glided through still water, heading towards the setting sun. It was a moment that made her want to sigh, at the same time not knowing quite what for. Something beyond the next lock, perhaps? Even beyond that… She looked to the right, towards the district of Ballybough, Poor Town. But it can't be any worse than Summerhill, she thought, which had to be faced again on the way home; however, before Summerhill ran out, James brought her down the Twenty-Seven Steps that led into the

Diamond, the intersection of Gloucester Place and Lower Gloucester Street.

'Why this way?' she asked.

'No reason…just another change.'

'You're all for change tonight.'

'It's just that we haven't been this way in ages.'

Looking about her, Lily said: 'And, with good reason.'

By now he was feeling guilty over leading her into a trap, for they were coming close to the address that Seán Brady had given him. He stopped outside the building and said: 'Your friend, May Sheridan, must live along here somewhere?'

'Yes, it's somewhere along here…but, I couldn't be sure…'

'Maybe, she's out of hospital?'

'I doubt it. If she were home, I'd have heard.'

'Will we go in and check? just in case?'

'No! It would look bad.'

'I don't follow?'

'She'd think we were anxious to get rid of Mary Theresa, that we were minding her with only half a heart. I don't want that.'

'But the baby has to go back sometime.'

'Yes, but I'm the one that told her to take every care. "Give yourself plenty of time to recover," I said. In any case, she wouldn't be out of hospital that quickly.'

'The least we can do is go in and ask after her,' he said.

'No, it's too late in the evening now. The boys will be wondering where we got to.'

'They're old enough.'

'It's late. We shouldn't take advantage.'

They walked on past the house and went home. But, lying in bed that night, James was worried. The baby lay across the room from him; it was time for action. A plan fixed in his mind. Tomorrow, instead of coming straight home from work, I'll slip round to the Diamond on my own.

CHAPTER FOUR

May Sheridan had been fussy about the men she'd gone out with and over time had lost interest in getting one to suit her, becoming resigned to the role of being an aunt to her married sister's children. The brother-in-law was a little man, who spent more time in the pub than at home, and where he got the money for it was a mystery. However, so far, he had found time to give Florrie six children, and May believed that she'd heard all six of them being made, as the wall separating her bedroom from theirs was paper thin. She cleaned for a living, scrubbed floors in the homes of the well-to-do and this gave her enough to pay her sister for her keep (without loss of pride) and still have money left for herself and the important odd treat.

James didn't think she looked like someone that Lily would be friendly with. He introduced himself, then said, 'You know my wife...Lily, Lily Clancy.'

'Did I work for her?' she asked, pushing wisps of hair from her face.

'I can't see how,' he said. 'Would there be another May Sheridan living about here?'

She called inside to her sister. 'Did yeh hear that, Florrie? He wants to know if there's two of me?'

Florrie came to the door and inspected James. 'May, darlin', how could there be two of someone like you? One of yeh is bad enough!' They laughed.

'I must have it wrong,' he said. 'I was looking for the May Sheridan...the May Sheridan with the small baby.'

A cloud crossed the woman's face. 'Is there someone making false insinuations about me?'

'No one is,' he said. 'You're safe – but I think I've been led up the garden path.'

'How can yeh get a thing like a name wrong? Tell me, who's been putting out stories about me?'

He stepped away from the door. 'I'm sorry –' he mumbled.

She advanced on to the landing, hands on hips. 'You ought to be sorry –'

He rushed down the stairs pursued by the women's jeering laughter. When he got home, Lily had the baby in her arms. 'You're late, James – me and Mary Theresa were worried about you.'

'Where's Peter?' he asked.

'He's fast,' she said, nodding towards the cot.

He looked at Mary Theresa: she was smiling, and it would have been so easy to lean across and kiss her little forehead, pretend she were theirs, but he knew what he had to do.

'She likes you,' Lily said.

He put his hand out, absentmindedly toying with a soft, pink finger. 'This cannot go on.' His words drew no reaction, as if she hadn't even heard him. He said it again. This time she looked at him as if he were a stranger and drew the baby even closer to her.

He said: 'I've been to see May Sheridan.'

She turned away.

He tried to be gentle. 'We'll have to return the child. The Ganlys must be in a state…'

'She's mine…ours.'

'You're fooling yourself, Lily.' He regretted his brutal words and moved around her, until they were face-to-face. But she refused to surrender her eyes and looked steadily elsewhere. Then there were silent tears and her body went into a rocking motion. Again, still being gentle, he said, 'Lily, you *know* she has to go back.'

She didn't answer, but continued the rocking motion – a double action, to soothe both herself and the baby in her arms. He looked on, unsure of his next move. Suddenly, like a steam valve blowing, he threw up his arms in exasperation: 'Lily, what've you done! Don't you know that whatever you're suffering, the poor Ganlys will be suffering twice as much!'

His outburst had got through to her, like a cattleman's prodding stick. She spat back: 'But they couldn't care for her like we can!'

At that moment there were footsteps on the stairs; the boys were coming in. 'We'll talk later, Lily.' He picked up a shirt of his that had been airing in front of the fire and used the tail to wipe a tear from his own eye. Just in time, for seconds later the door was flung open and Stephen and Bernard ran in.

James had decided to wait until early the following morning when there would be less people on the street to witness what he was going to do. However, he still had to get through the night; he could hear Lily beside him sobbing into her pillow; it went on all night, which didn't help.

He rose as daylight was creeping along Marlborough Street and lifted Mary Theresa from the cot. In doing so, he disturbed her sleeping partner, Peter, but the boy flung himself on to his opposite side, back into deep sleep. He wrapped Mary Theresa in two blankets and, knowing that Lily was watching, he hurried from the room before she could break his resolve; his footsteps echoing on the stairs seemed to be accusing him of treachery.

That walk to Ganly's was the saddest and loneliest one of his life. He knocked on the door of the pub and the sound carried down the street, but there was no answer. He knocked again. Upstairs, a curtain was pulled back and the publican's face was stuck to a glass pane as he struggled to see who was down below, then, there were cautious footsteps on the stairs and the door was opened.

'I've someone who rightly belongs here,' James said, rolling back the blanket to show the baby's face.

Ganly was amazed and flung the door open to its fullest; he wanted to say something but couldn't speak. The baby was thrust into his arms, and he accepted the bundle, unsure of what he should do next. He looked at James, hoping for an explanation. Finally, he found words: 'Where did you find her?'

'It's a long story, which I'd rather not go into.'

The publican said, 'Don't I know you?'

'You've probably seen me around.' James turned away with eyes so full of tears that the footpath was a blur. He felt as if he had abandoned the baby, but at the same time he imagined the excitement that he'd brought to the Ganlys; yes, he thought, pain in one household meant happiness in another. But how will I now face Lily? Rather than return home, he rambled the streets until it was time to go to work.

~~~

Lily had never felt so low. She wanted to take to the bed, detach herself from the cruel world; however, she still had to see the boys off to school, then, take up Peter and feed and wash him. Because she hadn't been out for three days, her home now felt like a prison. She had to escape, for every place she looked she saw reminders of Mary Theresa: the rumpled sheet in the cot, the feeding bottle that had been borrowed from Peter, the boys' baby clothes she'd dug out of the hole-in-the-wall press – they had fitted perfectly, made her look like a doll.

Lily left the house and pushed Peter in the pram to Talbot Street. The flower-seller at the corner called to her, 'Do yeh want a bunch, missus? Only ha'pence.' She passed her in a daze and went into the Food and Drink Emporium, filled the bottom of the pram with messages and stuck in a bottle of gin, as well. She imagined that Peter was spying on her. 'It's Mammy's medicine,' she said, as if he understood.

She waited until he was put down for his nap before opening the bottle – she was drunk at lunch hour when Stephen and Bernard came in from school. Stephen considered running to the tram depot to tell his father, then, dropped the idea; he would loyally stay at home with her and Peter. He prepared the lunch, and afterwards told Bernard to go back to school, but he resisted: 'If you're staying, I'm staying!'

James Clancy was in dread of facing his wife. He imagined her eyes questioning him, looking at him as if he had just committed a foul crime like murder. He climbed the stairs, wishing it had all been different, that he hadn't caused her this, or any other type of unhappiness. When he entered the room, he was surprised at how quiet he found her. She was looking at the floor, as if she had just been handed an excommunication notice by the parish priest. He had expected trouble but now he worried that something else had also happened.

'Did anything strange happen today?' he asked Stephen, as he was the eldest.

'No, Da.'

Suddenly, Lily looked up. 'Why are you quizzing him?'

'I have a right to know what goes on in my own –'

'He's a good boy and doesn't deserve to be quizzed like that.'

He looked closely at her: she seemed sober. Then he noticed that she had already prepared his work lunch for the next day; it was wrapped in paper, ready for going out the door. For the rest of the evening, neither one spoke of what had happened, and James began to feel that maybe she had put the episode behind her, but he was wrong, for later when they were in bed her voice came to him in the darkness: 'Did Mary Theresa cry this morning?'

'She slept all the time,' he answered.

'That was at least something, I suppose...' She was silent for a moment, then she asked, 'Did they say anything?'

'No. It was all over in seconds. I just handed her to him, Mr. Ganly, and went off.'

'Did he know you?'

'I don't see how.'

'I miss her.'

'It was a terrible...' he said. 'And, I pray...never again.'

There was a long pause before she said: 'But, what will I do without her?'

He let that question hang in the dark.

She was silent now, not asleep yet, for he hadn't heard her gentle snore. He asked himself, why is she like this? Hasn't she her own family? Are we not enough?

~~~

Next morning at the Ganly's, Biddy had forgotten the initial euphoria of Mary Theresa's safe return. Instead, she was angry, dead set on having someone arrested for taking her. 'Have you no idea who the man was?' she quizzed.

Tom had only a feeling that he'd seen the man before, but he couldn't place him. He shrugged his shoulders.

'You could at least have asked his name,' she continued.

'It happened so fast. But, isn't it enough to get her back safe and sound?'

'You're too soft, Tom Ganly. A kidnapper should be put in jail. And look at all the trouble and upset we've been caused.'

'Kidnapper is a bit strong, Biddy. Can't you be happy just to have her back?'

'I am happy,' she said, picking up Mary Theresa and cuddling her. 'But we still have to find out who took her – someone will have to pay for this!'

~~~

'Mr. Kershaw wants to see you, Mr. Clancy,' the messenger boy said.

James left the workshop floor and climbed the metal steps to the offices. Kershaw, his boss, nodded to him as he entered the room. It was unusual that he wasn't sitting in his leather throne but instead he was standing to one side of the room, obviously making way for a stranger who now was in his chair, positioned behind his desk, as if he were the rightful occupant. Kershaw made no introductions, instead he laid an overly friendly arm on James's shoulder and steered him to a window, which gave a view of the workshop.

'Do you see all this, James?'

'Yes...'

'Well, I see it too. I can walk from my desk and stand right here. But there's one big problem, James.'

'What's that, sir?'

'I don't really know what goes on down there.'

'You mean on the shop floor?'

'That's it precisely, James. Oh, I know they're all honest-to-goodness workers and all that – or so everyone would have me believe – but I don't know what they're thinking. I want to know what they're thinking. What the talk is between them.'

'I don't understand,' James said.

'My man, you're in a good position to hear what's going on.'

'All I hear is the usual stuff.'

'There's rumours they've been meeting again with a trade union …and that troublemaker Larkin.'

'I've heard none of that, Mr. Kershaw.'

Suddenly, the stranger spoke: 'Perhaps, you haven't been paying enough attention, Mr. Clancy?

James turned to him. The stranger was perfectly groomed, steel-grey hair, thin moustache, a delicate, gold watch chain peeping from a waistcoat; his cane with an ornamental silver handle had been laid, out of place, across some mechanical drawings on Kershaw's desk and he looked as if he had just stepped out of one of those gentlemen's clubs on St. Stephen's Green.

'Please leave this to me, Mr. Lambe.' It looked as if Kershaw was trying hard to assert that this was his office, his territory.

'Oh! Get on with it, then!' the stranger – Mr. Lambe – snapped back.

Kershaw turned to James. 'We don't want any more trade-union rot setting in.'

'I don't know how this affects me,' he answered, though in his heart he knew it did.

'God, Clancy, you're a foreman!' Kershaw had raised his voice, as if he had to make a show for Lambe. His tone was threatening: 'That means you know which side your bread is buttered on!'

James was uneasy. Before his promotion, he had been one of the men on the shop floor. He knew he was now expected to make hard decisions and already had made some, like giving men a warning if their work wasn't up to scratch, and he had even sacked a man he knew well, a man with mouths to feed at home, but it had to be done, because it was part of the new job. But this was different. They were expecting him to spy on the men.

'So, James, you'll keep a sharp eye out and report back to me anything you hear.'

Suddenly, the mysterious Mr. Lambe added, 'And, my good man, keep your ears open too.'

On the way out, James stopped to speak to Kershaw's secretary. 'Tell me, Eileen, who is this Mr. Lambe when he's at home?'

She looked uncertain. 'I shouldn't talk to you about him.'

'Come off it, Eileen, you've known me for years.'

'Okay, Mr. Clancy...the man is some sort of a shareholder. I've come across his name in correspondence, but to tell the truth, this is the first time I've ever laid eyes on him.'

'He certainly has Kershaw jumping.'

'You're terrible, Mr. Clancy. Tell me, did he have much to say?'

'Not very much, Eileen, but full of his own importance.'

Suddenly, she stiffened. 'You better move along. Kershaw is looking at us.'

James returned to the shop floor, the noise of hammering and the sound of machinery running were normally comforting to his ears, now he was in a daze, and didn't notice them. An apprentice, one he had helped to get employment with the tram company, came up to him with a requisition form to be signed. He scribbled his signature and said: 'Listen, son, this is to be only between you and me. A secret. Right? If you hear any man talking about a trade union, come and tell me about it, in private. Can I depend on you?'

'Yes, Mr. Clancy.'

The boy went away, whistling, and James felt the weight of treachery. He walked past a team of workers hammering rivets into a chassis. Although Kershaw had reminded him that he was now part of management, he still felt that he had more in common with these men. He knew that any friendliness that Kershaw and his likes would show him, any 'old boy' stuff, was probably put on, a mask.

He asked himself: And, what about this Mr. Lambe? He decided he was of a type more suited to mixing at the Governor General's garden parties in the Phoenix Park.

~~~

Lily no longer had Mary Theresa; nevertheless, she still felt they were together (even though it was all in her mind). Of course, there were dark periods, but a tipple soon banished these, and after a few drinks she was even having imaginary conversations with the baby. And, because Peter was always there, he also was encouraged to talk to his baby sister: she soon found that his baby talk made a real contribution to their three-way conversations. 'You don't say, Peter.' – 'Did you hear that, Mary Theresa?' – 'Did you hear what your big brother just said?' Often, when the weather was dry, she would go to the window, lean out as far as she could, almost to the point of falling out, and look towards Ganly's pub, where frequently she saw that Mary Theresa had been left outside the pub's door in her pram, Biddy being a woman of habit, a great believer in fresh air.

~~~

The month of June came, men went about with jacket slung over the shoulder, women threw off coats, cardigans with no elbows to them, dogs in the streets got lazy, searched out shade – summer had arrived. In the schools, children still sat in classrooms, bored out of their minds, and stared out the window at every distraction and longed for the holidays. It was a time when mitching increased, boys sent off to school but who hid their satchels and went wandering up the canal looking for adventure. The truant inspectors knew the favourite spots and lay in wait. A regular mitcher faced a court appearance and the mother or a jobless father would attend, but pleas for leniency were mostly ignored, as the boy was whipped away to Artane Industrial School for a period sometimes lasting years to be taught to change his wayward ways. ARTANE. As a word it seemed to have a life of its own and the stories about it would have made sure that only the brave or foolish would risk missing the school roll call; yet, there always seemed to be plenty of them, hard chaws, those prepared to take the risk. Stephen would have tried mitching, but he knew Bernard would have told on him, not out of disloyalty or spite, it was just the way he was.

They were breathless with excitement the day they ran home with the news that the Ganly's baby had again been stolen. They found their mother cuddling Mary Theresa. Lily didn't react to their news, instead she spoke to the baby, 'Look, sweetheart, your brothers are in from school.'

It was a great puzzle to Bernard. 'Isn't she the baby from before?'

Lily answered: 'Come and talk to your sister.'

'She's not our sister,' Stephen said, rebelliousness in his voice.

'Bernard, don't mind him,' Lily said, 'come and talk with her.'

Bernard moved closer and held a tiny hand. He knew she was the baby from before, but, at that time, no one had said that she was his sister. His brother stayed at a distance, wanting nothing to do with her. Bernard asked: 'Ma, can we go out to play?'

She nodded and returned to cooing at Mary Theresa. On the stairs, Stephen caught Bernard by the arm. 'Keep your mouth shut about the baby when we go outside,' he warned.

'What?'

'Don't you see?'

'See what?'

'The baby – she's belonging to the Ganlys.'

Bernard didn't believe him. 'You're codding…'

'Are you thick, or something? I tell you, she's the Ganly's baby.'

Bernard finally understood. 'Janey!' he gasped.

He knew there was going to be trouble over this.

CHAPTER FIVE

The boys were outside on the steps when James came home from work. He could tell something was wrong from the look on their faces. He asked no questions but passed inside. The boys followed him up the stairs and listened on the landing, waiting for a row to start; however, to their surprise, there were no raised voices, no commotion. Inside the room, James was sitting across from his wife, by the fire, watching while she held Peter on one knee and a sleeping baby on the other, the picture of motherhood. Without saying a word, he stood and took Mary Theresa from her grip, causing the baby to wake and emit a small cry.

'What are you doing?' Lily said, as if woken from a daze.

'I'm taking her home.'

'But…here is her home…'

'I'm taking her home,' he said, 'and that's the be all and end all of it.' He covered the baby with a rug and started for the door.

On the landing, Stephen was at his elbow. 'Can we come, too?'

His father didn't answer, instead he hurried away, the boys following him. He hadn't noticed them, and when he entered Ganly's pub they were right behind him. It was their first time in a pub and, wide-eyed, they watched him walk to the bar and hand the baby across the counter to Mr. Ganly; the pub had gone silent, stories were dropped in the mid-telling; all the customers had heard about the 'kidnapping'.

Tom Ganly spoke: 'It's you again.'

All eyes were now on James; they were waiting for him to say his piece, say something that would explain his action, then everyone could go back to drinking and talking, in that order. But all he said was: 'Mr. Ganly, I don't know what to say to you…'

At that moment, Biddy came down the stairs, spotted Mary Theresa and ran across the bar and whipped her from her husband's arms, then, with a look of disgust, she removed the rug wrapped round the baby and let it fall to the saw-dust covered floor, as if it were a beggar's rag. She looked all over the child, making sure she wasn't hurt or marked in any way. James was annoyed by the examination and said: 'She's perfect – no need to worry on that count, missus.'

Biddy had hatred on her face. 'You better be right!'

His instinct was to jump to Lily's defence; his wife had taken the child however he would swear before a crucifix that she hadn't mistreated her. 'I'm sure she was well-cared for.'

Biddy turned to her husband, and shouted an order that rang across the pub, like a command across the square of a military barracks: 'Tom, send someone to Store Street for a DMP!'

'You don't have to,' James said. 'I'm going there myself.' He turned and walked out and was on the pavement before the boys realized what had happened and they chased after him.

His sudden leaving shocked the Ganlys. The customers in the bar looked on with mouths agape. Biddy rounded on her husband: 'Don't let that kidnapper outa your sight!'

He ran out after James, as if chasing someone who hadn't paid for a drink and gripped him by the arm.

'I can't let you go,' he said.

'Don't you trust me, sir? I said I was going to the station.'

Tom Ganly looked at him, at the upturned faces of the boys standing close by. 'These your boys?' he asked.

James was surprised to find them there.

The publican made a quick decision, knowing it could bring his wife's anger down on him. 'I'll have to go with you.'

'It's your right, Mister Ganly.'

They walked towards Store Street Barracks, followed by Stephen and Bernard; the boys had seen the inside of a public house and now they were going to see the inside of a police station. The blood raced in their bodies until James stopped at the corner of Talbot Street and faced them: 'Go on home, boys, and sit with your mother till I get back.' It was a steely command, and they turned and trudged home, disappointed that the adventure had ended.

~~~

Constable Tuohy was on desk duty. He knew the men to see, Tom Ganly from going into his licensed premises, James Clancy from the monthly sodality in the Pro-Cathedral, two respectable figures. The publican, impatient to speak, made his complaint first. The DMP man slowed him down and asked him to repeat certain parts of the story so that he could write it into the Day Book. Then he turned to James, shaking his head. 'I can't believe this is true, Mr. Clancy, please tell me it's not.'

James felt humiliated, his first time ever to be questioned formally by an officer of the law. When he spoke, his voice didn't sound like his own. 'I can't deny what Mr. Ganly says.'

'Are you sure, Mr. Clancy? A serious charge is being made here.'

James bowed his head.

Suddenly, a slight smile came into Tuohy's naturally red face. 'I know what this is. This has to be some form of misunderstanding.'

'What type of a policeman are you at all?' Tom Ganly interjected. 'Do you think I've time to be wasting?'

'There's no need to be taking that line, sir.'

'Listen, I've said my piece and I thought I was clear about it and for the life of me I can't see how you can call it a bleeding misunderstanding! I want to see someone in charge, someone to take serious note of the complaint.'

Tuohy took a deep breath, gave him a long look, then said, 'Two things, Mr. Ganly: first one, I've no time for bad language in this station, especially from someone who should know better; second one, right now I'm in charge of the station, but, if you care to return in the morning, you can speak to my sergeant.'

'And, let this kidnapper go scot-free? Not likely. I want him locked up.'

Tuohy turned to James, hoping for a way out. 'Mr. Clancy, unless you can give a good account of yourself…?'

James thought of Lily back home. He wasn't going to draw her into this and remained silent.

Tuohy was uneasy. 'This is shocking,' he said. 'Are you sure you've nothing to say for yourself?'

'Do what you have to do,' he said.

'Then, I'll have to keep you here overnight.'

In the meantime, the boys had reached home. Lily was washing socks in a basin, and she smiled at them as if nothing had happened earlier.

'Da had to go to the barracks,' Stephen said.

The smile left her face and for a moment she just stared into the basin; all she saw were grey socks that looked like dead fish. Then, the panic began, and she grabbed her hat and coat. 'Stay and mind Peter till I get back.'

She entered the police barracks just as James was being escorted away to a cell.

'You can't do this!' she said to Constable Tuohy. 'I'm his wife – Mary Theresa was with *me*.'

'And who's Mary Theresa when she's at home?' the policeman asked. He felt it was going to be one of those nights.

'She's the baby who was taken,' Tom Ganly said in exasperation. 'Our baby – I gave you the name twenty minutes ago!'

Tuohy checked his notes with deliberate slowness. 'So, you did, Mr. Ganly, so you did.'

Lily spoke up: 'Mary Theresa is not belonging to them. She's mine!'

The constable looked across at James, who was now on the threshold of the heavy door leading down to the cells, the large hand of a policeman on his shoulder. 'Mr, Clancy,' he called, 'what's this good wife of yours saying? She claims the baby is part of –'

'But she is ours,' Lily pleaded.

'No, she's ours!' Tom Ganly said. 'You stole her from us!'

The constable dropped his pen and placed his head in his hands. 'I can't make head nor tail of this. A baby can't have two mothers.'

'My wife only thinks that she's the mother,' James said, moving back closer to the desk, the hand on his shoulder not holding him back (the policeman assigned to lock him up wanted to hear more).

Tuohy's face lit up. 'Ah! So Mrs. Ganly is definitely the mother?'

Tom Ganly hesitated.

'Well?' Tuohy probed.

'Not exactly, not the mother…'

'What do you mean, sir?'

'We took her in off the streets; gave her a home; she's treated like one of our own.'

'You're her legal guardians, then?'

'Not yet, Constable, but we soon will be.'

The note of respect that had suddenly come into the publican's tone pleased Tuohy. But this is a vexing puzzle, he thought. 'If neither Mrs. Ganly nor Mrs. Clancy is the mother of the baby in question,' he said, 'will someone kindly enlighten me and tell me who is?'

It was Ganly who spoke. 'Constable Tuohy, I can half answer that question…you see, the name Moore was mentioned, but we know nothing else about her, which I now know was –' He had a sudden feeling that his case was weakening, and he pointed towards the Clancys. 'But you can't let this pair get away with this! They had no right in snatching the baby…'

Tuohy was getting uneasy, yearning now for a simple case of fighting or drunkenness. He looked at the two parties and wondered if they expected him to make a Solomon decision. 'This is complicated,' he said. 'Now, Mr. Ganly, if you and your missus were the guardians of the baby, I'd run these people into a cell and lose the key, but you're not the guardians and that puts me in a fix.'

'But I told you the baby was left in our care.'

'True, Mr. Ganly, however you never even got the mother's name. 'Do you even know where she lives? Can she be contacted?'

'That's the point, constable. The girl...the mother was homeless.'

Tuohy had a plan forming in his mind; he would make a minor decision and leave the big decision to others. 'I find it hard to lock up Mr. Clancy and his good wife,' he said. 'From what I know of them, they're respectable people, and I feel they're not the type to do what you've said, at least not deliberately. I want all of you to come back at nine o'clock in the morning to meet my sergeant. He'll want to decide this one personally.'

Tom Ganly wasn't pleased. And, on top of everything, he would also have to face Biddy, who would be livid at the idea of the 'kidnappers' – now, plural – being free to go. He took his time going home, not keen to face her.

Meanwhile, James and Lily were also making their way home. They didn't speak until they were on the landing outside their door.

'I don't understand you, Lily. Are you trying to wreck our lives?'

'I'm sorry, James.'

'And you ought to be.'

'I was so frightened in the police barracks...'

'We still have to face it again in the morning'.

The boys heard them talking on the landing but couldn't make out what was being said. When they came in, James told them to do their homework and instinct told them that this wasn't the time to ask questions; otherwise, it was as if nothing had happened. When the boys were asleep, James and Lily prepared for bed, without any further discussion. During the night James woke up from a dream in which he was being chased; it was impossible to go back to sleep. Eventually he got up and stood at the window for a long time. The street was quiet, given over to cats on the prowl. He thought he heard Lily moving in the bed and was sure that she also was awake, although she never spoke.

Next morning, they had no one to mind Peter, so they took him in his pram to the police station, where Constable Tuohy met them and asked them to take a seat, pointing to a bench in the hallway. The Ganlys arrived soon afterwards, full of self-righteousness, and kept their distance. Biddy stole a look at Lily and wasn't sure if she knew her (she failed to connect her with the woman who had plucked Mary Theresa from the pram the day of the rat incident, having paid scant attention to her at the time).

Constable Tuohy returned and announced that they should all follow him. His direct superior was Sergeant Farrell, a neat man whose fair hair was turning to grey. He smoked a pipe and at one end of his desk stood a pile of Manila folders (he never seemed to have enough time to clear them).

'I'll be brief and to the point,' Farrell said. 'The barracks here at Store Street is one of the busiest in this godforsaken city. Here we deal with the underbelly of life: thievery, public order, murder, assaults on the female, to say nothing of keeping an eye on Sinn Féin…you're not Shinners, are you?' Before they had a chance to answer he continued, 'I didn't think you were. Now, let's be perfectly clear. Constable Tuohy has given me his report and it's obvious to me that this isn't a problem for the Dublin Metropolitan Police. The care of orphans is the work of orphanages and matters relating to orphans have nothing whatsoever to do with my barracks. Do I make myself clear?'

He paused, a moment of silence, as if to pay respect to the death of police involvement in the case. Biddy was simmering, unable to withhold her anger, her cheeks showing giveaway red blotches. 'What kind of a policeman, are you?' She pointed at the Clancys. 'This woman and this man snatched a defenceless baby from outside our premises – now, to do it once was bad enough, but to do it twice! And you've now the gall to sit there all high-and-mighty and tell us they've done nothing wrong! That they haven't broken any law!'

Tom was silent beside her, unhappy that she hadn't kept her tongue in check, as he had advised on the way to the station. Sergeant Farrell took a long pull on his pipe. Generally, he disliked dealing with women, but what he disliked the more was to be challenged by one. At that moment, Peter woke up and started to cry. Lily took a bottle from the foot of the pram and asked, 'Sir, is there somewhere I can heat this?'

Farrell groaned. 'Take her home, Mrs. Clancy, and feed her,' he said, waving in the direction of the door.

'He's a boy,' Lily said. 'Peter –'

'Please, take the boy home before you turn this place into a nursery.'

Biddy went rigid. 'And you're letting them away with this?' Her voice was quivering, her cheeks now completely invaded by a red tide.

'Mrs. Ganly, I'm trying to be a patient man. You have the baby – what's her name…Mary Theresa – haven't you? So, all's well that ends well, now, please go home and look after your care.'

Biddy noticed that James Clancy and Constable Tuohy, who had stayed in the background, had now moved to the door of the room, and were chatting like men coming out of a football match. She poked her husband in the ribs with her elbow, 'Do something, man!' But Tom wasn't listening to her, instead he was thinking that if he hurried back to the pub, he would be in time to catch the draymen as he hated being left short on the delivery. Meanwhile, Peter was still crying from hunger; Lily pushed the pram towards the door and James cut short his conversation with Tuohy and caught up with her.

The two families left Store Street Barracks, keeping a diplomatic distance between them, and headed to their homes.

It should have ended at that, but three weeks later Lily again took Mary Theresa from her pram: James despaired; Biddy Ganly was incensed, for surely by now every wagging tongue between the Five Lamps and Nelson Pillar would know of the goings-on. 'That's the last time that woman will make a fool of me!' she swore, then she went back to Sergeant Farrell and demanded that the baby be placed in an orphanage.

~~~

It so happened that a first cousin of the sergeant, Reverend Mother Consilio, had recently been appointed by her order to direct their orphanage in County Wicklow. For Farrell it was a quick decision. It all fitted in, a happy coincidence. He summoned two constables and instructed them to go to the Clancy's home to bring the baby to the station. The men looked at him in amazement, wondering how it would look to have two burly DMPs sent on such a mission, one carrying the bundle and the other providing an escort as if the baby were a wanted rogue. But Farrell wasn't taking any risks – he feared the Clancy woman would be obstructive for he had heard of women like her showing animal ferocity when their young were snatched from them. Even though the baby wasn't even her own flesh and blood, the poor demented soul believed it in her head. He sent his men on their way and asked himself: Who'd want a job like mine?

CHAPTER SIX

The Lock Out

Life was no longer simple for James – his wife was an alcoholic and he never knew the state he would find her in when he got home from work. Also, he worried over Peter. When Stephen and Bernard were at school, the boy was totally dependent on her. As if his family problems weren't enough, he found himself in the centre of an industrial dispute that had turned into a storm. He was in the odd position of being in work, while at the same time the principal employers in Dublin had locked thousands of men out of work. This was the strategy of the business circle to break the spirit of Larkin's union members. Although the tram company had been kept open and James's wages were secure, he felt guilty when he thought of the families that had to do without. Some would soon be facing destitution if they weren't there already. And events were getting out of hand. A week earlier, protesters had stoned a tram in Camden Street and the driver was hit in the forehead. The police drew batons and there was a running fight on the street. It had fallen to James to oversee a speedy repair to the tram windows. There was a poisoned atmosphere in the works, with Kershaw, himself, walking the shop floor like a general and spouting company propaganda, 'We must stand together against this intimidation!' While many of the tram company's employees felt sorry for the locked-out men, none could afford to risk their own jobs by speaking out in their favour, except in the privacy of their own beds, when wives would be glad that their men folk hadn't done anything rash and choked the supply of money that barely kept them in the necessities of life.

~~~

Dublin's general lockout continued, but the trams were kept running. Policemen stood guard along the route to protect the drivers and conductors. On one occasion a protestor diverted two of the DMPs at the junction of Church Street and the quays by jumping into the Liffey. Thinking the man was drowning, one of the policemen pulled off his boots and tunic and jumped in to save him. The second policeman was gobsmacked as the 'drowning' man suddenly swam away from his colleague, using a powerful front crawl (later, it was found that the man was a regular entrant in the annual Liffey Swim). Meanwhile, other men had gathered at the now unguarded junction and they bombarded the next passing tram. Then an incident happened in Waterford Street, just around the corner from Marlborough Street; a crowd of protesters stoned the police, who drew batons and charged them. The crowd was scattered and some of the protesters ran through the open front door of a tenement building, and the police chased in after them. During the scuffles, up and down the stairs of the building, an old woman – with the misfortune to be curious – stepped out on to her landing and in the excitement and confusion a young member let loose with a baton and left her bony arms black and blue.

James was shocked when he heard what had happened (the story had been magnified a thousand times by street talk). It had occurred around the corner from where they lived; the boys could easily have been caught up in it, or, Lily out with Peter could have walked straight into it. What was the city coming to?

And it didn't stop at that; a protester was killed in a baton attack; Larkin, the union organiser, was in Mountjoy Jail. All the while, James hated being on the side of might but he had a responsibility to his family and felt that no one would give him credit for throwing away a good position for the cause of others, or even notice it; yet, it was getting harder by the day to ignore the misfortune of others. Travelling on the tram to and from the depot, he felt more and more isolated from his fellow Dubliners. One night, he had to stay late at the tram sheds to get the Donnybrook car back into service for the following morning, as an obstacle placed on the line had damaged it. Kershaw's instructions: 'Keep the men's noses to the grindstone – the directors don't want Larkin's mob to gain any type of moral victory.'

Near the end of the repair work, he suddenly felt unwell and went to his office and collapsed into his chair, as if forced down by a heavy weight. He had a strong pain across his chest and was afraid to move. Meanwhile, the fitters completed the repairs to the Donnybrook tram and went home, unaware of his condition. He kept thinking of Lily and how she would worry, because he was going to be late. After a while, the pain eased, and he decided to make his way home. But he'd no energy and it took him almost ten minutes to reach the main gate of the tram works. The last tram had left, and he shuffled along the road until a passing hackney coach picked him up. Sitting in the swaying carriage, the clip-clop of the horse on cobblestone in his ears, his constant thoughts of Lily and his boys, Stephen, Bernard, and Peter turned to fear, and he couldn't wait to see them again. The carriage stopped at his house, and the jarvey, realizing that his fare wasn't a drunk, yet still was stumbling, offered to help him inside.

James again felt strong enough to go it alone and put a handful of coins in the driver's hand, hoping it was enough. He eased himself up the steps and went inside. The hallway was in darkness, not even a glimmer of light from beneath Mrs. Hanley's door, but that didn't matter for he knew every step by heart. Soon he would be home in the safety of his family. His heart gave out on the first flight of stairs. Barney Cullen fell over something on his way out to the pub for a nightcap. He cursed as he fumbled in the dark for a shoe he had lost in the fall, then, he realized that someone was lying on the stairs. He thought it was a tramp that had somehow got past the hall door but, when he lit a match, he saw it was his neighbour, James Clancy.

'Are you all right there, fella?' he asked, giving him a shake. It was clear there was something seriously wrong and he went back upstairs to fetch his wife. Mrs. Cullen brought an oil lamp and sat down on the stairs beside him.

'There's no breathing,' she whispered. 'Better go for a priest.'

He found his shoe and hurried to the parochial house. Meanwhile, his wife had whispered an Act of Contrition in James's ear, then fetched a blanket and covered him, leaving only the surprised face staring out. She thought of Lily and her family upstairs, but she wasn't going to be the one to break the bad news. A flustered priest ran into the hall, however when he saw the body, he regained his composure and gave the parishioner a well-practiced Last Rites, then – at Mrs. Cullen's urging – he climbed the stairs to where the Clancy family lived.

Someone was at the door and Lily wondered who it was at that hour; Mrs. Hanley had been paid the rent; she knew that because she'd brought the money down herself. Unless, it was someone else in the house looking to borrow a cup of sugar…something simple like that, yet, it was rather late…

'Who is it?' she called through the door.

'It's Father Fitzsimons, Mrs.Clancy.'

'Yes?

'It's your husband, Mrs. Clancy –'

She pulled open the door. 'What about James?'

Suddenly, years of experience deserted the curate, and he hadn't the heart to tell her the truth, instead, he looked down into the gloom, the way he had come up, and said, 'I'm afraid James has collapsed on the stairs.'

Without giving a thought to the children, Lily pushed past the priest, who made a token effort to restrain her. She rushed down the flights of stairs, with her eyes now on the group below, huddled around a form, illuminated by oil lamps and candles. Stephen had woken and Father Fitzsimons tried to stop him following her, but he squirmed past and hurried after his mother. The group on the stairs had parted to let her through. She sat on a step beside him, stroked his head, and called: 'James, wake up!' Already, a knowing hand had closed his eyes and he could have been taken for a man sleeping, except that he didn't respond, didn't stir. She called him many times, as if she were trying to awaken an obstinate dreamer, her voice echoing up through the building. Finally, she looked to Mrs. Cullen and knew from her that he was dead. That it was time to stop. It was then she realized that young Stephen had managed to fit in beside her on the stair.

Soon, the word spread along the street and a band of respectful locals gathered in the hallway to stand at the foot of the stairs. A doctor and the DMP were sent for to record the death.

CHAPTER SEVEN

James was buried from the Pro-Cathedral, where he had given many years of service as a steward at the monthly sodality and as a collector at Sunday Mass. There were two priests on the altar, a small but impressive group of mourners, including members of the sodality, and representatives from the tram company, a mix of chosen workers from the shop floor and a sprinkling of management. They went in carriages to the cemetery. Stephen and Bernard sat in alongside their mother and Uncle Bernard; he was their father's only other surviving relative yet didn't really resemble him. Mrs. Cullen was minding Peter. Lily told anyone who would listen to her the story of how the priest had knocked at her door and how she'd ran down the stairs and called James's name until she knew it was futile. Young Bernard had noticed how each time at the same place in the story she had begun to cry, at the place where she'd stopped calling his father's name. And, as she repeated the story, he found himself anticipating the moment when the tears would come. It would be followed by a 'there, there' from the sympathising listener.

For Lily, the worst moment was when she arrived home after the funeral – James would never walk into the room again, would never again wash himself over the basin and make a mess on the floor. All the neighbours came in to see her, to help with the void; there were offers of help from all sides. Someone placed a drink in her hand, but it wasn't going to do anything for her, as she was already feeling numb.

Later, when the last of the callers had left, including Uncle Bernard, she put Peter into his cot and sat at the kitchen table with the boys. Stephen and Bernard didn't know what to say. The clock ticked, each second passed slowly. Suddenly, she said: 'What am I going to do?'

Bernard cried and Lily moved round beside him and held him. Stephen tried to be a man but couldn't stop his eyes from filling up. She saw this and reached across and drew him to her. She rocked the two boys in her arms, as if the motion would comfort them and make the whole thing go away. Soon, she also was crying, rubbing her wet face alternatively against the hair of each boy's head.

'What am I going to do?' she repeated.

'Don't worry, Ma,' Stephen said. 'We'll look after you.'

Bernard also spoke: 'Yes, Ma...me and him.'

When they were asleep, she forced herself to go to bed; she lay awake, angry with James for leaving her to fend for herself and the three boys. The next day the undertaker called with the bill. He was extremely polite, but behind it all he still wanted to be paid. He explained the various costs, but she was in no condition to follow what he was saying. Finally he got up to go and said, 'I'll leave the bill, Mrs. Clancy...you can drop into the office anytime in the next week to settle, or, if it suits you better, just send a message to me and I'll come by.' He hadn't mentioned paying it in instalments, as he needed the money to pay his own bills; anyway, he reasoned, James Clancy wouldn't have seen her short.

She was in a panic, for she hadn't found any money in James's drawer, nor could she find a savings book. All she had was a small sum to feed them. She went to her brother-in-law, Bernard, hoping he would help her; however, she had never got on with the wife, Moira, who for some unknown reason had always been cold towards her.

'Can't you go to your own family, Lily?' the brother-in-law said.

'We don't speak,' she said, for after setting up home with James she had cut all ties with them. Now, she couldn't face going back, cap in hand.

'What about the tram company?' Have you thought of asking them?'

She said she would, and as he was showing her to the door, he slipped two crumpled notes into her fist, away from the wife's gaze. 'I'd help you more,' he whispered, 'only you know what she's like.'

~~~

Lily had never been inside the tram company's premises before. James had worked there since joining the company as a runner, then he'd been offered an apprenticeship, after that he had worked as a master craftsman maintaining the carriages, until he was promoted to management, rare for a Catholic.

She was escorted by the gateman to Kershaw's office. His secretary, Eileen, who told her that she had always found James to be 'a lovely man', greeted her with kindness. She brought her in to meet Kershaw, who jumped up from his desk and, hand outstretched, showed his best funereal expression.

'Your husband will be sorely missed, Mrs. Clancy,' he said. 'I don't think we've ever had a supervisor as conscientious as him.'

'It's good of you to say that, Mr. Kershaw. James always said the tram company was a big part of his life.'

There was a moment of embarrassed silence.

'Is there something special you've come to see me about, Mrs. Clancy?'

She was uncomfortable, unused to the formality of a big office, although she had been slightly surprised at its untidiness, for engineering drawings were scattered across the desk, and spare parts from trams lay propped against a wall, looking out of place. She couldn't control the trembling in her hand as she took the undertaker's bill from her bag and handed it across to him.

'What's this?'

She hesitated.

He flattened out the account and read it. Then he folded it and handed it back. 'Dying is an expensive business,' he said, 'but it appears to be a normal enough sum.'

'But, I haven't the money…'

'Oh! I understand…' Kershaw lifted a large notebook from his desk and consulted it; little did Lily know that he was looking at a blank page. 'Well, Mrs. Clancy, you'll certainly have James's wages for the few days before he died…but nothing like enough to settle an account of that size.'

'I thought there'd be more.'

Kershaw studied her. He hated having to deal with situations like this. 'Perhaps I can convince the wages office to pay a full week's wages,' he said, shifting the blame onto anonymous clerks. 'You'll still be short, but it's probably the best that can be done. You know how it is, with this trouble on the streets and everything. People are beginning to stay off the trams, even though we've put guards –'

'But how will I get the rest?' she blurted.

Kershaw was surprised. Because Clancy had been a foreman, part of management, he'd expected his wife to know how to conduct herself.

'That's not for me or the company to say, Mrs. Clancy.' He thought for a moment, then said: 'Perhaps you could sell some belongings?'

Kershaw led her to an office, where a wages clerk got her to sign for a small manila envelope. He called a runner to guide her through the shop floor and its obstacles to make sure she reached the front gate in safety. She couldn't shake the fear she'd felt when Kershaw had suggested selling some belongings, for it had made her think of the women going to the pawnshop. A bottle of gin was bought on the way home.

That evening she let the boys out to play and put Peter down in the cot; she needed time to think about her problems. She poured a drink and looked round the room. The carriage clock on the fireplace mantle was given an executioner's stare. Maybe, I could sell that? It must be worth a few shillings but who'd buy it? Between strikes and workers locked out of their jobs, everyone seems to be skint nowadays. The obvious answer was to go to the pawnshop, but she couldn't bear the thought of having to queue with all those wretched women carrying their swollen pillowcases. She took another drink.

Next day, Lily sent the boys back to school (since the funeral she had kept them home for company). From her window she watched the comings and goings at the pawnbroker's. A lull came in the traffic of clients, and she guessed there was only a handful of people inside at that moment. She wrapped the clock in an old newspaper, put a coat on Peter and headed out, him under one arm, the clock under the other. She wasted no time on the stairs, afraid she would bump into a neighbour: if she met someone, how could she cope with the embarrassment? Her heart was thumping, as if she were doing something illegal, like an act of burglary.

She hurried into the pawnshop and, not knowing what to expect, she hung back from the counter. A man, probably younger than herself, beckoned her forward. The wrapped clock was put on the counter. 'I want to pawn this,' she said, surprised by the brazen sound of her voice.

'What is it?' he asked, then seeing Peter in her arms he took the initiative and drew apart the newspaper wrapping. He studied the carriage clock, clicked his tongue, and gave a professional, 'Hmm'.

'It belonged to the Queen herself,' Lily said.

'Did it, now…' He had heard too many ridiculous claims in the past and no longer gave them consideration.

'I tell you it did. It was my late husband's, but he got it when a distant cousin of his died. She'd worked in the royal household and got it when leaving service.'

The pawnshop employee went through the motions of examining the clock. Suddenly, he tensed, rubbed at an inscription. He read Osborne House and looked again at Lily. 'You're not a regular here, missus. However, the face is familiar – do I know you from somewhere?'

'I live next door.' She quickly added: 'But I've never been in here before.'

'That's it! I've seen you pass outside. I knew I knew the face.' He placed the clock back down on the counter. 'It's a nice clock, missus, and its provenance makes it a little more interesting. But that's all, just a *little* more.'

'Provenance?'

'Where it came from.'

'Then, you'll take it?'

The man examined it again. 'You do know how a pawnshop works?'

She had a blank look.

'I can only give you part of its value and if it's not redeemed and the interest paid before six months, it'll be sold by us.'

'Then, you will take it?'

He drew a docket book to himself and filled in the details. From experience he could tell which person would come back for their necessities or their treasures – he didn't think this woman was one of them. His boss would be happy with him, for if she never returned then the item would be sold to the trade at a good profit. He remembered an early lesson from his employer – 'Never feel guilty at making a profit!'

Lily went straight to the undertaker and paid the bill. 'It's a pleasure to have dealings with you, Mrs. Clancy. You won't believe the number of people that take us for a charity…they want their loved one buried but keep us waiting for our money.' He escorted her to the door, unaware that she had only a handful of shillings left. Walking away, she wondered if she should have reneged on the bill, used the money for other pressing needs; the truth was, she was too respectable for that and wouldn't have people thinking badly of her.

She stopped in Talbot Street to buy food and then went home to prepare the lunch. Mrs. Hanley sprung out from her room when she heard her come in, as if she'd been crouched behind her door, waiting for her.

'It's Friday, Mrs. Clancy. Will yeh come and see me later with the book?'

Lily realized she was talking about the rent.

'I will, Mrs. Hanley. I'll send young Stephen down with it later.'

The landlady retreated into her room, like a spider retreating into a dusty corner. Lily climbed the stairs, angry that she now had to deal with such matters, for money had never been her worry when James was about, as he had dealt with the weekly rent, getting the rent book scratched by an inky scrawl. She counted out what money was left. There was enough, with something remaining to feed them, but what would she do for next week's rent? When the boys came in, she sent Stephen downstairs with the money. When he came back, he pointed to where a fresh scrawl had been made.

'Ma, I'll do this job for you every week,' he said.

'You're a good boy, Stephen.'

Bernard didn't like being excluded and said, 'I want to do it next time!'

'We'll see, Bernard.'

'No – I'm the oldest!' Stephen said.

'Boys, I said, we'll see.'

Later, when they went outside, she poured herself a drink. She looked slowly round her home, somehow seeing it with fresh eyes, not missing any detail: she had been proud that she and James had managed to make a comfortable living area for their family. But now, he was wiped from the space, like a figurine snatched from a Christmas crib never to be seen again, and, if the money dried-up, their home could be stripped of any comfort and, worse still, it could be taken from them – it was a terrifying thought. She could end up like one of the women who regularly stood in the queue outside the pawnshop on a Monday morning; indeed, because she had pawned the treasured carriage clock, she'd almost become one of them. She quickly emptied her glass and poured another drink.

Friday came round again, the weekly circle of debt. She went to Mrs. Hanley and nervously told her she couldn't pay the rent, at least, not for the moment. The woman tightened the stained cardigan she was wearing by opening a safety pin, then, she pulled the garment together and re-clasped it. Only then did she speak: 'If yeh can find money for drink, yeh can find money for me!'

There seemed to be no mercy beneath that dirt-ingrained face.

~~~

Parnell Street was as busy as usual. Among the greengrocers, public houses, a chemist shop (famous for cure-alls) and a milk bar with its own dairy behind it, stood Abie's Second-hand Furniture Emporium. Lily was waiting for the pavement to clear, as she couldn't be seen going into the shop. She moved up and down the street several times, looking aimlessly in other shop windows. After what seemed an age, the moment came when the street went quiet, and she hurried to Abie's, only to hesitate outside, for deep down she didn't want to part with her furniture. Her thoughts raced: If I sell it now, how can I ever hope to replace it? It felt like selling an arm. But if Hanley doesn't get her rent, we'll be on the street, and what good will the furniture be to us then without a roof over our heads? She decided that James would have wanted her to do this and was about to enter the shop, when a man, a stranger, politely took her arm and guided her to one side.

'Excuse me, madam,' he said, tipping a bowler hat, 'but are you buying or selling?'

She stared at him a moment, surprised by the question. 'I'm selling, but what's it to you, sir?'

'You're not going into old Abie, are you? You know what they say about that rogue?'

'No.'

'Abie wouldn't give a fair price to his own mother!'

She stalled.

'Madam, you look a good sort and I'd hate to see you taken advantage of. Listen, if you've something to sell, I'll give you the best price.'

'How am I to know that?'

'I'm an honest dealer, madam, many years in the business. You can trust me, but not someone like that Abie fellow. How do you think he can afford this big fancy shop? This Emporium?'

For dramatic impact, he pointed to the sign above the door. She could see the sense in what he was saying. 'You'll give a good price?'

'As God is my witness, madam.' He produced a calling card:

Patrick Lee, esq.

Dealer in Fine Furniture

She said, 'I suppose it won't cost me anything to show it to you.'

'A wise decision, madam, you won't regret it.' He steered her away from the front of Abie's and asked, 'When can I call? I could go with you right now?'

'Not now, but can you come when it gets dark?'

'I understand, madam. A wise decision; let's keep our business to ourselves.'

She gave him the address and started for home, taking care to hurry past Ganly's for fear of having to come face-to-face with either him or her. Stephen and Bernard were allowed stay up late, as she needed them to keep an eye out for the furniture man and to bring him up when he arrived.

Patrick Lee had high praise for the furniture and was interested in the sideboard, the mirror, a mahogany table, and matching chairs. 'I'll give you three guineas for the lot, Mrs. Clancy.'

The price seemed good to Lily.

'I'll even give you ten shillings on account and fix up the rest when we come by tomorrow to collect them.' He pressed the money into her hand.

While the boys showed him to the hall door, she sat on one of the sold chairs and wondered on what she would be sitting on the following day, and, the day after that. She stayed up late that night, occasionally stroking her furniture.

Lee came back early the next day with two helpers, young men with the broad chests of farmers' sons. He supervised the work, shouting directions – 'Mind how you go, lads' – 'Don't damage that corner.' When they were moving the heavy sideboard down the stairs, they grunted and strained. Lily had hoped to sneak the furniture out, but now the whole house would know her business. From her window, she watched her prized objects being placed on to two handcarts. When they were ready to push off, Lee came to her to settle, but when she put out her hand, she saw only five shillings. He explained: 'I've given you money on account, Mrs. Clancy, and I'll be back with the rest when I sell your fine furniture.'

'But you never said that before?'

'That's the real world, Mrs. Clancy. It's how it works. You get the rest when I get my money.'

She was confused; she'd never had to deal with someone like this before; it was moments like this when she needed James at her side.

Patrick Lee had been a gentleman until now but suddenly he became impatient. 'Missus, do you want me to sell the furniture at all, at all? I can get the lads to take it off the carts right now, and no hard feelings.' He waited with confidence for her answer.

'You know I want to sell.'

'Then, trust me, Mrs. Clancy. I'll be back.'

She watched her furniture rattling on the handcarts as they were shoved up the street. Then, when the cortege turned a corner (it had felt like another funeral), she faced the room and was shocked at its sudden bareness. We must get something to sit on, she thought, and Stephen and Bernard were sent across to Moore Street to hunt for any wooden boxes that the dealers on the street might have cast aside, warning them as they left, 'And, be careful crossing Sackville Street!' They headed off – apprentice scavengers – and she sat on the floor, with Peter on her lap, a drink in her hand. The boys came back, clutching their 'finds', and, after she had made a fuss of them, she instructed Stephen to go out for a bottle of wine.

'What if they say I'm too young?'

'Pretend to the man behind the counter that your ma is sick, and just smile.'

Bernard didn't ask to go with him, as he normally would, for his mother had given him the important task of arranging the empty fruit boxes, their new seats. She sat on one as a test; it stayed together; however, she failed to notice that Bernard was watching her, downhearted that her face had taken on the silly look that came when she drank, the look he hated.

~~~

Patrick Lee, esq. never came back with the rest of the money.

Only then did Lily realize that there was no address on his calling card. She began to hang around Parnell Street on the slim chance that she would see him again, especially outside the second-hand furniture shop. But he never appeared. She was tempted to go into the Emporium to ask its owner, Abie, if he happened to know Patrick Lee, but she couldn't see herself doing that without revealing the full story. To make matters worse, ever since she had been swindled, she'd heard that the Jew was a fair man; she was now certain that she'd been a fool.

And, to report Patrick Lee to the DMP, she would have to go to the barracks at Store Street, and she certainly wasn't going in there again.

~~~

Lily managed to keep the family in Marlborough Street until the following spring – then was faced with looking for a cheaper place.

Mrs. Hanley gave her a month's grace, a sum she knew Lily couldn't pay. 'It's all I can do for yeh,' she said. 'I'm a poor widow woman and it's me rents that keep me going. You have to understand…' Lily hadn't expected this act of kindness. The family moved a short distance to a tenement room in Waterford Street. Lily had always dreaded the possibility that one day she might have to live with the poor, now she had no choice, for she'd become one of them. Her family had to have shelter, and there was no space left in her life for pride and choosiness; she even washed floors in a hotel on Great Denmark Street, and, after school, the boys joined the many other youngsters scouring the streets for firewood, and the chance to earn a ha'penny.

To console herself, she knew she could have been worse off – at least, she had been able to bring the beds with them from Marlborough Street, for the family in the room below slept on homemade mattresses stuffed with straw. During the night, Lily would wake up and hear the noises of tenement life: the talking, the crying, the arguments, and noisy lovemaking. It came through the plaster-crumbling walls, the gaps in the floor planks and the once-ornate ceiling that told of former genteel times. Sometimes, to get back to sleep, she would try to count the number of people living in the building and always gave up at about sixty. With only one toilet out the back, the chamber pots, or buckets or whatever was being used in the rooms during the night caused a smell that lingered throughout the building. In the morning you would cover the receptacle and carry it down the stairs and out to the toilet. And there was always a deep coughing coming from somewhere in the building. Tuberculosis was in the air, Lily thought, and everyone was breathing it. Sometimes, thinking about the position they were in would get the better of her and she would cry herself to sleep.

As the months passed, she knew there was no way they would ever get out of Waterford Street; nevertheless, even though all pride had been squeezed from her, she still had memories of the days when times had been good for them, especially when she passed Mrs. Hanley's house and looked up at the windows of their former home. The new tenant had put up lace curtains, and she always expected them to part and a stranger's face to appear, where once hers had been.

Peter was now running about, a stubborn boy, testing his will against hers; Stephen and Bernard were companions for one another, still attending school in Marlborough Street. She knew that sooner or later they would be separated when Stephen would walk out the school gate for the last time and look for a fulltime job and she worried about Bernard being left to face the hazards of the school playground without the protection of an older brother, who already was working after school for the Food Emporium, delivering groceries on a messenger bike.

Lily allowed herself one treat a week – she went to a bar along Summerhill on Saturday nights and sat in the snug with the other women, drank porter and forgot the world outside; however, she didn't abstain between her nights out. No, there was always a drink to be had in her tenement room, no matter how bad things were.

It was on one of those Saturday nights in Summerhill when she first met Jemser Flood.

She had waltzed out of the public house on her own that night, feeling that the world could do her no harm, but when she hit the cold air, she started to wobble, her legs refusing to accept the brain's directions. She managed to cross the road and a homing instinct took over, taking her on her regular short-cut through a laneway off Rutland Street, where she fell and couldn't get up, her body robbed of all its strength. She looked up at the frosted rooftops and the cold stars; that was all she knew, until a man pulling at her shoulder woke her up.

Jemser Flood was also on the way home after a night's drinking. At first, when he saw the woman crumpled on the ground, he feared she was dead. Then, he heard gentle snoring and through a cloud of drink he decided that he couldn't leave this person lying out all night in the freezing cold – otherwise there certainly would be a corpse in the morning.

He managed to wake her. 'Are yeh all right there, missus?'

She gave him a blank look, then, glanced round her, trying to figure out where she was and who this man was.

'We'll have to get yeh out of here, missus. Where's your home?'

'There,' Lily said, pointing in the vague direction of Waterford Street. Her mouth couldn't form any more words and she realized she'd wet herself and started to weep. Jemser got her upright, but her legs buckled beneath her; another effort, this time throwing one of her arms across his shoulder, and, struggling like a shaky old gatepost, he managed to keep her on her feet. Eventually, he got her walking and they swayed to the bottom of the laneway.

They rested against a wall, then he asked in gasps: 'Which way, now?'

Again, she pointed, no words.

He checked with her at every corner; finally, she stopped outside a tenement and sat on the granite steps.

'It's here, missus? Well, thanks be to jaysus…' He hauled her up the steps, through the open entrance into the dark hallway, and, not knowing which door to knock on, he decided to try the first one he met. He propped her against the wall and by accident felt her breast beneath his hand; he pulled it away and knocked on the door and a young girl with a candle answered. She looked at him, then, she saw Lily.

'Ma,' she called back into the shadows of the room, 'it's that Mrs. Clancy again, and she's stocious!'

A large woman, who looked strong enough to haul coal bags, appeared. Jemser said, 'She was lying on the ground…I don't know her, at all.'

The woman came out and steadied Lily. 'We'll get her up to her place.' She called an older daughter to give a hand.

'I'll leave her with yeh, then?' he said, glad to pass on the burden. Outside on Waterford Street, there was a heavy frost, and he made his way towards his room in nearby Gardiner Street, all the time thinking of the soft feel of the woman.

He asked around the next day and found out that she was a widow.

Lily was surprised when the stranger knocked at her door.

'Yeh don't 'member me at all?' he asked.

'Should I?'

'Last night. I brought yeh home.'

'I'm sorry, but I don't remember...'

'You're all right, then?'

'Why wouldn't I be?'

At that moment, Peter called to her from inside the room.

'I have to go to the child.'

'Don't let me stop yeh.'

She took him at his word and shut the door. Jemser lingered on the landing for some moments, then skipped down the stairs, his mind full of the woman.

On the following Saturday night, he headed to Summerhill to look for her. He guessed which pub she was at and opened the door of the snug and peered in – she was among a group of biddies in black shawls, and he signalled for her to come to the door. All eyes were on him.

'Who's your man?' one of the women shouted.

'Our Lily's a dark horse!' another one roared.

Lily recognised him but had no idea what he wanted.

A toothless woman took a pipe from her mouth and declared to the group: 'It's only Jemser Flood. He's no catch!'

Lily went to the door, knowing she was the centre of attention, and hating it.

'Will yeh drink with me?' he asked.

'Why would I drink with you?'

'For company's sake.'

'I'm in company,' she said, nodding back into the snug towards the upturned faces of the women. 'And besides, I don't keep company with men.'

'I don't mean anything by it...'

Lily looked back at the women in the snug and declared, 'Ladies, did you hear that? He wants me to drink with him.'

'Yeh didn't have to tell that lot,' he said, looking pained.

She left him at the door and went back to her place among the women and took up her drink and the conversation resumed at where it had left off, as if he didn't exist.

He knew he could do no more, at least not on that night, and moved along Summerhill to a different public house. However, he wasn't one for giving up. During the following days, he hung about Waterford Street hoping to come across her; it had to look like a chance meeting. Eventually, he spied her coming out of the tenement; he felt excited, and his heart was beating loudly. He rushed along the far side of the street, then, when he was ahead of her, crossed the road and turned back to meet her, trying to appear natural.

'It's yourself,' he said, nodding at her. His hope was that she would stop and talk; instead, she looked straight past him. On another day, he followed her to Mass in the Pro-Cathedral and sat in a pew directly behind her. When she was leaving, he placed himself beside the holy water font, hoping she would notice him. She came along and dipped her hand in the water, made a quick sign of the cross, and went out the door. He wondered if she seen him but just hadn't shown it.

Jemser kept this up for a while, trying to attract her attention without going straight up to her, but weeks passed by, and, in the end, he accepted it was hopeless and stopped hanging about Waterford Street.

He wasn't to know then that another opportunity would come along.

CHAPTER EIGHT

The rebellion of Easter 1916 meant little to Lily Clancy, for as far as she was concerned, she couldn't see how it was going to change her lot. She knew it was dangerous on the streets, especially as they lived so close to Sackville Street, where the General Post Office had been snatched by the rebels and was now under siege.

Stephen was now aged thirteen, Bernard eleven and Peter seven, and the boys amused themselves by counting the rifle cracks and artillery booms. Lily followed the news of what was going on outside through the talk in the tenement. Then word ran through the building that the crowd was taking things out of Clery's.

At first, she didn't want anything to do with it; but when she saw others running to their rooms with armfuls of 'free items', she became caught up in the excitement. Leaving Stephen in charge, she ran out into the dark street, ignoring the curfew, and joined up with a voracious mob heading for the department store. She was carried along, amazed that she had no fear, like a placid dog caught in a pack of sheep-killers, and when they rounded the corner into North Earl Street, she even stepped across the body of a dead soldier, as if he were only a stiff cat. Ahead of her, she could see flames leaping and sparks flying into the night sky. 'Jaysus, the GPO's on fire!' she said, but no one had time to listen to her, all were rushing to the large gap in the broken display window at the side of Clery's. She picked her way across the shards of glass, passed a fallen mannequin that had been stripped, its female contours shown to the world, an eerie smile on a china face and a head at a funny angle where it had hit a wall. Then she was inside the store, following the crowd, the way lit by a dull, yellow-orange light, coming through the front windows on Sackville Street from the flaming GPO. People were rushing past her, breathless to get their hands on a prize, or, as many prizes as possible, things they would never have been able to afford. It was all there for her, too. She ran like a child through the aisles of goods.

Within minutes, she had collected a fur stole, a hat fit for a garden party at the Governor General's, and, also, she was tottering in shoes with a high heel, a giddy new experience. She stopped and stood in the centre of the chaos, undecided as to what else to take – then she remembered an item she wanted. She headed for the jewellery department and searched the shelves for a carriage clock like the one she had pawned (never to be redeemed). There was only one left on display, and she grabbed it just as another woman went to lift it.

'I saw it first!' the woman shrieked. 'Give it to me!'

Lily tightened her grip.

'I said, it's mine!' the woman said, trying to take it, but Lily wasn't letting go. The woman was pulling Lily's hands apart, and because she was a bigger and stronger woman, it was certain that she was going to win in the end. By now, Lily's hat was on the point of sliding off her head and the fur stole was about her ankles. She felt her hold on the clock weaken and was about to concede, when an arm came between them and a voice roared at the woman, 'Get on with yeh! There are plenty of other things for yeh to put your greedy eyes on!'

The woman swore at Jemser Flood and moved on, sulking like a child denied a toffee.

Jemser Flood picked up the fur stole and placed it round Lily's shoulders. 'I'll take yeh back,' he said, smiling in the flickering glow. 'That's if your shopping trip is finished?'

'It's finished, but I can make my own way home, thank you.'

At that moment repeated cracks of rifle fire came from just outside and Lily jumped with fright, her newfound bravery suddenly leaving her.

'Come on!' Jemser said.

She followed him as he pushed his way past laden looters; there were so many now in the store that they crammed the aisles. He had turned his own jacket into a makeshift bag and, as they fought their way through, he stopped every so often to pick up an item that had caught the eye. They burst out of the store into the street and when they were clear of broken glass, she took off the stilettos and ran behind him. The hat came off and he went back and picked it up for her. She was breathless and strangely excited by the time they got to Waterford Street. They stopped to gather themselves, and she put the shoes back on, adjusted the fur stole, allowed Jemser to place the hat on her head, and, clutching her new clock, she wobbled along the cobblestones.

'It's Lady Muck from Foxrock!' he said.

They laughed all the way up the stairs to the room. Jemser had seen rooms like this before – where his sister with her ten children lived was as bad as this, maybe worse. Lily was passing the fur stole round her children, inviting them to touch it. 'And did you see the new carriage clock?' she said. 'I wouldn't have it if it weren't for this man.'

Peter was too young to care, but the older boys were already wondering who this man was?

Then Lily said, 'Oh! My old shoes…I left them behind me.'

'I'll go back for them,' Jemser said.

'And risk getting shot at?'

'If yeh want them, I'll go.'

'No such thing,' Lily said. 'They're not worth dying for.' At that moment she realized that Jemser Flood was then actually inside their room, in their home. She backed away from him and pointed to the door. He could see the change in her; she was again the woman who kept giving him the cold shoulder. He gathered up his own bag of loot and left her standing in her squalid little home, surrounded by her three sons. He was on the landing, when he heard her call after him: 'Thank you, Jemser.'

Anyone passing him on the stairs would have seen a broad grin on his face.

~~

Lily hadn't changed her mind about what was happening in the streets; it wasn't her concern; all she knew was that the family was now hungry. The gunfire stopped, and it was safe to go outside again. Rather than drawing attention to herself by struggling with the stilettos, she went out in her bare feet but found the shops empty of food. In no time her feet were sore, and she wondered how other people managed to do it. She knocked at the side door of a convent and because they knew her, was given a pair of cracked shoes that had cardboard inserts to cover the holes in the soles. The nuns told her that an elderly sister who had just been buried wouldn't need them anymore and asked her to pray for her.

Meanwhile Stephen had gone scavenging. At Summerhill he found a crowd surrounding a farmer's horse and cart, where the horse had slipped and couldn't be made to stand. The unfortunate man could only look on as the crowd dived on his cargo of vegetables bound for market. Stephen arrived home in triumph with cabbages under his arms and carrots and potatoes bulging his pockets.

A few days later, Lily heard urgent banging on her door. It was the woman from down below. 'They're searching all the houses!' she yelled. 'It's the DMPs!'

Lily ran back into the room and stuck the stilettoes up the chimney, then took a lingering look at the fur stole, the garden-party hat and the carriage clock and threw them out the window. She saw the fur stole light on the railings round the area; the hat was caught by a gust of wind and blew down the terrace and the clock bounced off the footpath, its workings spilling on to the road. Suddenly, two baton wielding DMPs burst in and looked round the room. They prodded the worn bedclothes, even kicked a bed over, then seeing no sign of newfound prosperity they thundered upstairs to the next landing.

She had been lucky; others hadn't been as quick as her and ended up in Store Street Barracks.

When Jemser called again, he said, 'At least you're okay, you've shoes to your feet to take yeh to the pub, that's if yeh can learn to walk in them.'

She looked at him and thought how she'd never have done anything like this if James had been still alive. Certainly - rebellion or no rebellion - he wouldn't have had anything to do with breaking the law, whether the law of the land or God's law. This man in front of her wasn't as fine a man as James, but he *was* a bit of a daredevil...

Lily became his Saturday night drinking companion. It didn't go further than that, for a while at least; at first it seemed he just wanted someone to talk to, that is until the time on the landing outside her room he tried to kiss her.

'The boys will hear us,' she said, pulling away from him.

'Forget the boys, Lily, think of yourself for once.'

'Don't talk to me like that. You're not thinking of me, you're thinking only of yourself.'

'I thought yeh liked me?'

'I like the company, any company.'

'Well, yeh won't have mine if yeh keep treating me like this.'

'What?'

'Yeh heard me. We should be closer. Yeh know? Close...man 'n' woman, like.'

'I couldn't do that with you nor anyone else, not after a good man like James Clancy, God rest him.'

'God rest him, is right. I must and I will respect the dead, but he's not here, is he? I don't see his ghost anywhere about. I'm the one that sits with yeh in the pub, makes yeh laugh, listens to yeh going on 'n' on about your boys. He can't do that for yeh, Lily, can he?'

'I have memories.'

'Are yeh going to waste the rest of your life on your memories?'

'If I want to waste me life, I'll waste it any way I see fit.'

Jemser stood back from her in the gloom, his hands deep in his trouser pockets, and he knew he couldn't win against a ghost. 'Well, here's one won't be hanging round to see it.' He turned to the stairs and left.

She listened till the echo of his hobnail boots evaporated into the tenement, then went into the room. The boys were still up, and she guessed the two older ones had heard and probably understood all that had gone on outside.

'That's the end of him,' she said.

It was Bernard who went to her. He stood beside her and rubbed her arm and smelled porter from her breath when she leaned to kiss his cheek. She looked tired as she plopped on the side of her bed.

'Who's going to help Mammy with her stockings?' she asked.

Peter ran to her and yanked off her shoes – they fell to the floor. Bernard then came and pulled off the stockings and she lay back on her elbows while he rubbed her toes. Stephen helped her wriggle from her topcoat.

'I don't need anyone else,' she said, 'as long as I have my three sons. Isn't that right?'

She fell asleep in the rest of her clothes.

~~~

Lily started feeling a bad pain in her knee. She didn't go to a doctor, but when she brought it up in the snug, they said in a chorus, 'it's rheumatism!' She went to the chemist in Parnell Street for a 'Cure-all', to be rubbed on and covered with a bandage, but, while there was less pain, she still found she couldn't stay on her knees and wash floors for the same number of hours as before. Suddenly, her small income was shrinking.

Stephen gave up school and went fulltime as a messenger boy, and without telling his mother Bernard also tried for work at the Food Emporium. The man laughed at him. 'You should be at school, sonny. Come back in a few years when there's more meat on you.' After that, he resigned himself to taking Peter to school, just as Stephen had taken him. He now saw more of his mother than Stephen did, and sometimes he came home from school and found her drunk. Then, he would mind his younger brother until the effects of the drink wore off, or, until Stephen came in from work. He was in trouble in school for poor homework, for there was no one to keep him off the streets at night.

One night, he saw a man being attacked by a gang. They kicked the teeth from his gums and left him lying with blood oozing from his shattered mouth. Bernard and his street friends gazed at the crumpled moaning figure. The man turned on the ground and, at that moment, a watch chain caught the light from the street gas lamp. It led to the man's waistcoat pocket. One of his street friends ran forward and tugged at the chain – a watch shot out and rested on the moaning man's chest. Someone dared Bernard to go and get it. He darted over and undid the watch and chain, just as he had done when he'd played with his father's timepiece while sitting on his knee (then his father had let him hold it to his ear and listen to the movement). Now there was no time for anything like that, only time to run and escape. Grasping the watch and chain, he raced up the street and straight into the long arms of a DMP man on patrol.

Lily heard the commotion down in the street, rushed downstairs and met the policeman holding a sobbing Bernard by the collar of his gansey. 'Are you the mother?' he demanded.

'I am, officer…what's he done?'

He held up the watch and chain. 'He's gone and committed the seventh sin, missus.'

She looked at Bernard, whose eyes were downturned. 'He's only a lad,' she said. He wouldn't –'

'Sorry, missus, but I saw him, myself.' The policeman's free hand pointed to the man who'd been attacked. People from the street were helping the victim to stand unsupported; he was in a daze, exploring the damage to his mouth with a finger. 'That unfortunate man was set upon, and your boy – rather than being the Good Samaritan – thought it better to rob him.'

'I still can't believe it.' She cupped Bernard's face in her hands and looked into his wet eyes – something in his look said all she needed to know. She had a sudden terrible feeling that her husband James was watching from the afterlife. I have failed him, she thought. 'Can't you turn a blind eye, officer? Let him go? He's only a young fella.'

The policeman said, 'Hold on to your son a minute, missus, while I see to the other man'. He ambled across to the victim, handed him back the watch and chain, and then took out his notebook. Surprisingly, the man didn't want to answer any questions and hurried off, like a Mass-goer leaving the back of the church early. The policeman came back to Lily, took a long hard look at the snivelling boy at the end of her arm, and said: 'Missus, this is how it starts. For his own good, it has to be nipped in the bud.'

She was almost blind with panic. A woman from her building said she'd mind Peter. Lily followed the oak-like figure in uniform and the stringy figure of her son through the streets, on her way again to the barracks at Store Street. She imagined someone there exclaiming, 'Mrs. Clancy, what've you done, this time?' Thankfully, no one on duty knew her; Bernard was placed in her care for the night; she was to bring him to the Children Court, at Smithfield, in the morning. She gripped him as they walked back to the tenement. Stephen, who on seniority had convinced himself he should take on the role of his dead father, met them at the top of the stairs and went to give him a clatter.

Lily stepped between them. 'He's your brother, Stephen.'

~~~

Lily stood with Bernard outside the Children Court waiting for it to open. It was cold on Smithfield, worsened by a chilling wind unrestrained on the wide space, a delivery cart from the whiskey distillery trundled past. Eventually, there was a rattle of keys from within as a porter opened the door. He pointed to the waiting room, and it wasn't long before the room was filled with boys closely guarded by worried-looking fathers or mothers (mostly mothers); the faces of the young offenders were gleaming from a recent meeting with soap and water, yet their clothes were worn thin from too many rubbings on a washboard.

Bernard's case was called, and he couldn't control his shaking knees as he stood before the judge. He was glad that his mother was standing with him, his only friend in this austere place. The judge – not in robes, but a grey suit – was expressionless as he listened to the policeman deliver the evidence in a monotone courtroom voice. It was all so matter of fact and this seemed to add even more seriousness to the account. Bernard sensed that his mother was weeping.

'Well, Master Clancy,' the judge asked, 'what do you have to say for yourself?'

Bernard hadn't the confidence to speak.

'Look at the shame you've brought on this good woman.' At that, the judge acknowledged Lily's presence in the court with a polite nod. 'Your poor mother and all who belong to you,' he continued. 'I'm sure you were never reared to be light-fingered. Please, tell me, young man, that this is the case.'

Bernard still couldn't speak, never expecting to be asked direct questions.

'He's a good boy, really, your honour,' Lily said, glimpsing some sympathy from the judge. 'I don't know what got into him – I blame it on the boys he was mixing with.'

'Mrs. Clancy, I'm inclined to agree with you, and your son has an honest face.'

'I thank you, your honour. Thank you, thank you...'

'But, Mrs. Clancy, I feel obliged to protect...' – he consulted the charge sheet – 'young Bernard from the influence of the streets.'

'Your honour, I'll keep him off the streets, I promise. And it'll never happen again, I swear to it.'

The judge considered her words. He asked, 'Where's the young man's father today?'

'I'm a widow, your honour, but I do look after my boys.'

'How many children do you have, madam?'

'Three sons, your honour...that includes Bernard...'

'Hmm...widowhood never made it easier for any woman.'

'I can raise my son, your honour.'

'I would like to believe you, Mrs. Clancy, however, I'm inclined towards sending him to the industrial school at Artane, purely for his own good.'

'But, your honour, he's a good boy. I'll make sure –'

'Madam,' the judge said, his tone hardening, 'the industrial school will protect him from the evils of the street, and he'll be taught a trade. Surely, that's what any mother would want? For her son to become self-sufficient?'

'But, your honour, he's only a child and –'

'Mrs. Clancy, the court has made its decision.' The judge called impatiently to the clerk of the court: 'Next case, please!'

The policeman took Bernard by the arm.

She cried out, 'Where are you taking him?'

'I'd advise you to be quiet in the court, missus,' he whispered, 'otherwise the judge could round on you.'

'C'mon, lad,' he said, leading Bernard out to the entrance hallway, where he was made to sit beside three other boys, also waiting to be taken to Artane. A covered-in carriage, drawn by two horses with jingling harnesses arrived. The boys followed another DMP member outside; one boy tried to make a run for it, but the carriage driver was wise to it and had taken up a position to block any escape effort. The four boys climbed aboard and took their places, sitting opposite each other on wooden bench seats that ran the length of the carriage. The door was slammed shut. They tried to catch sight of a friendly face through any aperture they could find; Bernard saw his mother, who was waving a blind farewell at the carriage. The DMP man threw a bicycle on to the roof of the carriage and climbed up beside the driver.

Lily stood out on the cobblestone and watched the swaying carriage as it moved up Smithfield. She had caught one last glimpse of her son before he went into the carriage. Such a lost look, she thought. She was now crying freely, crying from shame, the shame of letting Bernard down, the shame of letting the good name of her late husband down, and, as the carriage turned the corner and vanished from sight, she mouthed the words, 'I'll be out to see you Bernard.'

CHAPTER NINE

The boys were still and silent, except the one who had tried to escape. He couldn't stay put and peered out at the passing countryside, reporting back to the others everything he saw – 'It's all bleedin' fields out here.' – 'We're out with the culchies!'

The horses laboured on the long hill from the city. The carriage-driver kept them to the task and knew that when they passed the tilled fields of Donnycarney the animals would sense they were near Artane and would find a second breath. True to form, they livened up and soon they passed between large gates, and, with a smart clip-clop, they were on the avenue that led to an enormous grey building: Artane Industrial School.

The escorting policeman unlocked the carriage. 'Out you get, boys,' he said, 'and, don't be looking so worried. Artane will make men of you and by the time the Brothers are finished with you, your families will be proud of you.'

They were lined up beside the carriage, and Bernard watched the policeman go to a group of men standing on the steps at the front door. They wore black soutanes down to their ankles and sizeable rosary beads fell from wide black belts: these were Christian Brothers. They were laughing and joking among themselves, which was a relief to Bernard. The policeman seemed to know them well and shook hands all round, then recovered his bicycle from the roof of the carriage and disappeared down the avenue: it would be downhill all the way to the city. The carriage moved away, round the back of the building, the horses heading for their oats, the carriage driver for a mug of tea, maybe with something stronger added.

A brother sauntered over to Bernard and said in Gaelic, 'Dia dhuit.'

Bernard's reply to the greeting was automatic – 'Dia is Mhuire dhuit' – basic Irish drilled into him at Marlborough Street School.

Another brother overheard and came across; he was smoking, and his hair shone with Brillantine, and he wore glasses; the top of a black leather strap stuck out from a side pocket. 'So, we've a scholar in our midst,' he said.

Bernard didn't know if he should answer, instead he looked down at his shoes, leather split and open to weathers, ready to fall apart, then, he looked across at the feet of the brothers, solid footwear, shining.

'I'm Brother Lowry,' said the one with the oily hair. 'And this is Brother Morgan.'

Brother Morgan was tall and thin, his face the colour of cold dripping. He crossed his arms and looked down on Bernard, a look to make you worry. 'What's your name, boy?' he asked.

'Bernard, sir.'

'Bernard, hmm... You must have done something really bad to end up here.'

Brother Lowry spoke: 'Don't be putting the heart crossways in the boy, Brian.' He placed nicotine-stained fingers on Bernard's shoulder, a promise of protection. He looked at the other three boys, who were silent, relieved to have gone unnoticed. 'These are a fine crop of young men – let's turn them into Artane boys.'

'The sooner the better,' Brother Morgan agreed. 'You'd smell them a mile off!'

'That's the smell of the streets, Brian. They haven't come from the fields of Offaly, like you have.'

Brother Morgan returned a steely smile, then barked at the new arrivals: 'Form a line, boys!'

Automatically, one went to the front and the others fell in behind, like they had learned in their school playgrounds.

'Now, follow us. Clé, deis, clé, deis, left, right...'

They marched up the steps and through the front door of the main building, not realizing it was a privilege to enter by this way, the chances of using it again being slim. They were in a large hallway, where the parquet floor was polished to a gloss and tall religious statues and heavily framed holy pictures made a guard of honour. Without warning, Brother Morgan shouted, 'Stad!', and they came to a halt in front of a large painting of a white-haired man.

'Do any of you bright sparks know who this is?' he asked.

There was only silence.

'This is our founder, Brother Ignatius Rice,' he said, contemplating the portrait. 'We pray every day for his canonization. This will be your prayer, too.'

They went outside again through the main entrance and then along the edge of the building, until they came to a door at the back.

'Johnny, where are you, you old codger?' Brother Lowry called out, as they entered a room where clothes and boots were stacked on shelves to the ceiling.

'Hold your horses, will you, I'm coming!' The voice came from behind a shelf; then, a smiling face with spectacles appeared, the frame of which was held together with black sewing thread.

'Brother Dempsey, we have some fine young men here for outfitting,' Brother Morgan said. He winked at the veteran brother, who had been retired from classroom duty and placed where he could do least harm. 'And, you be sure now, Johnny, to let them have their choice of colour.'

The brother ran his eye over Bernard, figuring his size. 'So, which colour would you like, master?'

'I don't know...'

Johnny sniggered. 'Then, you won't have any objection to the colour grey?'

'No, sir.'

The brother went to the shelves and came back with a neat pile of clothes and put them on the counter, all grey. Then he peered at Bernard's rough footwear. 'You've small feet... I'd say size six.' As if by magic, he pulled a pair of black, hob-nailed boots from under the counter. He turned to the next boy and asked, 'Pray tell me, have you a favourite colour, sonny?'

'Blue, sir.'

Johnny vanished between the shelves and came back with the clothes, all grey.

'Have you no blue today, Johnny?' Brother Lowry said, snorting a quick laugh.

When it came to the two remaining boys, they had the good sense to ask for grey. They were marched to the barber, Brother Ryan, whom Bernard later learned had the nickname, 'sheep-shearer'. Bernard was shoved down on to a seat; the scissor blades whirled above him and then dived into his hair. Brother Ryan worked fast. One wrong move and blood would flow. When he stopped a mirror was mockingly presented, and Bernard thought, Ma wouldn't know me, if she saw me. The next stop was the washhouse, where they were made to strip naked and stand at troughs; the water ran as cold as the outside tap in the tenement did in wintertime; the bars of soap where the size of small bricks. The old clothes were scooped up by the brothers and dropped into a bin. Every so often, Brother Morgan shouted: 'Get rid of those scruffy tide marks!'

Brother Lowry laughed and lit a cigarette; he leaned against a wall, watching. Then, Brother Morgan instructed the boys to bend forward and he inspected the cracks of their bottoms. Just then Lowry stubbed out his cigarette and decided to do his own check. He drew a black-leather punishment strap from his pocket and walked between the naked boys, flicking it towards their genitals, making them jump back. He stopped in front of Bernard and stuck the leather under one of his arms. 'Up with it,' he said; the brother inspected his armpit. He was close enough for Bernard to hear his breathing and realized the leather was now being slowly drawn along his naked side. His legs were shaking. Lowry stood back and studied him for a moment. 'There isn't much mate on you, boy, is there?'

The boys were lined-up in their Artane outfits and Morgan said: 'They look like choirboys, now.'

Lowry said: 'Don't kid yourself, Brian.' He looked at his watch and sighed, 'I suppose we have to feed them now.'

They were marched off again, this time to the refectory. Clé, deis, clé, deis… They arrived at a noisy, large hall, where hundreds of boys – all dressed alike, all with the same haircut – sat on forms at long tables. Brother Morgan brought the new boys to the end of one of the tables and demanded space for them. Bernard jumped as a mug of tea was slapped down in front of him. He watched what everyone else was doing and took two thinly-spread jam sandwiches from a large plate in the middle of the table and as he hadn't tasted jam in a long time, he began to think that Artane mightn't be such a bad place, after all. He quickly changed his mind when two boisterous lads near him knocked over their mugs, causing tea to spill along the table and on to the floor. A brother appeared out of nowhere and Bernard heard a whoosh, the air split by a cane. It slapped on the table causing him to jump; it had landed in the centre of the spilt tea, and he felt splatters on his face.

'Who did this?' the brother bellowed. 'Have you no respect for God's food? Own up!'

No one owned up. Bernard knew who the guilty ones were, and so did the others round him, but they all kept their mouths sealed. By now, the entire refectory was quiet, everyone seemed to have heard the brother, all eyes were on him, waiting to see what would happen. He smacked the table again.

'This is the last chance. Say it, now, if you know…'

There was still no answer. Bernard was shaking. Anyone close to the spilt tea was yanked from the bench and caned on the back of the legs. His legs stung and he returned to his place on the bench. When the brother was finished, he stood to one side, a high colour in his face and sweat on his brow. The refectory returned to normal, again high-spirited talk filled the hall. Bernard no longer enjoyed the bread and jam, but being poor, he couldn't let it go to waste. Brother Lowry came across to the table and put his arm across the shoulder of the cane-happy man.

'Brendan, I see you've initiated some of the new boys.'

'I'll redden their arses for them,' the brother growled, before moving to the other end of the hall, looking for more victims.

Brother Lowry squeezed himself on to the form beside Bernard, causing two boys at the end to stand. He leaned down and rubbed his palm along the red marks on the back of Bernard's legs. 'I hope it didn't hurt too much?'

'It wasn't me,' he said.

'Nobody said it was, Bernard. Just try to forget it, it'll go away.'

Bernard bit into his bread and jam. The sting was easing.

'I can see you're different to the other boys,' the brother said. 'I can tell you're from a good family. What does your father do?'

'He fixes the trams, but he died.'

'I'm sorry to hear that, Bernard. But, then, I definitely know now that you've a good mother.'

Bernard didn't know what to say. He imagined the eyes of the rest of the table trained on him.

'And because you come from a good family, Bernard, I'll keep a special eye out for you. I'm sure your good mother would like me to do that.'

Lowry took away his hand, the pain had almost gone. He left, and the boys at the table began talking again, as if nothing had happened. Bernard was still in shock from the caning, and he wondered if any of the others had been as scared as he'd been. Not long afterwards Brother Morgan came along, clapping his hands. 'Brustaigh ort! Hurry up! It's time for chapel.'

Bernard copied everyone else: put his mug and plate on a trolley by the wall, went back and stood in a line parallel with the table; when their turn came, they marched out of the hall and across a square to the chapel. A brother stood at the door, watching the boys dip their hands in the holy water font. He hissed at a boy, 'Bless yourself properly – no lazy efforts!'

Bernard made sure he did it correctly, perhaps exaggerating the action.

He was directed to squeeze into a pew, as the chapel was full to the door. Brothers walked the aisle, demanding silence with a threatening stare. A priest came to the altar in white and gold vestments, clutching a monstrance. He was old, with a kindly face, and every so often he appeared to almost stumble, however two attentive altar boys were on hand to steady him. Bernard recognised them, for they had sat close to him in the dining hall. Benediction commenced, prayers in Latin floated on a sea of incense. Bernard copied the actions of the boys round him: kneel, stand, bow, sing; not knowing the words, he mouthed the sounds.

After Benediction, the priest reminded them to say their bedtime prayers. 'That way, my children, you'll be ready for God if you die in your sleep. But', he added, with an awkward grin, 'I'm sure something like that won't happen to any of *you*. You all look too young and healthy.' He shuffled off the altar, a signal for the brothers to begin emptying the pews. The boys marched to the main building, where the dormitories were.

After going to the toilet, Bernard was led to a bed by a Brother Salmon, a man with a red face and a bull neck. He tossed a nightshirt to him. 'On with this and not a peep out of you, or you'll hear it from me. Lights out in ten minutes, and don't forget your prayers!'

Bernard wasted no time in doing as he was told, then lay in the bed, listening to the boys round him: some were praying aloud, as if they wanted the patrolling brother to hear them; springs were still creaking, as the slower boys climbed into bed. Then it was darkness. Some coughing, but no talking, not even prayers said aloud. He curled up and shut his eyes, his mind possessed by Artane. He had heard that name so often. Exasperated mothers and fathers, teachers about to lose their temper, neighbours sick of hearing back-chat – 'Keep going the way you're going, sonny, and you'll end up in Artane!' An everyday threat, but not really meant, he hoped.

He woke up to the sound of movement in the dormitory. Early daylight was coming in the window. 'You better get up,' someone said to him. The warning tone broke through his sleepiness, and he swung himself out of the bed, ready to pee. There was a line for the toilets. While he queued, he saw Brother Salmon moving along the line of beds, his nose stuck out like a dog hunting for rabbits. He stopped at one bed and yanked away the blankets. 'Holy Mother!' he roared, his eyes searching the line of boys at the toilet. 'Where are you, Flynn?'

Bernard saw a boy ahead of him leave the line and walk stiffly to the brother; the colour had left his face. When he came within Salmon's reach he was grabbed by the neck of his nightshirt and his face was thrust on to a wet patch on the sheet. The brother was shaking with anger.

'What did I tell you before about this, Flynn? I like a clean dormitory and I don't want smelly mattresses.'

The boy said nothing, just stared at the wet patch, as if that look alone would cause the problem to disappear.

The brother seemed to have been through this before with Flynn, and with many other boys before him. He took a moment to compose himself, then said, 'Let's get this mess cleaned-up. Take that mattress outside to air. And be quick about it!'

Bernard watched the boy strip the bed and, crouching, draw the mattress on to his back and go outside, an ant with an oversized load. Meanwhile, the queue for the toilet had moved along and it was Bernard's turn to pee, then, copying what the others were doing, he washed his face and hands and went back to his bedside to dress. On his way out to breakfast, he passed Flynn standing in the cold in his wet pyjamas holding on to his mattress, like a hired man holding on to an advertising arrow on the corner of North Earl Street and Sackville Street.

In the refectory – as no one had told him to do otherwise – he sat where he'd sat the night before. When the hall was full, the boys stood for morning prayers, then Bernard took a bowl from a trolley and queued for porridge; it was cold and slimy, however the mug of tea that followed was hot, and it came with a slice of bread. He wondered if Flynn would be left outside for long, and felt guilty, for a moment.

Breakfast ended with Grace After Meals and the refectory started to empty. Flynn finally appeared, fighting his way against the flow of boys, anxious to see what food was left. Bernard was relieved to see him and wondered what had happened to the mattress. Eventually the 'newcomers' were the only ones left in the refectory. No one had told them what they were to do, and they looked at each other with uncertainty. However, shortly afterwards Brother Morgan came along, killing any hope that they might be left to themselves for the day. He asked one boy what his father did for a living – the reply was that his father didn't work.

'What do you mean? Is it that he can't get work? or that he just doesn't want to work?'

'I don't know, sir.'

The brother picked him to work on the farm. When it came to Bernard's turn, he replied, 'My father's dead, sir.'

Showing more interest than he had shown with the first boy, Morgan asked: 'And, when he was alive what did he do?'

'He was with the tram company, sir.'

'What did he do, boy? Drive a tram, collect fares, clean the carriages?'

'He fixed them, sir...I think he was in charge.'

'I'll send you to the fitting shop,' the brother said, then he moved on to the next boy. He later brought Bernard to the fitting shop, located in a cluster of buildings behind the chapel. Bernard hadn't been in a workshop before and was startled by the clanging and banging of the belt-driven machinery. A grey-haired man, in a faded-blue shop coat with a steel ruler sticking out of the top pocket came forward to meet them, clenching a pipe between browning teeth.

'Paddy, I've a recruit for you. This one should have a good pair of hands. He tells me his father was in the tram company.'

'In the Dublin United Tram Company, was he?' the man asked.

'Yes,' Bernard said, 'I think he fixed them.'

Morgan was smiling. 'I think he's playing it down, Paddy! I get the idea he'd charge of a squad of men.' He then turned to Bernard. 'Mister Walsh is one of our very few non-religious.' Then his tone changed, 'And he doesn't approve of hitting the boys, but I don't have that problem.' He was moving a thumb and forefinger along the top of a black leather strap, as if waiting for an excuse to use it. 'If I hear of any guff from you, any hint of backchat, I'll take pleasure in introducing you to this.' He pulled the leather completely from his belt and dangled it in front of Bernard's nose. 'Believe me, boy, you don't want to be doing that. So, do everything Paddy asks, and you'll have nothing to be sorry for.'

With a swish of his black soutane, Brother Morgan left. Paddy put an arm round Bernard's shoulder and steered him towards a bench. 'I want you to start by knocking the rivets out of this brake band,' he said. The boy had no idea what he was talking about, but he was soon to learn. He watched the man lift the brake band off the floor and secure it in a vice on the bench, his pipe still between his teeth. He produced a hammer and chisel and showed Bernard how to knock the heads off the rivets. After a short period, he stopped and handed the tools to him. 'Now, it's your turn, son. Simply, do as I've shown you, and I'll be back later to check.'

'But...I've never done anything like this before, mister.'

The man moved away, as if he hadn't heard him. Bernard looked at the tools in his hands; they felt strange to him, heavier than they had looked. He placed the edge of the chisel against a rivet and tapped it with the hammer. Nothing happened. Not even a mark on the rivet. He swung the hammer back and tried again, this time using all his force, but the face of the hammer was off target, and he struck himself on the hand. Instant pain, sharp, severe. The tools fell from his grasp, and he gazed at a growing red patch on the side of his hand; he wanted to kiss it and comfort it, like his mother had done for him when he was a young child. His eyes watered, he had trouble seeing. He wondered were the others in the workshop sniggering at his effort, but no one said anything nor came near him. As his vision slowly cleared, he saw again the mocking shape of the brass rivets waiting to be beheaded. He lifted the tools off the floor and found that he could barely grip the chisel from the soreness in his hand; nevertheless, he wanted some success before Mr. Walsh came back to him.

He resumed with caution, still failing to break a rivet head. When he thought he had the measure of the hammer swing, he steeled himself to apply more power. On his next try, he felt the solid impact through his arm – the rivet had been shaken but wasn't defeated. He struck again, this time he saw the sheared rivet head slap on to the bench, however, at the same time, he watched in horror as the follow through of the hammer skinned his knuckles. His cry of pain went through the workshop, even above the noisy, slapping drive belts. Walsh looked up from the group of boys he was instructing, and then returned to what he had been saying, as if nothing had happened.

Bernard was forlorn. He stared at his enemy, the brake band with hardly a dent to its territory, his hand hurting more than it ever had from any teacher's punishment. Only one rivet had been sheared and there were nine more to go! Suddenly, he regarded the hammer as something dangerous, not to be meddled with, and he put it on the bench and contemplated it. Never once when he had seen his father or other men use one, had he known how tricky and treacherous a tool it could be.

He expected that Walsh would have something to say, since there hadn't been progress, but he hadn't the stomach for another bang on the hand. Five minutes passed before he returned, pulling hard on the pipe. He looked at the intact brake band, then at Bernard. 'At least you tried and, son, a trier will always get on with me.' He spotted the skinned knuckles and he brought him to a medical cabinet, where he cleaned and dabbed iodine on the area. 'There you are now,' he said, giving a chuckle. 'It'll hurt for a spell, but you'll survive.'

Again, Bernard didn't know what to say or what was expected of him.

'Anyway, you're only a bit of a lad and you've plenty of time ahead of you to master a hammer 'n' chisel. In the meantime, let's see if we can get something easier for you.'

Bernard found himself arranging nuts and bolts in the fitting shop's store. It wasn't hard work nor complicated, allowing his mind time to think of home. He could see the tenement room, his mother looking out the window and he imagined she was watching out for him, waiting to see him walk up the street, his brothers Stephen and Peter elsewhere in the room, doing everyday things. In the evening, Mr. Walsh came along and dismissed him. 'Just follow the other boys to the refectory and you won't get lost, and I'll see you back here at half eight in the morning.'

Bernard took his place at the table. Although, there was chatter all round, he was the outsider, unsure about joining in. Then, unexpectedly, a boy said to him, 'You're in the fitting shop, then?'

'Yes...where are you?'

'Tailoring – we make the trousers you're wearing, and the likes.'

'Sounds difficult.'

'It's a cinch when you get the hang of it.'

'Are you here long?'

'A year...maybe two...I forget.'

'Does anyone come to see you?'

'Me Ma...she comes now and again. But it's a long way, the other side of the city. Ticknock, you know it?'

'No, but it sounds a bit like knock-knock,' Bernard said. The boy gave a polite laugh, as if he'd heard it a thousand times. Bernard added, 'I hope my Ma comes.'

'Hey, do you want to be my pal?'

'I don't mind...'

'But we'll keep it to ourselves. The brothers don't like it when boys are pals.'

Bernard finished his meal in silence, making eye contact now and again with his new friend. He knew his name was Seán because he had heard others say it. After tea, they were again marched off for Benediction. A boy fell asleep in the pew directly in front of Bernard and a patrolling brother woke him up with a clip to the ear. The boy let out a puppy's cry, more because of a sweet dream interrupted than any pain he felt, but the noise carried to the altar and the priest eyed him with annoyance. The patrolling brother glowered, a look demanding silence and respect for the Holy Presence. The priest gave a cough of acknowledgement to the brother and resumed. For Bernard, the ceremony seemed to go on forever.

Later in the dormitory, he again wasted no time in getting ready for bed. But after light-out he found it hard to fall asleep, no matter how tightly he closed his eyes. Eventually he became drowsy and was on the point of drifting off, when he heard a man talking in a low voice. Without thinking about it, he raised himself on an elbow and looked about. In the gloom, he could make out a shape kneeling beside a bed not far from him. There was no more movement, just that large figure. Bernard paid no heed to it; he lay back and curled himself into a ball; soon afterwards he was asleep.

The next day had a more frightening start than the one before. Brother Salmon went straight for Flynn's bed and this time he used the leather on him, it bending into a banana curve as it was raised behind the shoulder, straightening out as it whipped down, slapping onto the bedwetter's palm. The noise at that early hour was unreal. He heard the brother say, 'Suffering is part of your training...' but it was as if he was speaking to himself, for by then the boy was scurrying off, toting his wet bedclothes and mattress with resignation while the brother pushed back into place a length of oiled hair that had fallen on to a face red from the burst of exertion. Bernard watched the brother straighten his cassock, adjust his belt, replace the leather to its place of readiness, then, suddenly, he knew Salmon was now looking at him. There was a second of eye contact, and Bernard dived into making his bed. He sensed the brother coming towards him, panting at his elbow. Salmon pushed him aside and lifted the blanket. Even though there was no cause for worry, Bernard could hear his own heart hammering. Deprived, the brother rushed off to check other beds. Bernard was in the queue for the toilet when he heard a roar of discovery at the other end of the dormitory. Another boy was heading outside, mattress across his back.

Later, when he reported to the fitting shop, Walsh said, 'Let's see if we can find something that'll keep you out of harm's way.' He surveyed the workshop, running the stem of his pipe between his teeth. 'I'll put you with Larry on the lathe. He's one of the older lads; watch and learn and if he needs a hand, you row in and help him'.

Bernard followed him across to a tall, thin boy, who stood on a wooden platform beside a long, cold-looking bulk of a machine. This must be a lathe, he thought. He felt the older boy's eyes examining him.

'Look after Bernard,' Walsh said, then turned his attention elsewhere.

When they were alone, Larry pulled a nearby switch, and suddenly they were surrounded by a clatter of noise as an electric motor was awakened from sleep; an overhead shaft went into wild motion and it in turn spun another belt that sent a river of energy to the lathe. Bernard watched him spin a bar of iron in the machine, shaving thin ribbons of metal from it. Suddenly Larry said, 'Quick, pour on some coolant.'

Bernard didn't know what he was talking about.

'The coolant!' the boy shouted. 'In the bloody squirting can!'

Bernard spotted the squirting can on the floor and picked it up, not knowing what to do next.

'Squirt some out, yeh thickhead...on the shaft and the cutting tool.'

He pressed the trigger and a white, milky-looking liquid shot out, but missed the target. He tried again and this time the liquid sizzled as it met the hot metal.

'Now, keep doing that till I tell you to stop.'

When he did stop, Larry examined his handiwork: the iron bar had been worked down to a thinner, shining diameter. Bernard stood by, can in hand, waiting on his next instruction. The older boy looked at him and sneered. 'You have to be fast round me, thickhead.'

Bernard looked down at the squirting can, still dripping white liquid from the tip of its long neck, and knew he didn't like Larry, who, throughout the day persisted in trying to make a fool out of him at every turn. By evening, Bernard was miserable. Walsh came up to him and said, 'I hope Larry looked after you today?'

Bernard didn't speak.

'I know the older boys can be tough on new boys,' he continued, 'but behind it all, they don't mean anything. They were once new boys, themselves, now it's your turn.' Bernard couldn't avoid that sneer of Larry's that came to him over the man's shoulder.

In the refectory, he was happy to find that his new friend, Seán, was now sitting next to him at table. 'I swapped places,' Seán grinned, pointing to a boy. 'All it cost me was a square of toffee.'

Bernard told him about his day.

'They like to throw their weight around,' Seán said, 'and some of them will even belt you one, just for fun! That fellow, Larry, he's just a tosser!'

'You're right, he's a tosser.'

Bernard still had a worried look, and Seán asked, 'What's the matter?'

He confessed: 'What's a tosser?'

'I give up on you, Berno...that's what I'll call you from now on: Berno. It has a ring to it.'

'But, what's a tosser?'

'That bleeder in the fitting shop – he's definitely one! Now, the thing to do is just let on he's not there; do as your told, keep the head down. That's how to do it.'

Later, after lights out, a figure came to stand beside his bed. Even though it was dark, he made out the shape of a soutane, but he didn't look up to search for a face, instead, he pulled the blanket up past his nose and pretended to snore. He could hear the brother breathing; then, he heard him move away.

CHAPTER TEN

Lily Clancy's conscience was at her. It was almost three months since Bernard had been sent to Artane and she still hadn't brought herself to go and see him. She could make a hundred excuses, one of them was that she had heard from other women that it was no use just turning up at the gate. They said, 'You have to write a letter, Lily.' This was another time when she wished James were still alive, he'd have written a lovely letter. Then, someone advised her, 'Get the priest to write one for you – they write letters for people all the time.'

One day after Mass in the Pro-Cathedral she went into the sacristy; the priest was removing his vestments, shadowed by Paddy Gill, the sacristan. Gill saw her standing in the doorway and gave her a nod of recognition. After all, hadn't he and James Clancy been ushers together in the sodality, but seeing Paddy Gill made Lily suddenly self-conscious of her appearance; no longer was she the wife of a highly respected parishioner; instead she felt like a nobody, a nobody who lived in a tenement in Waterford Street. Instinctively, she attempted to tidy herself, but she knew in her heart that her neglected hair and old clothes were beyond salvation.

She stood in the doorway for several minutes, but the priest either ignored her or simply didn't notice her waiting. Paddy Gill had gone to a press in an inner room to put away the vestments, and on his return, he saw that Lily was still unattended. 'Father Leahy, one of our parishioners Mrs. Clancy wants a word,' he said, indicating her presence. 'Her husband, God be good to him, was a pillar of this church.'

Lily mouthed a thank you to the sacristan. Father Leahy came forward with an outstretched hand. 'I'm fairly new here, and it's always good to meet people from the parish.' Despite his friendliness, she felt her appearance was being examined.

'How can I help you, Mrs. Clancy?' he asked.

For a moment she wanted to run out of the church, but being there, in the sacristy at the heart of the workings of the parish, she took strength from James's memory – this was a place he'd have known well. To save her any embarrassment, Paddy Gill slipped away to the inner room, pretending to be about his sacristan duties. Lily spilled out her full story to the priest, her fall from respectability and the utter disappointment of seeing her son being carted off to Artane. Father Leahy gave his fullest attention, but it was plain to see that he wasn't going to jump to Bernard's defence, probably thinking that no one is sent to Artane without good reason. This frightened her, and all she could think of saying was, 'It isn't easy when you're left without a husband.'

It made her sound pitiful, and she knew it.

'Mrs. Clancy, Jesus always had time for the widow,' Father Leahy said. 'Can you come back tomorrow? The letter will be ready, then.'

'Thank you, Father, I'll do that.'

Paddy Gill returned just at that moment and saw her to the door.

~~~

Lily sat with her son on a polished bench in the great hall, beneath the benign gaze of Brother Edmund Rice.

'This looks a nice place,' she said, looking around, struggling to say something that wouldn't cause pain to him or to herself.

'I suppose it's all right,' he replied, remembering his first day, his introduction to Artane. 'We never really come into this part.'

Silence fell on them, except for a ticking clock, then Lily said: 'They told me you'd learn a trade here. Have you started, yet?'

'I guess so...I'm in the fitting shop.'

'Just like your Da when he started...he'd have been pleased.' She stole a glance at his hands and saw the scratches and skinned knuckles. He had small, sensitive hands, not made for pushing and pulling and rough work.

She wanted to reach out and massage the skinned knuckles, but knew he would pull away, like any boy his age.

Then she said, 'Jemser Flood, you remember him? Well, he says you should try and get into the Artane Boys Band.'

'I'm okay where I am, Ma.' He remembered his pal Seán pointing out a group of tables in the refectory where most of the band boys were seated, an island of musicians. He called them 'nancies' but at the same time admired them for wangling a way to be treated better than the rest of the boys.

'You're right, Bernard,' Lily said, 'keep up the training in the fitting shop – a trade is a trade, after all – but, maybe you could be a band member, as well?'

'But, Ma, I don't know any music.'

'Chance your arm, son...they'll teach you.'

They were quiet again. Lily had said her piece and was now blank; Bernard wondered what that man Jemser Flood was doing talking to his mother. Hadn't she already sent him on his way? There was no need for him to be butting in, throwing his advice around their family.

'I suppose you get plenty of praying here,' Lily said, in desperation. She didn't want to walk out of Artane without having had a decent chat with him – that would be a wasted trip. Saying anything at all seemed the right thing to do.

'Too much,' he said.

'Say some for your ma, Bernard...God knows I need them!'

She had been told that the visiting time was for one hour, but never imagined that it would be such hard work trying to fill it with conversation; it wasn't until the last ten minutes when they started to talk about Peter that words came freely, and by the time she was ready to leave, she'd come to realize that he missed home life more than she'd imagined.

'You will ask about joining the band?' were her parting words.

Later, in the refectory, he told Seán what his mother had said.

He waited for him to jeer him, move away from him as if he stank. Instead, he went silent, his eyes fixed in the direction of the colony of band boys. It was a surprise when he said, 'If you're joining, then I'm joining, too! We'll both be in the fancy uniforms!'

For the rest of the mealtime, Bernard caught him glance more than once at the band boys.

The next day, he went to Mr. Walsh, his legs shaking. Even though he felt he was someone he could trust to be fair, he couldn't forget that he was still the man in charge. Walsh's pipe was chewed and moved along the teeth as he listened to Bernard's account of his mother's visit and her wish that he should try to join the band, yet still stay in the fitting shop.

'You like it here, then, son?'

'I'm learning. Me ma says I need a trade above everything...'

'And she thinks you also have the making of a musician?'

Bernard nodded.

'And what do you think?' Walsh asked.

He hadn't an answer. Instead, he stood, as he had stood in front of the judge in the Children Court, waiting on someone else to make the decision.

'Your mother's a wise woman,' Walsh said. 'She's right – youngsters should make the best of their time here. I'll speak to the brother in charge of the band.'

'Thanks, Mr. Walsh.'

'Now, get on with you, and let's get some work done.'

He suddenly remembered his friend Seán, and finding courage he didn't think he possessed, he said: 'And, Mr. Walsh, can you ask for me pal, too?'

A puff of smoke went up towards the roof beams of the fitting shop. Bernard waited for Walsh to erupt; but instead he said, in a friendly tone, 'We should look out for our pals. I'll speak to Brother Smith about him, as well.'

Next day, he came back to him and said, 'Brother Smith wants a chat with you.'

'Is that good?'

'Very good if he likes you.' Walsh was about to move away, when he said, as if it were an afterthought, 'But, your pal Seán – he hasn't a hope in hell.'

Bernard wanted to ask: why? But held back. However, Walsh knew the question was just below the surface, and added: 'It seems your friend has blotted his copybook once too often. He's good at the back answers, hid a brother's leather and was found out, and worst of all he skipped from the farm when a brother's back was turned. A few days later he was discovered at home by a DMP man. The Brothers give you a chance, maybe a few chances, but run away like that and they can take a strong dislike to you.'

Bernard felt sorry for Seán. He had decided that if his pal couldn't join, then he wouldn't join, either.

'Your ma will kill you,' Seán said. 'You go and be a nancy...I never really wanted it.'

'We'll still be pals?'

'Sure,' he said. However, Bernard worried that he mightn't have meant it. 'Anyway, I won't be round here much longer.'

'You won't?' he gasped, frightened on his behalf, yet in awe of his bravery.

'I've found another way.'

~~~

Bernard tried to blow a trumpet, but not a sound came out of it. He thought, that's it – I've failed the test already. Brother Smith took the shiny instrument from him and returned it to its bed of purple velvet. 'The breathing will come in time, boy,' the brother said, smiling. 'I've a good feeling you'll make it in the end, that's if you really want to?'

Bernard realized that he had been accepted into the Artane Boys Band; one part of him was happy, but the other part was worried about being branded as a nancy by the others. The brother added, pointing across the band-room, 'I think you know one of the other boys.' His heart dropped when he saw Larry from the fitting shop.

'Mr. Walsh tells me that Larry likes to throw his weight around. Well, he carries a heavy drum for us – so, there's a place for everyone in life.'

In his mind, Bernard already saw Larry jeering his feeble effort at blowing the trumpet, and he wished that Brother Smith had chosen an easier instrument for him, even perhaps a drum, but the band-room turned out to be a different world than the fitting shop, here Larry was too busy looking after his own corner to be bothered with annoying anyone else. Bernard flung himself into his daily breathing exercises, and after a short while the shiny instrument began to give out a hesitant and constipated sound, then, by the turn of a season, he had moved on to practising scales, like a child taking first footsteps. In the refectory, he sometimes sat with the band boys, a group he now viewed differently, or, he sometimes moved back to his old table, where a new boy now sat in place of Seán, for his pal had absconded.

The runaway was caught after a short time and handed back to the Christian Brothers; yet he never reappeared in the refectory. There was a rumour he had been taken to hospital with a broken arm. None of them really knew, no one had seen him depart. In the fitting shop, when Walsh came to Bernard to inspect his work – he was now operating a lathe of his own – he asked, 'Any word of your friend?' Bernard told him of the talk, of the rumour.

Walsh couldn't hide a look of surprise, the pipe was taken from the mouth, put back in again, as if he couldn't decide whether to smoke it or not. 'Are you sure of this?'

'It's what said.'

'Then, you're not sure? You see you must be careful about what you say. You can't be smearing the good name of the Brothers without being certain. It's the law of fairness.' By now, the pipe needed to be relit, and Walsh sucked on its stem, waiting for the light to catch.

Bernard turned back to the lathe, feeling angry and frustrated; however, he remembered Seán's words: 'Keep your head down.' But his friend hadn't followed his own advice; he was, in his own words, 'Afeared of no one.' Bernard felt that something bad had happened. He missed being called 'Berno' and kept to himself after that, as if he couldn't trust any new friendship.

~~~

Lily finally gave in to the persistence of Jemser Flood. She wasn't sure about it yet felt that somehow there had to be the promise of something better, after all, the man with the whiskey nose had a steady job – lighting the gas-lamps on the quays – and, at last, she could lose that dreadful feeling of not knowing what would happen to her and her remaining family. (Bernard was in the care of the Christian Brothers, so, he was looked after). But there was a high price to be paid.

The price: Jemser Flood moving in with her.

Afterwards, she didn't dwell on it; instead, with his money she turned her hovel into a room that was, to her mind, fit for living in. She told the curious he was paying rent (few believed it!). A new curtain was bought to make a private space, a private space taken over by a new double bed. It wasn't love but it wasn't poverty. If he smelled of drink when he rolled over on top of her, pulling up his nightshirt, it was probably no worse than the smell she herself gave off, for they both were regulars along the bars of Summerhill. In fact, the act only happened when she wasn't sober. The memory of James was now a habit, a spirit that walked with her. As for Jemser, it was a matter of timing; he knew he was competing with the dead.

Her two sons slept behind a curtain, and, while Peter was too young to be bothered by Jemser's arrival, she knew that Stephen wasn't happy sharing his home with a man he saw as a stranger, a stranger who in a clumsy way tried from time to time to act as his father. Stephen couldn't hide the fact that he wanted nothing to do with him.

Sometimes, in the middle of the night, Lily would be awakened by Jemser's snoring. Finding it hard to go back to sleep, she would listen for a sound from beyond the curtain, a sound from her boys, and, inevitably, also would think of the son not in the room, but in Artane. She hadn't visited him now in six months. How has it come to this? In her heart she knew the answer. It was the feeling of letting him down; it stabbed at her as soon as she entered through those large ornate gates and started up the avenue; it was the look in his eyes she had seen at the end of the last visit, the unspoken accusation that said: You're abandoning me. It was also the heavy guilt that came from not telling him about Jemser Flood hanging his trousers on the end of her bed.

Little did she know the trouble she was storing up by keeping it from him, particularly when she went that step further and decided to marry the man with the whiskey nose, but she wouldn't be doing it to fasten down tightly any feelings she had for him, no, she would be doing it because she had become terrified that her God would do something ugly on her, turn on her for going to the altar rails while in the state of mortal sin. She had stayed away from confession because she couldn't promise the priest that she would avoid the occasion of sin; yet she'd joined the queue for communion, as if church rules had meant nothing. She had tormented herself countless times. How can I make a promise I can't keep? Jemser was her security, and she wasn't going back to the blackness of uncertainty. Surely, God would understand that? There seemed only one answer – Marriage.

At first Jemser took fright at the notion, for he had been content with his life. After all, he was still a free man, able to walk out of Lily's life at any time, and he liked that feeling, however, she kept talking about marriage. In a sense she wore him down, and over a few weeks he came to not only accept the idea, but also to look forward to this new change, even new status, in his life. So, dressed in their best, they went one morning with their witnesses to the Pro-Cathedral; they went before dawn, a suitable time for a couple not wanting to trumpet their wedding; during the ceremony, she remembered that this was the same altar at which she'd made her vows to James.

And she hoped he would forgive her.

They came out the side door of the church, where there was no one to shower them with confetti, unlike when she had married James openly in front of family, relations, and friends. It had rained that day and they'd dashed in high spirits the short distance to Moran's Hotel in Talbot Street for the wedding breakfast, confetti circles stuck to their wet and breathless faces, however, it was to be different this time round, only four people, counting themselves, newly-weds who were over-mature like two overripe bananas. They went for a session at an early-opening pub on the quays, that smelled of cattle drovers and spilt porter, where Jemser slapped his money on the counter with the confidence of a regular. The party broke up sometime in the late afternoon and the newly-weds parted from their witnesses – slobbering an accentuated 'Thank you' at them – then, arms linked, they swayed up the quays in the direction of a drinking hole in Summerhill.

Afterwards, Lily was relieved that she could now go to the altar rail with a clear conscience, also, she could stand erect and look any woman in the eye, especially the other women in the tenement, when she would run into them on the stairs. Meanwhile, Jemser had started to act like the man of the house, having a long face if his dinner wasn't put on the table as soon as he came in, barking at Peter as if he felt he had to. As for Stephen, he stayed out of his way, much to Jemser's annoyance. Lily felt it would all settle down, eventually, and everyone could be happy together. She was shocked when Stephen came home one day and said that he was going to sea.

'I'm afraid for you, Stephen,' she said. 'You're only...'

'Ma, I am old enough.'

'First it was Bernard, now you. What will I do without me boys?'

'Ma, it's not forever – there'll be shore leave when we're back in Dublin.'

He left a few days later, a bag slung over his shoulder, imitating the jaunty walk of a hardened seaman. She waved after him from the steps of the tenement until he turned the corner to go into Marlborough Street, and, at that moment, she remembered the many times she had watched the boys make their way to school along that same street. An indescribable feeling came on her, stretching from her throat region all the way down to her waist, a sad emptiness that wanted those days to return. It caused her to shudder, to feel like throwing-up.

She trudged upstairs and, as Jemser was at work and Peter at school, entered an empty room. She looked round her, like she used to do when she lived in old Mrs. Hanley's house, hoping to draw some consolation from the few pieces of second-hand furniture which she had managed to buy over a period of months, a small measure of comfort back into life. But, today, it didn't work for her, for she may as well have been looking at a collection of stones. She made up her mind to spoil Peter with attention when he came in from school.

~~~

Jemser no longer had a job. The changeover of Dublin Port's gas lamps to electric lighting meant he was no longer needed, for one pull of a switch could now trigger immediate incandescence along the length of a quay. His boss didn't even say he was sorry when he told him he was fired (Jemser believed he had it in for him).

Lily found out about it when he came in after midnight almost paralysed from drowning his sorrows. It took a while to make sense of what he was saying but the full importance of it didn't really hit her until he surfaced late the next morning, hungover and overflowing with self-pity.

'What a state I've landed meself in,' he moaned. 'I'll be broke...' He looked around the tenement room, then fixed an aggressive look on her. 'And, into the bargain, I'll have to support you and your snotty-nosed chiseller.'

'There'll be other work,' she said.

'Don't be a fool, woman! This city's fucked...there's nothing for the likes of me. I should have stayed single...'

'Please don't speak like that, Jemser. Haven't I made you a comfortable home?'

'We'll be lucky to keep it,' he said, spitting on the floor and going for the door.

'Where are you off to?'

'The bloody pub, woman!' he roared. 'Where else is there to go?' He slammed the door, and she knew that his roar had carried out on to the landing, up and down the stairs, the tenement telegraph. The neighbours won't say anything directly to me, she thought, but I'll know from the look in their eyes that they'll be gloating, just waiting to see me pulled down a peg or two.

It didn't take long for Jemser's money to go, and they had to sell the few pieces of furniture that Lily had brought into the tenement; respectability was again washing out of her life, an inevitable ebb tide. Just as Jemser had been doing, she also wanted to lose herself in drink, but he had confiscated the few shillings made from the furniture. If she said she wanted to go with him to the pub, he would go into a tantrum, blaming her again for all his woes.

This was a side of him she hadn't seen before. As a result, she never insisted, never tested him. Every so often, she saw a look that frightened her, warned her that she was within an inch of the back of an arm being swiped across her face; nevertheless, she still had to live with him. When he came home at night and fell on the bed, she waited until he was snoring to raid his pockets, and any change she could scavenge she used for food and if there was anything left over, she put it to a bottle of wine, hidden away and downed in the privacy of her own misery.

Young Peter lived with this continuous tension in the home. He went to school in clothes that he knew were cast-offs, his shoes let in the rain and hunger was never far away. This had fashioned him into a pale, thin boy, who, despite everything, was getting taller like a young, fruitless apple tree. He dreaded returning to the tenement room, the constant arguments between his mother and Jemser, the walking on eggshells when he was around.

Meanwhile, less than an hour's walk away, Bernard was coming to the end of his time at Artane. Mr. Walsh from the fitting shop had used his contacts outside the school to arrange an interview for Bernard. 'You go and see them. Be respectful, in fact, just be your normal self, that'll do. I've told them you've done well here, and they'll take my word for it.'

'Thank you,' was all he could say. It didn't seem enough, for he knew the man had gone out of his way to make things better for him.

Before they parted, Walsh said, 'Walk out the gates and be happy that you're going home. Think of it – tonight your mother will make you a coddle in your own place!'

He didn't say it to Walsh, but Bernard hadn't had a visitor in months, and he wondered if anyone from the Christian Brothers had even bothered to inform his mother of his homecoming, given her a chance to even think about making the welcoming coddle.

There was no special send-off from the Artane Industrial School – boys came in, boys went out. Nothing special, one among thousands. Before leaving, Bernard had to attend one last practice session in the band-room (he had recently been entrusted with a short solo piece at group rehearsals); then, after putting the instrument back in its case, he went and gathered up his belongings and pocketed an impersonal reference from the Brothers. The carriage to take him back into the city was waiting.

The horse trotted the long avenue; Artane was being left behind. Bernard was surprised at how quickly they reached the gates, then, he felt the carriage gathering speed as the horse pulled with excitement as it saw the open road. Bernard was going home.

But no one had told Lily about it.

CHAPTER ELEVEN

Bernard stood in the middle of Waterford Street, taking in the buildings, the women – some he recognised – still gossiping on the steps; he imagined one poking another in the ribs, saying: 'Isn't he the young fella that was sent to Artane?' Children were running and shouting, reciting rhymes from street games, but they were too young for him to know them. He looked for pals from the past, boys from school, boys he had scutted on the backs of carriages with, even girls whose hair he had pulled and who later treated him to a playful kiss, but he saw none of them. He asked himself: But why should I expect everything to be as I left it? He stepped on to the pavement and looked up at the tenement building, at the room that was his home.

He went lightly up the stairs, a notion in his head to surprise his mother, to see her face light up when she realized he was finally home. There was no need to knock, as the door was slightly ajar. He pushed it open and eased himself into the room. She was kneeling, her back to him, arched over a tub while she washed clothes, humming a tuneless sound. She looked thinner than he remembered. Her hair down to the shoulders was grey at the edges. He thought she would have heard him by now. He considered creeping up on her, and then decided it would be too much of a shock; instead, he gave a deliberate cough.

Lily jumped to her feet and spun round, 'Bernard…what?' A hand went to her hair, pushed stray clumps back with jerky movements. 'I must look a state…' She came a step closer. 'I didn't expect –'

'A surprise, Ma. I hope a nice one.'

For some moments, she seemed to be stuck to the floor. 'I'd have tidied the place, if I'd only known,' she said, her eyes wandering all over her son. Although she had seen him from time to time in the industrial school, she'd never really noticed how much he'd grown. Now, he stood in the room as large as life, a young man looking like James, his father. The likeness made her want to touch him; her embrace was weak, almost fragile; her lips brushed his cheek and she repeated, '…if I'd only known.' She stood back and self-consciously adjusted her clothes and fussed again at her hair. 'What must you think of me? And look at the place, it hasn't been tidied…'

'Ma, it's Waterford Street, not the Gresham Hotel, and you look fine to me.'

'You'll be sharing a bed with Peter…will that be –?'

'Ma, don't be fretting – after where I've been, I can't be choosy.'

'That's good, that's good.' She smiled, but, inside, she was in a state. She agonised: How am I going to tell him about Jemser? As if saying something else, anything else, would solve the problem, she blurted, 'Peter will soon be in from school – he'll be so surprised to see you!'

'It's been so long he probably won't even know me.'

'Of course, he'll know you. After all, he's your brother. And it's a pity Stephen isn't here too, then I'd have all my sons at home.'

But this was wishful thinking on her part, as Stephen never came near the tenement because of Jemser; nevertheless, when he was in port, he would send a message and meet her at the Seamen's Mission. He always passed her an envelope containing some welcome cash, though never a great amount, as he still wasn't on 'full money', yet she was glad of it and would hide it from Jemser.

Bernard had moved past her and placed his small bag of belongings on the table. He took a moment to look around the room, this place called home, this place he had often thought about in Artane. Lily heard heavy footsteps outside on the stairs and got a fright as she thought it was Jemser coming home early. Instead, the footsteps plodded on up the stairs to the next landing and a door was banged shut. Shortly afterwards, Peter came in from school.

'Your brother's here, Peter,' she said. The boy was curious, but unsure, after all he didn't really know much about this brother of his. While his mother had spoken a lot to him about Stephen, about his exotic travels to the far reaches of the globe, 'Places where God's word hasn't even been heard', all he had known of Bernard was that he was away at a special school and that one day he would come home to live with them. His mother had never mentioned the word, Artane, but from hearing people talking, Peter had guessed that that was where he was. Now he was out.

Bernard attempted conversation with him. 'I think we'll be sleeping in the same bed,' he said, nodding towards the corner.

Peter went to the table and took a schoolbook from his satchel. He was settling down to homework, just like his older brothers had done in their day.

'Where are you up to?' Bernard asked.

'Peter is a good scholar,' Lily said. 'He loves the books, he's even read way past the page he's supposed to be on, isn't that true, Peter?'

The scholar kept his head in the schoolbook, feeling obliged to, seeing as his mother had praised him so highly. Later, Bernard noticed him stealing a glance in his direction. He caught his eye and smiled, and his brother smiled back. It was beginning to feel like home again.

In true Dublin style, Lily went to Olhausen's to buy the rashers and sausages for making the coddle. She had raided the hidden savings, the money that Stephen had given her, and soon the smell of cooking was filling the tenement room, and her reward was Bernard's look of anticipation, but at the back of her mind was the worry that Jemser would demand to know where the money for the treat had come from. However, I'll face that when the time comes, she said to herself.

She had expected him home around six o'clock and still there was no sign of him, which was a blessing for it postponed the hour Bernard would realize that he had a stepfather. At least, she thought, we can have the homecoming meal in peace. They sat at the table and Lily filled the bowls. They slurped the hot liquid, stabbing the bowls to secure a potato or a rasher or a prized sausage.

After the meal, they talked of the past, especially of the house in Marlborough Street. Even Peter joined in, warming more by the minute to this long-lost brother, even though he'd been too young to remember their time at Mrs. Hanley's. Lily was the happiest she had been for quite a while;

getting out of bed that morning she would never have guessed that the day would turn out like this, a true family get-together.

Bernard was lying in the bed, close to his sleeping brother. An image of the sprawling dormitories of Artane invaded his mind, and he shuddered. Beyond the curtain, in the comfortable light from the oil lamp, he heard his mother move about and, eventually, he fell asleep to her sound. He woke up suddenly when he heard a man shouting in the room and sat up in the bed and heard his mother saying repeatedly, 'Shh'.

An angry voice came back at her. 'In my own home? Don't "Shh" me, woman!'

'For God's sake, Jemser, you'll wake –'

Bernard lifted the curtain and came out.

'See what you've done, now?' she said. 'I asked you to be quiet…'

Jemser was full of drink and had planted himself in the centre of the room, defiant, like a soldier defending the flag. For a moment, he rocked back and forward, close to unbalance, then, sneering at Lily, he said, 'So, precious Bernard is here?'

Bernard searched his mother's eyes for an explanation.

'I meant to tell you, son… but I just couldn't.'

'Tell me what, Ma?'

If I don't tell him, she thought, Jemser most certainly will. Seeing no other choice, she put her shoulders back, steeling herself, and – because of her nerves – almost declared her words, 'Jemser and me are now married… and he lives here.'

Bernard couldn't believe what he had heard. 'Married? And he lives here? In our home?'

By now, Jemser had a broad smile on his red face, his eyes danced, seeming to say: So, what do you think of that bit of news, precious son?

Bernard wondered how this, his day of release from the industrial school which should have been a happy one had turned into such a nightmare. He had disliked Jemser when he'd met him before, and he still didn't like him. He thought: Does the bastard expect me to call him father?

Jemser came forward. He was now chin-to-chin with Bernard, his breath reeking of porter. He said, 'Yeh hate me. Don't yeh, young fella? You'd like to see the back of me…march me out of here?'

Bernard had learned in Artane to be silent.

'Just in case, yeh get any notions,' Jemser said. He grabbed Bernard by the arm and flung him across the room. His mule-like strength came from toting timber on the quays in his early life.

Lily screamed: 'Jemser, what've you done!' She ran to Bernard, who was now halfway to his feet.

Jemser mocked him: 'I like to get my blow in first, young fella. You haven't the muscle to move me, so yeh better get used to seeing me stay put.'

Lily said: 'Did he hurt you, son?'

He shrugged her off.

There was disgust in his eyes. 'Don't judge me,' she pleaded, 'please don't do that. I was alone, what was I to do? You don't know what it was like for me… without your father… without –'

They were interrupted by Peter's sleep-laden voice coming from behind the curtain. 'What's going on?'

Lily answered: 'It's nothing, Peter…just go back to sleep.'

Bernard said, 'I'm going back to bed, too.' As he passed, Lily made a clumsy effort to kiss him, but he looked ahead, as if he hadn't seen the movement. She was left standing like a statue, then she saw Jemser staring at her, his face like a fighting dog's. Her legs were fit to collapse beneath her.

The news had stung Bernard. He lay awake in the bed; Peter had gone back to sleep. The shouting had stopped, now there were lowered voices, drifting to him from the other side of the room, from beyond the curtain, but he didn't want to hear them, and there was nothing he could do about it, for his mother had made a decision and he would have to live with it. He closed his eyes and tried to concentrate on the noises coming from the other rooms in the tenement. He had swapped the sounds of Artane for the ones of Waterford Street.

CHAPTER TWELVE

1922

Bernard walked through the gates of Beggars Bush Barracks; the flag of the new Irish Provisional Government was aloft, where the Union Jack used to fly. He skirted a line of uniformed men who were being introduced to the basics of square-bashing. There was a queue outside the Recruitment Room, a handful of unsure young men, all looking just that few years older than him – this was his concern: that he would be turned down because he looked too young. He had learned that the age was eighteen and when asked he was going to lie.

Soon it was his turn, and he was standing before a middle-aged officer, who looked conflict-hardened from the guerrilla struggle of the preceding years. The man was in the green uniform of the new National Army and was seated at a desk left behind by the British garrison, and because he was tall, his legs were thrust out to one side, the shine on his brown boots matching the deep colour of his Sam Brown belt. His pistol, bursting out of an undersized holster, was a reminder to all would-be recruits that this was a serious place, that he was a serious soldier. He took down Bernard's details, not even hesitating at his age. When he stopped writing, he asked: 'Why do you want to join the National Army?'

Bernard had rehearsed some answers. 'I believe in Mr. Collins.'

'Is that all? Our Commander-in-Chief is but one man.'

'I side with the Treaty, Sir.'

'Why?'

He had heard questions like this in Artane, when the Christian Brothers tried to catch him out. Devious questions. In those days, an answer would determine if you got a reddened ear for nothing, or, escaped for another day.

'It's the right thing to do, Sir.'

'And you think that's a good enough reason?'

Bernard didn't answer.

'And you'd give up a good job to join us?'

'Yes, Sir.'

'That's certainly a change – some of the misfits that have come through that door are unemployable.'

The military man studied the toes of his boots for a moment, then said, in a formal manner, 'Bernard, I'm accepting your application to join the Army of the Provisional Government of Ireland.'

He wasn't sure how to react. One part of him wanted to cheer. At least, now, he thought, I can pack in the fitting job and get out of Waterford Street, but another part of him was chilled by the reality of enlisting.

'Now, move along into the next room and see the corporal. He'll get you to sign all the papers.' He stood up, looked Bernard square in the face and shook his hand. 'I wish you well,' he said, before summoning the next hopeful from the queue outside.

~~~

Lily was shocked by his news.

'But you're getting on so well at the tram works. You're not going to throw away a good trade, just like that?'

'It's something I want to do, Ma.'

'Don't say that – you don't fool me, son. You're gentle, too intelligent for soldiering.' She paused for a moment, then said, 'It's living here, isn't it? It's me and Jemser you want to get away from?'

'You're wrong, Ma. It's just...well, I want to do something different with my life.'

'God, first it was Stephen, now you. And you'll be in danger –'

She started to cry and collapsed on to a chair. Bernard wanted to kneel beside her and place his arm on her shoulder, but he held back. He went to the window and looked down on some children playing in the street. They're oblivious to what's going on around them, he thought, just as I once was. He listened to her sobs and was moved, but not enough to make him change his mind. Anyway, he reminded himself, it's too late now. I've signed up, and that's that.

~~~

Bernard walked up the gangway of the SS Lady Wicklow, kitbag on his back, tight grip on his Lee-Enfield rifle, nervous he would drop it into the river Liffey. The training was over; he now knew how to shoot the weapon; clean it, oil it. The range instructor had barked, 'Look after your weapon and it will look after you.' Bernard came to a stop – a logjam had built-up at the top of the gangplank, and he took a moment to look round. It was almost dark, a summer's night, the prostitutes should have been about, but a cordon had been set-up to keep onlookers away from South Wall Quay.

The way ahead became unblocked. When he stepped on to the commandeered passenger-ship he found that the men ahead of him were shuffling towards a companionway and disappearing below deck: a sergeant was positioned to make sure no one dallied. As Bernard moved forward, he spotted two tarpaulin-covered shapes and could just about make out the contour of the armoured car and the 18-pounder field gun (swung aboard earlier by a dockside crane).

Following instructions, he made his way below deck and found men piled into cabins, sitting in the passageways, sprawled in the saloon, and occupying any space that could be found. It amazed him that so many of the company, IRA-hardened and raw recruits alike, had become used to the tight space in no time at all – card games were already in progress, and he watched a soldier undo the top two buttons of his uniform jacket with one hand, and, at the same time, hold his rifle and his hand of cards in the other, while a lit cigarette dangled from his mouth. It all looked so casual, unreal.

The embarkation was delayed because more troops were due. In the meanwhile, it became hot below deck, and escaping abovedeck was off limits. Bernard had found a place to sit, where he could rest his back against a bulkhead and where he had space to lay his rifle to one side. He dozed off, then woke when he felt a tremor in the floor; he looked to a porthole, it was still dark. They were pulling away from the dock. The SS Lady Wicklow was moved into the centre of the river, making the space her own, steered towards open sea. Bernard wondered if anyone were about at that early hour to see the passing ship; nobody would ever think it a troopship.

As they passed the Poolbeg lighthouse, the river met the sea, and, suddenly, men had to hold on tightly to keep from being tossed about, while the stakes in card games were scattered. There was a constant rumble from the engine room below. The ship was pointed south, its destination a closely guarded secret, because officers in the National Army saw a potential spy in everyone (during the War of Independence against the British, many of them had been masters of spying): when the time was right, the men would be told.

The smell of vomit was strong. For some soldiers this was their first time at sea, and there were no tablets distributed to prevent seasickness. Bernard, too, felt queasy yet managed to keep his stomach under control; he stared ahead and smoked his Woodbines, a habit begun when he had started to earn a wage, small though it had been.

He was asleep when his foot was kicked; they were to be allowed on deck. The night was warm, with running clouds and a half-moon. He leaned against the deck railings, smoking a cigarette, and wondered where they were heading, but it was a private's lot to be patient – they would all be told, sooner or later. He guessed it wasn't going to be pleasant, wherever it was. The first streak of dawn came on the horizon, which at its own leisurely pace opened into a yellow stain. The sea made him think of his brother Stephen, whom he had seen only once since his release from Artane. He had been enthralled by his stories of far-off places, names with an exotic ring, so much so that for a time he also had thought of going to sea, however, something he couldn't explain had stopped him from following suit. He wondered where Stephen was at that very moment. New York? Crossing the Equator line? Far East?

They were ordered back down into the belly of the ship. Trying to sleep he squeezed shut his eyes and tried to block out the noise from the engine room, but it didn't eliminate the warm, stuffy air of the below-deck, with its ill smell. Minutes went by, then, perhaps an hour, but sleep wasn't coming.

Word spread that breakfast was coming out of the galley, but some pale-faced soldiers, newly trained and ready to fight the enemy with a venom, looked as if they would rather swim ashore in full-kit than face greasy eggs and bacon. Although Bernard was feeling better, he decided to only attempt tea and bread.

Afterwards, he passed the time by keeping an eye to the portholes and to his wristwatch, and tried to figure out the distance they had covered since leaving Dublin; but, while he knew the hours involved, he didn't know the speed of the SS Lady Wicklow, all he knew was they'd already travelled quite a distance.

During the day, the sea flattened out, welcomed by those with seasickness. Bernard took the opportunity to check his rifle, still an item of curiosity, still not proven to be the loyal and trusted friend the range instructor had shouted about. His use of it hadn't been tested. Despite all the training he still didn't know how he would react if a flesh and blood person were in his sights: would he squeeze the trigger with calmness? He was further worried by the thought of fixing bayonet and charging madly at a Republican, at a man and not at a stuffed, swinging sack. Would he thrust it into his bowels and turn it? Automatically, he mentally corrected himself for using the title 'Republican' – instructions were to call them 'Rebels' or 'Irregulars' or 'Mutineers', but nothing that smacked of legitimacy. But it was hard to forget that they were Irishmen like himself.

It seemed to be an eternal day; eventually, the sun went down, nightfall came. Across from him a man produced his rosary beads and began to mouth his prayers. This was the last image he saw before he went to sleep. He awoke with a start. Word was circulating that everyone was to assemble on deck. An officer addressed them: 'Men, the time has come to brief you.' He waved an arm towards the dark shape that was the land. 'Out there is County Kerry; tomorrow we're going to give the enemy a surprise. We'll land in their backyard; show them what a real army is made of.

'We'll sail early into Tralee Bay, with no military show. Fenit is our landing point, but it's imperative that we're taken to be a cargo boat, that we dock without anyone suspecting our true purpose. Only on command will you break cover and storm the place. The enemy will have sleep in their eyes and won't know what hit them. Now, go back down below and be ready. Your officers and sergeants know the plan of attack and will apprise you of your part. He finished by saying, 'Also, the cook will soon have tea, bread and bacon for us all. It'll be a long day and it could be some time before you see other rations.'

Bernard waited below for the moment of action – he was alert, ready, but also nervous, uncertain of what lay ahead. Suddenly, a Baby Power was dangled in front of him. He looked up and saw a grinning face looking down; he recognised the soldier from seeing him at Beggars' Bush barracks. He was one of the experienced men who always seemed relaxed and who always looked as if he knew what he was doing. 'You're welcome to a few swigs,' he said, handing him the small bottle of whiskey.

The drink gave a delayed warm kick. Bernard went to hand back the bottle, but the man said, 'Go on! Have another swig…it'll help.'

'Thanks, but I'm not used to drink.'

'Son, you will be, in time. Did you know that going back centuries when a warrior went into battle, he always took a swig for courage?'

Bernard looked closely at him, at a wizened face cut in two by a wide smile, then he took another drink, wiped his mouth then handed back the bottle. 'There's not much left,' he apologised.

'Keep it,' the soldier said, with a wink. 'There's more where that came from.' At that he drew another bottle from his kit bag and sat on the floor beside him. 'I'm Corrigan,' he said, offering a hand.

'Bernard.'

'Good on you, Bernard, but that sounds stiff to me – I'll call you Barney.'

For a while they sat, saying little, waiting like the rest for something to happen. Suddenly, Corrigan poked him in the arm. He nodded towards a passing officer who seemed in a hurry. 'God help anyone that's captured and brought to that fellow!'

Bernard saw the officer move down the passageway. 'Yes? And who's he when he's at home?'

'Kinahan – he's inner circle, secret of secrets.'

It was getting light. A sergeant came along and demanded: 'Who's the corporal here?'

Corrigan inched an arm upward.

'Corporal,' the sergeant said, 'you'll take the second party of men. Pick the privates you want, but make sure they're of the right stuff. This has to be quick and smart.' The sergeant moved on to the next group.

Most of the men had never heard of Fenit. It was later that Bernard learned that the invasion plan for the 2 August 1922 had been hatched in Dublin by the Military Council, who saw the small port and village as a stepping-stone to Tralee. And, after that, the force of over 400 men would take the town of Killarney, then join up with a similar invasion force that would fight its way through County Cork; they hoped to deliver a massive blow to the rebel force, that's if all went to plan.

But first they had to land at Fenit.

As the SS Lady Wicklow drew closer to the target, its deck was cleared of uniforms, for binoculars would soon be trained on the ship. Corrigan had picked Bernard, and they waited below deck, close to the companionway. Bernard saw that the soldier who had been praying was at it again.

The ship slowed down to take on the local pilot. Bernard could hear discussions above on the deck; then, there were raised voices and an anxious moment when it became obvious that the pilot had tumbled to the SS Lady Wicklow's real mission. There was a commotion. Then, everything went quiet, seemed normal. Bernard had no way of knowing what was going on outside. He guessed that the ship was being manoeuvred into place. All he could see from where he stood was a chunk of clear, blue sky – a summer morning in County Kerry. He suddenly heard the hobnailed boots of the lead party on the gangplank and knew that the assault had begun.

'Right, men,' Corrigan barked, 'it's us now!'

They broke cover and rushed down the gangplank. Bernard saw Corrigan running along the pier towards a long, exposed viaduct that crossed a channel. Soldiers from the first assault group were already on the viaduct, pushing a loose railway wagon ahead of them, using it as a shield against gunfire. He ran in a crouched position, eyes fixed on Corrigan's back, hoping the man knew what he was doing. He heard unusual whistle sounds going past him, and realized it was the sound of bullets. They didn't teach me that in training, he thought.

They reached the lead assault party and caught their breath in the shadow of the railway wagon. Bernard looked back and saw the third wave of men run off the ship and on to the pier. The officer leading the advance group shouted: 'Let's get on with it!' and the men broke from behind the railway wagon and ran for the shelter of a house at the end of the viaduct. Bernard still hadn't fired his rifle; intent on moving forward, he hadn't had the time to identify a target.

It wasn't long before that changed.

He was in the first group to reach the safety of the seaward side of the house at the end of the viaduct. He saw Corrigan dash for the cover of the next building and was ready to follow, when, suddenly, he was pinned down by heavy fire. It lasted some minutes. When it eased,

Bernard was about to move forward when he noticed two men bearing rifles off to one side of him, dressed in civvies, yet draped in bandoliers. They stopped and whipped a tarpaulin cover from a detonator box. One was leaning on the plunger, the other was looking at the viaduct. The plunger went down.

Bernard uttered: 'They've mined the bloody viaduct!'

He looked back, soldiers were still emptying from the ship and were strung along the viaduct; he froze, waiting for the explosion, waiting to see the distant, green shapes fly into the air and drop into the sea. But nothing happened. He saw the plunger being hastily reset by the rebels, and slapped down again, harder. Still no explosion.

He lifted his rifle and fired. All his training was forgotten, the shots were wild, going only in the general direction of the bandolier-wearing men. Suddenly, he heard firing from directly behind him. He glanced over his shoulder; it was the praying soldier. His shots were more accurate than Bernard's, the first one pinged off the detonator box, successive ones scattered clay at the feet of the Irregulars, who retreated to a boreen and disappeared into the surrounding countryside.

Meanwhile, Corrigan and a group of men were being held back by a hail of gunfire coming from a house. Suddenly, lumps started to jump off its walls, hammered by rounds from the Lewis gun mounted on the armoured car, which finally had been unloaded off the ship. The National Army soldiers stayed low until the Lewis was paused, then rushed the building. The enemy had escaped out the back door.

In the space of fifteen minutes the first part of the mission had been completed – Fenit was in the hands of the government force. Bernard reported to Corrigan and told him about the detonator box. 'Show me,' he said.

Bernard led him to the abandoned detonator box. Corrigan followed the cables leading from it; they were concealed by a covering of clay and led to the viaduct. They clambered down to where they had a clear view of its supporting timbers. The trap was visible now. Corrigan counted three mines. He let out a soft whistle and said: 'Someone has done us a favour.' He pointed to a spot within arm's reach. 'See where the cables have been snipped. Someone has saved us!'

Bernard was puzzled. 'Who would do this?'

'It doesn't matter,' Corrigan said. 'We have to keep going.'

By now the force was assembling in the centre of the village, preparing to march on Tralee – they had been lucky so far, but needed to push on with the surprise attack before the enemy had time to reorganise. Corrigan reported the mines, and a small detachment stayed behind to close the viaduct and guard the SS Lady Wicklow. As they marched out of Fenit, Bernard glanced back at the ship at rest in the harbour. It was a picture book setting, a high summer day, a day made for pleasure, not a day for war.

CHAPTER THIRTEEN

Bernard hadn't a mark on him and knew how lucky he had been. Nine comrades had already died, their bodies sent back to Dublin, and, as well, there had been many wounded.

He was on a wooden bench seat in the back of a Lancia lorry holding on to an upright stay to stop himself from being tossed about, part of a detachment sent out from Killarney to investigate a rebel sighting in the vicinity of a large house a half-hour drive from the town. They stopped a safe distance from the building; Bernard had seen similar deserted homes belonging to wealthy Protestant Irish who had fled their property for the safety of Dublin or even the comfort and security of a London drawing room.

The soldiers spread out and crept towards the house, expecting to hear the sudden crack of rifle fire or the dreaded rattle of a Thompson machine gun, but the only sound came from crows that had taken flight and were squawking above the treetops. Two soldiers were sent to investigate an outbuilding and the rest of the patrol gained entry to the house by an unlocked window. They rushed through the rooms, however there was no evidence of current or past use by rebels; the house was as its optimistic owners had left it, everything in its rightful place, furniture covered in dust covers and ready and waiting for the family's return from exile. The men who had been sent to check the outbuilding also had found nothing.

Kirby, an experienced former Dublin Guard, who believed intelligence to be accurate until proven otherwise, led the detachment. 'Search the place again! Leave nothing unturned – you're looking for weapons, cigarette butts, pieces of left-over food, any sign they were here.' Soldiers opened every press and yanked out drawers, scattering contents on the floor. Neat order turned to chaos. Bernard pulled open the drawer of a bedroom dressing table; the contents – ladies' underwear – fell softly to a mat; but then he heard a thud and knelt to examine a small mound of soft clothing and fished out a pistol. Small, delicate, made for a purse, yet, a real pistol. He fingered it, examined the chamber, bullets were sitting in place waiting to be fired.

The men regrouped downstairs, all reporting no sign of rebel presence. Kirby still wasn't convinced. He barked: 'Outside and search the grounds, the ditches…'

Bernard showed him the small pistol.

'Why are you showing me that thing, soldier?' Kirby asked impatiently.

'It's a weapon, Sir.'

Kirby had fought alongside the anti-Treatyites and knew them as you would know a comrade. 'Do you honestly believe that a toy like that would interest the type of men we're after?'

'What will I do with it, Sir?'

'I don't care what you do with it!' Kirby stormed off, talking to himself.

Bernard slipped the pistol into a flap pocket.

Outside, he joined with the rest of the men, combing the garden and the land close to the house, all under the anxious gaze of Kirby. Bernard felt sure that they were wasting their time, but it wasn't for him to speak up; he had to obey orders. He was now searching alongside another soldier at the bottom of the avenue, just inside the entrance gates, poking at ugly bramble with the butt of his Lee Enfield. The man beside him was complaining, repeating what Bernard had thought: 'This is a pure waste of time!'

He hoped for the private's sake that Kirby hadn't heard his remarks. This was his first time on duty with this soldier, however, he had seen him on the SS Lady Wicklow and knew his name was Ron. Suddenly, a single shot rang out, the sound carrying across the countryside. Bernard flattened himself and scanned the rising ground across the road. He was looking for the shooter's position, for a tell-tale puff of smoke, for a moving figure. He saw nothing unusual. He had heard private Ron fall over and now he turned to look at him. A crimson spring had erupted at the side of his throat. Bernard stuck his thumb against the hole, trying to plug the flow of blood. It continued to run down the man's neck. His eyes were open, looking wildly at the sky, as if looking for a lost cloud. Bernard heard footsteps running towards him. It was Kirby. 'Christ! What a mess!' He shouted an order: 'Give us cover here.' Two soldiers jumped into action and fired blindly towards where the hill met the horizon. 'Hang in there, trooper,' Kirby said, 'we'll have you right in no time.' He looked at Bernard, making him a co-conspirator to the lie. The officer drew a bandage roll from a satchel on his belt and wrapped it round the soldier's throat; on contact, it flooded red. The more times he tried to encircle the neck, the wider the red stain became.

Then, accepting the inevitable, Kirby removed the soldier's hat and stroked his hair – turmoil had seized the rest of the body. Bernard watched and idly thought that Ron had nice hair. Then, as moments passed, the eyes were no longer darting, the breathing was shallower, and, overhead, crows were madly screeching.

He had never seen a man die before, though he'd seen his mother lay out an elderly neighbour in Waterford Street. He watched Kirby close Private Ron's eyes; no longer would they search the sky. A soldier volunteered to whisper an Act of Contrition in his ear. Meanwhile, Kirby looked through binoculars at the field across the road, clearly worried that they were sitting targets. He ordered a retreat to the Lancia. They used both sides of the road, looking for better odds if they came under fire; the men on the side with the most tree cover carried the body.

The truck bounced all the way back to Killarney, with a clay-encrusted rough canvas covering Private Ron. His body lay lengthways in the truck, between the boots of the soldiers. Back at the private hotel that had been commandeered by the National Army, grim-faced men unloaded the corpse. Next day, before the coffin was placed on the train to Dublin, Kirby asked Bernard to play Last Post as part of a farewell ceremony.

'Why me?' Bernard asked.

'Limerick Command has robbed our musician for a few days. I hear you can play.'

'I don't know the Last Post...and I'm rusty.'

Kirby said, steely-voiced, 'Soldier, you'll learn it and lose your rustiness by this afternoon.'

When the time came to honour the dead comrade, every soldier and officer not on guard or patrol duty lined up in respect. Bernard didn't like the idea of having to play in front of so many men; he imagined the wisecracks if he were to play a bum note. He closed his eyes and saw himself back in the band-room in Artane. While he played, he realized that this wasn't about him, but about some mother's son, a son who was being sent home to her in a crude wooden box. It could have been any one of us, he thought, completing the final note, with relief.

Later Kirby came up to him. 'You did well, Clancy. But, don't get used to the music thing. It's fighting men we need.'

Bernard couldn't believe that Kirby had grouped him with 'fighting men'. Surely, a wild exaggeration, he thought.

~~~

Bernard sat in the mess and nursed a pint of porter after a day out on patrol. The army had taught him to drink, just as Corrigan had told him it would. Jack Brady and Anto Coffey – fellow privates –came to join him. Brady took out a soiled deck of cards and spun out three hands of twenty-five, part of their mess routine, then Anto drew out cigarettes and passed them round. Brady had matches ready and lit up, then passed the light to Anto, who was on the point of giving it to Bernard, when Brady warned: 'Careful, it's the third light. Unlucky!'

Bernard snatched it and caught the last of the flame, then, leaning back with his lit cigarette, he grinned at Brady. 'I don't believe in that stuff.'

'It's true – you know the story?'

Bernard nodded, but just to annoy his friend he blew out a smoke ring. He knew well the superstition. It had come from the trenches: at night, a sniper would spot the flame, and by the time the third unfortunate soldier had sucked on the cigarette, the marksman had already aimed. Bang!

'When your time's up, it's up,' Bernard said, 'and, it'll have nothing to do with a third light.'

'Scoff, if you want,' Brady said. 'But you wouldn't see me accepting one.'

Anto interrupted: 'Can't you talk about something else? My arse is sore from sitting on a bouncy lorry all day, and I came in here in the mistaken belief that I was getting away from army talk.'

'Sounds good to me,' Bernard said. 'What'll we talk about, then?'

Brady said: 'Girls, women, what I'd give for a go at a busty country girl.'

'You couldn't trust them in these parts,' Anto said. 'The looks they throw us when we pass them on the road and they'd drop a grenade down the front of your trousers as quick as look at you, then go on to Mass.'

'Yes, but they've lovely ankles…all the way up,' Brady said, putting on a dreamy face. He turned his attention to Bernard, mischievously winking at Anto: 'Tell me, pal, have you had much luck with the women, yourself?'

'You know me,' Bernard replied. 'I've led a sheltered life.'

'Pull the other leg,' Anto said, attacking from the flank. 'Not even with a quare one? I hear you'd trip over them round where you live.'

He grinned back at him. 'That's between me and confession.'

'Go on!' Brady was trying to egg him on. 'You can tell us. It won't go any further than Tralee!'

'That's what I'm afraid of!' Bernard said.

He took a moment to retreat to a secret place in his mind, where a female *did* exist, but he certainly wasn't going to tell this pair of jokers about her. Before the mobilisation to Kerry, he had gone walking in uniform with Conroy, a recruit he had trained with at Beggar's Bush, and, while crossing O'Connell Bridge, his companion had stopped to talk to a girl he knew. She had a friend, who hung back, stayed quiet, however, in a fleeting scarlet-faced moment, the girl had looked Bernard in the eye, then, turned away, and fixed her gaze on the river below. When they had moved on, he had quizzed Conroy about her.

'Are you interested?' he asked.

'I could be…'

'You should've put your spoke in when we were talking.'

'I didn't want to cramp your style.'

'I'll find out all I can for you,' he said. It wasn't until two days before sailing, during the lockdown when they were all confined to barracks, that Conroy had met him and announced: 'Madeline'.

Bernard at first didn't make the connection.

'Your one on the bridge,' Conroy said, 'the one you were asking about.'

'Madeline', Bernard said, pronouncing the name with deliberateness. He was surprised. He would never have guessed that name. Madeline. Afterwards, when he thought about it, it seemed perfect for her.

'She says she'll meet you, but not on her own. Guess she must have heard stories about you!' Conroy was grinning. 'We can't do anything about it now, but I'll fix you up when we get some leave, whenever that'll be.'

Since then he had often thought about her – Madeline. Already months had gone by. Would she still be interested in meeting him? He wondered where Conroy had ended up, for the last time he'd seen him was on the SS Lady Wicklow. I hope he doesn't get shot, he thought.

'Another drink, Bernard?' Brady had broken into his thoughts and was heading for the bar.

'Last pint, then,' Bernard said. He felt the ladies pistol resting in his trouser pocket, his 'find of war', not booty, as he hadn't gone looking for it. The small weapon had become his rabbit's foot and touching it had become a comforting habit, something he did unconsciously. In fake embarrassment, his hand would shoot out if a pal quipped: 'Bernard, at the pocket billiards, again?'

Later he set out alone to walk to his sleeping quarters, which had been a former ground-man's house close to the hotel. He had scarcely gone fifty yards, when there was a muffled shot. He felt a searing pain in his leg and crumpled to the ground, like an empty flour sack. A guard saw what happened and ran to Bernard. He gave shrill blasts on a whistle and trained his rifle at the roof of the building, searching out the enemy. Reinforcements spilled down the steps of the hotel, and someone called for lights to be trained on the roof.

Frantic helping hands had meanwhile followed a medic's instructions and carried Bernard inside and a table for him to lie on was cleared with the swipe of a rifle barrel. The medic cut down the trouser leg and exposed the wound; it was in the groin. Bernard heard him say, 'That's a neat little hole.'

The garrison was now on full alert, a detachment was sent up through the building to the roof. A quiet night in Killarney had changed to one of pandemonium. It was unthinkable that the Irregulars would dare to infiltrate the very grounds of the National Army's operations centre.

The medic was talking to himself as he peered at the wound, which gave out only a trickle of blood. 'It must be quite a small calibre...'

Bernard had an awful thought. He didn't know whether to speak up or keep quiet. Finally, he had to confess. 'Look in the pocket,' he whispered to the medic. The man was surprised at the request, yet he did what Bernard had asked. He fished out the small pistol, warm to the touch from its recent firing. He spilled out a bullet, looked at the calibre, and sized it against Bernard's neat entry wound.

'How did that go off?' he asked.

Bernard returned a look of embarrassment, realizing he must have been fiddling with the trigger.

The medic laughed – 'You plugged yourself!' He spent some time examining the wound, prodding the leg with his finger; every so often he couldn't suppress an urge to giggle. An officer came along, looking to be briefed on the extent of the injury. 'He'll live; it's only a flesh wound. You can stand down your search for a gunman.'

'Oh?'

'An unfortunate case of self-infliction,' he said, pointing to the innocent-looking ladies pistol.

'That?'

'Fatal, if you were shot in the wrong place, Sir.'

The officer hurried away to call off the alert.

The medic stood over Bernard. 'Now, what am I going to do with you?' He thought awhile before reaching a decision. 'I think we'll leave the bullet where it is. It's lodged deep in a harmless place and it'll save you being cut open.'

'What if it moves?'

'If I were you, I'd be more worried about taking a *real* bullet.' He dressed the wound, disappeared for a moment, and came back with a crutch. 'Keep the weight off the leg for a while,' he said. As Bernard was hobbling away, he grinningly pointed to the pistol. 'Don't forget your property, soldier.'

~~~

Bernard was now without duties, as he was no longer able to climb in and out of lorries and run through the fields and hike the Kerry mountains in search of elusive rebels. Brady and Anto came to see him at his quarters, bearing a bottle of whiskey.

'Pal, do you believe me, now?' Brady said.

'About what?'

'The third light, you scoffed at the idea.'

'But I shot myself…'

Anto said: 'It's the same thing, Bernard. You got the bad luck!'

CHAPTER FOURTEEN

He was sitting outside his billet, when an officer he recognised from the SS Lady Wicklow came up to him; it was Kinahan, who according to Corrigan wasn't someone to be messed with.

'Trooper Clancy isn't it?' he asked, smiling. Bernard was cautious, as the friendly approach went against what he had heard.

He stood up, straightening himself as best he could. 'Yes, Sir.'

'At ease, man, this is only a chat.'

Kinahan drew a silver case from his pocket and offered him a cigarette. They smoked for some moments, there was a polite enquiry after his wound but, all the while, Bernard felt that he was being assessed.

'Clancy, can you write?' Kinahan said.

'Yes, Sir,' he answered, showing surprise at being asked such a question.

'I mean, is your handwriting legible?'

'It is, Sir,' he said, with confidence, having taken naturally to it at Marlborough Street school.

Kinahan seemed satisfied. 'Good, good.' He turned to one side, and stood looking towards the middle distance, his strong face was in profile, an image on a coin. He looked to be coming to a decision. 'While you're recuperating, young man,' he said, 'the Army is going to make good use of you. You'll work with me in Intelligence. I need someone dependable to record what's said during interrogations, as every scrap of information is important to us.' All the while, the officer never lost the friendly manner, a charm offensive, but Bernard remembered Corrigan's opinion of Kinahan, and, despite his best efforts, couldn't conceal his uneasiness.

'What's the matter, soldier?'

'Nothing, Sir.' The reply had been automatic, again Artane training, the survival instinct.

'Good, for a moment I thought you were hesitating. I'll let you rest for the remainder of today, and you'll report to me first thing in the morning.'

'Yes, Sir.' They exchanged salutes and Bernard watched Kinahan saunter away, a swagger stick under an arm, taking the odd kick at pebbles on the driveway. He looked more like a man who had come to Killarney on a short holiday, than a soldier at war.

~~~

Lying in his bunk, Bernard heard a patrol return, then a commotion outside. He sensed something important was afoot and went to the door; one of their men – the uniform was obvious – was being lifted from the back of the Lancia. He thought that the man was being carelessly carried, for he was drooping in the middle like a wide, rolled rug and appeared in danger of being banged off the ground. He then realized that the soldier was past being hurt, already dead. He hobbled over to see who it was. He met Anto coming towards him, the colour was drained from his face. With a weak motion, he pointed to the body being carried to the hotel, and uttered: 'It's Brady.'

'How?' Bernard asked.

'The murdering bastards – they'll pay dearly for this.'

'But how? what happened?'

'We were ambushed. We stopped to help a fellow with a broken axle on his cart, and there was a hail of lead. Poor Brady was plugged. He never knew what hit him.'

'I can't believe it,' Bernard said. 'It was only –'

'I know, I know.' Anto was quiet for a moment, then said: 'What'll I do now? We were the best of friends... and they got Flanagan too. Mercy of God, he isn't too bad.'

Bernard saw the other trooper, Flanagan, walking towards the hotel, his arm in a makeshift sling, refusing help from a comrade. Meanwhile, across at the Lancia, a man was struck to the ground with the butt of a rifle and then pulled to his feet and taken away at gunpoint.

'Who's that?'

'A prisoner, he's the one we stopped to help. Imagine. Falling for a trap like that!'

Anto rushed off, keen to ensure his friend's body would be treated with every respect; the driver hopped into the Lancia and took it to wash the blood from its floor. Bernard felt a great rage. This surprised him, as prior to this he had only felt a vague sense of cause, but he now knew hatred, hatred for the enemy, the enemy that had done this to a friend. He was now in a military family and Brady had been part of that family; for Bernard – as it was with the entire garrison – the killing had become personal.

He reported to Commandant Kinahan the following morning. The interrogations were conducted in the basement of the hotel, in a spartan room containing a table and chair, which were placed in its centre, and there were two extra chairs placed along a wall. There was a small rectangular window high up on the wall, which let in minimum daylight, and hanging from the ceiling was a single naked electric bulb. Kinahan said: 'Private Clancy, the prisoner that was captured yesterday is being brought to us. Just watch and take notes. If I ask you a question, it'll probably be just for effect, I won't be looking for a reply. Just nod. Understood?'

'Yes, Sir.'

The prisoner was being held in a makeshift cell, a short walk away. A 'halt' command outside in the corridor, and the door swung open. An affable Kinahan, acting like the host of a house party, greeted the prisoner. The guards were dismissed, taking up positions outside, and Kinahan closed the door with a flick of his boot and invited the prisoner to sit down. Bernard had an opportunity to study the detainee: he was in his mid-forties, well built, one who looked accustomed to hard, physical work, and he was coatless, despite the cold outside. He was already seeing the man as the enemy. Brady would be alive today, he thought, if it weren't for the likes of him. Then, his mind wandering, he thought of Michael Collins, the 'Chief', who also was recently killed in an ambush.

Kinahan began: 'I trust our soldiers are treating you properly, sir?'

The man seemed unsure of how he should reply. Kinahan continued: 'We pride ourselves on being a disciplined army – the Army of the Provisional Government – and we have high standards to maintain, not like the men you'd be used to running with.' He smoothed the pocket flaps of his immaculate uniform, then paused for a moment, as if for effect. Nonchalantly, he produced his silver case and lit a cigarette, then, as if an afterthought, offered one to the prisoner.

'I don't smoke, sir.'

'That's a pity,' Kinahan said, waving his cigarette in a theatrical motion. 'I find they relax me.' He looked over at Bernard. 'Private, would you like a smoke? But of course, you can't, for you're going to be writing down every word this good man is going to say to us.' He looked back at the prisoner. 'That *is* what's going to happen, sir, isn't it? Now, before we start, let me just tell you something important.'

Kinahan was still smiling, but Bernard had a sensation that the basement room was suddenly shrinking in size. 'Have you heard of the Special Emergency Powers granted to the National Army?'

'Is it a Dublin thing?' the man asked. 'A new tax?'

'I wish it were as everyday as that, but these Special Emergency Powers have placed a great responsibility on the shoulders of mere mortals, such as me.' He paused again, blew a smoke ring, and placed a hand on the man's arm. 'Let me explain the position, sir – now, why am I calling you that? Tell me, what is your name?'

'It's Pat…Pat Murphy.'

'Well, Pat, let me explain the position to you. We now have the authority to execute anyone found taking up arms against the State and, also, the authority to execute anyone else we suspect of giving help to such people. However, we also have the power to be lenient, even forgiving, to any good man who'll provide us with information. So, I want you to remember this when you answer my questions.'

Kinahan watched another smoke ring rise towards the flaking ceiling and then patted the prisoner's arm. He looked towards Bernard. 'Private, are you ready to start writing?'

Bernard nodded.

Kinahan asked, 'Are you, or anyone you know, connected with this rebellion against your government?'

'Sir, what happened on the road... when the soldiers were attacked had nothing to do with me and no one I know has time for politics and fighting – we're all only plain people going about our business. I was coming back from the fair in Castleisland when the axle broke. I didn't ask the troops to stop...'

'But, to our troops, you would have looked helpless, in a spot of bother. Wasn't it certain that they *would* stop? Good Samaritans, and all that.'

'Sir, I'd nothing to do with the troops stopping, and –'

'Pat, I could believe you, if it weren't for one action you took that has left me puzzled.'

'Huh?'

'It's reported you ran to the front, using the horse as a shield from the shots that came immediately afterwards, as if you knew what was coming.' Kinahan's eyes were now cold and unblinking. 'You knew it was an ambush because you were part of it!'

There was a pause and Bernard had a chance to catch up, as the words were coming so fast.

Kinahan leaned back in his chair, watching for a new crease of anxiety on the prisoner's face, a further slump in the shoulders, a sign of terror in the eyes.

The prisoner said, 'Any man would duck for cover if he saw men with guns, sir'

'Did you recognise any of these men?'

'They were too far away for that.'

'How many men?'

'I didn't wait to count.'

'You ducked for cover?'

'I did, sir. Two soldiers fell, one was near me, his eyes staring like… I was terrified of being shot.'

'And, after that?'

'There was a cry for help from the other soldier who'd been shot, and I thanked God and his Holy Mother that the man was alive. Next thing I knew, the rest of the soldiers turned on me, and I couldn't believe it. I was put on the back of the lorry and the dead soldier was put on after me and placed at my feet.'

'In case you're interested, his name was Private Brady. The men have taken this very badly. They say you'd time to shout a warning but didn't.'

'It was all so fast, I was scared outa me wits, sir.'

'Are you scared, now, Pat?'

Bernard had trouble hearing the prisoner's answer and put a long dash on the notebook page.

Kinahan stood and called the two soldiers on guard duty. 'Take him back,' he ordered. 'We'll see him again, later.'

The man was agitated. 'Sir, I've told you all I can. When can I go home? Me poor mother is left with the milking…'

Kinahan patted him on the back, as if they were old friends, but his words were the opposite. 'The way things are, Pat, I don't think you'll ever see your home or your mother again. That's how serious all this is. But it's up to you. Good information could change all that.'

With the prisoner gone, Kinahan glanced over Bernard's notes. 'He's told us nothing, except a pack of lies. Take a break for the rest of the morning, and we'll turn the screw on him when we come back at two o'clock.' As they were walking outside, he asked: 'Tell me, Clancy, do *you* think he's telling the truth?'

Bernard's instinct was not to answer, but he felt that Kinahan wouldn't settle for that. 'I'd never make a judge,' he said.

'Not a judge, but certainly a diplomat.' Kinahan went off, laughing to himself.

Bernard stood alone, glad to be free of the claustrophobic basement, out again in the open air, and it didn't matter that the Kerry sky was today an unyielding grey, that the cold from the lakes got into your bones. He took deep, grateful breaths, and, for no reason, had an image of what it must have been like before the fighting, when a hotel guest would praise the view of the mountains, perhaps take a jaunting car around the lakes, with a blanket across the knees and a brandy flask in the pocket. Someday, he thought, I'll come back here when all this is over. Maybe, I'll bring that girl Madeline with me.

As he went for lunch, he tried to put the morning's interrogation to the back of his mind, but it refused to settle there. A thought came: Could our lads be wrong about the prisoner? Then, he remembered Brady, whose coffin would be sent back to Dublin on the train, a package from Killarney to the Top Brass. His murder would have to be paid for.

CHAPTER FIFTEEN

The prisoner was returned and shoved on to the chair. Bernard saw Kinahan matter-of-factly produce a sack, a coil of thin rope and a pliers and lay them out before him as a tradesman would do before starting a specialised task, then the smile appeared, but there was a betraying ugliness about the way he ran his tongue between his teeth. 'Pat... dear Pat, I've given you plenty of time to think about your position. The trooper here is ready to write down the names and whereabouts of the mongrels that attacked our patrol. The question is, are you ready to provide us with this information?'

The prisoner was breathing deeply. 'Why don't you believe me?' he pleaded. 'I tell you, this had nothing to do with me...I was caught up in it, just like the poor –'

Kinahan slammed down the side of his fist against the table. 'Don't insult my intelligence. I know you're one of them or at least one of their supporters!' He tossed the rope to the guards, who this time had remained in the room. They tied the prisoner to the chair, leaving his right arm free. Kinahan lifted the sack, solemnly like a priest on the altar, and signalled for the man to be hooded. Just before the sack was dropped into place, he took up the pliers and said, with a mock shrug of the shoulders, 'We've tried the easy way, you leave me no option.'

The prisoner stood up, lifting the chair with him. He was struck on the shoulder by a rifle butt and fell back. Kinahan grabbed the man's resisting free arm and with the help of a guard it was wrestled to the table. The palm was facing downward, and Kinahan tapped the back of the hand with the pliers.

'You've one last chance,' he said, speaking close to the hood. The prisoner struggled to get his hand free, but the guard was heavy-set and leaning down hard on it. No answer came. Kinahan tapped the man's nails. 'Don't you know what you're forcing me to do?'

~~~

Once he got outside, Bernard vomited. He loosened his tunic to let cool air down his front. He had been shocked by what had happened. The prisoner had screamed, despite clearly trying not to, his cry amplified by the confining walls of the basement, yet he still hadn't changed his story.

Kinahan emerged from the building and stood a few feet away.

'Don't be ashamed, soldier. I was like that my first time.'

Bernard buttoned up and handed the notebook to Kinahan, who balanced it on his palm, as if he were weighing it. 'We got nothing out of the prisoner,' he said, a friendliness jumping back into his face. 'I doubt if the notes are of any value; nevertheless, get them typed up, as you never know.'

Bernard knew he was being studied. He took the notebook and went to go back inside, but Kinahan reached out and gripped him by the arm. 'You really don't have a clue about this war. Do you, Private?'

'What do you mean, Sir?'

'We have to win this. Otherwise, all that's been gained will be lost.'

Bernard didn't answer, waited for him to loosen his hold. Then, Kinahan strode away, whistling a dance tune, and re-entered the hotel ahead of him. A typewriter belonging to the hotel had been removed from a back office and placed in the reception hallway. A soldier called Quigley, who had a talent for always landing the easy jobs, was on typing duty; he one-fingered the Remington while Bernard dictated.

When finished, Quigley asked, 'Is this the fellow they caught for Brady's killing?'

'Yes. He's being interrogated but he may be innocent.'

'None of them are innocent! I hope he gets what's coming to him!'

Bernard took the typewritten report and went to lie on his bunk. He had a tiring pain from the bullet wound and was worried that the piece of lead had moved, but he knew the pain would pass and that it was a mere insect bite compared to the state of the prisoner who had been flung back in the cell with his hand crudely swathed in a bloodstained dirty rag. Bernard became unsettled, but he gave a shrug and swung his feet to the floor and sat by the window and let his eyes take in the green and blue mountains, and, gradually, the feeling went.

Later, when he took the typed notes to Kinahan, he was surprised when he said, 'I'm finished interrogating the prisoner – he's either unbreakable or innocent.'

Bernard was relieved for the man, and equally for himself.

Pat Murphy was brought up from the cell, and Kinahan paraded him in front of fellow officers and proposed his release from custody. Bernard noticed that one of the officers was becoming agitated; clearly, he wasn't happy to let the prisoner go. 'He's a rebel!' he shouted. 'You just haven't broken him!'

Kinahan didn't see fit to reply, but guided the prisoner to the front entrance, where he left him at the top of the steps, as if he were releasing a captured fox back to the wild. The man stopped to look round, and then glanced back inside the hotel, disbelieving that his hell was over. He tottered, then gathered himself and any pride he had left and started down the steps. Suddenly, the dissenting officer stormed past Kinahan, drew his revolver and shot the released man, once in the back, then when he spun around, he shot him again, this time in the chest, then, he fired a final bullet almost at point blank range which thumped into the right shoulder. Pat Murphy, a farmer, and a son, fell as if he were a bag of animal feed tossed from a lorry, and came to rest on the bottom step. He was dead, and a surprised look on his face seemed to ask: 'How did that happen?'

Bernard had earlier thought he'd seen the worst when Kinahan had tortured the prisoner, but this act was beyond all reason.

The officer holstered his weapon. 'Now, we're sure,' he said, straightening his cap.

'You're a savage and a fool!' Kinahan said.

Another officer said, 'Fuck! How'll we explain this?'

It was agreed that a false report would be drawn up and everyone present would stand by it, including Bernard, who resented the fact that he wasn't even consulted on this decision. Kinahan stood on the steps, watching the body as it was carried away. He left the building and signalled for Bernard to follow him. As they walked along the driveway, Kinahan kicked-up some gravel and said, as if he were both talking to himself and, at the same time, talking to Bernard, 'This is what happens...'

Bernard wasn't listening, because he was in a state of shock, unwilling to even try to make sense from the senseless. Later, he ran into Anto, who said, 'I hear they did in the prisoner. Only right, I say.'

'I think tonight we both deserve to get pissed,' Bernard said.

'Yes, in memory of Brady.'

Bernard thought: And in memory of that poor fucker, Pat Murphy.

They drank at their regular table, and every so often their eyes were drawn to a vacant chair that they had deliberately pulled up, out of respect.

'This has to be the worst day...' Bernard said, his words now slurred.

'Poor Brady,' Anto said. 'The poor bastard.'

In the early hours of the morning they got to their feet, heads spinning from a mixture of porter and whiskey. Bernard felt his legs buckle, and Anto staggered round the table to support him. They swayed for some moments, an indecisive dance, Anto straining to keep him upright; they moved outside, past the envious look of a sentry, and stumbled across the driveway. Every so often, Bernard said – 'Bang!' He saw the man from Kerry slump and fall and then, to block out the image, he remembered the ridiculous time he had shot himself; the very idea of it made him giggle uncontrollably. Anto got him as far as his billet, opened the door, and Bernard stumbled inside and collapsed on the floor. His friend, in his own drunken haze, tried to get him upright and found him to be a dead weight for such a slight man and soon gave up. Bernard was left where he lay, a blanket yanked from a bunk thrown across him.

Some weeks later, with snow settled on the mountains, the Killarney garrison acknowledged the official birth of the Irish Free State with a march-past, but Bernard didn't march, even though his wound had healed (at times, he even forgot the bullet in his leg), instead, he was entrusted with hoisting the Tricolour. The green, white, and orange was caught and straightened by an icy wind. The assembled men looked to it and saluted. An officer in a formal address warned the men that the country's new status would change nothing, that the guerrilla attacks hadn't stopped and that the war still had to be won.

Later in the day, Bernard reported for duty to Kinahan, who had dressed for the march-past with immaculate attention to his uniform.

'Clancy,' he said, 'we've carried out many interrogations in this short period of time and under a lot of pressure as well. I know you're probably just obeying orders and all that, and I suspect you probably hate this intelligence work, yet I've never heard you once complain.'

Bernard wondered what was coming next. He stayed quiet, waited.

'That's what I like most about you, Private. You've a quiet disposition, you've never interrupted me, though at times I've had the impression you may have wanted to. So, I've pulled a few strings and organised furlough for you over the Christmas. You'll have four days with your family in Dublin, then come back to Killarney a refreshed man. You'll need to be, for the Irregulars aren't beaten yet, not by any means.'

'Thank you, Sir.'

'You deserve it, Private Clancy. You deserve it.'

Bernard was provided with a travel coupon, and he prepared for the trip. He wrote home telling of his plans and hoped the postman would get to Waterford Street before him. On the morning of departure Kinahan came to him and said: 'You'll be in uniform in Dublin, and you could be a soft target, especially if they come to know you work in Intelligence.' He handed him a pistol and holster. 'The sight of a weapon will make anyone think twice about coming after you.'

He remembered the warning as he waited at Killarney train station, and patted the pistol hanging on his side, a feeling of comfort. However, he wasn't quite sure which prospect made him the more nervous, a surprise attack by an assassin on a quiet Dublin street or the coming visit to his family home.

CHAPTER SIXTEEN

His mother came to the door and hugged him. 'Your letter only came this morning, and I hadn't time to prepare the place.'

He followed her inside and found that little had changed since last time. He had expected it to look smarter, especially for Christmas; instead, it had a cold bare look, no sign of paper chains or tasty treats.

'I'll put on the kettle for a cup of Rosie Lee,' she said. 'You must be famished after the long journey. Oh! You are handsome in uniform! And, let me tell you, son, the moustache suits you so.'

While they drank tea at the table, he looked around the room, skipped past the double bed with the long johns hanging from the brass post, on to the corner, where he had shared a bed with Peter. She saw him looking. 'You'll have it all to yourself,' she said.

'Why? Where will Peter be?'

'He's in Artane.'

He didn't ask her, why? or, how? but waited for her to explain.

She was fidgeting with her hands and looking everywhere except at him. Finally, she said: 'It was getting too much, eat you out of house and home he would. I tell you there was never enough shillings.' As if inspired by his presence, she added, 'And, Artane didn't do *you* any harm. Look how you've got on!'

'Mother, I signed a form saying you'd get most of my army pay. Do you not get it?'

'I do, Bernard. You've been the best of a son.'

'But surely that helps?'

'It does…it did…but, then again, there's never enough.'

'How long has he been in Artane?'

'Not long, two months, maybe. I hated doing it, but it was all for the best.'

'So, he'll be there for Christmas?'

'I tell you, I hated doing it!'

He wanted to ask if she had been to visit him but was afraid of hearing the answer. He thought of his own time there and hoped the Christian Brothers would be easier on Peter, but he doubted it. It annoyed him that his mother didn't see the harm in what she had done.

He heard heavy footsteps on the stairs. His mother's expression altered, a look of panic in the eyes. It must be *him*, he thought, the owner of the long johns hanging like a declaration of occupancy on the bed frame. The door opened and Jemser stumbled in, the pupils of his eyes wide and dark and glassy. The squat figure, looking as immovable as a cast-iron pillar post-box, scowled at Bernard. 'The toy soldier,' he said. 'Come home to Mammy, have we?'

Bernard turned to Lily. 'So, this is where the money's going?'

'What's that you're saying?' Jemser said, struggling to remove a soiled topcoat. 'I can hear you and your conniving…what have you being saying about me, woman?'

'Don't you go accusing me, Jemser; I said nothing.'

Bernard said, 'She doesn't have to say anything. I can see how you've pissed the money away.'

'That uniform of yours won't save you from these fists.'

Jemser's big labourer's hands which had once pushed and pulled with the best of them on Dublin's dockside had changed into white-knuckle weapons, ready to strike. Instinctively, Bernard remembered Kinahan and how he would act in a situation such as this. He felt himself adopting the officer's persona – he forced a smile, gave all the outward signs of friendship, like someone coming towards you in a bar who you felt sure was going to stand you a drink.

'Jemser,' he said, 'you're correct, I'm not a fighting man. I know you'd make mash of me. I'm not a fool.'

The man's eyes narrowed. 'Respect, that's what the man of the house deserves, and gets. Respect.'

'And the man of the house holds the purse,' Bernard said.

'Only right,' Jemser said.

Bernard continued smiling, but in a smooth, almost undetectable movement, he drew the pistol from its holster. He broke the Colt and withdrew its bullets, all but one. Jemser was unable to take his eyes off Bernard's dextrous fingers. Then, Bernard snapped the pistol together and held the gun up to the ceiling and examined the chamber. He then brought the gun down again to chest level and spun the chamber and rested the barrel against his free hand, and all the while he maintained a 'Kinahan' persona.

He said to his mother, 'You should move out of the way.'

'Jesus, Mary and Joseph!' she said, making a frantic sign of the cross. 'Bernard, what are you at?'

'Go on, Ma, move,' he said, directing her towards the other side of the room.

Quickly sobering up, Jemser said: 'You don't frighten me, you know that; you don't –'

Bernard interrupted: 'I'm giving you a fighting chance. There's only one bullet and a pull of the trigger could fire it, or maybe not...'

'You just can't shoot someone; there's army rules, even I know that.'

'True, true.' Bernard paused for some moments, never dropping the friendly face, and then added, 'But *I* know I can.'

Lily shrieked, 'Gawd, Bernard, you're not going to shoot him?'

'He hasn't the balls,' Jemser said, his face contorted with rage.

Bernard pointed the weapon at him and pulled the trigger. Click. Nothing happened. Lily screamed. He put the gun on the table, within easy reach. 'There's always a next time,' he said, 'that's if you're still around.'

'What do you mean?'

'It means I can't shoot you if you're gone from here, you, your smell and all your filthy belongings.'

'Gone? Why would I go out of me own place?'

'That's exactly it, Jemser. This isn't your place, and it has nothing to do with you. So, I'm telling you, take all your stuff and get out.'

He turned to Lily. 'This son of yours is mad, woman.'

'I didn't put him up to this, I swear.'

'Well, talk to him...Tell him he can't.'

'You're my husband, Jemser – but I can't turn on my own flesh and blood.'

'I'll see about that,' he said, making a sudden rush for the table. He wasn't quick enough. Now, he was staring at the muzzle of the Colt. He saw empty gaps in the chamber and had an awful feeling that the lone bullet was snugly in place, just waiting.

Bernard saw Jemser's hand leaning on the table, palm down, and brought the butt of the gun down hard on his middle finger. A roar of pain and the damaged hand was sent to an armpit, looking for comfort.

'I don't want to be doing this, Jemser,' he said, 'but you give me no choice.' All the time, he never wavered, kept the Colt trained.

Jemser looked worried. 'Where can I go?' he said. 'I've no other bleedin' place?'

'I don't care, so long as you pack up and go and never come back here.'

Jemser shot a frantic look at Lily, hoping to appeal to her, but she had slumped to the floor and turned her face away. 'So that's the way it is!' he said. He turned back to Bernard, sneering. 'I'm going, I'm going. But get this, I'm going because *I* want to.'

'It makes no odds, as long as you're gone.'

Jemser sent an ugly glance in Lily's direction. 'I'm sick of humping that skinny body, so it'll be no loss.'

'Keep that up and I'll kill you, whether you go or not!'

Under Bernard's scrutiny he pulled a sheet from the double bed and began to toss his belongings on to it, starting with the long johns on the bedpost, and when he was done, he drew the corners of the sheet together and went to the door, the bundle over his shoulder. He took a last look around the tenement room, then, from his depths brought up phlegm and vehemently spat in Lily's direction and slammed the door behind him.

'Good riddance to him,' Bernard said, picking the bullets off the table and returning them to the revolver.

Lily was crying. He knelt beside her, patted her shoulder.

She said, 'He said things no son is meant to hear...I'm so ashamed...'

'That's his type, Ma – he's from the gutter.'

She stayed on the floor; her sobbing rose and fell. After a while, he said, 'Ma, I thought you'd be happy to see the back of him?' To his relief, she nodded, and clutched his arm.

'Son, my mind is in a state. One part of me is happy over the way you stood up for me. I know you care. But the other part of me is frightened. Even though Jemser was a bastard, at least I always knew where I stood with him. Now, there's no one...'

'Mother, you deserve better than him and you know that in your heart. Just compare him to Da, there's no comparison. We're a family and we won't let you down.'

'It's all well and fine saying that, but Da is above in Glasnevin, and you'll go back to the army and I'll be on me own. I don't know if I'll be able for that.'

'It won't be forever, Ma. And remember Stephen, I'm sure he'll be home on visits, and you can go and see Peter in Artane, and I'll be home as often as I can get leave. And I'll write every week...'

'I know all that son but I'm just not strong like you.'

He wanted to say, 'You are, Mother, you are'. But deep down he doubted his own strength and his right to be dishing out advice. Lily held on to him and lifted herself off the floor and dried her eyes. She looked round the tenement room, suddenly seeing it for what it was. 'It's Christmas Eve and look at the state of this place! Jemser was to give me money to get in the Christmas dinner. There's nothing –'

'Don't worry, Ma, tomorrow we'll go somewhere swanky.'

'But there's no money,' she said, feeling ashamed.

'Don't worry, I've something kept by.'

'But I've only rags to wear.'

He looked at his watch. There was still time to get to Talbot Street before the shops closed for Christmas.

~~~

They were seated in the Dolphin, having arrived in style in a hansom cab. Bernard was amused to see his mother behave like an excited child as she smoothed the already smooth white linen tablecloth and fiddled with the delicate, ornate cutlery; perhaps, he thought, it reminds her of days past, when the family had money. They had been lucky to gain entry to the dining room, thanks to a porter at the front door –a former classmate of Stephen's at Marlborough Street School – who'd recognised Bernard and spoken to the maître d'hôtel. Bernard was in uniform, and the man raised his hands in horror when he saw the pistol. 'We don't want to frighten our regular old dears! They're insulated from all this violence.'

'I'm sorry,' Bernard said. 'I can't part with the gun.'

The maître d'hôtel thought for a moment, then realized he was too busy to get involved in a row over detail on a frantic Christmas Day; he went off and came back with a large brown paper bag. Mother and son dined on turkey and ham and all the trimmings, while the concealed Colt was placed on the floor between them.

Bernard made a toast: 'To Stephen and Peter, whatever they're doing at this very moment.' He imagined that his seafaring brother was anchored off some exotic-sounding port, beads of sweat on his face from the equatorial sun, as for Peter, he saw him in the refectory in Artane, his heart in his mouth in case some bully would elbow him off his seat to claim a second Christmas dinner.

They clinked glasses. 'And, to Da, too,' she said, her eyes moistening. 'He would have loved to have taken me to a place like this.'

Christmas pudding eaten, the dining room became noisier; a group of people at adjoining tables began a singsong and a stout woman appeared at a piano at the other end of the dining room. He heard the words of a song, '*By Killarney's lakes and fells*', and an image jumped into his mind of Kinahan holding a pair of bloodied pliers. He glanced at his watch. It was already late afternoon, mid-winter darkness had closed in, and he with somewhere else to go to later that night, for by chance he had met Conroy the week before in Castleisland and pressed him for more information on the girl who'd sustained him for months — Madeline.

'Clancy, you've got it bad,' Conroy said. He hadn't the number of the house but was sure she lived on Langrishe Place.

Bernard was surprised at this. Her home had been but a few minutes' walk from Waterford Street and he couldn't believe that he hadn't set eyes on her before that brief encounter on O'Connell Bridge, however, now armed with Conroy's information, he was determined to find her. A waitress enquired if they needed more sherry, and her voice brought Bernard back into the dining room and he looked across at his mother and saw that her contented eyelids were drooping. It was time to be leaving and he asked for the bill. Outside, a man carrying a parcel under his arm passed them on the pavement. He stopped abruptly and turned back. Bernard tensed – the pistol was in the paper bag under his arm. The man raised his hat. 'Mrs. Clancy, I must wish you a Happy Christmas!'

Lily was puzzled for a moment and then she realized it was Paddy Gill, the sacristan from the Pro-Cathedral. 'And a Happy Christmas to you, Mr. Gill and all that belongs to you.'

Gill looked towards the inviting doorway of the Dolphin. 'You've been doing the Christmas in style then, Mrs. Clancy?'

For the first time in years, Lily had something to brag about. 'This is my son Bernard. "Nothing is too good for me", he tells me, spoiling me rotten he is.'

He turned to Bernard. 'Young man, look after this fine woman.' Then, pointing at the uniform, he shook his hand and said, 'I salute you for the job you're doing.' Bernard was too surprised to reply. Then Gill tugged his coat collar up against a sly wind that had whipped up and strode away.

'Such a nice man,' Lily said, 'a great friend of your father's.' She wanted to walk home by the Ha'Penny Bridge and linked him for support all the way back to Waterford Street. He knew it was a special moment, one to be treasured. Later, when she was dozing, he would go to Langrishe Place.

~~~

Not a long street – houses on both sides and lights from parlours making a pattern on the granite pavement. He went up one side and back down the other, eyes searching the windows, heart thumping. A young girl pushing a hoop ran out of a house ahead of him and came in his direction. He asked her if she knew a woman named Madeline. An arm shot out like a water diviner's rod and pointed to a hall door directly across the street. 'Over there, Mister.'

'There?' Bernard pointed, wanting to be sure, but the hoop-rolling girl had moved down the street and he was just in time to see her go into another house. A door slammed and the street was empty again, except for him. He crossed to the house and cautiously looked through the parlour window; indiscernible figures moved behind the net curtain, voices came from the room, Christmas gaiety. He hesitated. Knocking on the door seemed a big and irreversible step. It must be taken, he decided. He lifted the knocker and felt the door give way and move inwards; it was off the latch and it now stood ajar, the mouth of a dark hallway. Suddenly, the parlour door was opened, releasing light into the hall. A young woman came out of the room and turned to go deeper into the house. He somehow knew it was her. 'Madeline,' he said, his voice urgent, yet barely audible. She stopped and turned.

'Yes?'

'I'm Conroy's friend...remember you and your friend met us on O'Connell Bridge?'

She came slowly to the door. 'Yes, I remember.'

He was suddenly tongue-tied, and took his cap off, passing it back and forward between his fingers. The streetlamp behind him bathed her face, she was now close, eyes like pools, as he had remembered her, no, she was better than how he'd remembered. He now saw softness in her – he wanted to touch that softness, be swallowed by it.

'Bernard isn't it?' she said.

'Yes,' He was delighted that she had remembered; he knew he was staring. How could he not? Then, as if he were about to pose a question: 'Madeline...'

'Yes?'

She had moved forward to look outside, and her face was now only inches from his. He wanted to tell her that he had thought about her many times when in Kerry, especially when trying to fall asleep after a bad day. Suddenly, a man's voice came from within the parlour – 'Who's out there, Madeline?'

'It's only a friend, Daddy.'

'Friend? Who is it? Bring her in to the fire.'

'She's a *him*, Daddy,'

'Oh! Nevertheless, bring him in…It's Christmas Night.'

He allowed himself to be drawn into the hallway and next thing he knew he was in the parlour, the centre of attention. 'This is Bernard,' she said.

'Pour Bernard a drink,' her father said, pointing to a small table against the wall, which was covered in festive, red crepe paper, upon which, beside a small Nativity crib with chalk figures, stood a bottle of whiskey, golden amongst a gathering of different flavoured mineral waters. Madeline poured a drink and handed it to him.

A woman appeared at his elbow, carrying a plate of Christmas pudding. 'Bernard, you must have something to eat with your drink!'

'Mammy, he mightn't like pudding,' Madeline said, 'not everyone likes pudding.'

Bernard took a slice from the top of the deep festive pile, smiled at the mother, and was guided to a chair at the fire, a stranger thrust into the heart of their home life. They talked round him, but a natural reserve, cautiousness, even shyness, kept him quiet. However, everyone was friendly, and soon he found himself adding bits to the conversation, yet all the time his eyes were following Madeline as she moved about.

She left the room and her two sisters pounced with questions about the army and about his gun. Unused to such attention he was relieved when she came back; she had put on a coat and hat. 'We're going out for some fresh air,' she said to the family, fanning her face with her hand while sending a look of blame towards the innocent blazing fire in the grate.

Her mother squealed: 'Maddie, your only divine in the new Christmas coat!'

'Don't be embarrassing me, Mammy,' she said, steering Bernard towards the door. 'We're going!'

Outside on the pavement, he said, 'I feel terrible, I don't even know your family name.'

'It's O'Shea.'

'Your home is…well…it's friendly.'

She had a quizzical look: 'What a strange thing to say, I imagine all homes to be friendly.' A cold wind blew up Langrishe Place and she shoved her arm under his and they started walking. Bernard had earlier worried about what he would say to her, after all, she was almost a stranger; but he didn't have to worry. While he was quiet, she was vivacious. Her words were bright and buoyant; she seemed to be bent on taking life lightly. He could have found that annoying, but he allowed himself to be drawn into her world, to be lost in her world. When they paused under the portico of the General Post Office, light from a streetlamp lit up her eyes and he had a feeling that she could read his whole being. He wanted to kiss her, fall into those eyes. A simple movement of the head would do it, but his neck muscles wouldn't do what his mind wanted.

'What's the matter?' she asked.

'I don't deserve you.'

'What silly talk.'

'Silly?'

'Yes, it's silly. You've come looking for me, and I'm delighted you found me.'

'Really?'

'I don't tell lies, Bernard.'

'Can I kiss you?'

'You're shaking, are you cold?' She opened her new Christmas coat and her white blouse shone in the lamplight. 'Put your arms round my waist to keep you warm.'

They moved against a wall, still marked from the bullets of the 1916 rebellion, and kissed, and kissed, and kissed...

A member of the DMP on patrol saw them and passed without comment. Normally, he would have moved on a courting couple from such a hallowed place, but he spotted the holster and walked on; he wasn't going to spoil an officer's fun. Bernard hadn't even noticed him.

CHAPTER SEVENTEEN

B ernard took out Madeline's letter and reread it.

My dear Bernard
Your letter came this morning and Bernard my heart jumped with
relief when I saw it for the newspapers had me scared out of my wits
as they said more men had been killed in Kerry but now I know you
are safe I can sleep tonight and dream of you and your letter with
your beautiful words will be under my pillow so when will you be
back to me? forgive me darling I know you cannot answer that but
you are never out of my mind and I must tell you I saw your mother
yesterday shopping and I'm glad you pointed her out to me as I feel
closer to you when I see her and I nearly said hello to her but I will
wait till you come home and you bring me to see her
I wish it could be tomorrow
Your loving heart,
Maddie,
X X X X X X

He put the letter to his lips and returned it to his breast pocket. Although he lived for her letters, their arrival would deflate him for the rest of the day. It was the sense of not being with her. He shook himself and hurried towards the interrogation room, for an Irregular had been captured in a skirmish the night before and Kinahan would want to drag as much information out of the prisoner before letting the firing squad boys at him. The commandant was his usual affable self, like someone meeting up with a bunch of old chums at the races, but Bernard now knew the steeliness of the man.

A hooded prisoner was brought in and seated, and the interrogation started. In recent times, Kinahan's technique had changed. The prisoner couldn't see him, and he avoided introductions. No preamble, only hard, urgent interrogation: Who? Where? Why? Tell us all you know you scum!

This time, the prisoner stayed silent.

'I've broken bigger and braver men than you!' Kinahan roared. 'You men are a beaten lot – you *know* it's a lost cause. Tell us all you know, and we'll think about going easy on you.'

Still no response. He went behind him and hit out with a police truncheon, a souvenir from an abandoned RIC barracks. There was a cry of pain and the prisoner slumped forward, but like a man who caught himself in the act of nodding off in church, he jerked upright. Bernard wanted him to pass out; then he would be safe, at least for the moment. Kinahan went to walk away, a tight smile on his lips, then as an afterthought he swung the truncheon again.

'Christ!' the prisoner let out a cry and failed to stop his torso bending across the table.

Kinahan spoke down to the hood. 'You're not so strong after all, are you? I'll give you a chance to think over your precarious position and then I'll be back like the bad penny.' He turned to Bernard. 'Private, give this man a cigarette...I do hope for his sake he comes to his senses.'

Bernard was left alone with the prisoner; the guards were outside the door. He raised the hood until it cleared the man's mouth, lit a cigarette, and placed it between blood-crusted lips. The prisoner inhaled and then blew out the smoke round the cigarette. Bernard asked, 'Can you manage?' The prisoner nodded and took another draw of smoke followed by an outburst of coughing. Bernard took the cigarette away and let him recover. Then the prisoner said, 'Go again, pal.' Bernard fed him the cigarette, surprised that the voice had a Dublin accent, as he didn't think that fighters from the capital would be this far south, certainly not into Kerry.

He withdrew the cigarette. 'What's your name?'

'Another drag, pal.'

Bernard looked again for his name.

'I wouldn't speak to the other bastard, and I'm certainly not going to speak to you.'

Bernard thought he knew the voice but needed to hear more. 'I'm Dublin too...Waterford Street. Do you know it?'

'Of course, I know it,' the man said, as if insulted by the question. 'But that's all you're going to get outa me! Now get on with what you have to do.'

Bernard lifted the hood higher; the prisoner blinked from the brightness of a naked electric bulb. He was right – memories of Artane Industrial School, of rubbing shoulders at the refectory table. Glancing towards the open door, he saw that the guards were locked in conversation. He put a finger to his lips, then whispered, 'I'll speak, and for God's sake don't answer me.'

The man looked at him with suspicion.

Bernard said: 'Artane.' He saw the prisoner's eyes search his face, and he prompted him: 'It's Berno.'

'Berno?' The voice was croaky.

'Keep it low, or they'll hear,' Bernard said.

'I don't believe –'

'Yes, Seán, it's me.' At that moment, he heard Kinahan returning and pulled the hood back into place; he had just enough time to whisper, 'I'll come and see you tonight.'

Kinahan sauntered in, saw the half-smoked cigarette burning on the table, picked it up as if it were something dirty and squashed it with the heel of his boot. 'Well, my friend, are we ready to talk?' he said. 'In a matter of weeks – and that's all it will take now – your crowd will be coming out of the ditches waving white flags and you, sir, you'll be dead, and all for nothing. You're not going to save, alter or contribute anything to the outcome by playing the hero. Tell us something important, some good information, and I'll recommend a spell behind bars for you instead.'

Bernard had hoped that Seán would cooperate but should have known better; his friend wasn't going to bend easily. The guards were called and Kinahan ordered them to place the prisoner's hand on the table and despite his struggling they overpowered him. Kinahan lit a cigarette and kissed it against the back of Seán's hand, playing with him, as an inquisitive child would poke an insect with a stick. Bernard knew what was coming and wanted his friend to be weak, not strong, for being strong would only have a bad ending. Then, Kinahan drew on the cigarette until it glowed and placed it on the back of the hand, this time with pressure. The prisoner jerked yet stayed silent. Five more burns and the back of Seán's hand looked as if a plague from ancient times had infected him. Still he held out – no words, only muffled gasps of pain. And Bernard felt each stab as if it were against his own flesh.

Kinahan became impatient and called for the man's other hand to be placed on the table. He resumed the torture, not stopping until the prisoner passed out. Bernard hoped Seán would take his time in coming to, and Kinahan paced the room as he waited to continue. He looked at his watch and barked at Bernard, 'Private, I've a command meeting in two minutes and must go. When this weakling comes around,' he said derisively, 'see what you can get out of him. Otherwise, I'll grill him again in the morning.' He hurried away, a man with a war to be won.

Bernard asked one of the guards to get some water. Seán was groaning, coming back to consciousness, back to the reality of the grim interrogation basement. Bernard got him to sip from a metal mug.

~~~

It was after midnight when Bernard made his way to the cells. He found the guard cleaning his boots out of boredom. 'To see the prisoner,' Bernard said, clutching a notepad and hoping to sound official. He added, 'Commandant Kinahan doesn't want him to fall asleep.'

'Fat chance,' the guard said. 'He's nursing more wounds.'

'Oh?'

'The commandant came by an hour ago, thick over something and put a couple of digs into him.'

'I don't blame him,' Bernard said, 'those scum have a lot to answer for.'

The guard unlocked the door, however, rather than remaining outside, he went to follow him into the cell.

'The prisoner is tied-up?' Bernard asked.

'Trussed up like a turkey.'

'Then, there's hardly need for the two of us.'

The guard hesitated, then said, 'Shout if you need me.'

The cell was a converted room, with bars built into place on the window and a sturdy grille added a second layer of security to its door. There was no sign of a bed, not even a straw mattress. Seán was curled up in a corner. Bernard knelt beside him and touched him on the shoulder. 'Hey, pal…it's me…Berno.'

Seán said, 'Is this supposed to make it easier?'

'What?'

'Having someone I know –'

'No, it's not like that. I've come to see you, nothing else.'

'Yeah, pull the other one.'

Bernard sat on the floor beside him, his back resting against the wall. 'At Artane, I never imagined we'd meet again in a place like this.'

'On different sides,' Seán said, at the same time forcing himself to sit upright.

Bernard lit a cigarette for him. 'And which of us is on the right side?'

'The one that wins,' Seán said.

He fed his lips with the cigarette, occasionally drawing on the stained paper himself. 'How did you get tied-up with this Kerry mob?'

'The police were calling to the house looking to shove me back into Artane, and me Ma was desperate. Her people are from hereabouts and to keep me out of trouble she sent me here, down to the muck savages.'

'And the fighting?'

'It's a republican house. The cousins taught me how to shoot and I joined up. Then, when your lot sold us out, I just kept doing what I'd always been doing, except it wasn't against the English, but the likes of you.'

Bernard joked: 'The Christian Brothers would never have got their hands on you down here.'

'Berno, they'd have had to come prepared for a fight. And how come *you* signed up?'

'No real reason…they started recruiting and I was ready. It just happened.'

They sat in silence for some moments, their short accounts out of the way. The gap in conversation let the reality of the situation descend on them: Seán would be shot the following morning, unless…

'I've come to know Commandant Kinahan quite well,' Bernard said, 'and I'm sure I can get him to stand by his word if you just give him some information. It doesn't have to be important stuff, just look like you're cooperating. Can you do that, Seán?'

He stared at his bound feet. 'I thought you and I were friends?'

'What?'

'If I'm not shot, then the others will think I squealed. They'll say that the Dublin fella wasn't up to it! Do you think I'd live with the shame of that? If a cousin didn't shoot me, I'd shoot myself.'

'Aren't you afraid?'

'Of course, I'm afraid. But keep that under your hat.'

Bernard realized that his friend didn't want to be saved; that even if the cell door were to be left open and unguarded, he still wouldn't scarper. 'Is there anything you want me to do for you?'

'Go back and beat up some of the Christian Brothers for me, but it's probably too late for that.' He laughed, holding his ribs in pain.

'Seriously. Anything?'

'Well, you could make sure they tidy me before I'm given back to relatives and be sure to nail down the lid real tight if I look too bad. They'll be writing to Ma in Dublin, and I don't want her to suffer any more than is necessary.'

'I'll make sure of that.'

'Berno, don't you feel bad about this. I'm still the enemy and if you or any of your lot were lined-up in my sights I'd still pull the trigger.'

'Some friend you are!'

'I'm the friend who's really an enemy.'

'Friend against friend.'

'You could sing that if it had a tune.'

~~~

There was to be no magic reprieve. Kinahan had another fruitless session with the prisoner before he handed him over to an obedient but unenthusiastic firing squad. Bernard did what he had promised; he intervened and prepared his friend's body as best he could; he had seen too many Kerry women wailing at the return of disfigured corpses to know how important it was. Later in the day, Bernard was summoned by Kinahan, and he found him reading a week-old Freeman's Journal, which he dropped and folded at his arrival.

'Private Clancy, I hear you visited our prisoner last night.'

Bernard guessed that Kinahan had been talking to the guard and knew it was pointless to lie. 'Yes, Sir, I did.'

'I won't ask your reason, Private, but I must tell you I'm disappointed.'

Bernard stayed silent.

'You deceived a fellow-soldier and, without authority, spoke with the enemy – that could be construed as treason.' As if to reinforce his remark, the officer stared at him, emotionless. 'I like you, Clancy; you get on and do what has to be done, no fussing or complaining from you. But what you did last night was a breach of my trust and I don't like that, which is a pity because when this war is over there'll be a country to be run and because we're the ones making it all happen…well, I expect we'll be in key posts and be in a position to help out our loyal friends. Unfortunately, I worry now that you mightn't be loyal anymore.'

He rose and went to a window and looked down on the hotel's driveway, his back to Bernard, who, to remove himself from the situation had begun to think of Madeline and the hours they had spent together just before his return to duty. He could almost feel the warmth of her, the softness of her: the Christian Brothers' stern warnings now history as he wandered into what they had branded as impure thoughts. Kinahan interrupted the daydreaming: 'Private Clancy, I've decided to overlook last night's breach and let you stay on my team, for all the reasons I said earlier. But, remember this, and remember it well, I have the power to make your life a nightmare; equally, I can make it easy. Understood?'

'Yes, Sir.'

'Good. Now tell me, did the prisoner tell you anything that will help us finish this damned war?'

'No, Sir,' he said, omitting to say anything of Seán's rebel cousins. And if the fighting was nearly over, what did it matter?

Neither man was to know that Kerry was about to boil over.

CHAPTER EIGHTEEN

1923

Bernard awoke to a commotion outside. It was still dark. He went to investigate and by moonlight saw a squad of soldiers preparing to march five prisoners away. A trooper told him that the men were being taken to remove a suspicious obstruction on a bridge located on the outskirts of the town. He wasn't surprised by this action, not since the recent explosion at Knocknagoshel in another part of the county, where five of their men, including three officers, had been killed in a booby trap. It was accepted that Irregular prisoners would now clear obstructions, particularly if there was any suspicion of a similar tactic. The five prisoners chosen for the task had already been interrogated, and Bernard knew that some of them were in a poor state, with one even having a broken arm. However, better one of them be blown up than one of us, was the general reasoning. He watched them leave, ghostly figures by moonlight, herded to the barks of the excited officer in command.

Early next morning the squad returned – minus the prisoners. Word went around that there had been an explosion at the bridge. A fresh force was despatched, and it brought back the bodies of four of the prisoners; apparently, one Irregular had survived the blast and, in the confusion, had luckily escaped. Coffins were brought from an outhouse, and Bernard inspected the corpses to see who had got away. He was shocked by their condition and couldn't identify them and, as if the blast hadn't been enough, he saw that the bodies also had bullet holes.

A soldier stood behind him, waiting to close the coffins. Bernard asked him: 'What really happened out there?'

The soldier looked about him, and, satisfied they were on their own, he said, 'What do you want to hear, the official version or the unofficial version?'

Bernard offered him a cigarette.

The soldier wanted to talk. 'First, I'll give you the official version, the one we've been told to say, in case we're asked. We went to the bridge; there was a barricade of stones blocking our path; the prisoners were ordered to pull away the stones; and…boom!'

'And the truth?'

'The road blockage had been erected and booby-trapped by our own side. When we got to the bridge, we took up positions at a safe distance. The prisoners were sent to dismantle it, the mines were triggered and any man that was still moving after the blast was riddled. But you didn't hear it from me.'

'And the one who escaped?'

'I think we hit him, but he kept running. He knew the countryside better than us.'

'You better screw down those lids,' Bernard said.

A priest came running up; someone in the garrison had had the decency to send for him. He prayed for the men, turning a blind eye to his own church's stance, a stance that condemned the anti-Treaty republicans from the pulpit and denied them the sacraments.

The news of the deaths would spread through the town and a crowd would soon gather.

Likewise, they would be gathering in the town of Tralee. Word had come through that eight Irregular prisoners had been killed the previous day at a place called Ballyseedy. Local people in Tralee were calling it murder, a reprisal. Bernard could well believe it, for since Knocknagoshel he had sensed a wild thirst for blood among the officers.

~~~

My Dear Bernard
My heart jumps with joy when your letters arrive and of course if
you knew me at all you would know that my love your last letter
made me cry and I know you did not mean it as you would never on
purpose say something to worry me but I cried Bernard because I
felt behind your words there was sadness and I wanted to wrap my
arms around you darling and save you from whatever is making you
sad but I'm so far away from you and can only keep you at all times
in my thoughts and in my prayers so no more of that and I should
be cross with myself for I should be writing only happy words to you
and sharing happy thoughts with you and talking of the day when I
will kiss you again when will you have leave? I know you cannot
answer that so please forgive your darling for being anxious to see
you God bless you and protect you I'm looking at the clock and must
rush out now to catch the post
Your loving heart
Maddie
X X X X X X X X

~~~

The atmosphere in Killarney was tense. When the relatives had unscrewed the lids of the four coffins and saw what Bernard had seen they were shocked and furious. This was not what the people had expected when they had gone to the polling stations and voted in favour of the pro-Treaty party. Revulsion spread among the townspeople, hatred against the Free Staters. A week later, Bernard was sitting in the mess with Anto Coffey, and his friend pushed a newspaper in front of him and stabbed at a news item: 'Read that!'

It reported that in future all prisoners who die in military custody in Kerry are to be buried by troops where the death took place.

'Now, they bloody well want us to be gravediggers, as well!'

'Keep your voice down,' Bernard said, glancing round the mess. 'Here, let me get another one in.'

'Drink won't sort me tonight.'

'What's up?'

'I'm truly sick of this place, that's what's up.'

'Who isn't?'

'When Brady was killed, I wanted to cheer whenever one of our lads plugged one of theirs. Now, I want to throw up when I see or hear of someone being killed, even if it's one of *them*. I met Cooney out on patrol yesterday. You know Cooney?'

Bernard nodded.

'He was at Ballyseedy,' Anto said, 'and he swears he'll never forget it. They were ordered to gather the bits of bodies. They even had to climb up into the trees for them. Can you imagine?'

'Kinahan says it'll soon be all over. They've made him a colonel; he's in on the command meetings, so if anyone should know, he should.'

They silently looked at their porter and occasionally took tasteless mouthfuls. Some minutes passed, then Anto said, 'Did I tell you I wrote a letter of condolence to Brady's missus?'

'That was a nice thing to do.'

'She replied, thanking me. It seems Jack had told her about me in his letters, about how we were such pals, and all.'

'That's how it was, Anto.'

'If I were such a pal, how come I couldn't protect him?'

'You can't be blaming yourself. It wasn't you pulled the trigger.'

'I know, but that doesn't help.'

'As I said, Kinahan thinks it'll soon be all over. Then we can all go back to normal living.'

During the following week Colonel Kinahan was in Tralee, and Bernard was transferred back to patrol duty until his return. Free of the interrogation room, the unrelenting way that Kinahan gathered intelligence, he would rise early, and the patrol would leave Killarney before the townspeople were moving about. They travelled in convoy through scenic countryside made for landscape artists, sheltering under a tarpaulin sheet when it rained, throwing it off when the sun appeared. Two troopers were assigned lookout duty, watching the surrounding hills, forests, fences, stonewalls, any hiding place where a rifleman might be waiting to shoot at them. In the cab of the lead lorry, a young captain sat keen-eyed alongside the driver, watching the road ahead for a mine. The squad searched abandoned houses and derelict farm buildings; they fanned out across fields and mountain land, hunting for rebel fighters. When tired, Bernard limped from the piece of lead lodged in his leg, but he carried on, happy to be out in the fresh air, despite the threat of a sniper.

His first three days back on patrol passed without incident; Killarney and the surrounding areas were deceptively calm, as they had been in former days when this countryside had been a favourite with moneyed tourists from London, and the like (after all, it had been good enough for Queen Victoria), now, however, walkers in tweeds and deerstalkers hadn't been seen for years, not since 'that impudent rebellion!'

On the fourth day, they rounded a bend and came upon two men crouched behind a Ford motorcar. They had weapons drawn, pointing not at the army convoy but in the direction of a further bend along the road; plainly, their target was coming from the opposite direction. The lorries came to a halt and the patrol spilled out and took up positions on either side of the road. Bernard placed the stock of his rifle against his shoulder, found and held one of the men in the gun sight and watched for a hostile show. They waited for a command from the officer. There followed a moment of uncertainty, with nothing happening. Sheep were moving on a hill beside them and Bernard could hear the gurgling of a stream somewhere close at hand. Then, unexpectedly, the two men placed their guns on the ground and moved away from them. The young captain stood up and gave Bernard and two others a signal to advance. They moved up the road, rifles trained on the targets, trigger fingers at the ready.

As they neared, Bernard was surprised at the calm demeanour of the two men, as if they had been interrupted while doing nothing more than playing a game of pitch-and-toss. The officer strode the last steps with confidence; waving his pistol he shouted: 'Hands over the heads and clearly in view!'

They were dressed in city suits, strange for a remote part of Kerry. One of them said to the captain, 'Don't be a fool, we're on the same side!' The other one was casually looking about, unimpressed by their arrival.

'What do you mean?'

'We're Dublin Guard, as well,' the first man said.

'Keep your hands where they are!' the officer said. 'Move and you'll be shot.' He studied the two men and then examined the car. 'Do you have papers to prove what you say.'

'No.'

'Then, we're taking you as prisoners until you prove who you are.' He blew a whistle and the other soldiers advanced in support, leaving two behind to guard the rear of the convoy.

'You're making a fool of yourself, Captain,' the second man said, as if he were offering friendly advice.

This irked the officer. 'I can shoot you where you stand. Don't you know that?'

'It's as we told you,' the first man said, 'we're all on the one side.'

'In that case, where are your uniforms? Who do you report to? Where are you stationed?'

'It's none of your business, Captain.'

Bernard, rifle trained on the chest of one of the men, saw that the young officer was losing patience. 'Handcuff these men and put them in the lead lorry!' he ordered.

At that moment, a car came around the bend, the bend that the two men had been watching. It slowed and a man crouched over the steering wheel peered out at them. The captain stepped out and waved him on. The driver had to mount the grass verge to pass the lorries, and once the car had a clear road it sped away and went from view at the next bend. A soldier called Monaghan, who fancied himself as a motor mechanic, was directed to drive the prisoners' car back to Killarney. Back at base, while the prisoners were being unloaded, a senior officer came out of the hotel and recognised them and drew the young captain to one side. Bernard couldn't hear what was being said, but the captain looked as if someone had put a bayonet through his football.

Meanwhile, the two prisoners were grinning and looking confident. The captain reluctantly signalled for their handcuffs to be removed, and the men were conducted away as if they were visiting dignitaries. Bernard and the rest of the patrol were left looking at each other: the young officer, reeling from the put-down in front of the men, gave a feeble order to dismiss. Later that night, Anto said that he had heard they were Oriel House men.

'What does that mean?'

'It means they were out to kill someone – a murder squad. They do dirty deeds that can't be blamed on anyone.'

'A car came by shortly afterwards,' Bernard said, 'just one man in it. Was he the target?'

'If he were, he'd a lucky escape.'

~~~

When Kinahan returned from Tralee, he summoned Bernard.

'Private Clancy, bring me any interrogation notes you have, no matter how trivial they may seem.'

'I will, Sir.'

'Good. I'll expect them on my desk by this evening. Make sure you bring me everything.'

At that moment, Bernard expected to be dismissed, but Kinahan pushed back his chair and studied him. 'Private Clancy...Bernard, isn't it?'

'It is, Sir.'

'Bernard, we've been through a lot, you and me. There's been hard things done that had to be done. Dublin will protect us if there's any accusations made against us...but, just to be sure, you should take it upon yourself to forget all that's happened here. That's what I'll be doing, and I'll expect you to do the same.

'And I've being thinking about putting you forward for corporal. You deserve it and it'll happen when we're back at Beggars Bush once things settle down. I feel that you could have a promising career in our army; and it will be peacetime, not like now, not like it is here.'

Bernard didn't respond, for he had that old feeling, the feeling he used to get in the industrial school when standing in front of a Christian Brother. At the same time, he couldn't forget his friend Seán, his dignified walk to the firing squad. He asked himself: How could I ever deny what went on here?

'We're agreed on this, then?' Kinahan was waiting for an answer.

Seeing no other option, he nodded.

'Good, and I look forward to receiving those notes.'

A week later, Bernard saw a group of excited officers run out to stand in front of the hotel; they discharged their pistols into the air. 'It's over!' was the cry. The rumours were right, he thought. Now we can all go home. But it turned out that it wasn't going to be that simple.

Dearest Madeline,

You'll have read the good news in the papers and soon I'll be with you.

Unfortunately, it'll only be for short leaves at first, and I'm as disappointed as I feel you'll be when you read this. I've put in for a transfer, but it has been turned down for the time being at least. But don't be down at heart darling, for soon all of us Jackeens will be home for good.

Now, I'm waiting on dates for my first furlough and a letter will be
speeding to you as soon as I know. Keep me deep in that treasured
spot in your heart for soon I'll be holding you for real.
Your Devoted Love,
Bernard.

He dropped the letter in a green post box, which up until recently had been coloured red; however, the cast initials GR still showed through, a branding from the British past. He walked slowly back to barracks. Normality was returning to Killarney. With the cessation of fighting the haunted look seen in the townspeople was disappearing, and the singing chatter of Kerry voices was getting stronger by the day. He passed a number of inviting pubs, full of high and low-brow talk, but still off-limits to the soldiers for you never knew who could be in there, someone still grieving over a relative killed at the hands of the Free State forces, a grief that might only be assuaged by revenge.

CHAPTER NINETEEN

Bernard wondered where his mother was. He had gone straight to Waterford Street from the train, but she wasn't at home and when he asked the people downstairs if they knew where she was, they'd shrugged their shoulders, and from the look in their eyes he'd known it was an awkward question that they didn't want to answer. Back upstairs, there were minor signs of improvement in the room; he wondered had he the right to expect more, after all, she wasn't getting a fortune from the Army Paymaster. He waited an hour before going to look for her. He tried Talbot Street, hoping to catch sight of her in one of the shops she frequented, then he moved towards Summerhill and began to search the public houses.

Lily, wrapped in a black shawl, was in the second one he entered, sitting alone in the snug. She looked thinner and older, however, on seeing him, her face lit up and she began to look better. He sat beside her, as if they'd had a longstanding arrangement to meet there. The barman pulled the hatch open and stuck his moustached red face through and asked him for his order.

'Give me a bottle of stout and a whiskey and the same again of whatever her ladyship here is having.'

'That's nice of you, Bernard. Isn't this cosy, you and me like this, away from the rest of the world?'

'It is, Ma'. He realized that this was the first time he had ever sat with her in a pub. 'Did you get my letter?'

'I did, Bernard. I was so pleased.'

'Sorry it can't be for longer.'

'Don't worry, I'm getting used to being on my own. Whenever you come home for good or Peter gets home or Stephen comes home, I won't be alone then, but, as they say, you can get used to anything.'

The barman poked two arms through the hatch with the drinks, rescuing Bernard from his feelings of guilt. 'Sláinte, Ma,' he said, raising his glass to her.

'Your good health, son.'

They sat quietly for some minutes, as if they had suddenly become complete strangers, with nothing in common. He was thinking of Madeline. She was probably in Langrishe Place, maybe helping her mother prepare the evening meal, unaware that he was here, in this snug, almost within shouting distance of her.

Suddenly, Lily said: 'Did I tell you that Jemser took up with someone else?'

He shook his head.

'He was only a wet day out of Waterford Street when he'd his feet under another one's table. A widow woman as well, down in Portland Row somewhere. Bad cess to him and her.'

'He's low class, Ma...better off without him.'

'You're right, son, you're right, but the time hangs when it's only you and the walls and you want to be consoled and saying your prayers and rereading letters isn't enough.'

She was opening her heart to him, and he couldn't think of a suitable response. Two beshawled women came into the snug and sat opposite them. One of them asked Lily: 'Is this one of your lads, love?'

'This is Bernard.'

'Son, I suppose we should be thanking you,' the woman said to him. 'Shouldn't we, Moira?'

Her companion seemed puzzled by the question, but answered: 'Whatever you say, Rita.'

Rita explained: 'These lads in uniform are keeping us safe in our beds.'

Moira, still looking mystified, said: 'But this one is a soldier, not a policeman.'

'Do you think I'm thick or something? Of course, I know he's a soldier! But he's still to be thanked. Isn't that right, son?'

'There's no need, missus,' he said. 'It's my job.'

'Did you hear that, Moira? Hasn't he the humbleness of a saint?'

'And what,' Moira asked, 'are you fightin' for now?'

He smiled at the question, thinking that the county of Kerry might as well be in a different country. And, as for the politics...

Lily said, 'The shooting's over now, thanks be to God, and Bernard will soon be home for good, won't you, son?' She placed a bony hand on his and he nodded.

'Ma, will you be staying here with these good ladies for much longer?'

Lily corrected the shawl on her shoulders and, winking at the two women, answered. 'Well, it *is* comfortable here...' Then, as if she had only just remembered, she added, 'I'm sorry, Bernard, you must be starving from the journey. Is the stomach falling out of you?'

'Not at all, Ma, I ate at the railway station. I've a friend I must visit, not far from here. Will I come back here for you? Or will you be home by then?'

'Such a considerate son,' one woman said to the other.

'I'll be home, Bernard, and I'll have the pan on.'

Before he left, he got a fresh round of drinks for the three women.

He hurried along Summerhill towards Langrishe Place, yet when he entered the street, he had a sudden fear that his built-up expectations, his daydreams, his yearnings might all evaporate into nothing. He moved up the street and stopped at the hall door; his knock was polite, uncertain. No answer: he knocked again, louder. A curtain moved in the parlour window, and he heard a door inside being opened and footsteps in the hall. The hall door was opened, and she was standing there and every sense in his body was directed towards her, magnetised, drawn into those pools of eyes of hers. For a moment nothing was said. It was as if they were examining each other, like a couple in an arranged match who were meeting for the very first time. Finally, she murmured: 'Bernard.'

'I should have been here sooner...my mother...'

She reached out and touched his arm, an innocent gesture to the curious eyes that might be looking out from behind net curtains on the opposite side of the street, yet it was a touch charged with a form of magneto electricity. 'I can't believe you're here in the flesh,' she said, her eyes drawing him further in, a step that had to be taken, an indefinable sensation in his chest that had him on the point of trembling.

The spell was interrupted by a voice from inside. 'Madeline, who's at the door?'

'It's Bernard, Mother.'

'Bernard?'

'You remember, Bernard, from Christmas Night…'

'Oh! Well, don't have him standing out there, bring the chap in.'

'Not now, Mother, we're going for a walk. We'll probably stop by the church for the devotions.' She disappeared inside and came out wearing a lemon-coloured cardigan. He had his hand in his pocket and was gladdened when she thrust her arm into the hook of his. They walked down the street, unaware of the squinting windows, and turned onto Summerhill and never noticed the passers-by, the horse-drawn carts, a messenger boy peddling like fury on his last delivery of the day – they only had eyes for each other. They reached Parnell Street and lingered at a shop where the wedding cake for Michael Collins and Kitty Kiernan had once been displayed; an anti-Treaty bullet had stilled that dream and the cake had vanished from the window shortly afterwards. 'It was such a shame,' she said. 'I never saw him in the flesh, only photos. He was so handsome, and we all cried when we heard. Sometimes, when I thought of you, I thought of that cake, and it brought the danger home to me, and I panicked and prayed you'd be safe.'

'Your prayers were answered, darling.'

'Bernard, I won't stop worrying till I know you're back for good.'

'I hate it when I cause you worry, but I'm happy you care.'

She squeezed his arm and they walked on. They entered Sackville Street and passed the General Post Office, a reminder of their long and deep embraces in its shadows. It wasn't necessary to mention it. They lingered at O'Connell Bridge and gazed into the dark flowing river, and he put his arm round her to protect her from a stiff sea breeze. He remembered the night he had boarded the SS Lady Wicklow; it seemed a lifetime ago, yet it had only been ten months. They watched the river for a while, then he said, 'You do know why we've stopped here?'

'It's where we first met.'

He pointed to a spot not far from them. 'We were standing just there.'

They would have stayed happily on the bridge, only Madeline started to shiver, and they decided to go back. As they passed Cathedral Street, he spotted people going in the side door of the Pro-Cathedral. 'I thought you wanted to go to the devotions?' he said.

'I'll tell Mother we went. God will forgive me; it's not often I skip them. I want to spend my time with you, your leave will be over before you know it.'

They walked on a few paces and then without warning he stopped.

She turned to him. 'What's wrong, Bernard? You're looking sad. Is it something I've said?'

He lit a cigarette to distract her gaze. He was looking away, at a cabbie picking up a fare outside the nearby Gresham Hotel, at a DMP man moving on two drunks who had started a scuffle between them.

'This is all strange to me'.

She looked at him, unsure of what he meant. A tram came to a halt close by and passengers were alighting, while those on the street waited anxiously to board.

He searched for words to explain. 'I've never known such...such tenderness...'

'Don't be like that, Bernard,' she said. 'If it's been hard for you, then I'm here to make it easier.'

She had let her cardigan fall open, and the shape of her breasts was pushing against her dress, not coquettishly, but in a comforting, motherly way; her eyes now had a look that reminded him of a picture of Christ showing his Sacred Heart, which he'd seen hung in the refectory in the industrial school. He offered her a pull on his cigarette. The intake of smoke was deep, and she started coughing and thrust the cigarette back at him. She took a moment to recover, then cried: 'Never again!' They laughed and moved on, gripped together.

~~~

Later, in Waterford Street, Lily reheated the food in the pan, and they sat down to eat. Afterwards, he said, 'I've something to tell you, Ma.'

'Yes, Bernard, give me a moment.' She was clearing the table.

'That can wait, Ma.'

'I want to make it nice for the breakfast,' she said.

'Please, Ma,' he said, pointing to her chair.

She sat in mock indignation. 'So? What's so pressing it can't wait?'

'I've met a girl.'

'Yes?'

'Well, I like her…I like her a lot, Ma.'

Lily was twisting the end of her apron. 'Who is she, a country girl?'

'No, Ma, she doesn't live far from here – Langrishe Place.'

'Oh, I don't think I know anyone at all up there.'

'She says she knows you, at least she knows you to see. Since I told her about you, she's seen you about but didn't want to appear forward by going up to you.'

'So, this has been going on for a while?'

'There's been little "going on", as you put it, Ma. I know her mostly through writing to one another.'

'And this is the friend you went to see earlier?'

'Yes, Ma, she is. She's a lovely person and I know you'll like her. Her name is Madeline.'

'Sounds like a Protestant name to me.'

'It might be, but she isn't. In fact, we were at the devotions tonight…her family are very devout.'

'Oh…'

'I'd like you to meet her, Ma.'

Lily had a moment of consternation. She suddenly saw the tenement room for what it was, rough and neglected. 'You can't bring her here, son. I'd be embarrassed to bring anyone here.'

'She won't mind. She's an ordinary person, down-to-earth.'

'Still, she's not coming in here.'

'Don't worry, Ma. We'll arrange a place, somewhere that suits – maybe a hotel?'

'That'd be nice,' she said, masking her thoughts. She had banked on him coming home in a matter of months, then, in time, Peter would be let out of the industrial school and, who knows, even Stephen could come back, and the family would be together again. But now this...this Madeline one had sprung up from nowhere, and worst of all she'd never expected it.

At bedtime, the curtains were pulled to divide the sleeping areas, the gas mantle was choked and, lastly, the bedside candles were blown out. Bernard wandered in the fresh memory of Madeline: Lily felt a slow-moving tear head for the pillow.

~~~

The lorry bounced along the road, the driver no longer fearing a mine or a felled tree; the hostilities were officially over and if there were to be a shot fired it would probably come from a defiant, isolated fighter. Bernard was in the back of the lorry, one of a party sent to arrest one of those die-hards. They had good intelligence that he had abandoned his mountain hiding place and was lurking close to his family farm, like a fox creeping in by cover of darkness for supplies. It was twilight and the soldiers had left the lorry to advance on the farmhouse by foot, the plan being to trap the rebel in the dark.

As they got closer to the farm building, it became clear that something was wrong. Bernard saw two women in the yard, one standing and wailing to the sky and the other on her knees, sobbing into her palms near the door of the house. The party advanced, rifles at the ready in case they were walking into an elaborate ambush. The woman who was standing shrieked when she saw them. 'Don't shoot us, don't shoot us!'

'No one's going to shoot anyone,' a sergeant said.

A trooper beside Bernard said, 'Christ, what's happened to her?' Thick black oil had been poured over her head and it covered her face and stuck to her clothes. He kicked at a metal container guiltily lying close by; it gave a hollow drum sound and rolled across the farmyard. The other woman was also covered in oil; they tried to lift her to her feet, but she resisted. 'They said they'd shoot us if we moved.'

'Who said?'

'They're out there, watching...'

The soldiers had encircled the farmhouse and the sergeant was quick to say, 'Miss, there's definitely no one out there.'

'Check the house, then get these women inside,' the sergeant barked. The men rushed through the doorway, ready to shoot anything that moved: it was empty. The All Clear was given and the women were brought inside. Bernard and a comrade set about cleaning the clinging oil from them by lantern light. Firstly, they worked on the faces, clearing round the eyes, nostrils, ears, and mouth. Skin appeared and soon they were again recognisable as humans, strong-featured Kerry women, clearly sisters, one, they discovered later, five years older than the other. Towels were found and the younger sister pressed one to her face, while Bernard used another to clean her oil-sodden hair. By now the older woman had steadied herself, and she pushed Bernard aside and took over the task of cleaning her sister. 'There, there, Florrie, it'll all wash off, a little soap and hot water and you'll be right as rain.'

The sergeant came back to question the women. 'Who did this to you?'

'They had scarves up to their noses,' the older woman said.

'How many?'

'Three of them; they held us – they had guns.'

'You've no notion at all who they were or why they did this?'

'They wanted our brother Seamus. They kept asking where he was, and we kept telling them we didn't know. Then they did this to us. They said it was a message for Seamus.'

'We're talking about Seamus Coyle?' the sergeant said.

The woman nodded.

'And you're his sisters?'

'You're well informed, sir.'

'The army is after him, Miss Coyle.'

'He's not here!' Florrie the younger woman said.

The sergeant thought for a moment, then spoke aloud his thoughts: 'But he *will* be here tonight.'

The Coyle sisters clung together. The sergeant divided the patrol in two, half would stay in the house and the other half would hide outside in the dark. He sent Bernard and another soldier upstairs with the women. 'Draw the curtains, tie them up and gag them. I don't want to hear a squeak from either of them!' The trap was set.

Following orders, Bernard and the other soldier tied up the Coyle sisters with strips they had cut from sheets. 'You're the brave one now, aren't you?' Florrie hissed. Bernard hated having to manhandle the sisters, particularly this younger one, as she reminded him of Madeline. He was gentle with the gag but when he tied it in place she suddenly panicked, struggling for a breath. He loosened it and assured her that she wasn't going to suffocate. She calmed down. 'I'm sickened by what happened to you,' he said. 'Have you no idea at all who did this?'

The older sister's mouth was still free. 'It was your lot!'

'What do you mean?'

'They were soldiers like you, only they wore high shiny boots.'

'Officers?'

'You'd know better about them than us.'

'How did they sound?'

'Just like you, soldier.' At that moment, the other soldier bent forward to gag her. Although she smelled of oil, and her hair was a tangled mess and her dress was stuck to her, she managed to stiffen her back in defiance.

'You won't catch him, you know. Seamus can smell Staters a mile off and he won't come near the place!'

'So, he's out there?'

'You seem to think –' The gag cut short her words, then Bernard took up position at the bedroom door and the other soldier went downstairs.

They waited.

CHAPTER TWENTY

He tried to stay alert, but time dripped by. All quiet except for the barking of a fox and the hoot of an owl out there in the dark, somewhere. To kill time, Bernard thought of that final night of furlough, the one before returning to Kerry.

Madeline had brought him to a house on Berkeley Road where a friend of hers named Ellen was babysitting. The man of the house and his wife weren't expected home until after midnight, and the children were sleeping and Ellen's boyfriend, Tommie, had made himself comfortable in an old armchair beside the kitchen range. He was lanky, fair-haired, and his limbs had outstretched his clothes. They played cards, drank only tea because Ellen wouldn't allow anything stronger and chatted and all the while Madeline sat on Bernard's knee, an arm crooked round his neck and, now and again, she turned and kissed him, which sent shrieks of mock disgust from Tommie. 'I can't play cards with the goings-on of those two!' he said, with a female-like giggle.

'Quiet!' Ellen hissed. 'You'll wake the children. Anyway, this pair have good reason – Bernard goes back to the army tomorrow and Madeline won't see him again for who knows how long.'

'Sorry pal,' Tommie said, 'you're making up in advance for lost time?'

'Something like that,' he answered.

'If you want to be alone,' Ellen said, 'you can go inside that room.' She pointed to a door off the kitchen. 'It's a bedroom; I don't think they ever use it. Just leave it as you find it...you've a good half-hour.'

Bernard looked at Madeline not knowing if this was a step too far. He had no idea what would happen, alone with her, with no disturbance. She sprang off his lap, making the decision for him. It was a small room, an iron-frame bed taking up almost half of its width; it had an old pink coverlet. The electric light on the ceiling had a matching pink lampshade that was scorched, and a faded picture on the wall had been made from the top of a chocolate box. They sat on the edge of the bed and embraced; in a matter of minutes they had fallen backwards, and he was looking down into her eyes, ready to give up his soul to drown in them. They kissed and hugged and rolled, and the movement disturbed her clothing, showing the valley of her breasts. He wanted to kiss that valley and she let him. (He remembered she had once said to him: 'I'm here to make it easier.') He opened the dress down the front to her waist with trembling fingers and –

Bernard tensed, shoved his thoughts aside. He heard the soldiers below move into a position of readiness. They must have heard something. He checked his rifle and looked back at the two sisters. They looked pitiful, for although the worst of the oil had been rubbed off, they still needed a proper cleaning, maybe even a bath. It angered him to see them in this condition, for he couldn't get over the violence of the act against them. They were struggling against their bonds, their eyes full of terror, and he was certain it wasn't for their own safety but for their brother's. He strained to hear what the men downstairs had heard. The distinct call of a cuckoo came in from the night outside. A few minutes later the sound was repeated, this time coming closer. There was silence again, a silence that seemed to go on eternally; in reality, it lasted only about five minutes. Then a shot rang out and there were shouts outside and the soldiers on the ground floor burst out of the house and ran into the farmyard. Bernard looked around – the sisters were dementedly rocking themselves back and forward. He went to the top of the stairs, rifle trained on the hall below. The activity continued outside, shouts, men running, but no more shots. Shortly afterwards the sergeant came striding in, his face red with fury. 'Bring down those women, Private!'

Bernard untied the sisters and removed the gags from lips deadened by pressure. He helped them to their feet then went ahead of them on the stairs, descending backwards. The women, stiff from being tied up, collapsed on to chairs at the kitchen table and the sergeant took up a position facing them. 'I want you to tell me,' he said, 'where your brother might have gone. We know he's hiding in the hills behind here. You must know where he goes?'

'We're saying nothing to traitors and murderers,' the older sister said. 'You sold us out on a republic! And now you expect us to give up Seamus, our only brother?'

'Miss Coyle, the fighting's over. Your side has given up the ghost. Your brother Seamus is living in the past and can't hope to fight the whole of the National Army – it'll only end badly for him. And you wouldn't want that, would you?'

'And what mercy can he expect from Staters?'

'I can promise nothing, Miss Coyle. Probably, we'll just beat the shite out of him and throw him in jail, with the rest of his pals.'

'And then shoot him,' Florrie Coyle said.

'That's up to higher authorities but, if you want my opinion, I think that they'll all do some jail time and then be let home. The Government can't execute every prisoner.'

The sisters exchanged looks. The older one said: 'How can we believe you?'

'You have to...I'm not making any promises, though.'

Again, the older girl spoke: 'The men that came here earlier, the soldiers that did this to us, they were out for blood. They'd have murdered my brother on the spot if they had caught him.'

'I know nothing of that, Miss Coyle, and I'll just have to take your word for it, but if your brother gives himself into my custody, I'll guard him with my own life.'

This seemed to satisfy her, somewhat.

'We don't know where he is', she said, 'but we know someone who might be able to make contact. I'm sure Seamus won't want to give in, but we can try.'

'When? How soon can you make contact?'

'We certainly can't do it with Staters around. Leave us and we'll do it tomorrow.'

The sergeant considered the woman's proposal: he thought of the vast tract of land behind the house where a man could hide forever, and at this mopping-up stage of the war he didn't want to be leading men up and down mountains on a probable wild goose chase. Finally, he said, 'Ladies, I'll leave it to your persuasive powers, and we'll be back to hear what he has to say.'

The younger woman spoke up: 'We won't be trying to persuade him. We'll just tell him what you said. Seamus will be making his own mind up.'

The sergeant shrugged his shoulders and walked outside.

The patrol would wait until daybreak before heading back. Meanwhile, the sisters disappeared to boil water and bathe, taking turns in a galvanised tub placed in front of an open fire. Bernard stood guard at the door in case the temptation to spy on them became too great for any of the men. They emerged soft and shiny in a change of clothes. And when he looked at them, he thought of Madeline and the room in Berkeley Road and how her face had reddened from passion and how he couldn't believe that something so wonderful could have happened. Then there had been bangs on the door, Madeline's friend warning them that the owners of the house would soon be home.

Daylight broke. There was a last-minute conversation between the sergeant and the Coyle sisters, and then the order was given to leave. As Bernard walked from the house, he spotted a button on the ground and picked it up; it was familiar to him, the type used on the breast pocket of an officer's uniform. He kept it and boarded a lorry. They moved out from the farmyard; the air smelled fresh, sheep were rambling on and off the road ahead. As they rattled along, Madeline came back into his mind. On that last night, they had walked slowly back to Langrishe Place, an unspoken contract forming between them. He had even had a crazy notion of breaking his furlough and staying with her; however, he knew it was out of the question, unless he wanted to end up in Arbour Hill Jail with deserters, and their like.

They had lingered at her corner, each unwilling to break the spell. Finally, her father shouted from the hall door and Madeline broke from his arms and walked away, constantly glancing back. Then the door slammed, and she was gone inside.

~~~

The patrol returned to the Coyle farmhouse, where the sisters took delight in declaring that their brother would have nothing to do with the 'Staters'. On this occasion a captain was in command of the party and the sergeant was more than happy to hang back, but the officer made no headway with the women, who were now behaving like hostile ganders. He went around the back of the farmhouse and pessimistically scanned the hills and above them the mountains, more fit for goats than humans. The party left empty-handed: the sisters looked triumphant.

Some days later, Colonel Kinahan was called back to Dublin to take up his new posting. The night before he left, Bernard was invited to his farewell event in the mess. The room was crowded with Dublin Guard officers from across the Kerry Command, and the urbane Kinahan was jokingly presented with a shillelagh. There was a speech and when he was over-praised for 'the part he had played in taming Kerry' he was the first to laugh; in the same breath the speaker reminded him 'not to forget his bar bill'. It turned into a party when a group commandeered the piano and started a singsong.

During the night Kinahan was speaking to Bernard when the officer who had made the speech stopped to talk to them.

'Kinahan, you're the lucky sod, getting back to dirty auld Dublin. Guess we'll have to sit it out here till we're sent for.'

Bernard was introduced. The officer imperiously inspected him, then, remembering he was having a rare 'night with the boys', he gave Bernard a brotherly grin. 'Soldier, I hope you learned something from this man, cutest whore in the whole army!'

They all laughed. Then Bernard noticed a button missing on the man's uniform – left hand side, top breast pocket. The Coyle sisters had said that the men wore long, shiny boots: officers. He fingered the button in his pocket, feeling sure he was looking at its twin on the officer's other breast pocket. He was tempted to produce the found button and politely ask, 'Sir, by any chance did you lose this?' However, being tempted and doing it, were two different things, a lesson learned in the industrial school. Besides, he had a sneaking regard for Kinahan and didn't want to spoil his evening. The colonel was gone the next day and the basement that had been an interrogation room was cleared, its guilty table smashed for firewood. A fresh visitor would never guess its previous use, nor hear the echo of men's cries muffled by the weight of the hotel above them. It was turned into a store for excess files, for a proper army of fifty thousand men can't exist without rigorous paperwork.

~~~

The pleas in Madeline's letters became more urgent – *Are they not going to give you furlough at all my darling?* He carried her latest letter on him, sneaking a read whenever he had the chance, even while out on patrol, rolling from side to side with a lorry's movement. Bernard's at his love letters again! a fellow soldier would jeer. He knew better than to raise his eyes. Jealousy will get you nowhere, he would reply. He takes them to bed with him, another would say, and who knows what he does with them there? Ugh! Mock disgust from someone else. Banter was predictable, as it is with men when they're bunched together and become easy in one another's company, no one takes offence as it serves to pass the time, entertainment, often close to the bone but a relief from boredom. The fighting had now stopped long enough for even a hermit in the deepest cave to know of it. Bernard read that some Irregular prisoners had already been freed, returning to work the land or to whatever work they could find. For the garrison at Killarney, the patrols had become monotonous. Out in the morning, back in the evening, all was quiet in the Kingdom of Kerry.

And receiving mail from Madeline didn't help Bernard. Here he was stuck in Kerry, where life was returning to normal, an adventurous American tourist had even been spotted in the town. It galled him to think that Dublin could be reached in a day, if the railway line weren't sabotaged, yet he couldn't leave his posting. He had submitted request form upon request form to the adjutant in charge of granting furlough, all to no avail. Eventually, the besieged man's patience gave out: 'Listen, Clancy, I'm sick of your requests! What makes you so different to the rest of us? Dublin needs us here to fly the flag, every man must obey these orders and you're no exception. Don't you think that I too want to get home?'

A week later, Bernard dropped another request on his desk.

August came, and to mark the anniversary of the landing at Fenit, the garrison paraded through Killarney to attend Mass. There wasn't any fuss, not many townspeople came out to see them, except a group of children playing at being soldiers who tailed them. The soldiers filled the front half of the church and listened to a priest congratulate them on bringing peace back to the country. It was followed by a return parade to the hotel for drinks in the mess. It was there that Bernard reread the unsettling part of the latest letter: ... *but I worry about your mother for only yesterday I saw her in Moore Street looking the worse for wear...*

He wondered what it meant. She's getting the money from the army, and Jemser's no longer a parasite on her. Is she sick? Another thought was that Madeline might have seen her drunk in the street. He knew he hadn't sent a letter to Waterford Street in a while and felt guilty about it, his mind more taken with writing to Madeline. He penned letters that night to the two women and posted them but, afterwards, he had an awful fear that he could have put the letters into the wrong envelopes; his love words for Madeline were for her eyes only and he only relaxed when she wrote back within days saying that certainly she would call to visit his mother.

~~~

Madeline had met her just that one time in a hotel. They'd drank tea from pretty cups and eaten dainty sandwiches in strained silence. That day, Bernard had tried to be all things to all men, but in the end had given up and just sat there smoking a cigarette. It wasn't that Mrs. Clancy had been unfriendly or anything, she was too respectable for that, it was just that her eyes didn't seem to want to meet hers; instead, the woman had spent more time looking around at the confident regular customers and the busy serving staff. Outside on the street, they had talked of meeting again, but it never happened. Now she was in Waterford Street, climbing the stairs of the tenement to call on her. She heard her shuffling across to open the door; a slot appeared only wide enough to see who was calling. 'Good morning, Mrs. Clancy!'

She sensed that the woman was having trouble placing her, and an awkward moment passed before she added: 'It's Madeline. Bernard's friend, we met that day for tea.'

'Oh! Yes, I remember.' Lily turned back into the room and Madeline took it as an invitation to enter, gently closing the door behind her. They sat at the table and Madeline did everything she could to ignore the state of neglect in the room, she wasn't there to judge, but to lighten Bernard's concern, if she could.

'There's nothing the matter with Bernard, is there?' Lily asked, tramlines of concern on her forehead. 'I'd a letter from him and all seemed well.'

'Don't worry yourself, Mrs. Clancy. There's nothing wrong...Bernard asked me to call, that's all.'

'Oh! That's friendly of you.' Lily was looking round the room, now clearly worried at its appearance.

'Isn't this nice, you and I meeting again?' Madeline said, fearing her remark sounded silly. She struggled for something else to say, something intelligent. She hadn't expected to be so nervous. 'Mrs. Clancy, shall I make tea for us?'

Bernard's mother seemed surprised at the idea.

'Why should you be making tea in *my* home? You wouldn't know where to – '

'You just sit there and point out everything.'

Lily sighed, laid a tight bony grip on Madeline's arm. 'That's not the way it's done here, child.' She got to her feet, steadied herself as if her brain needed to be balanced, and moved towards the kettle.

Afterwards, Madeline asked: 'Is there anything you need? anything which needs doing?'

Lily returned a look that was almost a stare. Eventually she said, 'Like what?'

'I don't know, Mrs. Clancy…anything at all. Going for messages, or doing some washing, or even going with you to the dispensary? Like I said, anything at all.'

'And why would you do all that, Madeline?'

At least, she says my name, she thought, but then, maybe she's known it all along. 'I'd be doing it for *you*, Mrs. Clancy, just to make things that little bit easier.'

'That's very thoughtful of you, but I think I can manage.'

'I didn't mean you weren't, Mrs. Clancy…I'm just trying…'

'I know all that, and you're good to ask, but I like to do things my own way. And it won't be long before Bernard's home and I'm expecting his two brothers to also come in that door any day soon.'

Madeline gathered her coat to leave. 'It's been nice spending time with you, Mrs. Clancy. I could call to you again, but only if you want me to?'

'You know the house. And if Bernard wants you to call…'

She hurried down the stairs, shielding her nostrils from the smell of the tenement. On the pavement, well clear of the earshot of any locals, she let out her frustration, her real opinion of Lily Clancy – 'The auld rip! If it weren't for Bernard…'

On the way home, she started to mentally compose a letter to her sweet husband. Well, he *was* her husband, she thought, in all ways except marriage, and she was sure that Bernard felt the same way. It was always meant to be like that, so his mother will just have to get used to it.

CHAPTER TWENTY-ONE

At last, Bernard had been given a four-day pass. He went to meet Madeline and when he arrived at the house, she was at the window watching out for him and she ran to the door before he could knock, and before she brought him into the living room they embraced in the hall, a snatched moment of hungry kissing and breathless body pressing, then, flushed in the face, she took his hand and brought him inside. Her mother sat him down as if he were a long-standing friend of the family, made tea and produced a slice of gur cake. He was touched by her welcome, her friendliness, even though she probably suspected what they had been up to in the hall. Madeline hovered round him and every so often their eyes met, and he couldn't wait to be alone with her again (so much stored-up, so much to tell).

Over the next three days he juggled his time with his mother in Waterford Street and where he really wanted to be: with Madeline. On the last night of leave – they called it 'parting night' – Bernard called to the O'Shea's. He kept watching the clock and was becoming increasingly anxious as time passed. Madeline was sitting on the other side of the room, and every so often they looked at each other, waiting. He wanted to take her somewhere quiet, where he could live-out the erotic thoughts he'd had about her on those long nights in Kerry. Finally, they escaped, hurrying arm in arm down Langrishe Place. At the first laneway they met, even though it was still daylight, they fell against a wall, and he kissed her, hard, soft, then hard again, breathless, her warm body against his, her cheeks burning as she turned from his mouth to take in air. He suggested the canal bank, and they skipped along Summerhill and came to the canal bridge at Ballybough and went down on to the towpath. They walked along it towards Croke Park, looking for a spot away from eyes on the bridge. Dusk was falling. They could contain their passion no longer and fell to the ground on a grassy patch and she murmured, 'I've been waiting for you.' Again, those eyes, those deep pools in which he wanted to submerge.

There was a rushed movement of clothes. Suddenly, Madeline heard a sound in the nearby bushes. 'What was that?' she said. Bernard peered in the dim light and discerned a crouching figure. 'Who's there?' he shouted, a sentry-post tone.

A man stood up, and ran towards Binns Bridge, his legs flying outwards, giddy snatches of laughter coming back over his shoulder.

'A bloody busher!' Bernard said.

'You mean he was watching us?' she said, getting to her feet and straightening her clothes.

'That's what they do,' he said. 'But, he's scarpered, so there's no need to – '

'I have to go,' she said. 'I couldn't, not after that.'

They hurried from the canal bank, then, once back on Summerhill, Madeline lost her fluster and they walked slowly back to her home, downhearted that he had to return to duty.

~~~

A late-autumn chill had come into the Kerry nights and Bernard was standing at the foot of the hotel's steps, smoking a cigarette, and wondering when the waiting was going to end. It was rumoured that the men of the Dublin Guard would soon be transferred back to the capital, but he hadn't mentioned this in his letters, not wanting to build-up Madeline's hopes, nor his mother's. In the closing light, he noticed Anto approaching, kicking up gravel, hands deep in his pockets, the tunic open at the neck.

'Smarten up there, Private!' Bernard said, 'or we'll drill you into the ground.'

He smiled back. 'That's about all we seem to be doing these bloody days, drill formations.'

'Aren't we getting paid for it, Anto? Sure, isn't it like an extended holiday?'

'Shut your face and buy me a drink.'

They headed into the mess for their first drink of the day. Anto threw a copy of the Freeman's Journal on the table. 'I kept this to show you,' he said, opening the newspaper and stabbing at a title. 'What do you make of that?'

Before picking it up, Bernard said, 'Aren't you the great man for the newspapers?'

'One of the officers left it down and I sort of borrowed it. Anyway, I read what interests me…us, this is about us. Go on, read it!'

The piece was short and concise:

Since hostilities have ended and the Free State's position looks secure, the Government is preparing to reduce the National Army to a size more in keeping with the country's peacetime needs. At its height, the fighting force reached 56,000 men, whereas, it is now considered that we could operate in these new conditions with a much smaller figure. The number of 16,000 men has been suggested to this correspondent by well-placed sources.

When Bernard put down the newspaper, Anto said: 'They're going to turf us out! Imagine, so many going into Civvy Street, all at the same time, and all looking for work. It'll be mayhem! We fought for a Free State and they go and do this to us.'

'How do you know it'll affect you? You could be worrying over nothing.'

'You know how it is. If you're in the know you'll be kept, and I'm certainly not one of those.'

'Anto, it's not the British we're talking about, it's our own army. It won't depend on who you lick up to.'

'Pal, for a clever man, you can be very naïve; just you wait and see. And do you think the officers will take this sitting down? If they're getting rid of the troopers, they won't need heads at the top. It stands to reason.'

Bernard had to agree with him, but didn't tell him so, as his friend was agitated enough. They stayed until late, then Bernard found his way back to his billet, undressed clumsily in the dark, flopped on to his bunk and closed his eyes to allow Madeline to come to him, his nightly luxurious pleasure, and he roamed in her company, until he drifted to sleep.

CHAPTER TWENTY-TWO

Bernard was finally back in Dublin, for in early October, without warning, he received a transfer to Intelligence at General Headquarters, Portobello Barracks, a posting which he suspected Kinahan was behind.

Upon arrival, he was told to report to a Colonel Moran, whom he knew nothing of. Little had changed in the colonel's office since the British had left, even down to the same desk and chair, except that George V's picture had been taken back to England and replaced by a photograph of Michael Collins, not the usual one of the 'Chief' in uniform, holstered pistol swinging on his thigh, but a stately portrait as a cabinet minister. Bernard gave a smart salute and followed Moran's direction to stand at ease. The officer went back to reading a slim file on his desk and after some moments he looked up again and studied Bernard.

'Private Clancy, I've a request here from Kinahan that you be approved for corporal's stripes. It seems he is anxious to keep you in the fold; I think I can guess why.'

Bernard tried to look impassive.

'It says here that you made a valuable contribution to our efforts in Killarney. How would you describe this *valuable contribution*, Private Clancy?'

'I did little, Sir, except take notes of the interviews conducted.'

'Is that what we're calling them now – interviews? How inventive.'

Bernard didn't answer.

Moran continued, stifling a yawn: 'I suppose you know we're thinning out the ranks, so I'm in the sticky position where I should be releasing men from service, not promoting them. But if Kinahan wants to keep you, then I can only congratulate you and tell you that the Paymaster will be giving you a modest increase in wages. Is all this to your satisfaction, Corporal?' The officer looked down at his desk, a signal that the meeting was over.

'It is, and it isn't, Sir.'

'What do you mean by that?' The colonel had quickly looked up again.

'I feel I'm not really an army man, Sir. You see, I've been promised my old job back in Civvy Street, Sir.'

'No, I don't see, Clancy. That's hardly enough reason to leave the National Army, especially since I've just promoted you!'

'Sir, I don't mean to be disrespectful…it just isn't –'

'That's enough, Clancy! I've heard all I want to hear. I'll speak to Kinahan and see what he's got to say.' Moran's patience had run out; he considered the soldier to be an ungrateful nobody who couldn't see a good thing when it was put in front of him. He added, 'And, forget what I said about you being promoted to corporal.'

He dismissed Bernard with a deliberately lazy salute and watched him turn for the door. Curious, he called after him, 'Trooper, have you already put in a Request of Discharge?'

'Not yet, Sir.'

When the door closed, Moran looked up at the photograph of his late Commander-in-Chief and said: 'Mick, what's it all coming to?'

Now that he was stationed at Portobello Barracks, Bernard was able to give time to his mother and the tenement room. He made simple repairs and brought in better furniture from a second-hand market, including a good bed for himself for the times when he wasn't sleeping at the barracks. He saw her start to look healthier, to take more care in how she dressed; her hair was never out of place and she seemed to be losing that stooped look; yet, at the same time, she still had the need for a night or two in the snug with the shawled drinking biddies of Summerhill. Bernard, when he was about, would break from an embrace with Madeline and be at the pub at closing time to help her home. Always she would lean on him and tell him he was such a good son.

It was a slap in the face when the army wouldn't release him. When he looked for a reason from the adjutant processing the forms, he was told that the instruction had come down from above – they insisted on keeping him. It was useless arguing with a man who was merely following orders;

still hot with annoyance, he went off to write a letter, laying out his case for discharge, saying he hadn't attested for service beyond the war. He delivered the letter and went to Langrishe Place to tell Madeline what had happened.

A few days later, Bernard was summoned to the Adjutant's Office.

'You sent for me, Sir.'

'Yes, Private.' He shuffled some papers and found a typed letter which he placed on the desk in front of him. 'I don't know what you've been up to, Clancy, or why the sudden change of heart by Intelligence, but I'll read this bit to you, which you mightn't like. *We recommend his discharge* – they're talking about you here – *as he is of little use to the Army, either as a soldier or a clerk.*'

'If it gets me into Civvy Street, I'll be happy, Sir.'

'Very well, Private, take it as done.'

~~~

Wanting to surprise Madeline, he waited until they were out walking together before he told her the news.

'Bernard, I'm so relieved! I've had nightmares of you being killed.'

'It's finished,' he said. 'Now I can start a normal life, with a job…and perhaps a wife?'

'A wife?'

'Yes, Madeline, we should get married. That's if you *want* to be called Mrs. Clancy?'

She looked nervous. 'You make it sound so easy, Bernard. As if there's nothing to it.'

'Well, what's your answer? Don't leave me wondering.'

'Sweetheart, I've always seen us as being married: surely you know my answer?'

They were standing in Capel Street, and they kissed, oblivious to passers-by.

'I don't have a ring, but we'll get one.'

'What does it matter?' With a gentle tug she turned him back towards Langrishe Place. 'We must go and tell Mother and Father!'

'And after that, we can go and tell my mother,' he said. He didn't know how she would receive the news but didn't tell that to Madeline. He didn't want to spoil her deliriously happy mood.

Excitement filled the O'Shea household, a manly handshake from the father – a good reason to take down the whiskey! – giddy hugs and kisses from the females; Bernard felt another door had been opened, admitting him deeper into their family.

Lily heard the two sets of footsteps stop on the landing and wondered – Madeline walked in ahead of Bernard.

'Ma, we have news,' he said. 'We're getting married.'

'Oh?' She glanced at Madeline's belly. No sign. She tried to force a smile, show enthusiasm for his news, their news, and all the while she was hoping that her face wouldn't betray her. 'I'm happy for you both and wish you a long life together. Where will you live?'

'We hope to find somewhere close to everyone.'

'You could stay here. I could make –'

Madeline interrupted, 'Thank you, Mrs. Clancy, but we'd like to start out in a place of our own. You know what it's like.'

'Very well,' she said, remembering the early days with James. 'We'd have been the same ourselves.' A memory of carefree times past was knocking to enter.

Later, she surprised him by saying, 'I *am* happy for you, Bernard.'

He lay down to sleep that night thinking that army life in Kerry had been a lot simpler.

CHAPTER TWENTY-THREE

Nellie the vocalist had sung the last line of the song and the seven-piece band was now bringing the dance number to its gradual conclusion, like a carnival roundabout slowing to a standstill. The band leader George Hooper, founder and owner of the George Hooper Dance Band, seemed to make a magician's motion with his arms and the music stopped, but the energy of the tune continued to vibrate through some of the dancers on the Metropole's flexing maple-floor, causing them to shuffle on a few extra steps after the last note. Bernard wiped his trumpet with an unconscious movement as he tracked the tall man in officer's uniform who had danced past the stage several times, whisking an elegant-looking woman through anti-clockwise circuits of the floor; now he was escorting the female to a table on the balcony, his arm snaked round her waist. Bernard watched him lean forward and whisper in her ear. Her head went back in laughter, while the officer stood by, a grin on his face. Bernard wondered if Kinahan had recognised him.

During the interval he went to the rest room and as he stood at the urinal, he heard the unmistakeable voice behind him: 'Clancy, I thought it was you, blowing the horn!'

'Colonel Kinahan', he said. He moved to a sink and ran his hands under a tap. Kinahan had taken his place at the urinal, and Bernard studied his back in a mirror, the polished Sam Brown, the immaculate uniform.

'So, Clancy, this is what you're doing with yourself?'

'Not full time, Sir.' His use of the word 'Sir' was automatic, and he was annoyed with himself for using it. He added, 'It helps the finances.'

'What else are you up to then?'

'I'm back with the Tram Company; they kept my job open for me.'

Kinahan stood beside him at the mirror, drew out a comb and reset his hair where it had been upset by a jerky turn during the tango. He said, with an air of self-assuredness, 'It's the least they could do for one of our boys.

They're not a bad sort at the Tram Company, but they can't be paying you enough when you have to come out and moonlight in a band?'

'They're a good employer...' (He caught himself at the last moment and didn't use the word: Sir.) It's not their fault I've a family to support.'

'Good on you, Clancy! You went and got yourself married?'

'Right after discharge.'

They came out together and stood looking at the stage, where the downed musical instruments were like so many creatures at rest, waiting for the band members to return. Kinahan glanced towards the balcony and waved to the elegant woman who had gone around the floor in his arms. He was smiling and Bernard remembered how he had used the same smile at the beginning of the interrogations in Killarney.

'Children, Clancy?'

'Two. One of each...' He mentally chastised himself for almost saying 'Sir' again. He felt Kinahan would have loved to hear him say that.

'You didn't waste time.' A cigarette was offered from the silver case (Bernard remembered it). They smoked, and for a few moments both seemed content to let their eyes wander round the ballroom, as if they'd nothing on their minds. But Kinahan wasn't the sort to empty his mind. 'It's a pity you never stayed with us. I could have done something for you.'

'The Army wasn't for me.'

'That may have been the case, Clancy.'

'Everyone to their own.'

'True. But now that things here are under control, I'll be moving across to the police force. There has to be privileges, you know.'

'Congratulations, Sir.' He cursed himself; again, the military habit.

'Thank you, Clancy. If you'd have stayed in my camp, I could have helped you.'

He didn't answer. The smug bastard's putting me down, he thought. He noticed George the bandleader had returned to the stage.

'I'm on,' he said.

Kinahan offered him a handshake. Surprisingly, the grip felt genuine.

'I suppose we'll never forget Kerry,' Kinahan said, as if talking to himself, then he turned and moved across the floor towards the stairs leading to the balcony. Bernard watched him resume the company of the elegant woman and caught her glancing his way; he felt she would see him as a curiosity, nothing more.

~~~

1927

Peter had gone to Artane as a bright boy, her baby, and returned home as a brooding young man, with full eyebrows almost meeting and a downy shadow above the lip. Despite putting brand new linen on his bed and cooking all his favourite meals, Lily found that when she tried to talk to him all she would get in reply would be cursory answers. She knew it was on account of Artane, and wanted to explain how difficult life had been for her with Jemser, but was never able to get far with the subject, because he would see it coming and clam up – he wasn't going to let her off that easily.

She saw him bringing home second-hand carpentry tools. A collection was built up daily. A hammer, a saw, a plane, a hand drill, and the like. Some of them were rusted and blunt and he spent hours cleaning and sharpening them, then they were placed in an old canvas tool bag that he put under the bed. When she asked about them, he said that he simply liked refurbishing the old tools.

But Peter had a plan. While in the industrial school, he had learned the rudiments of carpentry, and he now was putting together a collection of second-hand tools to give him the credibility of a tradesman. They were to be his passport to emigration. He told her of his plan the night before he left for England.

'I'm sick of this country!' he said.

'But…when will I see you again, son?'

'Ma, it's a pity you didn't think like that when I was in Artane.'

He softened when he saw the hurt in her face, and added: 'Who knows, Ma?'

~~~

Tom Ganly was sitting in a corner of his pub, waiting for the cleaning woman to finish so that he could pay her (a habit had been formed of daily cash). She had been with him now a good many years, a wiry woman who had never let him down, and even her 'arthuritis', as she called it, couldn't stop her and she still had the brasses shining and the floor clean, despite moving round with the slowness of a grazing old goat. For her part, she knew every inch of the premises, the places to put your back into to impress Ganly and the places to skim over. She was surprised to see a young woman carrying a scuffed suitcase standing in the entrance, and asked her, 'Are you looking for someone, love?'

The girl hesitated. She could easily make a fool of herself if she were in the wrong place. 'I'm looking for Mrs. Bridget Ganly. Do you know her?'

The cleaner signalled with her grey head towards the corner where Tom Ganly was sitting. She would have followed her, except that she was running behind and had to stay harnessed to the last piece of cleaning. The stranger stood in front of Tom with the same question.

He squinted up at her. 'You mean, Biddy?'

'The name I wrote down is Bridget, but I suppose Biddy is the same, isn't it?'

'What do you want from her?' he asked. 'And who are you?'

She placed the suitcase on the floor, looking like an emigrant in the waiting room of a railway station, and fiddled with a button on her coat. She wore respectable plain clothes, no sign of patching on her coat or stockings, full heels to her shoes; her hair had an institutional look, a convent style that ensured she would pass unnoticed.

'I'm Mary Theresa,' she said, with the familiarity of a second cousin, who had just come up from the country.

'So?' His memory was whirling, trying to remember why the girl's name meant something to him.

'I've been living with the nuns. I was told I must now make my own way and I was shown the door, but I have no family or place to go to.'

'And?'

'Well, before I left the orphanage, I asked who my mother was, but they told me nothing. Then, I happened to see that the register had been left open in the Reverend Mother's office and the page was there, staring up at me, with my name Mary Theresa Moore on a column and I moved my finger across the page and found the name Bridget Ganly and, further across, this address. I *have* come to the right address, sir?'

'You have, but I don't see why?'

'I've come to see if …I'm desperate to find family, sir.'

'And you think that we might be your family? Well, that's a quare one.'

'Look, sir, I've written down the name.'

'You've got the correct name, okay, but that's all.'

'I don't understand.'

'We never had a baby girl,' he said. 'Biddy was always after one, but it never happened. God's will, I suppose. But sons are a blessing, too; that's if you can get them to do any work.'

'Please don't get me wrong,' she said. 'I know the names are different and I would never think that Mrs. Ganly was actually my mother. It's just that I thought there might be a connection.'

She went to lift the suitcase up, feeling that she had made a fool of herself. Tom was still trying to remember why her name meant something. The old memory was letting him down again: at times life was very confusing. He spotted the cleaning woman rinsing a worn, grey rag into a bucket and, knowing that she would have caught every word, he called across the bar: 'Can you help this young girl? She's looking for our dear Biddy, God rest her soul.' He quickly made a sign of the cross and the woman copied. She dropped the rag into the bucket and came over, wiping her hands on a soiled pinny. He's getting worse, she thought. How could he ever forget that name? 'Don't you remember, Mr. Ganly? The trouble you had over her? and that Clancy woman that lived beside the pawn?'

'Clancy, now that name rings a bell.' He was searching the past, a series of blind alleyways. He hated being put under pressure.

She reminded him: 'Clancy was the woman who kept taking the baby from the pram.'

'There was trouble,' he said, 'you're right.' He looked again at the girl, wondering what she'd had to do with it.

'Don't you realize who this girl is?' The cleaning woman was losing patience.

Ganly's mind was in turmoil. This woman's getting at me again, he thought. She expects me to remember everything.

'Mr. Ganly, this girl is *that* baby. I remember the name. It must be her, it all fits.'

Mary Theresa's face brightened. 'I'm in the right place, then?'

'It has to have been you,' the cleaner said. 'You were but a baby.'

'Did you tend me?'

'God, no! Biddy kept you all to herself, but I did steal a cuddle now and again when her back was turned.'

'And Biddy's not here?'

'Child, didn't you hear him? She died, and himself here,' she pointed to her boss, 'hasn't been the same since.'

Mary Theresa turned to the publican. 'Mister Ganly, would you happen to know who my real mother is?'

'Huh?' Tom was again fruitlessly searching.

The cleaner came to his rescue. 'I saw her, a slip of a thing, blue with the cold. She stayed for a time, then she went, and you were left.'

The girl was excited, a prospector hacking at a promising seam. 'Do you remember my mother's name?'

Bony fingers combed away untidy wisps of hair from around the cleaner's face. 'It was a good while ago, child. It was just an ordinary name. Mary, or Ellie, or something like that. You know what I mean? It didn't stand out.'

'Mary would be good,' the young woman said. 'That's me, Mary Theresa.'

'I don't know, girl. Maybe it wasn't Mary, after all – it could've been any name.'

Tom was listening, trying to be of help, but he couldn't swear on a name either. The girl noticed his upturned face and asked, 'Did she say where she was going when she left here? Did she mention a place, sir? Anywhere at all?'

'I'm sorry,' he said, putting up his hands in a gesture of frustration. 'It may have been said, but – '

Without warning, Mary Theresa began crying. She'd had high hopes that Bridget Ganly would point her to her mother. 'What am I going to do?' She looked round the pub. 'Can I stay here, sir? I can work – clean, cook, bake, whatever you want.'

'You wouldn't fit in here, child,' the cleaning woman said. 'Isn't that right, Mr. Ganly?' She had to protect her own interests.

Tom nodded in agreement. 'A pub is no place for a nice, young woman like you.'

'Where will I go? What'll I do?'

The woman said, 'Why don't you try that Clancy woman? She wanted you badly when you were a baby. She might still be glad to have you.'

'Where can I find her?'

'I know where she lives,' the cleaner volunteered.

Mary Theresa left, carrying her orphanage-issued suitcase.

~~~

Father Swift was the only priest in the parochial house when Mary Theresa called after leaving Waterford Street. When the housekeeper had disturbed him at tea, he'd stamped up the stairs holding a tight rein on his annoyance. He was full of self-pity and thinking: Doesn't anyone at all appreciate that I've been running around the parish all day? That I didn't get to bed until after three this morning because I was sitting up with that dying woman in

Montgomery Street? Can't a body have a meal in peace? Arriving in the hall, he was intent on brusqueness. This shouldn't take long.

He was surprised at the young woman he met at the door, for she was clearly not local, and while one side of him was impatient to return to the sanctuary of a set tea-table, his curious side got the better of him, and, afterwards, he was glad he hadn't given short shrift to her story; instead, he had asked, 'Have you eaten at all today, miss?'

Mary Theresa realized she was hungry and in a dumb motion waved her head from side to side.

'Follow me, child,' he said, 'and close the door behind you.'

She entered and eased the heavy hall door until the latch clicked then hurried after the priest who was about to disappear down a flight of stairs. He called the housekeeper and instructed her to get a meal together for the visitor. The woman gave Mary Theresa a disapproving look, a look to make her feel that she was nothing more than a charity case in her eyes. She wanted to wolf down the thin slices of ham placed on a plate edged with a flower pattern, but, remembering the many times she had heard 'Table manners!' from the nuns in the orphanage, she took her time and busied herself spreading butter on neat slices of bread which had come on a separate plate the housekeeper had slapped on to the table. Father Swift wondered what had gotten into the woman and, trying to make up for her rudeness, he poured tea for Mary Theresa, then he sat back to watch her.

~~~

The next day, Bernard dropped into his mother's and heard the story of the surprise visitor. She told him how the stranger had called, and how at first, she hadn't had a clue as to who she was or what she wanted. Then the girl said that the people in Ganly's bar had sent her. 'Before I knew it, she was telling me she was looking for a bed, and then she tells me who she is – I could have fallen over with the shock.'

Bernard was mystified. 'But who is she?'

'It's Mary Theresa.'

'Where have I heard that name before?'

'It was a long time ago. She lived with us when a baby.'

He suddenly remembered. 'You used to say that she's our sister.'

'That was years ago. You can't just turn up and expect a widow woman…'

'So, you didn't take her in?'

'How could I? You never know when one of your brothers could walk in again and need it.'

'Then where did she go?'

'I sent her round to the priests'.

'You've heard nothing since?

'She never returned if that's what you mean.'

He was taken aback when he heard this. By now, it had all returned to him; he was too young at the time to know the full details, yet he remembered the uproar in the home and how sad she'd been when the baby went. Despite this history, she now seemed unconcerned.

When Bernard returned to their own tenement room at the other end of the street, he found his mother-in-law Mrs. O'Shea had called in for a visit. He relayed the story to Madeline and her about Mary Theresa turning up at his mother's door. They were hungry for all the details; however, all he had were teasing pieces of what had occurred fifteen years ago, not enough to complete the jigsaw.

Mrs. O'Shea said, 'The poor girl! What state must she be in?'

'It's up to the priests to look after her now,' Bernard said.

'We must find a place for her,' she said. 'It's only Christian and the right thing to do.' Already in her mind, Mrs. O'Shea was moving the beds around in the daughters' bedroom.

'Madeline and I will go to the presbytery tomorrow,' she said, closing the subject.

When they called to the presbytery, the housekeeper gave them directions to a lodging house on Talbot Street, but she couldn't let them away from the door without saying: 'Father Swift must be soft in the head, spending his own money on a complete stranger!'

At the lodging house, the landlady allowed them to use her drawing room, and Mary Theresa sat with her visitors not knowing why they had come; her first impression of them was their remarkable likeness to each other

After the niceties of introduction, Madeline said, 'I happen to know Mrs. Clancy, the lady you went to in Waterford Street.'

'Yes, but I only met her for the first –'

'We know that, child,' Mrs. O'Shea said, 'and we heard about you from the lady's son Bernard.'

'Bernard's my husband,' Madeline said.

Her mother was impatient to get to the point. 'Young lady, I know you've been disappointed, pushed from pillar to post, and I'm not going to be the one to criticise anybody, but we've come to offer you a roof over your head, at least until you've a chance to get your life in order. It's not a palace, but it's our home and I'm sure you'll be happy with us.'

Mary Theresa said, 'Praise God for all the favours He's put on me today.'

Mrs. O'Shea asked, 'Does this mean you'll come to us?'

'Of course, yes, yes.'

'Bernard will be happy,' Madeline said. 'Now he can meet you; he says he remembers you as a baby.'

Mrs. O'Shea took command: 'Now young lady, pack whatever you have, and we'll be on our way! I'll explain everything to your landlady.'

Back in Waterford Street, Lily withdrew from the window and slumped into a chair. How can God be so cruel to me? He wouldn't let me have her as a baby when I really wanted her and needed her. She turns up now out of the blue and it's as if He's handing her to me. But I've missed all those years when I could've been putting ribbons in her hair, dressing her like a doll. At that time, I'd have starved myself to see her look well, but too much has happened since and I've neither the heart nor the energy for it now. Mind you, she seems to have turned into a nice girl. Speaks well. I'd never have guessed it was her, not in a month of Sundays. I hope the priests found her somewhere safe to stay. In her mind, Lily was now back in Marlborough Street, sitting on the steps outside the house, holding Mary Theresa in her arms, admiring the soft skin of her sleeping face as she waited for the eyes to open, eyes to brighten a world.

CHAPTER TWENTY-FOUR

Mary Theresa – whom his mother had once called his 'baby sister' – had fitted in to the O'Shea household like a new tablecloth, so much so that a stranger would have taken her as a family member. Mrs. O'Shea insisted that Bernard sit and talk with her; however, despite the past connection, he found her to be a total stranger. She talked about her life in the orphanage: he judged it against his own period in Artane and felt she had got off lightly.

He looked for Madeline to rescue him and heard her in the kitchen with her mother and their children – Granny O'Shea always gave them lemonade when they visited. Madeline's youngest sister Gertie came behind him and started to comb his hair, as she often did during visits to their house. 'It needs a haircut,' he said, speaking over his shoulder at her. She laughed, happy that he was letting her do the combing. Suddenly, Mary Theresa said: 'I'll cut it for you.'

Madeline came into the room, the children in tow. The sight of Mary Theresa cutting Bernard's hair gave her a turn against her. Then, as if Gertie and Mary Theresa were only stage scenery, she said, 'Bernard, we're ready to go.'

'In a moment', he said.

'Yes, we won't be long,' Mary Theresa added.

There was silence. Bernard sensed Madeline's annoyance; Gertie must have felt it too, for she also went quiet; meanwhile, Mary Theresa's fingers clicked away, the sound competing with the ticking of the clock on the fireplace mantle. When the cutting stopped, Gertie stepped in with the comb, looking to bring his hair to the point of perfection. 'Look in the mirror, Bernard,' she said, breathlessly.

He stood up and went to the mirror. 'It's a professional job. Thank you, ladies.'

Gertie giggled, Mary Theresa put away the towel and scissors, and Madeline moved in to stand beside him, looking at their reflection. 'You're so handsome,' she said, reaching down for his hand. By now, she had managed to shove her demon to one side.

~~~

1932

Bernard had come forward in the carriage to see what the delay was. The tram had stopped on O'Connell Bridge, the way ahead blocked by a swollen election-rally centred on the GPO. 'Not more bloody politicking!' he muttered. Can't a working man go home in peace? not have his journey blocked by politicians? He could avoid the crowd by taking to the quays; instead, he decided that no one was going to keep him from his usual route. He hopped off the tram and entered O'Connell Street. From the signs carried aloft, he could see it was a rally on behalf of the governing party, Cumann na nGaedheal. He jostled his way forward and hadn't gone far when he was surprised to see Mary Theresa standing in his path, bearing a placard, her face flush with excitement.

'You be careful,' he said, 'these rallies can get ugly.'

'What do you mean?'

'Believe me, this is no place for you; ditch that silly placard and get off home.'

She stiffened. 'I'm not afraid if that's what you're thinking! Everyone should do their bit – you should grab one and stand with us!'

'I played my part,' he said. He skirted round her, again warned her to be careful, then heard her call after him, 'I'm entitled to know my own mind!' From a loudspeaker, the rasping voice of a political candidate pursued him into Lower Abbey Street, and he ducked into Denis Hayes's pub, where he ordered a pint of porter.

The pub was busy; a rally needs a good watering hole, he thought. He turned to his drink and started thinking about his latest run-in with Egan, his foreman at the tram company; he was getting sick of his taunts. Egan was a Cavan man, with hedgehog hair the colour of grey shale, and spectacles which magnified the size of his protruding eyes. The man seemed to believe that the Fianna Fáil party was going to bring him into the Promised Land. Confident of change, he strutted about the shop floor, keen to take on anyone with a different political view to his. For a while he had been jibing Bernard over being a Free Stater; this had recently got worse. If he hadn't needed the wages, Bernard would have hit out, but the constant niggling was chipping away at him, and he wondered if he could control himself for much longer. When he told Madeline about it, her fear-filled reaction was, 'Don't give him an excuse to fire you!'

Now he had a strong feeling that it would be only a matter of time. He took a slow swallow of porter and looked at his reflection in the bar mirror. From old photographs, he knew that the receding hairline came from his father. If it keeps going the way it's going, there'll be little left to comb. His thoughts were interrupted when a man ran into the pub holding a bloodied handkerchief to his nose. 'There's fists flying up there!' He was pointing vaguely in the direction of O'Connell Street.

Bernard suddenly remembered Mary Theresa and left his unfinished drink at the bar. He made his way against the crowd and spotted her, no longer carrying a placard, her wine-coloured coat askew and half off the shoulder. He grabbed her under the arm, the way a member of the DMP would perform an arrest, and marched her away, his only thought being to get her back to her home, to the safety of his in-laws.

He hurried with her down Lower Abbey Street and turned left into Marlborough Street, where she suddenly wheeled round and refused to move any further. 'I didn't ask for your interference,' she said, catching a breath, 'I'm well able to look after myself!'

'Look at the state of you,' he said, pointing to her coat. It was then he saw her grazed knees and realized that she must have been knocked to the ground. He saw the open door of a milk bar and pushed her inside. The woman behind the counter, silver hair combed back in a neat, tight bun, peered at Mary Theresa. Bernard hastily explained that she had been caught up in the crowd and needed to tidy herself. Then thinking that the woman might be more sympathetic if he bought something, he added: 'And, you can give her a glass of milk.'

'The young lady can go in the back and clean herself up,' the woman said, going to a churn and drawing up a ladleful of milk. She poured it into a tumbler and placed it on the counter.

'Thank you, but it's not that bad,' Mary Theresa said, straightening her clothes and wiping her knees with a hankerchief that she had wet from her spit. She then ran her fingers through her long chestnut hair, until she was satisfied that it fell evenly to the shoulders. She took up the glass of milk. 'It's lukewarm.'

'It's fresh,' the woman said.

Mary Theresa drank half a glass, put it down and wiped her mouth. 'I've had enough', she said. He paid for the milk and, as they were preparing to leave, the woman said: 'I hope your wife is feeling better, now.'

He was quick to say that she wasn't his wife and wasted no time in moving Mary Theresa out on to the street. A man came by, bleeding profusely from a gashed hand, consoling himself with a string of oaths.

Bernard said, 'You see what can happen!'

She stood looking at him, a smile on her face, fingering a strand of hair. It annoyed him that she hadn't seen the danger, and for a moment he thought that he should have left her on O'Connell Street. But if she had been injured, he knew he could never again call to Langrishe Place. 'This should teach you not to get involved in politics,' he said. 'It's a nasty business…you could get hurt very easily.'

She had a look of disbelief. 'Why wouldn't I back my party?'

'Do you think the politicians care about you?'

'Bernard Clancy, you've certainly changed your tune! People say how brave you were sticking up for Collins's side, and all.'

He was frustrated. 'That doesn't come into it, and we're only standing here because I couldn't leave you to your own devices. It's no place for a'

– he was about to say, slip of a girl, but caught himself in time – 'young woman, like you. There are men who come to these rallies only to cause trouble. You could be hurt, and no one would notice.'

'And you care?'

He looked at her. It wasn't so much what she had said, it was the luscious way she'd said it. Then, as if she suddenly needed the chilly February night to swallow up her words, she turned away, leaving him with a sense of having been ambushed, and mystified as to why. For an instant he had seen an alluring look, one known to prowling soldiers at certain street corners in Killarney, but now she was walking ahead of him like a saintly sodality girl, and he was trailing some paces behind her, reluctant to catch up. He decided to shepherd her home, and only came to her side when they entered her street, when there was no time left for further conversation. When they reached the house, Mary Theresa had a latchkey ready and she hurried inside; he turned for Waterford Street, relieved. Also, Madeline would be wondering why he was late for dinner – she was like that, and he didn't want to worry her. He thought about telling her why he was late, and then decided there was no point in causing trouble where trouble had no right to be. Or so he hoped.

~~~

Buoyed by the election result, Egan, the foreman, went after Bernard with the zeal of a greyhound being blooded. He spoke of 'Mister deValera' in reverent tones. Each time Bernard signed in for work he knew that another day of baiting lay ahead. Madeline's words of caution held him in check, until the day he threw a spanner at Egan and hit him over the eye. Blood spurted, Egan dropped to the floor and screamed for assistance, giving a performance fit for the Abbey stage. He was taken to Jervis Street Hospital for stitches. Bernard sensed trouble. The tram company sided with their foreman, and he was sacked, without a reference.

Madeline knew something was wrong when he arrived home in the early afternoon; more revealing, his eyes betrayed that he had stopped at a pub.

She had to drag the words from him. It seemed unreal, impossible to absorb. She looked round the tenement room at their sleeping arrangements – their own double bed and a rickety single bed that compressed two growing girls and the straw mattresses stacked in a corner that were pulled out at night for the older two boys. Despite their best efforts at restraint, four children in ten years: how many more in the future? Bernard looked broken, but she was too numb to hold and comfort him, even though she knew he wouldn't have lost his temper without good cause. How would they manage with no wage coming in? In the end, all that she could say was, 'How unfair...'

Later, she had an idea. 'I can do char work.'

Bernard remembered his mother going out to clean, and the drained look of her on arriving home. He remembered how she would raise the front hem of her skirt to rub her knees, then get one of the family to rub her aching back. He smothered Madeline's suggestion. 'Don't worry; I'll find something, do anything. I need you to hold together and back me.'

She was touched by his pleading look. 'Of course, I'll back you, my love. You're my husband, aren't you? You're still my beautiful Bernard, so, whatever happens, remember that.' She held out her arms and invited him to the comfort of her pinafore, which was threadbare from being washed too many times.

Bernard couldn't get a job with a decent wage, for he had no reference and was viewed as a troublemaker. Madeline still wanted to go out and clean, and still he resisted. 'I've my pride. No wife of mine will be a skivvy!' Then the savings ran out and Mrs. O'Shea came to them offering a handout. He felt wounded and said he wouldn't be beholden to anyone. She rounded on him: 'It's okay for you, Mister High and Mighty, but *I* can't stand by and see my daughter and grandchildren go without.' He looked away as she pushed the money into Madeline's closed hand. Some minutes passed in embarrassing silence, then Granny went to play with Patrick, the youngest. He saw how much she doted on the child and felt ashamed for even thinking about turning down her money.

Later, Madeline's father told him of a stevedore on the docks who might have casual work for him. He was to ask for James Cremin, and he found him sitting in a small hut at a makeshift desk full of shipping documents. 'My world's upside down because of these custom vultures,' he complained. 'They sit on my shoulder making sure every penny of tariff is collected!' Cremin had red and purple blotches on his face due to a biting east wind that too often whips up the Liffey in winter, and due also to his strong liking for whiskey. 'And, you say Billy O'Shea sent you?' he said, tidying a sheaf of papers and placing a weighty shackle pin on top to hold them down. This distraction was needed so that his brain could turn the problem over, for the man in front of him didn't look like he had the makings of a dockhand. Cremin again studied him and, almost apologetically, sent him with a gang of seasoned hands to empty a flour boat.

Bernard descended into the hold of the ship and felt as if he were being sent into exile. Its cold steel walls, and the grey-pudding sky above now set the limits of his world. He pulled heavy sacks of flour on to his shoulder and toted them to a frame, trying inexpertly to keep apace with the other workmen. When the frame was filled, it was hoisted and swung out on to the quayside, somewhere out of sight, above their heads. Then, a brief rest, long draws on cigarettes, until the frame was back in the hold and it was back to hauling sacks. Many a time during that endless day he felt like giving up, but he stuck with it, partly out of obligation to Mr. O'Shea, partly out of pride, but above all it was the promise of payment for work done that made him forget his aching muscles and back – he had no intention of going home empty-handed.

Finally, the last sack was cleared, and he stood on the frame with the other men and was hoisted back on to the quayside. His legs barely carried him to the stevedore's hut, where he collected his wage from Cremin and headed home; he hoped no one he knew would see him, as he was shuffling like an old man. He guessed there was something else odd about his appearance when a group of passing children laughed at him, then a man from his building passed him by without recognising him. When he got home, Madeline's first reaction was to laugh, then her face changed as she realized his true state. 'You're like Lazarus coming out of the tomb!' She fetched a mirror, and he didn't know his own face, eyes looking out from a coating of flour dust. He was too exhausted to wash and change, and could only collapse into a chair, arms hanging limply, fingers almost touching the floor. The children gathered round him, but he was too tired to talk. Madeline said, 'Leave off your Da.' At dinnertime, he hadn't the energy to go to the table; instead, Madeline brought his plate over and set it upon his lap. A weak smile creased the white dust round his eyes. 'Thank you,' he said, with the gratitude of a hospital patient.

'One thing for sure, Bernard Clancy,' she said, standing back to take a long critical look at him, 'not for love nor money am I letting you next nor near those ships again!'

He was happy to have her take over. A phantom, the colour of the sacks he had hauled, he stayed immobile until the children were sleeping, then Madeline put him kneeling in a tin bathtub, and gently washed him down. She dried him and he fell into bed. Although he never went back to dockside work, Bernard used every chance he had to bring some money in, from washing cars for a car dealer, to making wooden household ornaments which he sold door-to-door in the better off areas. He wasn't going to see his family go hungry.

~~~

The ordinary people of the country were gripped by the coming Eucharistic Congress; the event especially engrossed Dublin, where it was to be hosted – imagine, the Pope's personal messenger, the Papal Legate, walking our streets! In preparation, the city was bedecked with the yellow and white colours of the Vatican. The street dealers had turned Nelson Pillar into a sight to be seen, with favours and flags of the Holy See on their barrows which surrounded the base of Horatio's column. Waterford Street was no different, with lines of bunting strung proudly from tenement windows and anchored at street level to the railings. If ever one could say that the street looked beautiful, it could be said then.

Mary Theresa came to Madeline: 'We must go to the Women's Meeting for the Congress.'

'What do you mean, Women's Meeting?'

'I don't know exactly,' she answered, 'except that there's a special evening for us on Saturday. Will you come? They've taken over the Fifteen Acres in the Phoenix Park, built a big altar there. There's going to be thousands!'

Madeline was doubtful. 'I'll have to ask Bernard to look after the children.'

'There's a day for the men too. On the Friday, or he can go Sunday, the final Mass Day. It's the biggest thing that will ever happen in this city!'

'Bernard's not so keen on the Church anymore. Don't get me wrong, he still goes to Mass, but he's lukewarm about it, and won't kowtow to cardinals and the like. He says they think they're actual princes.'

Mary Theresa paused for a moment, as if her efforts to convince Madeline had backed up, like a mountain stream suddenly narrowed by rocks. She caught her breath and continued: 'It'll be our special day. You'll be able to tell your young ones all about it in years to come! And we can bring a picnic…'

'It's a long time since I've had a picnic,' Madeline said, thinking of the days when her father and mother would take the family on the bus to Enniskerry in County Wicklow and they would walk awhile until they came to a grassy spot surrounded by brilliant yellow furze bushes and they would lay out a blanket and eat their sandwiches and drink cold tea from bottles amid the country sounds and they would loll there as if they had forever owned that patch of ground. That night she told Bernard about the meeting. He laughed and told her that she should attend. 'I'll mind things when you're off wearing out those beautiful knees of yours!'

She was already thinking of what she would put in the sandwiches.

Saturday evening came and the two women headed to the Phoenix Park, linking one another like schoolgirls. The North Circular Road was a river of women and young girls (old enough to stay up late), all going excitedly in the same direction, as if they were heading to a free variety concert, but as soon as they passed through the iron gates of the park, the atmosphere changed; officious stewards in suits with yellow and white sashes pointed the way and sodality leaders led groups that were either reciting the Rosary or singing hymns. Mary Theresa trapped her hair under a headscarf.

Madeline asked: 'What do you need that for? We're not going into a church, are we?'

'No, but we're in God's territory now. He's not coming Himself, nor is the Pope, but Cardinal Lauri will be here to stand in for them. Don't worry, I've brought a scarf for you too.' When they reached the altar site, she said, 'It's magnificent! It looks as if it were dropped down from Heaven itself!'

Madeline thought it was as big as the GPO. She heard country accents, for clearly many women had come a lot farther than Dublin. Mary Theresa grabbed her hand and led her towards the front, but a steward stopped them. 'Beyond this point is priests and nuns only,' he said, relishing the power, as if it had been bestowed on him by Rome.

'I thought this day was for women only,' Mary Theresa said. She had spotted the clergymen in black suits occupying the prime positions. 'And why are the priests getting special treatment, haven't we got even more right to be in the front than they have?'

The steward looked over their heads at the next approaching group; he wasn't going to be drawn into a debate on the matter. Two nuns and a monsignor came along with the confidence of royalty and the steward, with a sweep of the arm, made way for them, as if their very bodies were items of reverence. However, Mary Theresa wasn't going to have their outing spoiled by a mere steward; instead, she guided Madeline along the rope that separated the general body of women from the inner sanctum until they came to a steward who looked friendly. They held back until a group of clergymen were going through, and they dashed in on their tails.

The man spotted them but merely smiled, as if doing anything about it would overstrain his role as a volunteer.

Madeline said, breathlessly: 'I haven't had this much fun since the day I mitched from school. Mind you, it was only the once, but I remember it like it was only yesterday.' She took a moment to look back on the growing throng of pilgrims and wondered at their luck in getting so close to the altar. Up and down its steps, long-robed figures worked like ants to prepare for the arrival of the Papal Legate. Madeline spread the blanket for their picnic, and they giggled over the sandwiches, especially when a wayward piece of salty streaky rasher or a nugget of cheese escaped from the bread and fell to their laps. They would have liked hot tea but had to settle for cold milk from washed mineral bottles. Suddenly, someone said the cardinal had arrived. Music came from a distant end of the altar; an angelic voice sang out over the heads of the eager pilgrims, and everyone jockeyed for a good position so that they could relive in their old age the time that Rome came to the women of Ireland. Cardinal Lorenzo Lauri moved to the altar table and acknowledged the crowd with a tentative salute, then, clearly deciding it wasn't appropriate, he managed to convert it into the sign of the cross, which was copied without delay by the attendance. He tapped a microphone and said in an accent exotic to Irish ears: 'Women of Ireland.' A roar of approval came from behind Madeline, and she turned to see a female army determined to put its stamp on the day. A shepherding priest standing beside the cardinal was beaming, as if he, personally, could take credit for the fervour of Irish Catholic womanhood.

The ceremony started, and a bishop appeared at a microphone; he began to address the crowd in Gaelic. Madeline hadn't paid the slightest notice to the language when in school and couldn't wait for him to finish. She looked at Mary Theresa, who seemed transfixed, but Madeline doubted her ability to understand him, either. Then there was a hymn, and this was an opportunity for the women to sing out and show what they were made of. This was more like it. She was moved to tears and wanted to be back behind the barrier rope among the plain people.

Next, the crowd was introduced to the Archbishop of Edinburgh, who spoke on the 'grave dangers of Bolshevism!' Someone close by said: 'What's Bolshevism when it's at home?' Madeline wanted to hear the answer, but no one spoke up. She would ask Bernard, he would know. More hymns, singing with abandonment; then the crowd was asked to pray for an Italian priest who had been fatally struck by a lorry in Thomas Street while escorting a group of Congress visitors around the churches of Dublin. Everyone nodded in agreement at how sad it was. The Papal Legate spoke of the important role of women in the Catholic way of life, their special responsibility to give example. The ceremony continued with Benediction, a final blessing on the women of Ireland, after which all were slow to leave the park, almost reluctant to return to the ordinariness of life. Mary Theresa complained of a thirst and downed the last of the milk, then wiped her smiling satisfied mouth with the back of her hand and said, 'I haven't enjoyed a drop of milk like that since the night your Bernard took me to the milk bar in Marlborough Street.'

Madeline tried to look unconcerned.

Mary Theresa said, 'Hasn't he told you about it?'

She pretended to be absorbed in the people surrounding them, who were gathering themselves to go home, but her mind was racing. What's she on about?

'I'm sure he must have mentioned it,' Mary Theresa said. 'He thinks I'm a helpless female, and I let him think he was my knight –'

'He told me,' Madeline said, embarrassed into a reluctant lie.

'I didn't need to be saved,' Mary Theresa said. 'I can take care of myself. Then he brings me to a milk bar, of all places, so that I can straighten myself; then he starts preaching –'

'It's time to go,' Madeline interrupted, 'it'll be dark soon and we'll be on our own here.' She was racking her brains. Has he told me? No. I'm sure he hasn't. Why would he keep that from me? As they fell in with the throng leaving the park, she fought against a feeling of betrayal. The crowd was in high spirits, but her mood was heavy. A milk bar, she thought, and the very idea that he would give Mary Theresa so much attention had started an obstinate worm in her head and, as they walked, she rehearsed how she would tackle him over it.

He didn't know why Madeline was acting like this; all he knew was that she was upset. He felt it in many ways: at times when he was lucky enough to have some casual work, she used to kiss him before he went out, now this had changed to a lukewarm movement of the head which only allowed his lips to brush her cheek; or, when he came home for dinner, his plate was put on the table like it was an act of duty; furthermore, they would eat in stony silence where normally she would be bursting to tell him news of her day. Eventually he asked her what was wrong. She gave him a cold look and turned away to do a chore, but he spun her round and held her shoulders firmly so that she could not wriggle from the question.

'I know there's something eating you, and I'm not stirring from this spot until you tell me.'

'Why should I?' she said, her voice shaking. 'You're not the quickest to tell *me* things.' Her words hung in the air, refusing to dilute, refusing to merge into the cabbage-smelling air of the tenement.

'Madeline, what did I do?'

He still had a grip on her shoulders. 'You're hurting me,' she said.

He fell away from her. 'Jaysus woman, tell me what this is all about!'

She stared at him for some moments, then said: 'Mary Theresa told me about the goings on at the election rally.'

'And?'

'You tell me!' she spat. 'You're the one that's kept me in the dark!'

'Madeline, there's nothing to tell. She was in danger of being hurt, and I helped her. Did you want me to leave her?'

'I heard there was more to it than that.'

'She was in a state if that's what you mean. She had to be cleaned up somewhere, and I took her into the nearest place, a milk bar. What was wrong with that? Surely, you'd have wanted me to help her?'

'How can I pass the door of that place, without the woman there looking out and sneering at me?'

'You're making this into something it isn't.'

'You're the one that didn't tell me. Hid it from me.

'Madeline, I didn't speak about it because I knew you'd be like this.'

'What do you mean? *Like this*?'

'You know, sometimes your imagination runs away with itself...'

Her forehead creased; she was thinking over his words.

'What am I to do, Bernard?' she finally uttered. 'You're my life...'

He always felt guilty, undeserving, when she said such things to him.

'And you're mine,' he said.

'I couldn't bear the thought of losing you,' she said, 'and my mind goes crazy when I think I don't have all your love. I know it's not normal, I know I jump to wrong conclusions, but that's me. I'd be lost without you, probably want to die.'

'Madeline, there's no cause for you to worry over me, and most certainly there's no cause to worry because of Mary Theresa. Remember, for a short space in my life she *almost* became my sister. Thanks to the goodness of your own mother and father, she's almost become your sister, too. She's messing in politics, and I was only trying to protect her, as I'm sure your father and mother would have wanted me to.'

She fidgeted with her hands, undecided as to whether to leave them in or out of the pockets of her pinafore. She searched his face. 'Forgive me for being such an ejit.'

'Madeline, there's nothing to forgive. You can't do anything wrong in my eyes.'

~~~

Bernard hadn't played in a dance band for nearly three years, and when George Hooper came along saying that his regular trumpet man had broken an ankle, he didn't hesitate; but then he remembered that he had sold his instrument to put food on the table. 'Don't worry,' Hooper said, 'I'll get you a trumpet!' The bandleader was determined to put on a good show for the next booking, a Grand Dance for members of the National

Guard, and nothing was going to stop him. Relieved to have secured Bernard, he descended the stairs of the tenement building with as much speed as his short legs would allow, wondering how anyone could endure such living conditions and was thankful that his parents had owned their own house and kept him at a good school. Once he reached the street, he pulled loose his bow tie, opened the top shirt button for air.

On the night of the dance, Bernard arrived early at the Metropole, as he wanted time to get used to the borrowed trumpet, which had only been handed to him the day before – he had the stage to himself for half an hour of practice. The first of the other band members arrived. It was Stan, the saxophonist, eyes shining from drink. 'Good to see you back, Bernard!' he said. Nothing's changed, Bernard thought. Bet he was in the Palace Bar beforehand. Not wanting to look amateurish, he put the trumpet away, and chatted with Stan. The rest of the band came along in dribs and drabs, and, at the same time, the ballroom gradually filled with waiting dancers. A lot of the men were wearing the Blueshirt, the uniform of the self-styled National Guard, and even some of the women had swapped the evening dress for the inelegance of the military-looking shirt. He hadn't realized that it would be like this, and began to regret agreeing to play, but then he remembered that he'd had little choice (if he'd turned down Hooper on this occasion, he might never be asked again). He needed the money. He didn't like the Blueshirts, and he had already made his excuses when asked to join them by an ex-army comrade. Its aims seemed straightforward enough: stop disruption of Cumann na nGaedheal election rallies by rowdy elements, over-zealous supporters with different political views; yet he still wasn't impressed. He also knew that the Church backed the Blueshirts: 'Protect this Catholic country from the evils of Communism'. His own opinion, which tonight he would keep to himself, was that the Blueshirts were amateurs who liked playing at being soldiers.

The time came to strike up the music, the reflected light from a revolving crystal globe on the ceiling darted among the bobbing blue shirts. Suddenly, there was a flurry of excitement in the crowd near the door. Bernard couldn't see the reason for it until the tune ended and a man made his way through the dancers, like an ancient Irish chieftain being welcomed by clan members. Stan, the saxophonist, leaned over and whispered, 'It's O'Duffy!' The visitor was in full Blueshirt regalia, including a beret and a high-waisted belt, and he was flanked by no-nonsense blue-shirted bodyguards, who had the fighting build of Gaelic football midfielders. Hooper turned to the band and said, 'We'll hold off a minute, until the General finishes.'

Every so often, O'Duffy was met by an arm thrust upwards. Looking paternal and self-satisfied, he would return the fascist salute and move on. Bernard couldn't resist saying, 'Hail O'Duffy!' It was meant only for Stan, but Hooper heard it and glowered at them. The saxophonist took a fit of laughter and had to turn his back to the ballroom. Meanwhile, mesmerised women were waiting to be introduced to the leader and when their moment came, they had to hold in check an urge to curtsy, a throwback to regal times. He came closer to the stage, and Hooper offered him the microphone, but he declined it with a princely wave of the hand. Then, just as suddenly as they had appeared, he and his entourage moved purposely to the door and left. Hooper led the band into a set of frantic quicksteps, and soon the maple dance floor was flexing beneath the darting and whirling devotees.

~~~

It would soon be Mrs. O'Shea's 60th birthday, and she decreed that all family members were expected to come to Langrishe Place for a tea party. 'While I still have the health and strength in me to enjoy it!'

When Madeline mentioned it, Bernard said: 'A tea party?'

'It won't be all like that, darling. There'll be a drop of the cratur too; Daddy will make sure of that.'

The birthday arrived and Bernard found himself in the scullery with the men, where the whiskey bottle stood next to a jug of water on a scrubbed worktable. 'Help yourself,' O'Shea said, 'while it's still going!' They were summoned to the parlour for tea and cake and the blowing out of the candles. It was only then that Mary Theresa arrived, red-faced and breathless from running. 'Sorry, I'm late, Mammy,' she said, giving her a birthday kiss, 'but the parade went on longer than expected.'

Bernard saw Mr. O'Shea roll his eyes to heaven but didn't understand the reason for it, not until Mary Theresa removed her topcoat – she was wearing the Blueshirt uniform, with its badge of crossed red lines stitched over the heart area. Nobody passed remark for fear of spoiling the party. Bernard returned to the scullery to pour another drink and found that O'Shea had beaten him to it; he was staring out the window, into a small backyard. Bernard stood beside him. 'You don't approve?'

'She won't listen to reason,' he said. 'And, now the Government's talking of banning the uniform. She could be arrested. What if it came to that?'

'De Valera won't go that far,' Bernard said.

'Would *you* talk to her? She might listen to you... I'm sick trying...'

He remembered the night of the election rally, and the trouble it had caused with Madeline. He was on the point of making an excuse, when he became aware of a further ageing in his father-in-law, a degree of frailty. He hadn't the heart to refuse him. Madeline became agitated when he told her. However, on thinking it over, she said, 'I'll suppose you'll have to do it, if Daddy asked you.'

Bernard didn't know how to approach Mary Theresa and decided that he would meet her in a manner that seemed accidental, with no hint of a family plot. He waited outside her workplace until she appeared, then followed her as she walked among a group of chatting women. He needed her to be on her own and saw no other option but to get closer and to call out her name. She turned and looked quizzically at him – 'Bernard!' By now the rest of the females were scrutinising him, thinking this might be gossip for tomorrow's tea break. Mary Theresa could read them. 'He's my brother-in-law. You go on, girls, and I'll catch up...' Then, just to be sure they understood, she called out for all to hear, 'Is Madeline with you, Bernard?'

He shook his head, feeling guilty. The other women moved on; although one glanced back, still hopeful of a titbit.

'What are you doing around here?' Mary Theresa asked.

'Visiting an old army comrade. He lives not far from here.' He could speak with a straight face, as the excuse was partly true; although, he hadn't seen the man since the Kerry days. He added for good measure: 'He's been poorly.'

'That's nice of you,' she said. 'You're heading home now?'

'Yes. Maybe I can walk some of the way with you?' He pointed at the women who had gone ahead. 'Unless you want to catch up with your friends?'

'No, no, you can tell me everything that goes on in Waterford Street. I don't see enough of the children, and every time I do, I can't believe how much they've grown.'

'They'd eat you out of house and home, if we had a house,' he said, feeling uncomfortable with having to make chitchat. Suddenly, he found that he couldn't keep up the pretence. 'Mary Theresa, tell me, what do you see in the Blueshirts?'

She looked surprised and was silent for a moment. Then, she said: 'You've ambushed me. You only want to talk me out of the Blueshirts. That's it, isn't it? I don't have to explain myself to you!'

'Why do you persist in going to their meetings? parading around in the silly getup they wear?'

'You've asked a question and I'll give you an answer,' she said. 'For me, it's simple. They're saying from the pulpit that we must save ourselves from the evils of communism, and we will. And, before you say any more, the communists are here already...and they've friends in the IRA and the IRA have friends in Fianna Fáil and it's all part of a plot to make us turn our back on God.'

'I'm not going to argue with you, Mary Theresa, but I have to tell you that the O'Sheas are demented with worry, and it would break their hearts to see you arrested or something over a silly shirt.'

'It's not a "silly shirt", as you put it, Bernard – it's a legitimate uniform.'

'It can't be legitimate, not if the Blueshirts are banned! They're even saying now that a person might be arrested for simply wearing the damn thing! He hesitated before adding, 'What would happen if a guard stopped you in the street and demanded you take it off?' It was a bluff, a clumsy attempt to scare her. Now, he felt embarrassed and knew he shouldn't have said it.

'Bernard, I believe you're blushing,' she said, in the same teasing tone that had slipped from her on the night of the election rally.

They stood at a busy street corner, and even though he knew they could be overheard by passers-by, he wasn't going to make the same mistake of taking her somewhere private. 'Why do you carry on like this?' he said, in exasperation. 'I'm only doing my best to help, and you come out with something like that?'

She stood back and squared her shoulders. 'What do you mean, "Something like that"?' Unwittingly, she had stepped backwards on to the road; a carter cursed her as his wagon narrowly missed her.

He pulled her back onto the footpath. 'You know well what I mean. All that come-on stuff. I wasn't born yesterday.'

She was silent.

'What would the good people at home think of you talking like that? And remember, Madeline is almost your sister and you should treat her, and all the family, with the respect that's due them.'

'Bernard Clancy, I don't need you to tell me what to do. And you've some cheek saying I don't respect them.'

'Then, show it, stop acting like a spoilt child!'

Suddenly, she strode across the road; he had to dodge a telegram boy on a bicycle to follow her. When he reached her, she had tears in her eyes. I shouldn't have been so blunt, he thought.

'I'd never do anything to hurt the O'Sheas,' she said. 'Not any of them.'

He softened his tone. 'Then stop this Blueshirt stuff, and while you're at it show Madeline more respect.'

'I do try, I do try,' she said, 'but...'

'But, what?'

'It's too hard to explain.'

He didn't want to hear any more, but couldn't stop himself, 'You might as well spit it out.'

'Sometimes I never know where those words come from. Like it isn't really me that's saying them.'

'Aren't the O'Sheas everything you could want? You couldn't have asked for better, could you?'

She looked away, 'You're right, but I still can't help myself. Sometimes I feel they're complete strangers to me. I don't know whose blood I have in me, and you know all about that. You don't know how lucky you are to know where you come from. But I can't be blaming the past for everything...' She sucked in a deep breath and moved off. He kept up with her, pondering her words. Before they parted at his turn for Waterford Street, she said, 'Bernard, in any case you can relax. You won't have anything to complain about. I'll join a convent!' She was laughing now. 'And, as for the Blueshirts, I'd already decided to leave them. A bunch of farmers, anyway!'

'Good for you.' He was thinking that he could have saved his breath. 'And my lips are sealed about the rest...you know.'

'You're a gem, Bernard Clancy.'

'Get on with you,' he said playfully.

~~~

The interviewer tapped a ruler on his desk. Bernard sat opposite to him, knowing he had said too much, but when a smug bastard accuses you of being irresponsible because you have too many children, well, he thought, you must defend yourself. When he had said to him: 'Mind your own bloody business', he'd spiked any chance of getting the job (another rejection to add to the others).

'Mr. Clancy,' the man replied, 'I can see you think the world is against you, and I can tell you now that if you can't take honest criticism and keep acting the way you're acting, well, you'll only be making it harder for yourself to get a job anywhere.'

Bernard wanted to tell him that it was easy for him to talk, but he kept his mouth shut, and waited for the interview to be over. During the following weeks, a course of action grew slowly in his head, one he knew Madeline wouldn't like.

One morning, making up a story that he had a day's work, he took the train to Belfast, found the British Army Recruitment Office, filled out the application form, underwent a medical and was back to the station in time for the evening train back to Dublin. It was a lonely journey home. How would he tell her? How often had she poured out her feelings and said that he was her life? that she would die without him? On returning home, he hadn't the heart to tell her; furthermore, he kept putting it off, and the more the days passed, the more he worried.

The letter was expected, but the soldier at the recruiting office had told him that it would take three or four weeks. His plan had been to look out for the postman, catch him on the steps of the tenement, and then gently break the news to her. Unfortunately, the letter came early and was handed to Madeline by the boy from the ground floor who had taken it upon himself to run up the stairs and place it in her hands, hoping in return to be given its stamp. Even though it was only the King's head, and the eager philatelist had plenty of them already, it could be used as part payment for a more exotic swap.

Madeline looked at the envelope. She always opened his mail, but this formal looking letter she placed to one side for him to open when he came in. Every time she came near it or passed it, she felt its draw, but, for some unexplainable reason, it also made her wary. Eventually, its pull became too strong, and she slid a knife under the flap and drew out the letter. Her world fell away from her, as if the house had spontaneously started to collapse, and she slid to the floor, reading and re-reading details of his posting to Lincolnshire.

It took her a while to gather herself; the letter went back into its envelope and was left on the table. When he came in, she said, 'You're in the mail'.

He knew immediately what it was. He read the letter, then looked up, but she'd turned her back to him. 'You know already what it's about.'

She did not look back, nor did she answer him.

'I'm only doing this for us,' he said. He was receiving the 'silent treatment'. Some of the children were in the room and, to avoid upsetting them, he didn't attempt to bring her around to his way of thinking – it would have to wait until later, when he would begin to scrape his way back into favour. At bedtime, they changed in silence into their nightclothes, he sat on his side of the bed, facing away, and she sat on the other side, her back to him. When he could bear it no longer, he said: 'At least, let me tell you about it.'

It was a relief to hear her speak, even though the tone offered no hope of forgiveness. 'What's there to talk about? I don't know how you can say you love me.'

'But it's because I do love you, and the children, that's why I'm doing it.'

'Going to England! How is that for us? It's yourself you're thinking about, not us.'

They were still looking in opposite directions, he towards the sleeping boys in the corner, she towards the stove, for no other reason except that it was there.

'I have to do this.' His voice was quivering. 'We're going nowhere as it is...the children are getting bigger...there's no end...'

'We'll cope, as we always have.'

'Madeline, I'm sick of scraping by. Any man worth his salt wouldn't put his family through what we're having to put up with.'

'And your going away will solve that?'

'Soldiering is something I know. The British Army wants me, nobody else wants me. Every week there will be good money coming home to you and we can begin to see a way out of this place. Do you really want to spend the rest of your life in Waterford Street?'

She didn't answer.

'I have to start being a man again, start thinking about a future. Can you not try and see that?'

He knew she was crying, and he moved round the bed and sat beside her. 'Don't for a second think that I won't ache for you. Don't for a second think that, darling.'

'What am I going to do? You know I'm nothing without you. I won't be able to let you go. I know it.'

'Of course, you will. Your job will be here, mine will be there, it won't last forever.'

'A week from you is forever and God only knows how long it'll be before you get back.'

He extinguished the lamp and lay beside her, his cheek against hers, wet from her warm tears, whispering consolations to her, she full of worry.

CHAPTER TWENTY-FIVE

June 1944
South of England.

It was four days after D-Day. The Willys Jeep four-wheel drives were lined up in columns along the docks, waiting to be loaded for the Channel crossing; they would be driven onto the ships as soon as the order from Top Brass came down. Bernard moved along the line-up under his command. He was obsessive regarding the Military Police signs. Are they clean and clearly visible? At each stop he took time to make small talk with his men, some encouraging words, a cigarette shared, anything to kill the tedium of waiting, anything to calm any sense of terror that might sneak into the heart. They had been at this south coast harbour for almost ten hours, staring across grey, choppy waves in what they regarded as the general direction of Normandy.

Returning to his own vehicle, he sat in the passenger seat and took out a read-many-times letter from Madeline. It had come some weeks before, and he imagined her back in Dublin waiting for a reply, but he hoped she realized that there was a clampdown on sending mail home — 'Loose talk can lose lives!', so the slogan went.

He saw her at home at this hour, in Waterford Street, at the opposite end of the tenement terrace to his mother, close enough to look in on her, yet, at Madeline's insistence, a daughter-in-law's breathing space between them. He saw the scene at home, full of activity, the dinner over, the table cleared for the children to do their homework. He often drifted to sleep placing their names and birthdays in order; they now had eight children. Last time he was home, Madeline had accused him of leaving her with all the rearing to do, not only that, but also the caring for a cranky, alcoholic woman who'd taken to the bed and who in all probability didn't even like her. Also, Madeline hadn't a kind word to say about her brothers-in-law, describing them as a bunch of 'Pontius Pilates', wanting nothing to do with their mother's situation.

He again told her that their choice was either hardship or putting up with forced separation, which wouldn't be forever. She was never fully convinced by his viewpoint, but in the end, as usual, she gave it lukewarm acceptance. When the war came and conscription flooded the British army, his experience from the Kerry Campaign had been a surprise passport to a sergeant's stripes. Their orders as members of the Corps of Military Police were clear: control the junctions, keep the traffic flowing, no troop-carrying trucks colliding with weighty Sherman tanks, keep the men in order as if they were still on duty in Britain, no drunkenness and certainly no fraternising with prostitutes spinning seductive-sounding foreign words, feared by Command as a sticky web of sexually transmitted diseases, but, in reserve, in case the men ignored the warning, the Jeeps also had a box stuffed with hypocritical 'Johnnies'.

Bernard snatched a moment to re-read Madeline's letter:

How are you? all is good here with us so do not be worrying and we must be thankful to God for that and I could write a million words on our gang here but today I am down in my boots and missing you terribly and I want to keep you to myself for this letter at least am I being selfish? I hope not as I am already losing you to the army so I think I am right in looking for some private time with you my lovely man so when I wake in the morning you are the first person I think of and when I go to bed no night passes without falling asleep with you I am a hopeless case and half a person without you and not cut out to be an army wife and there you are since I started writing this letter I am already starting to feel my cloud lift as I feel I'm talking to you through this pencil I have to keep licking I want to tell you all in my heart because often I am taken by worry over you and I ask myself what —

He heard an American say, 'Let's get these wagons rolling!' He looked up at an MP with wrestler's arms, metal helmet sitting oddly on a large head, who was furiously waving them towards the nearest gangplank. Bernard's driver had already gunned the engine into throaty life, his boot poised impatiently over the clutch pedal. Bernard put the letter back in its special place and held on to the dashboard as the jeep jerked forward.

It was bizarre to see fields of green on either side of roads choked to a single lane where the urgent advance had shoved burnt-out German lorries to one side. For Bernard this was so unlike the Kerry Campaign, a different scale of war: no time to think, no time to dwell on the supply-line problems, no time to clear the roads of the abandoned debris of the enemy; that task would be for another unit somewhere behind them. The columns of troops slowly pressed on against strong resistance, guided by a horizon of rising black smoke and the almost surreal reports of constant shellfire and explosions in the distance.

Five weeks later in the city of Caen, his group came upon a fuel tanker that had crashed into a wall. The road was blocked, and the dazed driver was staring at a shiny slit in the side of the barrel-tank of fuel from which a relentless, flammable spill was threatening to snake into a nearby terrace of once-dozy houses miraculously still standing in the smashed city. Most people had fled, but the few who came to the doors were mystified by the barks of the military police, then a redcap who had once motored in peaceful times through France remembered the translation for petrol, *essence*, and, by repeating the word and pointing at the stricken lorry, the message got home.

By then the crash had backed up the advancing lorries – Operation Overlord stopped by a skid. Bernard commandeered a heavy truck close to the head of the logjam and, after explaining the situation to its driver, a rope was lashed between the two vehicles. The driver of the tanker stood a safe distance off and Bernard told him to get back in the lorry, as he needed him to steer it out of the way. The man hesitated.

'The lorry's your responsibility, soldier,' Bernard said. 'Come on, we haven't all day!'

'What if it goes up?'

'Then we'll all go up. Now get on with it!'

The driver picked his way to the cab, afraid his very footsteps could ignite the spilt fuel. A strain was taken on the rope and the assisting truck growled from the effort, giving off the smell of slipping clutch-plates. At first it looked as if the rope would break, but instead it seemed to stretch and then hold firm. The pull on the tanker was unyielding. Then suddenly it was yanked free and it shot back, narrowly missing Bernard. He pointed to a side road leading to open countryside and said to the tanker driver, 'Drive it up there, out of the way!'

'You mean, start the engine?'

'How else can you do it, soldier?'

The man was undecided. Bernard lost his patience and pulled him out of the cab and jumped into the driving seat, turned the ignition key, pressed the starter button, and prayed that no spark would catch the fuel. The engine roared into life and he slapped the truck into gear, and it bounced along the road. He abandoned it at the first safe clearing and ran back to the main thoroughfare, where the traffic was moving freely again. The driver of the tanker was close by, arms hanging.

'Am I going to be arrested?' he said.

'Hitch a lift from one of these lorries and find your company.'

'I thought –'

'It'll be a long tour, son. You'll have your day later.'

At that moment they heard an explosion and exchanged looks, knowing it was the tanker. The driver hurried off, ran alongside a slowing troop carrier, and swung himself on board. As Bernard watched it trundle away, he felt the outside of his breast pocket and tapped the place where Madeline's letter rested. It dawned on him that he could have been killed and the thought of the 'Regret Inform' telegram being delivered to Waterford Street made him angry with himself for being so reckless.

Strong resistance by the Germans had held up the advance, and Bernard had orders to stay at Caen for a further twenty-four hours. The MPs set up a traffic control position, working through the night in four-hour shifts. They took turns to snatch sleep on hard benches in the council chamber of the *Mairie*, one of the few large buildings left with a roof. At daybreak, a plane strafed the town, came back for another run, hitting three trucks; stretcher bearers ran with the injured to a field hospital and the disabled trucks were pushed to one side and the move to the front continued, a relentless tide of troops and supplies. A fresh contingent of MPs arrived in the afternoon permitting Bernard to assemble his team and move forward. Their jeeps slotted into the continuous convoy and, as they left Caen behind, he joked with his driver, 'Not even time to buy a picture postcard!'

They were travelling through countryside and every so often locals were at the crossroads waving to them, all smiles, but behind the smiles one could see that the eyes demanded revenge. Bernard saluted back, wondering if they knew that he and his men were MPs and not frontline heroes. He didn't feel guilty that on this occasion he wouldn't be lining up his sights on the enemy; instead, he remembered the words his commanding officer had said at the pre-embarkation briefing: 'Your job, men, is to bring order to this war. To defeat Jerry, we have to be organized.'

Road signs to Argentan had been destroyed, and Bernard studied a map and guessed at their position. He figured out that reaching the area before dark was unlikely and on top of that a downpour had started and the Jeep's solitary window wiper was failing to keep pace with the rain. They spotted a small village off the road and pulled over to wait for an easing in the weather. In the confusing conditions, the rest of their company had missed them turning off and had pressed on, leaderless. In the jeep, wrapped in their heavy waterproof topcoats, water dripping on them from an ill-fitting canvas canopy, they sat and waited. They were a short distance from a huddle of cottages, all in darkness except for a weak light in one of the windows.

One of the men, Bury, took watch while Bernard and the other two settled down to sleep to the sound of rain on the canopy, their legs hungry for want of a good stretch. Bernard was woken by urgent words, 'Sergeant, someone's coming!' He saw the figure and opened his holster-flap and rested the pistol on his lap. All four men were alert now. The driver started the engine, ready to speed away if need be. Something told Bernard they should wait.

He was an old man, shouting and gesticulating. Bury had a smattering of French and through the torrent of words he picked out: *'Violeurs!'*

'He's calling us rapists,' he said.

The old man started to beat the bonnet with his fists. Bernard jumped out of the jeep and Bury followed him. The Frenchman spotted the pistol and spat at him.

'Bury, tell him we're here to fight the Germans, not fight him.'

The soldier spoke to him in slow, uncertain French but the man showed no sign of calming down. He said something that baffled Bury, who asked him to speak slowly, nodding every so often as he tried to piece together what had occurred. The Frenchman was pointing back to the cottage, the one with the weak light in the window. 'Sergeant, he says his daughter was raped here two days ago.'

Bernard put away the gun. 'Follow us,' he said to the driver. Their path lit by the jeep's following headlights they went with the Frenchman. In the cottage the man lifted an oil lamp and led them through a rustic kitchen, where a worn, slight woman stared at them, her ancient face stamped with the confusion of war. The man opened an inner door, made for a smaller past generation, and stooped to enter a bedroom which lay in darkness. The light from the lamp spread into the room and revealed a bed with a figure lying under the covers, face to the wall. The figure turned to see who had come in and Bernard saw a woman who was perhaps the same age as Madeline. She quickly turned away.

'Bury, tell her we're sorry…ask if she needs medical attention.'

The soldier spoke and she turned to glare at him. Bernard didn't need a translation for that. 'Tell her we want to help and we're not responsible for what the Germans did.'

'You don't understand, Sergeant. It wasn't a German.'

Bernard had a sudden flashback to a farmyard in Kerry where two women cowered under a coating of thick obnoxious oil. Not rape, but a violation of their dignity. But this was a rape.

'You mean, one of us?'

'Looks that way.'

'You're absolutely sure she's been raped?'

'She says so, Sergeant, and I don't think she's making it up.'

'I agree,' he said. She looked too distressed to be lying. 'We'll need a medic to confirm.'

'Is there time for that?'

'No. Do you think you can take a statement from them?'

'I'm not sure, Sergeant…perhaps if they wrote them out themselves and signed them?'

'Good. Tell them I'll report this at Alençon.'

Bernard went outside the cottage and protected a cigarette from the rain while he looked at distant flashes of light from the combat zone. If it weren't for orders, he would take her to the field hospital in Caen, but they had to keep going. The downpour was easing, and it was time to be on their way. He went back inside and found Bury waiting for the statements to be completed. Bernard watched the old man move the pen down the page in crabbed handwriting.

'Have you the woman's yet?'

'I left it with her. She didn't seem keen. Perhaps, you could check, Sir.'

She was sitting up in the bed, using a heavy book to support the notepaper. Stealing a look, he saw she had stopped mid-sentence, as though the act of putting her ordeal into words had been too much for her. He realized she was crying, not sobs, just quiet tears which sat precariously on the cheeks, threatening to drop and smear the ink. It seemed right to put a comforting hand on her shoulder, no matter how inadequate, and he stood like that for some moments. Then, without warning, she started writing again in quick jerks of the nib and he went back outside to check on the progress of the old man's statement.

~~~

Bernard looked out the window and admired the classic garden; it was divided by a long driveway, and he imagined the satisfactory life its French owners would have enjoyed here until the day they were dispossessed in a rush of jackboots running into the grand hall where he now waited. The only sign that the chateau had been a German command centre was the ugly stain on the lawn where files had been burned as the Allies pressed closer. It was the Americans who had arrived first, an enterprising lieutenant of the US Army wasting no time in claiming it as their temporary headquarters.

A voice from behind: 'Sergeant Clancy, Colonel Hunt will see you now.' It was a large room, with Baroque-style plasterwork on its high ceiling, and the Colonel, tight haircut, yellowish complexion, sat behind an estate-owner's antique desk – he was younger than Bernard had expected. He rose and offered a handshake, like an enthusiastic preacher welcoming a lost soul to church service, then indicated a chair.

'What's this about, Sergeant?' He had a cowboy drawl.

Bernard told of the French woman who claimed that a soldier from the advancing troops had raped her. He produced the signed statements. The American scanned them, creases in his brow, long legs stretched wide of the desk, as if they needed the space. He looked up with a blank expression. 'I'm sorry, Sergeant, but I can't make head nor tail of the French language. Why are you're coming to me with this?'

'Sir, the woman remembered the man's uniform and, more importantly, memorised his dog tag information.'

'Let me get this straight, Sergeant, you're saying he's one of us?'

'I'm afraid so, Sir.'

The American studied him, as if he were an opponent. 'There must be proper channels for this? Why hasn't this come to me through those?'

'Too much happening, Sir. It's impossible to find proper channels…not immediately. I felt time was important, next week this could be forgotten.'

'You could've gone to our military police?'

'I felt I should go directly to you, Sir.'

Some moments went by. Straightening his long body, the colonel got to his feet and paced the room then came back and fell back hard on to his seat. 'You do know the harm this will do if it gets out, damn it, we're supposed to be the good guys! We can't afford to lose the moral high ground.' He stood again and went to the window, twitching his shoulder blades, as if working at tension release.

Without turning, he said: 'Sergeant, you do know we could lose a soldier to hanging over this?'

Bernard didn't think an answer was expected.

'We must win this war. We must be ferocious, even barbaric. And not a damned soul will thank us if we fail. Do you understand my point?'

'Not exactly, Colonel.'

Hunt returned to the desk and looked again at the crudely written statements. 'This incident could be viewed as a casualty of war.'

'You're calling it, one incident, Sir. But, what if this soldier...what if this soldier were to rape again? Then, there'd be –'

'Okay, okay, Sergeant, I hear you. Gawd, you Englishmen are so straight down the middle!'

He didn't correct him, feeling his nationality had nothing to do with the matter. Neither did he ask him if he had a wife, or sisters, or daughters, or a mother still living, instead he hoped the man just had a conscience. Meanwhile, the colonel seemed to be drilling his mind like a Texas oilman, looking for another option, as if there were one out there, somewhere – one that would remove this problem. He looked again at the statements. 'Sergeant, I presume you have a translation of these?'

He handed him a rough translation that Bury had written. 'I'm sure an official interpreter will tidy it up, but the main facts will be the same.'

A junior officer put his head round the door, apologised, and came forward with a sheet of paper; he eyed Bernard's British uniform with suspicion and placed the document face down on the desk. 'A despatch just came...' The man gave a smart salute and left. Hunt picked up the despatch and as he read it his brow was smoothed and a smile spread from his mouth. 'Sergeant, it's better news all round. Our infantry is gaining ground by the hour and it looks as if we'll be moving forward.'

'And this business?'

'In the first place, you shouldn't have brought it to me but, seeing as you have, I'll pass it on to our Military Police. As *you* well know, they're the guys for problems like this.'

Hunt went back to reading the despatch, a signal to Bernard that he had been dismissed.

He returned to his men on duty in the centre of Argentan. It was warm and dry, and they'd discarded their jackets; meanwhile the stream of vehicles heading for the front were thundering through at a steady rate. Unnoticed to him, although close to where he stood, a crowd using sticks had herded four women into the town square, as if they were cattle from the field. He only heard their shouts when there was a lull in the passing traffic. He went to investigate and saw a man come out of a house carrying a chair. The crowd bayed at the cowering women: '*Collaboratrices!*' Of the accusers the women were the most vehement; they saw the herded women as traitors not only to France but also to their gender, an unforgivable sin.

One of the accused women was pushed roughly to a spot beside the chair and the clothes were ripped from her and with insufficient hands she tried to cover her pubic area and breasts. A man advanced on the woman, an arm behind his back. He was concealing an industrial scissors more fit for cutting rough jute sacks than for cutting her treasured chestnut-coloured hair. He sprung the surprise, grabbed a fistful of hair and chopped at it, exposing a white stretch of scalp; meanwhile, the other terrified women huddled together, forewarned of what lay in store for them. The shearer looked to the mob for approval, as if he had single-handedly assailed a barricade of Hitler's crack infantry. He turned back to finish the humiliation.

Bernard was sickened and his instinct was to save the women but, as he moved forward, he felt his arm being gripped: it was Bury. 'I wouldn't do that, Sergeant.'

He glared at him, waiting for his explanation.

'We'd have a riot on our hands, Sir. Their blood is up, we won't change anything.' By now the first woman was shorn and the next in line was clinging to the remnants of her dress, as if that would halt the inevitable.

'We can't just leave...' Bernard's words were lost in the roar of the crowd; the second woman was being pushed into the chair. He realized that Bury was right and they returned to the town's main intersection to ensure that the war would not be lost on account of a bottleneck at Argentan. Later in the afternoon, the four women, one still in her teens, probably only guilty of an infatuation with a uniform, were loaded on to an open-back lorry and paraded through the town. As it passed the control point, Bernard averted his eyes.

CHAPTER TWENTY-SIX

May 1945

Bernard was in Germany. As with most people, he had only recently seen the newspaper photographs and the newsreel footage; the gates of the concentration camps had been opened, matchstick humans, stumbling about on the point of death. It got worse – reports of mass exterminations. Naked bodies piled high. The horror clutched out at him from the flickering black and white images, and, on first viewing, Bernard ran from an army movie show to vomit.

His unit had been posted to a city flattened by Allied bombs. He had everyday contact with Germans, the desolate old, and the stunned children, wandering and scavenging through the rubble of destroyed neighbourhoods. Here also words weren't enough to describe what he had seen. When this was all over, he knew he wouldn't be able to talk about it, about how it made him feel, not even to Madeline.

Lately, there had been rumours of his unit heading home. This started a spree of last-minute collecting and swapping of Nazi souvenirs, trophies picked up as the enemy line shrank backwards into the Fatherland. Items with a hint of an SS officer about it were especially prized. Bernard stuffed his collection into a kit bag, unsure of what he was going to do with them.

Weeks later, he was aboard a passenger ship on the Irish Sea in his demob suit and carrying a scuffed navy suitcase. He made his way to Waterford Street, looked along the symmetrical line of grand houses designed for the wealthy but long turned into tenements, took in the distinctive smells of the neighbourhood, and listened to the sound of children playing and the noise of horse-drawn carts running over the cobblestones. It was exactly as he had left it, and in one sense he was glad that it had stayed that way, as he hadn't wanted too much to change. A woman talking to a neighbour at the hall door recognised him. 'There you are, Mister Clancy.' She gave his suit and the suitcase a knowing look. 'She's in. I saw her earlier.'

Tipping his hat to her, he went inside and climbed the stairs. He stood outside the room and playfully listened at the door, and at first heard only children's voices and then Madeline's came to him and he delayed twisting the doorknob, just to listen. The talking stopped and it was totally quiet for a time that seemed eternal, then he heard the children again and he rapped the door with a knuckle. He heard Madeline say, 'Someone see to the door!'

It swung open and Bernard looked down on a girl, barely tall enough to have reached the doorknob.

'Yes, mister?'

'Don't you know me, Lucy?'

The girl ran back into the room, shouting, 'Mammy, Mammy, I think it's him!'

Madeline had been washing clothes and rushed to dry her hands. When she saw him in the doorway, she patted her hair and threw off her apron, uncovering a new frock. An anxious Lucy tugged at her and, too excited to speak, she pointed to Bernard, as if the emphatic thrust of an arm would compensate for her failure as a lookout, for Madeline had been reminding her all morning, 'Keep an eye to the window for Daddy coming up the street'.

He stood still and looked at Madeline.

She blushed, patted her hair again, pulled Lucy's hand from her clothing and smoothed the creases left behind. 'Close the door Bernard, before the whole world knows our business.'

'I'm happy just standing here, just taking in the view.'

'Some view,' she said, appearing to run herself down, however, if the mirror could talk, she had been up from early, getting herself looking perfect for him. She knew he was enjoying her, and she returned his gaze. The moment was broken by footsteps on the stairs, and he closed the door behind him and rushed to her. He kissed her, moving his hands to her backside.

'Bernard, the children!'

He looked to the far side of the room where Lucy now stood with Kevin, a dark curly-headed boy, and beside him was 'Young' Madeline who was fiddling nervously with a large bow in her hair; they waited, like unsure child actors needing to be pushed onstage into the spotlight. He held out his arms and they came forward slowly and slid into his grip.

'Where are the others?' he asked.

'They'll be in later, sweetheart. You won't know the bigger ones at all.'

'It isn't *that* long ago, Madeline.'

'It seems a lifetime.' She stood behind him, holding him about the waist, her head against a shoulder blade. 'I can't believe you're here.'

Turning to face her, he looked into those eyes that had lulled him to sleep so often when away, caressed her hair, which had begun to show grey, as a book page can start to discolour at the edges. Producing some money, he asked, 'Can Young Madeline take them to the shop for sweets?'

Her instinct was to worry, but now that he was home, she no longer felt that burden of sole responsibility. 'If you think she's big enough…well, okay.' Nevertheless, as the children headed for the door, she warned them, 'And be sure to stay together, and hold hands crossing the street.'

As their footsteps bounced down the stairs, Bernard's voice rang optimistically after them, 'And don't rush back.'

She giggled, 'You'll never get to heaven, Bernard Clancy.'

'Darling, I hope to be in heaven, right here, right now.'

'We'll have to be quick.'

Afterwards, he went to see his mother. It was seven in the evening and Lily was already in bed. He pulled up a chair beside her.

'What kept you?' she said.

'I'm only in today, Ma. You're the first person I came to visit.'

She gestured with her hand. 'Stand back and let me see you properly.'

He did as she asked.

'I expected you to have a look of your father, but, honestly, now I don't know who you're like. Maybe it's my side of the family you're from? I don't know. You've become a real man, I always liked the moustache, but you could do with more meat on you. That wife of yours will have to start going to a good butcher.'

'It's the way I am, even the army couldn't fatten me.'

He looked round the room; it was much as he remembered it, except for the arrival of a new crucifix hanging on the wall near her bed – all she had to do was lift an eyelid and the over-realistic image of the suffering Saviour would be there before her. She seemed more pessimistic than ever, reminding him of the soldier on a stretcher who wanted to dictate a farewell letter to his family, even though the wound was far from fatal. But, then again, he knew that she could act the part, play the sympathy card. However, he couldn't hold that against his own mother.

He struggled for words. 'You're comfortable, Ma?'

She ignored the question and asked him to pour her a drink, all the while watching him carefully. 'You pour like my father did. I hope you don't end up like him.'

'Army practice.'

Unexpectedly, she added, 'He wasn't a nice man, you know.'

'You don't have to tell –'

'Why not?'

'He's gone, and what he was is gone too.'

'That's a queer way of thinking.'

'Probably.'

An awkward silence followed. She was looking everywhere except at him. For something to say, he asked: 'Do you have many callers, Ma?'

'Mrs. Cummins from above comes in and wears the ear off me, but she's a body and it's company.'

'No one else?'

'Well, I see Madeline from time to time, but she only comes because of you.'

'Don't be like that. Madeline cares about you, we all care about you.'

She looked unconvinced. 'I was probably the same with your father's mother. It was never ordained that we should get on with one another.' She lay back on the pillow for some moments wanting to swim for a while in the old days, then, as if she had just remembered, she said, 'And, your friend Mary Theresa, she puts her head round the door every so often.'

'That's nice but remember she's *your* friend too.'

'Maybe – but you're the one that put her in touch with the O'Shea's.' She was quiet for a while, then added: 'I'll never forgive you for that.'

'What's there to forgive, Ma? I did nothing.'

'You deliberately showed me up.'

'It wasn't like that.'

He wanted to tell her in detail how it had all happened but held his tongue. As if nothing contentious had been said, he asked: 'Where does she live now?'

She looked irritated. 'It's your wife should be telling you these things. Since him and her died, the O'Sheas I mean, she lives with one of the other daughters…somewhere nearby, I forget. And she drops in magazines I think she gets in work. Old ones mind you.'

'At least, that's something.'

'I suppose it is.' It was a grudging compliment and the effort caused her to sit up and take a drink from her glass.

That night he lay quietly in bed beside Madeline, their passion spent from earlier in the day. She turned in her sleep, and he remembered how he had ached for comfortable moments like this when he was away. He listened to the night sounds of the tenement building and the sounds of the sleeping family. After leaving the Irish Army, he hadn't burdened Madeline with what he had seen in Kerry and, likewise, he wasn't going to burden her with what he'd seen this time. She was his life, the mother of his children and home life was to be kept separate. Even, kept sacred. In any case, how could anyone who wasn't there ever hope to understand? Instead, he would stare alone at his dark memories. But more pressing now was finding the money to replace his army pay; in the morning he would be out bright and early, looking for work.

CHAPTER TWENTY-SEVEN

He had secured a job interview.

'Don't you feel a bit of a traitor?' the interviewer said, looking up from the application letter.

Bernard was convinced that the man was sitting on a cushion, probably adding three inches in height to a weedy torso.

'In what way do you mean, Mr. McGloin?'

'I hate spelling out the obvious, but you *have* been in the British Army.'

'You'll see further on down, sir, that I also served in our own National Army.'

The interviewer held a cigarette between nicotine stained fingers, ash quivered on its end, then collapsed onto the letter. He swiped it away, then puffed it off the desk. 'Aren't men like you being barred from government jobs?'

'How do you mean?'

'Deserters who went to fight with the English.'

Bernard took a deep breath. Although years had passed, he had a sense that he was back at the industrial school and seated before a Christian Brother dressed in a black soutane. He wanted to get up and walk out of the interview but was restrained by the thought of the family he had to support. Struggling to be calm, he said, 'Mr. McGloin, you'll read in my application letter that it's twenty-two years since I left the Irish Army.'

McGloin glanced again at the letter. 'That fact looks correct, Mr. Clancy, I'll give you that much. But, still, you did join the British Army, not at all popular where I come from.' His finger hovered above the line where Bernard had inserted his Irish Army service dates, then, as if he had just realized their significance, he said, 'At that time – 1922 to 1923 – weren't you fighting against the good men who run our country today?'

He felt powerless. By now he knew the job was never going to be his, and couldn't believe it when he heard himself say, 'Mr. McGloin, I'm not afraid of hard work and I'd be grateful for any position, any work you might have going.'

The man sucked on the cigarette, his eyes going into slits. He gave the impression of rereading the letter, but he was skilled at putting the knife in and twisting it. 'Mr. Clancy, have you the language?'

Bernard decided not to answer.

Again, McGloin asked, 'Have you the language? The Irish? The Gaeilge?'

Leaving the interview, Bernard now knew that finding a job was going to be as difficult as ever. He went into a public house and nursed a drink at the bar. Money was going to run out soon, he could see that, a truth that couldn't be dodged or put back to a later date. A man in a dirt-ingrained peaked cap and a jacket too small for him, with a shine on it from over-wearing, came into the bar and went straight through to the outside toilet. He returned and stood next to Bernard and out of the corner of his mouth said, 'Pal, could you stand a fellow a scoop?'

'Sorry, friend, but I'm not in a position.'

'Oh! I wouldn't have asked, except you look all spruce.'

Bernard glanced down at his suit that Madeline's iron had dignified with razor-edged creases. 'I was at a job interview.'

The man let out a soft whistle. 'Like trying to find gold in the Wicklow Hills, did you get it?'

'I don't think so. But they may get in touch...'

'Don't believe it, pal. You need to be in the know. I've been one year and seven months looking. I tell you, one year and seven months, and I'm lucky to even get a foot in the gate to talk to someone and even at that, I know I'm wasting my time. It's diabolical, I tell you, diabolical.'

Just then the barman came along. 'I told you, Joe, not to be coming in bothering the customers.'

The man hitched up his trousers in a nervous motion. 'We're having a conversation here, what's up with that, Eddie?'

'I told you before, this isn't a charity and you can't expect to come in here without any money.'

The man shuffled his feet, looked towards the floor.

Bernard said to the barman, 'I was just about to order a drink for this man.'

'I can't have him coming in here and harassing clients.'

'He's not harassing me. It's like he said, we're having a conversation.'

The barman came back with a pint of porter and slapped it down in front of the man. 'It's your money, sir,' he said, lifting Bernard's coins from the counter.

Bernard enjoyed watching the man gulp down the drink, although he knew it was a waste he couldn't afford. The man set down the empty glass and with a jerk of his shoulders adjusted his tight jacket. 'Pal, I thank you. I'll do the same for you someday.'

Bernard watched him leave and saw the warning – he could end up like him if the money ran out. It was then that he thought of Kinahan. Maybe the colonel has some contacts that could help me? But he knew he wouldn't be easy to find, as the last he had heard of him was that he was doing 'something' in the Civil Service. Running into his army pal Conroy shortly afterwards was a fluke; it was almost predictable that he would know where the colonel lived. A hopeful letter to Kinahan asking to meet him was answered; it contained a sketch of how to find the house.

He took the tram to Ranelagh and using the neatly drawn map he entered a leafy avenue of semi-detached houses and took a turn into a cul-de-sac. He pushed open the gate of a red brick house, with roses in front – it reminded him of the south of England. He thought of Madeline back in the tenement in Waterford Street; she would only ever get to enter one of these houses if she came with a mop and bucket. Kinahan came to the door and ushered him into a parlour where, even though it was a mild evening, a turf fire was going. Bernard watched as he switched on a standard lamp with a burnt spot on its shade. It illuminated a print on the wall of red-coated huntsmen on horseback, and of hounds bearing down on a fox, its body stretched in balletic desperation. He thought that Kinahan hadn't worn well; the once tall and straight body now leaned forward like a tent pole bent by the wind and he had a habit of smacking his lips and running his fingers through hair limp and grey; Bernard was surprised at the change, he wasn't the man he remembered. A framed photograph of Michael Collins looked down like a guardian angel from a spot above him.

A woman came into the room and Kinahan said, 'Margaret, come and meet Bernard, an old comrade.'

'It's a pleasure to meet you, Bernard. I hope my husband doesn't bore you to tears. Get him talking of the old days and he never stops. You'll have a cup of tea, Bernard?'

Was she the same woman from the Metropole? He wasn't sure. 'That would be nice, Mrs. Kinahan.' She went off to the kitchen, leaving them alone, comfortable in the two armchairs placed either side of the fireplace.

'Bernard, tell me what you've been doing with yourself? I meet up with some of the old Dublin Guard crowd from time to time, and your name gets mentioned every so often.'

Bernard didn't believe he had been spoken of, and felt he was being deliberately flattered, but despite that he opened-up about his life since they had last met, surprising himself with the amount of detail he revealed. He paused when the woman came back with a tray and poured tea from an ornate teapot into dainty cups. 'I'll leave you two soldiers to march down memory lane.' As she slipper-footed out, she added, 'Dan, don't let the fire die.'

While Kinahan put the sods in place, he spoke over his shoulder. 'After all that time out, you went back to the military. It makes no odds that it was to his Majesty's. I'd never have expected you to do that!'

'Needs must, Dan.' Bernard used his first name, encouraged by the easy setting of the parlour.

The colonel showed no sign of noticing anything different. 'But you, Bernard, of *all* people.'

'I even surprised myself. Back in Twenty-three, I couldn't wait to get out, but things changed for me.'

He told him of his recent efforts at finding a job and the way he had been treated by the last interviewer. Kinahan leaned forward in his fawn cardigan, brown darning on the elbows, and listened like a confessor. When Bernard had finished, the colonel sat back to give the problem some thought. A burnt sod of turf collapsed in the grate. He gave his opinion: 'That idiot is not on his own, I meet them all the time. Imagine what it's like for *me*: I fought alongside them for a republic, then, fought against them to protect the Treaty, and now they're in government they've hidden me away in a dusty, useless part of the Civil Service.

'A man of your experience and ability…it's a crime,' Bernard said, sensing that any faint hope he'd had of making a job-connection had disappeared.

'It's all politics now, no room for soldiers. And you're right, the knives are out for men who deserted and went to fight Herr Hitler. Okay, they shouldn't have deserted but you can't blame them either; unfortunately, for you, it looks like some ejit hasn't understood that the block is meant to be only on State jobs, or, worse still, he's putting his own interpretation on the Minister's ruling.'

'But I never deserted.'

'If someone's wearing blinkers, there's little you can do about it. And to tell the truth, back in our time, we probably did things like that to the anti-Treatyites. But there are very few jobs going in this country at present, that's the reality. It's on its knees, and we certainly won't be getting handouts now from the Brits or the Yanks – DeValera has made sure we've few friends. If I were you, I'd be thinking of going back into the British Army.'

'You don't paint a good picture.'

'It depends on you, Bernard. You could scrape the barrel here, or you could do better for that growing family of yours.'

He had to admit to himself that he'd had the same thought but had pushed it away. No longer was he so sure. He felt the colonel looking at him, examining him. Unexpectedly, Kinahan asked: 'Going back to our time in Killarney, how come you knew that prisoner, you know, the one you went behind my back to see – the one that was executed?'

Bernard thought the question typical of Kinahan. One minute he's on about me re-enlisting, the next minute he springs this on me. 'It was quite simple, Dan, we were in Artane together.'

Kinahan laughed. 'The industrial school, a brotherhood of delinquents.'

'Some would say that.'

'And, you'd have helped him, if you'd had the means?'

'He was my only friend back in Artane, but he never gave me the chance to help him – he didn't want to be saved.'

'A martyr, then?'

'He was trapped in many ways,' Bernard said.

It was getting late, a soft light was coming through the lace curtains from the streetlights, and Mrs. Kinahan returned and gathered up the tray. Bernard knew it was time to go and leave them in their southside security. He could imagine her tidying up when he left, then they would slowly climb the carpeted stairs to retire for the night (did Kinahan sleep with a clear conscience?) then, come the morning, she would see him to the door on his way to a neutered desk in the Civil Service, to wind down the qualifying years for a comfortable pension. Leaving the house, Bernard suddenly felt sorry for him, even though it should have been the other way around. He made a brief gesture of his arm that could have been interpreted as a salute. 'Good night, Colonel,' he said, and moved briskly to catch the last tram for O'Connell Street.

A week later, on their way to a cinema in Mary Street, he told Madeline that he had applied to his former barracks. She said nothing. Her fist was clenched during what seemed an endless film, and when he tried to take her hand in the darkened stalls, she moved it away, as if from a nibbling mouse. She didn't break her silence until they were on the way home, and what he heard was totally unexpected. 'I never told you I went to the fortune-teller, Madame Nora.'

'Oh?' He was thinking she wasn't normally that brave, would shy from such people.

'Mary Theresa wanted to go, but wouldn't go on her own, so she dragged me along. Madame Nora read my leaves too.'

'You shouldn't believe all that nonsense.'

'She told me she saw travel and… upheaval.'

They walked on, with the visit to the fortune-teller becoming a new knife between them.

'Anyone could say that,' he said.

'She seemed to know.'

'It's a business, she's chancing her arm.'

'It's what she didn't say that scared me,' Madeline said.

'What?'

'She saw something else. I saw it in her face, but she said nothing about it, and I was too frightened to ask her.'

'Madeline, it's all in your imagination.'

'I don't think so…'

He was annoyed. 'Mary Theresa had no right in bringing you to someone like that. They can tell if a person is easy to scare and they use it.'

'Don't speak badly of Mary Theresa,' she said, her tone icy. 'At least she's about when you're not.'

Wounded, he retreated. It was ironic that now she only saw goodness in Mary Theresa. It went back to the time of Madeline's serious dose of flu, when so drained and helpless she'd had to take to the bed. When Mary Theresa had heard of her situation, she had gone selflessly to the tenement room and nursed her, cooked the family meals, and washed their clothes. He had known nothing of it, not until he had returned from the war. They were almost at Waterford Street and he glanced at her. She had a faraway look; although he felt guilty, there was no going back on his decision. 'Anyway' he said, 'they mightn't even take me back.'

She didn't answer, seeing the clumsily thrown lifeline for what it was. Within a month he was reunited with his old regiment, which had shrunk to a peacetime size; the commanding officer had welcomed him, saying he needed some familiar faces around him.

But Bernard couldn't forget his last conversation with Madeline when she had accused him of preferring army life to living at home. He told her he wouldn't see his family on Poverty Street, his conscience was clear on that point. Still, on the day of departure, as he walked for the boat, he had avoided looking people in the face, in case anyone saw his tears.

~~~

The undertaker would hold back Lily Clancy's funeral until her sons arrived. He had already heard from the neighbours in Waterford Street how she must have felt unwell, got out of the bed, and collapsed before she reached the door. Her daughter-in-law found her, a shock for anyone. Still, he decided, the old bird had had a good innings. Already, he had met the eldest son Stephen, who was conveniently living across the city in Patrick Street, but the other two sons, Bernard and Peter, they were due in off the boat that very morning – he gathered that one of them was a soldier, the other working on the buildings in London. The undertaker rushed off to make sure everything was in readiness.

The three sons walked into his office just before noon, each wearing the black necktie and, as a further mark of respect, the black diamond patch sewn on to a coat sleeve. He offered them his condolences, telling how he'd heard that their mother had been a much-loved lady, almost an institution in Waterford Street. The brothers thanked him and listened in silence as he guided them through the final arrangements. 'Have you any other questions?'

Stephen gave a nervous cough (earlier in the pub he had been appointed spokesman). 'We want to give herself the best of send-offs,' he said, 'but we're embarrassingly short of the readies.'

The undertaker had already prepared estimates, one for prompt payment, and one slightly higher for credit. 'This is no time for a family to have extra worry, Mr. Clancy. You're a respectable family, and I'm not waiting on the money. We'll make a plan to deal with that side of it.'

~~~

It was agreed between the brothers that each would send their share of the weekly payment to Madeline. She religiously visited the undertaker's every Tuesday, and she was fussy about always getting a receipt. In due course the debt was cleared, and the Clancy family had no reason not to hold their heads on high.

On his next visit home, Bernard made a wooden cross. It's humble, he thought, but at least it will mark the spot. Madeline accompanied him to the cemetery where he shoved it into the earth at the head of Lily's grave. There was every intention of erecting a proper headstone, later.

CHAPTER TWENTY-EIGHT

Dear Bernard
My heart is breaking at the news but do not let them send you
overseas after all you only signed up for three years and I think I
would die if they do that and what will I do about our Michael he is
hanging round corners and I worry about who he is mixing with but
he will not listen to me and he needs a strong talking to from you
and I do not want him getting into trouble with the guards who will
put him in an industrial school and you know what those places are
like I am too upset to keep writing and yearn to see you darling
with everlasting love
Maddie
please please do not let them send you away XXXXX

~~~

Madeline's persistent visits to the Corporation's housing department to plead her case hadn't been in vain, for she now had a house.

Today, as usual, she was at the parlour window watching for the postman. Perhaps he has a letter from Bernard this morning? As she waited, she noticed a neighbour go down the road, dressed in topcoat and headscarf, carrying a deep shopping bag that looked full and plump and she guessed the woman was off into the city. If I'm not mistaken, this woman makes the same journey every week, on the same day and at the same time – I'm sure she's off to the pawnshop. Judging by the size of the bag she's probably also carrying for neighbours who don't want to be seen entering under the three brass balls. She looked for the postman again; he passed in next door, whistling the tune, *On a slow boat to China*. He came back down the garden path with a slight shimmy of the body, like he was steering a lucky girl across a crowded dance floor, then he pulled next-door's gate behind him and thumbed through the letters he held in his other hand and performed a light-footed chassis past Madeline's house and went in two doors further up. No word today, she thought. The net curtain was dropped, and she went back inside to the living room.

With a swipe of the hand, she evicted the dog from her fireside chair. It was part of a set, and she looked across at its vacant and unused twin, which she didn't allow any of the family or the dog to sit on, as it was waiting for Bernard. She heard their youngest child playing upstairs; next year she would be at school. The others were either at school or at work (one had emigrated). Those that worked in Dublin had left the house early, catching a bus to the city centre. The journey took twenty minutes, and she knew this because twice a week she also took the bus to go to her sisters. Even though she accepted that the brand new Corporation house in the suburbs was everything she needed, with fresh air for young lungs, gardens front and back, separate rooms with their own doors, an indoor toilet, a bath and a gas cooker, she still was drawn to the familiar air of the North Inner-City slums.

By now she had come to know some of her new neighbours (at least to chat with), mostly families like her own who had moved from Waterford Street and Summerhill. Other people on the road were harder to get to know, migrants from south of the Liffey, places like Fenian Street and Charlemont Street, who should have been offered a house in Crumlin or Drimnagh, but their loyalty to the southside had melted when a set of instantly available hall door keys had been dangled in front of them. Since moving in, the Clancy's new house had gone from being an empty shell – although the papered walls and the paintwork were a credit to the Corporation's workers – to one furnished with pieces of modern furniture, all standing on seamless linoleum floor covering, and all bought on credit, thanks to Bernard's army wage; however, she often felt that she would have returned the lot and lived on bare floorboards in exchange for having him there beside her. In one way it was meaningless without him, but in another way, she had to accept that they'd brought a big family into the world, and she'd vowed to herself that the children would never be denied anything within her power. Yet, it would be perfect if Bernard were here. If only…

She lit a cigarette, something she had taken up because Bernard had left her a packet of his army issue, saying at the time, 'To remind you of me'. The smoke rose to her eyes and stung. She took a few more puffs, without inhaling, then stubbed out the cigarette in a shamrock-shaped ashtray and went upstairs to check on the child.

England

It was hot in August in the New Forest, and Bernard was on a bench drinking ale outside a village inn. Top Brass had decided it would be good for the men to do some training under canvas, life in the rough. Everything was dry that summer – the forest floor only required a thoughtlessly flung cigarette butt to start a fire. Forest ponies came out of the shade and searched around the tents, nuzzling any pot or steel washbasin that had been left outside to see if it contained something to drink. Among the men there was a sense of playing at games, a feeling of being kept busy, without any sense to it. And to prove the point, the rules laid down for the camp were ambiguous. They had been sent on this manoeuvre and Command hadn't made it clear that they were to be confined to the camp – that is, when they weren't crawling through undergrowth on their bellies and disturbing the wildlife – and no one had bothered to look for clarification. A twenty-minute trek and even a City Slicker with a broken compass could follow the forest trail and hit the nearest village inn where the overworked landlord had been forced to recruit an extra barmaid.

Bernard was content to sit alone outside the drinking establishment. The other refugees from the boredom of tent living on a Sunday had gone inside. He could hear a noisy game of darts. No chaplain had been assigned to the camp, so the morning had passed without Sunday prayer; however, sitting at the edge of a tranquil wood, with a strong late-afternoon sun and absolutely no threat of a typical English cloudburst, Sunday observance wasn't something to fret about. He sipped his ale and smoked. Every so often a soldier would appear from the wood heading for the inn and, on passing Bernard, would offer a doubtful salute before disappearing inside. Unintentionally, it became like a changing of the guard for no sooner did one soldier go in, when another one came out, weaving his way across the narrow country road before disappearing into the trees, bound for the camp in a pleasant, alcoholic haze.

A singsong had started up inside the inn. It seemed to Bernard that there was always an order to the songs, with the sentimental ones coming near the end. The sun was starting to dip below the treetops, casting a shadow across the road, diving and swirling swallows were running riot through the insects. Inside the inn they had reached the sentimental verses. He heard a noise down the road and saw a pony break clumsily from the forest, then it found its balance and began nibbling on the grass verge. Bernard went back to watching the dive-bombers. The evening was closing in and he would soon have to break up the party inside and shepherd the remaining men back to the tents, otherwise in the dark they could end up as far away as Bournemouth.

Without Bernard realizing it, the pony had worked his way down the road to within a few feet of him. It was the sound the animal made shifting its weight that made him turn round. He slid carefully along the bench to get closer. He remembered the days in Waterford Street when he and his street pals would ask the ever-darting coalman, 'Mister, can we mind your horse for you?' Now, he was studying the animal next to him. If he reached out an arm, he could disturb the irritating fly that was walking unchallenged across the pony's face. A sentimental lyric was drifting out from the inn. Midges were filling the space about him. He suddenly had a sensation of utter loneliness. It was deep in his chest, sucking the joy out of the day, as if it were a vacuum. The horse was still, no sympathy in those eyes. Then a soldier's voice drifted musically out to him from inside the inn. The words of the song told of a desire to visit places of the past dear to the heart.

He thought of Madeline and the children back in Dublin. The darkening forest across from him became a foreign space. Rising to go, he moved a hand to disturb the fly from round the pony's eyes. The animal shied away, crossed the road, and vanished into the trees. It was time to round up the men.

Dublin, mid-1960s

Bernard's thoughts were interrupted by a group of noisy young people boarding the bus, one of them had a yellow transistor radio pressed to his chest as he listened attentively to the Top Twenty countdown. The others paid no attention and chattered like monkeys. A weary-looking conductor collected their fares, but made no effort to quieten them, as if he almost envied their youth. Bernard shut out the sound and let his eyes take in the passing streets; they seemed to doze in Sunday quietness. He fingered the red poppy in his pocket; he had heard of men being jeered and even spat upon for daring to wear one. It would be worn today at the National War Memorial, and the irony of it was that the labour used to build the memorial had been drawn from veterans of both the British Army and the Irish National Army.

He alighted at Islandbridge and, before he entered the War Memorial, he pinned the emblem to the outside of his topcoat. Groups of bereted British

Legion veterans (Irishmen like himself) were gathering for the annual parade, busily reconnecting with past acquaintances, however he didn't spot anyone he knew. But that didn't bother him and without fuss he slotted into the nearest group of ex-soldiers and soon he was striding in time to a marching tune that was running in his head.

They entered the grounds and moved smartly along a tree-lined avenue. On their right, the ground sloped away gently to the river Liffey, which today looked grey and sullen, reflecting the wintry November sky. The Dublin University Boat Club on the bank was deserted, no rowers wanting to compete against the cold wind on the water. The marchers came to the monumental temple in the centre of the avenue and, never forgetting the lessons of the drill square, they veered to the left and continued up the approach road to the memorial. The road was now sloping and some of the older men with dodgy hips and grating knees were falling out of step and beginning to trail behind, pursing their lips in determination. They went through the gateway on the left and arrived at the heart of the memorial where the path was flanked by tenderly manicured lawns and came to a halt in front of the Great Cross where each group assumed a designated formation. Wreaths were laid for the tens of thousands of Irishmen who had died in the First and Second World Wars. A chaplain came forward to say the prayers. To make it more real, he asked everyone to imagine the fallen men placed end-to-end in the memorial garden and to further imagine how they would fill the space many times. Bernard visualized the corpses lined along the ground, all as still as the granite of the memorial's stonework.

Ever since leaving the British Army, he had tried to attend the annual November commemoration. He also used it for his own purposes, for during the ceremonies, his mind would inevitably stray to fallen comrades from the Kerry fighting; he would see Jack Brady's face just as he remembered it, the nights in the mess, full of banter in Killarney; however, the most abiding memory was not of a Free Stater, not one of his own side. Instead, he would find himself back in the cell in Killarney, back with his pal from the Artane days, Seán. He saw him as the unbreakable Seán.

Two verses of *Abide with Me* were sung, after which the veterans marched back to the car park at the entrance, where the parade broke up. Spikes of November rain were beginning to fall. Old poppy-wearing comrades huddled together for a chat, then as the rain became heavy thought better of it. Bernard pulled up the collar of his coat and pulled his trilby down over his eyes. He removed his poppy and went into the Black and Amber across the road and sat on his own. He would have just the one pint, then maybe a chaser. It being Sunday, he had promised Madeline that they would later go together to evening Mass and then catch a picture show. As he waited for the drink, he quietly hummed a marching tune.

Author's Note

Waterford Street no longer exists – lost to development in the period 1970-80. This was unusual, particularly as the street had a long history. Previously it was part of Mecklenburg Street (1700s), then it was changed to South Tyrone Street (1800s) and finally renamed Waterford Street.

Desmond Gallagher has written about Local History, Aviation History and on the business subject 'Selling'. Short stories of his have been published, and Waterford Street is his first novel.